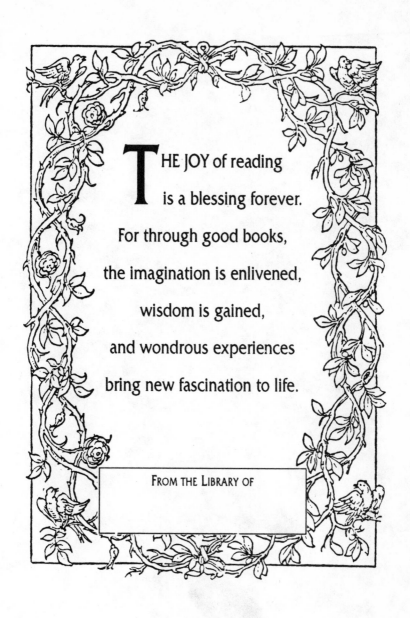

THE JOY of reading
is a blessing forever.
For through good books,
the imagination is enlivened,
wisdom is gained,
and wondrous experiences
bring new fascination to life.

FROM THE LIBRARY OF

Storm at Daybreak

The Daybreak Mysteries

STORM AT DAYBREAK
THE CAPTIVE VOICE
THE TANGLED WEB

B. J. Hoff

COMPLETE AND UNABRIDGED

Since 1948, The Book Club You Can Trust

Cover illustration copyright © 1995 by Ron Finger

Originally published 1986 by Accent Books / David C. Cook Publishing Co.

Library of Congress Cataloging-in-Publication Data

Hoff, B. J. (Brenda Jane).
  Storm at daybreak / B. J. Hoff.
    p. cm. — (Daybreak mysteries ; 1)
  ISBN 0-8423-7192-3 (pbk.)
  I. Title. II. Series: Hoff, B. J. (Brenda Jane). Daybreak mysteries ; 1.
[PS3558.034395S7] 1996
813'.54—dc20   96-12867

Printed in the United States of America

01 00 99 98 97 96
7   6   5   4   3   2   1

First combined hardcover edition for Christian Family Book Club: 1997

AUTHOR'S NOTE

The town of Shepherd Valley, West Virginia, is fictional. The majestic beauty of the mountains and the indomitable spirit of the people are wonderfully real.

My sincere thanks to the Governor's Office of Economic & Community Development and the Chamber of Commerce of West Virginia for their generous assistance.

Thanks, also, to Ms. Catherine W. Swan, The Seeing Eye, Inc., Morristown, New Jersey.

> *He heals the bird with the broken wing . . .*
> *He heals the child with a broken dream . . .*
> *He heals the one with a broken heart . . .*
> *Our Lord makes all broken things whole.*

—B. J. Hoff
From "Broken Wings"

Patches of ice checkered the pavement, barely noticeable beneath the drifting snow. The driver of a battered pickup swerved when the voice came over the radio, and the rear wheels skidded in response. With an edgy glance in the rearview mirror, he pulled off the highway, bumping and sliding over a frozen mound of snow. When the truck finally pitched to a stop, he let the engine idle as he turned up the volume on the radio.

He hated the voice, but he had to listen. It was important that he listen every day now.

His mouth quivered, and he wiped his hand across it impatiently. Kaine was at it again with his holier-than-thou hogwash.

He has his nerve. Who gave him the right to get on that microphone of his and tell the whole town—the whole country—what to do?

His head was beginning to ache from that fool's incessant yammering. He pushed a hunting cap farther back on his head, then tucked a limp strand of hair underneath it. *Thinks he's funny this morning. A real comedian.* Saturdays were always the worst. Other days Kaine mostly played that church music of his and didn't say much. But on Saturdays he talked a lot more.

Now he was talking about the big radiothon. The man ran the back of one hand slowly down his leg, snagging a split fingernail on the torn seam of his jeans. He licked his lips, then twisted them in a sneer at his own sour taste.

The voice on the radio made a few more comments about a nationwide campaign to increase drunk driving penalties.

The man snorted. *Something ought to be done about that big, mouthy ape. Got the whole town thinkin' he's so special, so important. Just because he owns a radio station. A* Christian *radio station. Just because he's different, not a normal man. Maybe everybody wouldn't think he was such a prize if they knew. If they knew about my kid.*

He squinted through the icy glaze forming on the windshield, his eyes watering as he listened. *Somebody needs to shut him up. He talks too much. He's got nothing else to do, that's his problem. So he spends his time preachin' over the radio.*

No wife or kids, of course. The man laughed aloud, a sharp, ugly sound. *No woman'd have the likes of Kaine, that's a fact. A woman wants a normal man. He'll never have himself any kids of his own, so he tries to take someone else's boy.*

He pressed his fingertips to his temples, trying to silence the pounding in his brain. *I'm sick of you, Kaine . . . sick of thinking about you, sick of the sound of you. One of these days, somebody's gonna pull the plug on you, shut you up for good.*

ONE

J ENNIFER glanced around the lobby of the radio station, hoping to see a receptionist. When she didn't, she walked toward the two glass-enclosed studios. A lanky teenage boy with mournful eyes was vacuuming the empty studio on the left. He exchanged a shy smile with Jennifer through the glass partition, then returned to his work.

Catching a glimpse of her reflection in an oak-framed wall mirror, Jennifer stopped for a moment to make a quick inspection of herself. Three hours behind the wheel of her aging Honda had left her feeling rumpled, stiff, and at a definite disadvantage for her interview with Daniel Kaine. She searched the cluttered depths of her shoulder bag for a brush. Finding none, she made a futile attempt to comb her hair with her fingers, then lifted one cynical eyebrow in defeat and shrugged philosophically.

Sensing movement out of the corner of her eye, she turned to the studio on her right. A lone disc jockey was sprawled comfortably in a worn brown chair, adjusting his headset as he spoke into a suspension mike.

The two years she had spent in Rome studying voice with Carlo Paulo had conditioned Jennifer to a steady parade of intriguing, attractive men. While not exactly immune to their appeal, she considered herself difficult to impress. At the moment, however, she was definitely impressed.

He wasn't handsome—at least not in the conventional sense.

He had the look of a vagabond prince, Jennifer thought fancifully. A hint of nobility subtly blended with a touch of the maverick. Even slouched as he was with one leg thrown idly over the arm of his chair, she could see that he would tower over her by several inches. At five-eight, she didn't run into that too often.

She moved closer, nearly touching her nose to the glass window. The disc jockey placed one large hand on the control board and the other on his headset to make an adjustment. His red V-neck sweater emphasized the breadth of his shoulders, and his faded jeans made his legs look even longer. His hair was an odd shade of charcoal—not quite, but almost black, a peculiar dusky color. A line of silver winged randomly from his left temple upward, a startling contrast to the thick, dark strands that fell over his forehead.

Jennifer dryly reminded herself that she didn't care for beards, although his was thick and neatly trimmed. His nose was a little too hawkish for her taste, and his shaggy hair could do with some attention. Still, she was intrigued by his profile, and what she could see of his features hinted at a sense of humor and a comfortable, friendly kind of strength.

Unexpectedly, he turned and looked directly at her. She let out an embarrassed groan and backed quickly away from the studio window, briefly registering the disappointing thought that he seemed singularly unimpressed. He hadn't blinked an eye when he caught her staring.

"May I help you, or are you just window shopping?"

The deep voice at her back halted her movement away from the studio. Jennifer jumped, then whirled around to encounter, almost nose-to-nose, a more conventionally handsome man than the disc jockey. His skin was sun-burnished, his blond hair streaked with gold. He wore a winter-white ski sweater, and his green eyes danced with mirth above a remarkably perfect nose and a dark mustache.

Jennifer was beginning to think she had somehow taken a wrong turn and ended up in an employment agency for male models instead of a Christian radio station. She gaped at the life-sized physical fitness ad who was smiling at her.

"Help me?" she stammered in confusion. "No—I mean yes!"

The green eyes twinkled with even more amusement. "Yes, you need help, or yes, you're window shopping?"

Jennifer stared at him. Her recovery time was slower than usual this morning, probably due to lack of sleep the night before. "I . . . I have an appointment for an interview. With Mr. Kaine."

"Ah! Then you must be Jennifer Terry." He offered his hand and continued to smile.

Jennifer adjusted her shoulder bag and drew a long breath of relief as she shook his hand. "Yes, I am."

"Gabe Denton. News director, gofer, and court jester. At your service." He paused. "You're a Buckeye, right?"

His smile was infectious, and Jennifer grinned back. "Yes—Athens, Ohio. Is everyone in West Virginia this friendly?"

"You bet. It's the altitude. You went to O.U., didn't you?" He didn't wait for an answer. "I almost went there, too, but Dan talked me into attending West Virginia U. He's forever talking me into something. I have no backbone, I suppose."

Jennifer's mind reeled from his high-speed verbal barrage. "I see."

"I reviewed your resume with Dan last week. He's very interested. Come on, I'll get you a cup of coffee while you're waiting for him. He'll be with you in a few minutes."

He led her down a paneled hallway to the left of the studios, carrying on a constant flow of idle chatter as they went. Turning, they entered a bright, informal lounge where the whisper from a heat register was the only sound. It was a cheerful room with hanging baskets, a floral chaise, and matching chairs. A large commercial coffee urn and a variety of cups rested on a white table.

"Did you drive down this morning?" Denton asked, pouring a cup of coffee that smelled rich and delicious. Jennifer's stomach reminded her with a growl that, in her characteristic rush out of the house, she had skipped breakfast.

"Yes, I left home about seven."

"No one should have to get up that early on Saturday," he said with a sympathetic grimace. "It's criminal."

"Actually, I'm used to it," she said, gratefully accepting the coffee. "Where I'm working now, I have to be at the station by six o'clock every morning except Sundays."

"No wonder you're job hunting." He extended a small plate of cookies to her, and she took a couple. "Well, Jennifer, I hate to desert you, but I have an insurance rep in my office who's expecting a stroke of advertising genius from me. Do you mind waiting alone? I'll go in and tell Dan you're here."

After a quick sip of coffee, Jennifer motioned him on. "I'll be fine. Go ahead. Oh—and thanks for the coffee!"

"It'll be great working with you." Denton gave her a quick wave and turned to go.

"But I haven't got the—," Jennifer stopped, her words trailing off as he dashed out the door.

She carried her coffee over to the window. If the lounge were indicative of the rest of the station, the place was definitely a step up. The small Christian station where she worked now was little more than a two-room warehouse a few miles outside Athens.

She liked the job, but the time had come to move if she were ever to make a dent in the loan her dad had assumed for her music studies in Italy. The salary quoted for this position was surprisingly good, and she was determined to make a good impression on Daniel Kaine.

Not for the first time, Jennifer wondered what to expect of the man who owned and managed the station. She already knew Kaine was young. She remembered what Dr. Rodaven, her former professor at Ohio University, had told her when he first contacted her about the job.

"I've only met the man twice, Jennifer, but I was impressed with him. He's in his late thirties, I suppose. Seems highly intelligent—a fine Christian, too, by the way. I don't suppose you'd remember, but Kaine made quite a name for himself and his community several years ago in the Olympics. He took a gold medal in swimming, as I recall. I watched him on television—a real powerhouse in the water. Great athlete. A terrible tragedy, what happened to him. . . ."

"What sort of tragedy?"

"He's blind. There was a car accident a few years ago—a teenager, I think. Drunk driver. Daniel Kaine lost his sight, and I believe the boy died."

Jennifer had nearly backed off then and there. A man with that kind of disability might be expecting someone to function more as a personal aide than an executive assistant. What Jennifer really wanted was to break into management and perhaps have a show of her own. The stark reality of financial need, however, had been enough incentive to lure her to Shepherd Valley for an initial interview.

So, here she was, though not without reservations. She sipped the coffee slowly, gazing out at the winter landscape.

I could learn to love this place in no time, she thought, enthralled by the mountains.

A town of approximately thirty thousand people, Shepherd Valley nestled peacefully at the bottom of a wide range of some spectacular mountains, white now with January snow. The entire community formed an oval, with only a few buildings fanning out into the surrounding woods. Since the radio station sat squarely on top of a hill, Jennifer had a breathtaking view of the Appalachian settlement below. It appeared to be very old and quaint and tranquil.

Her thoughts returned to Daniel Kaine. The only blind person Jennifer had ever known was Miss Rider, the elderly piano teacher she had seen for half an hour weekly while she was still in elementary school; she barely remembered her. What was it like, living without sight, knowing you would never see again?

According to Dr. Rodaven, Kaine's blindness was permanent, caused by severe damage to the optic nerve. Jennifer shuddered, trying to imagine how she would deal with a tragedy like that in her own life. Her mind went briefly to her younger brother, Loren, a victim of cerebral palsy. She had helped to raise him after their mother's death, and even now she felt a sharp twist of pain whenever she thought about the way her brother's condition had ravaged his body and trapped his mind. *Which would be worse,* she wondered, *spending your life in a wheelchair or living in continual darkness?* She pressed her lips together, resolutely swallowing a familiar lump of resentment.

She couldn't stop thinking about Daniel Kaine. Always curious, she turned and placed her nearly empty coffee cup on the white lacquered table beside the chaise. She shut her eyes and stood perfectly still for a moment to fix her sense of direction. Then, slowly and cautiously, she began to walk across the room, her hands flailing out and groping with every step. She felt something fall with a soft thump but refused to give in to the temptation to look. Weaving back and forth, she continued to walk, flinching when she heard something else topple, but still resisting the urge to open her eyes.

She should be close to the door by now. She turned sharply to retrace her steps—and collided so soundly with a hard, massive shape that her head snapped backward from the unexpected blow.

Her eyes flew open to encounter an incredibly broad chest covered with a crimson V-neck sweater—a chest her hands were now braced against in an attempt to steady herself.

The disc jockey! Her stomach sank with a thud.

Miserably, Jennifer raised her eyes upward, then higher still, to the dark, bearded face lowered toward her with a questioning stare. She felt her face heat with embarrassment.

"Excuse me." The voice was low, richly timbred, with a soft but definite drawl. "Am I, ah . . . in your way?"

Jennifer uttered a small groan of dismay. "Oh—no! I—oh, I'm *so sorry!*"

The big man smiled, and Jennifer had a fleeting memory of a sunrise she'd once seen from her window in Rome—slow and gentle and breathtaking.

"Did I run into you? Or did you run into me?" He laughed easily and continued to stare down at her with wonderful blue eyes.

Startled, Jennifer realized that her hands were still splayed against him. She yanked them abruptly away with a choked exclamation. "I—I definitely ran into you," she stammered. "Did I hurt you? Oh, I feel so incredibly *stupid!*"

Still smiling, he braced one arm above her on the doorframe, trapping her within his space. "You needn't. I run into things all the time."

He was being wonderfully nice, but she felt like such a klutz! Here she was, finally face-to-face with a man who could make her heart go wild, and she was walking around with her eyes closed, for goodness' sake!

"I'm not totally crazy, honest!" she blurted out. "You see, I have an appointment with Mr. Kaine for a job interview, and . . . well, I was waiting for him, and I started thinking about what it would be like, not being able to see. And I—well, I just shut my eyes to try it out for myself, and—oh, I suppose it *sounds* even more stupid than it must have *looked!*"

Jennifer knew she was chattering—she always did when her composure was shaken—but the disc jockey simply kept on smiling, as though he didn't quite know what to make of her.

Running his hand lightly over his beard, he finally spoke. "I don't think that's so stupid," he drawled softly. "In fact, I think it shows a lot of sensitivity."

"You do?" Jennifer stared at him blankly.

He nodded. "Absolutely. You were wondering what it's like to be blind, right?"

"Yes. But my brother told me I should say 'unsighted' rather than 'blind.' What does Mr. Kaine prefer, do you know?"

He appeared to consider her question carefully for a moment. "I don't think he much cares what you call it. So . . . you have an interview for a job here?"

"Yes, as Mr. Kaine's executive assistant. Have you been here long?"

"Mm-hm. A long time. You any good?"

"I beg your pardon?"

"At what you do. Are you any good?"

Really, wasn't he strange? "Well, I think I am. I have a degree in broadcast communications—and experience. What do *you* do?"

His smile was disarmingly boyish. His even white teeth flashed in dazzling contrast to his dark hair and skin as he moved away from the doorframe and took her hand. He placed his much larger hand over hers on his forearm and motioned her to the doorway.

"As a matter of fact, I own the place, Jennifer. Jennifer Terry, isn't it?" he said smoothly as they entered the connecting office.

"Now then, why don't you just come in and sit down, so we can talk. I've got a hunch you're already hired, so we'd better start getting acquainted, don't you think?"

TWO

J ENNIFER skidded to a stop on the other side of
the door, narrowly avoiding a second collision. Her
mouth fell open on a sharp intake of breath, and
she gaped at him in startled silence. He waited, a trace of mischief
scurrying across his features.

"You're Daniel Kaine?"

"Guilty." The man had a grin like a jolt of electric current.

She didn't know whether to groan with embarrassment or simply try for a fast getaway. "Well, if you'd only *told* me—," she muttered weakly.

"Told you?"

"Who you *are!*"

He nodded. "Sorry, I guess I got a little . . . sidetracked."

"Well, now that you've seen me make an utter spectacle of
myself. . . ."

"I wasn't looking—honest." A dry note of amusement edged
his words.

Jennifer slapped the palm of her hand against her head, moaning softly when she realized what she had said. "I'm so sorry," she
said miserably, wondering if she would have liked the job.

"Jennifer—sit down and relax, OK?"

His hand still covered hers on his thickly muscled forearm, and
he pressed it gently, moving her across the plush carpet to a chair
that sat directly opposite a large walnut desk.

9

Jennifer sat down cautiously. Glancing up, she encountered the curious, dark-eyed gaze of one of the most beautiful dogs she had ever seen. An elegant golden retriever resting casually beside the massive desk studied her with friendly interest.

"What a lovely dog!"

"Ah . . . she likes to hear that, don't you, girl?" Kaine eased his large frame into the chair behind the desk, then leaned sideways to stroke the dog's head affectionately. "Jennifer, meet Sunrise Lady of Shalimar. Her friends call her Sunny."

"Is she—"

"My guide dog," he finished for her. "One of the best—from the Seeing Eye in New Jersey." He skimmed his hands quickly over the right side of the desktop, stopping when he touched a slim file folder. Opening it, he began to run his fingertips lightly across the Braille letters of the top sheet.

The dog sat up, tilted her head to the side, and began to whine softly. "I believe Sunny would like to introduce herself to you," Kaine said, smiling as he continued to read the Braille file.

"Is it all right to pet her?"

He nodded. "It's fine when she isn't working."

Jennifer extended her hand, and the retriever immediately perked up her ears even more, then looked appealingly at her owner.

As though he could see her bid for approval, he inclined his head slightly. "Go on, girl."

Sunny shook off her dignified demeanor at once, bounding over to Jennifer and nudging her hand in an undisguised attempt to get her ears rubbed. Jennifer complied, laughing at the small sounds of pleasure coming from the dog's throat. "How old is she?"

Kaine thought for a moment. "A little over seven. But she thinks she's still a puppy."

He called the retriever back to his side, and the dog returned without hesitation.

"OK, Jennifer, I think I remember most of the information on your resume. Gabe went over it with me a few days ago." Kaine leaned comfortably back in his chair and locked his hands behind his head. "You're twenty-seven?"

Jennifer nodded, then caught herself and spoke. "Yes."

"Born and raised in Athens, Ohio. Nice town," he said thoughtfully. "I was there a few years ago with my teen ensemble. I noticed Carey Rodaven was one of your references. Did you study with him at O.U.?"

For the next few minutes he continued to mix his questions with casual, friendly comments. Jennifer was intrigued by the slow, rambling way he spoke, his words flowing smoothly in a soft Appalachian drawl.

As she listened to his mellow voice, she scrutinized his features. If one could accurately measure a person's character by his face, she would judge Daniel Kaine to be an extremely kind, good-natured man who had known more than his share of trouble, yet had come through it reasonably unscathed. Everything about his appearance, his voice, his mannerisms seemed to fuse together into a unique combination of unshakable strength, patient tolerance, and relentless humor.

He also possessed, she realized uncomfortably, a distinct magnetism. His size, rather than presenting the blustering threat of an aggressive grizzly, held more the endearing appeal of a comfortable, but powerful, giant panda. He appeared to be essentially pleasant; she would guess him to be a man who seldom lost his temper. And something in that youthful, mischievous grin told her he liked to have fun and might even be a bit of a practical joker.

But he also had a blunt, no-nonsense way about him that unnerved her. It occurred to Jennifer that Daniel Kaine would not be easily taken in. She suspected that he possessed the intuitive ability to go straight to the heart, to strip aside any superfluous layers of camouflage and pierce the depths of another's spirit.

It didn't help that his blue eyes—beautiful eyes, Jennifer thought—followed sound and movement and contributed to the overall impression of a highly developed intelligence and sensitivity. It was true that they lacked perfect focus, but this simply gave him a somewhat pensive expression, as though he were continually looking at or listening for something in the distance. When he faced her, Jennifer had the sharp, unsettling sensation that he could *see* her.

Kaine put her file aside and leaned forward, lacing his fingers together on top of the desk. "Why don't I fill you in on the job first, Jennifer? Then, if you're interested, I'd like to hear more about you." He smiled again, seemingly intent upon putting her at ease.

"The job description that was sent to you might have been a little vague," he continued in his soft, mild voice. "What I'm looking for is someone to function as an assistant station manager as well as my executive assistant. Gabe Denton, the comedian you met earlier, has more to do than he can handle. He's our program director and acting sales manager and—well, I've just got to get some help for him. There's a fellow coming in next week to interview for sales manager. If he works out, that will help, but we still—"

The telephone interrupted him with a shrill ring, and Jennifer glanced at the special instrument with its large, raised numerals. "Sorry," Kaine said. "My secretary doesn't work on Saturdays, so I have to pick up my calls. I'll try to make it quick."

Jennifer resisted the urge to study him while he was on the phone—somehow it seemed unfair, almost as though she'd be taking advantage of his sightlessness. Instead, she let her gaze roam over his desk. A large Bible, probably Braille, she thought, lay close to his right hand, and just a few inches away stood a clock with raised numerals and a machine that looked like a small record player. To his left was a battered IBM Selectric, as well as numerous Braille papers. Bookshelves held a state-of-the-art stereo system, and on the opposite wall hung framed photographs of Christian recording stars. Many of the photos, Jennifer noted with interest, included Daniel Kaine.

She was trying not to eavesdrop, but when she heard the agitation in his voice and saw his heavy dark brows knit into an annoyed frown, she couldn't help but wonder what was so disturbing about the call.

"Listen—" The soft, gentle drawl she had found so charming moments before now deepened. He sounded almost gruff as he went on. "I don't know what your problem is, but you're not going to solve it like this. If you want to come in and talk, that's fine, but—"

Surprised by his abrupt change of manner, Jennifer was even more puzzled when she heard a loud click at the other end of the connection and saw Kaine hold the receiver away from his ear. He replaced it slowly and quietly, shaking his head in puzzlement.

He managed a brief smile for her before he spoke again. "Takes all kinds, I suppose." He made no attempt to explain what had transpired, and Jennifer didn't ask. "So . . . where was I? Ah—I was interested in the job you're doing now, Jennifer. Gabe said you have quite a variety of responsibilities, that you're doing a little of everything."

"Yes, it's just a small station. Everyone has to be a jack-of-all-trades."

"Well, that could be a real plus around here," said Kaine. "Things get pretty hectic every now and then. It would help to have someone who could pitch in as needed." He leaned forward a little more.

"Let me explain something else before we go any further, all right?" His pleasant, good-natured smile was back to normal now. "Some people are intimidated by my disability. They simply can't relate to it, so they find it difficult to work for me. That makes it awkward for me, too. I've got to have someone in this job who isn't going to get all strung out about working with a blind man. Someone who'll be comfortable with me—so I can be comfortable, too. We're going to be together too much for it to work any other way. Do you understand what I mean?"

Jennifer considered her answer for only an instant. "I think so. And I've got to be honest with you, Mr. Kaine. I've never worked with anyone who . . . couldn't see. But I don't think it would be a problem for me once I learn your way of doing things."

Kaine nodded slowly, running the palm of his hand lightly across his beard. "Well, let me put your mind at ease about one thing. If you're afraid you'd end up as a nursemaid, you wouldn't. Most things, I do for myself. My little blonde here—" he leaned over to stroke the retriever behind the ears—"gives me a lot of independence I wouldn't have otherwise. And Katharine Chandler, my secretary, keeps me more organized than I'd like to be. I'm sorry you couldn't meet her today, by the way. She puts in so many hours through the week, I don't think it's fair to ask her to come in on Saturdays, too."

He crossed his arms over his chest, and his massive shoulders reminded Jennifer that the man had been an Olympic swimmer. She forced her attention back to his voice.

"I have a housekeeper to keep my place from turning into a condemned area. And I also have an overprotective sister who takes care of my social life—such as it is." He flashed his annihilating grin and pushed his chair even farther away from the desk.

"And, of course, I have Gabe. He's my right-hand man. And my best friend. He's also the best program director in the state." Another smile darted across his face. "Gabe's sense of humor leans a bit to the odd side every now and then, but he's a great guy.

He's also my part-time chauffeur and drives me to and from the station every day. Anyway, I've got all the personal attention I need—sometimes more than I can handle. What I *do* need is an assistant with some smarts and a healthy dose of common sense who can also take my blindness in stride." He paused for just a moment. "Since you've been working for a Christian station, I assume that you have some church background."

"Yes," Jennifer assured him. "I'm a Christian."

He nodded. "Good. Everyone who works here is. We try to function primarily as a ministry. Of course, we have to make a profit to pay the bills, but we try to keep our priorities straight. Did you grow up in the church?"

"Yes. My grandfather was a minister," Jennifer explained. "In fact, he started the church my family attends."

"With your background in music, I imagine they keep you real busy singing."

Jennifer swallowed hard, not answering for a moment. When she finally spoke, she deliberately kept her tone even and bland. "Actually, I don't sing anymore."

Kaine raised one dark brow. "Not at all?"

"No."

Jennifer waited tensely for the question he seemed about to ask, but after a brief hesitation, he simply smiled and changed the subject. "Well, now it's your turn to ask questions."

Relieved, Jennifer leaned forward a little. "What exactly would my responsibilities be?"

Kaine lifted a hand with an encompassing motion. "Helping me run the place, mostly. You'd coordinate programming with Gabe, do some public relations for us, cover a lot of the community stuff—you know, concerts, church activities, civic meetings, that sort of thing. I said you wouldn't be a nursemaid, but you *would* be driving me around some, I'm afraid. Would you mind that?"

15

"Not at all," Jennifer answered quickly.

"Good. I would need you to get going on one thing right away. We're the coordinating station for a nationwide radiothon coming up in just a few weeks. Gabe and I have been working on it for months, but we keep getting bogged down in other stuff. Consequently, we're not nearly as far along as we should be with the planning."

"What kind of radiothon?"

"We're hoping to generate more public interest and awareness regarding drunk driving laws. There's been a good deal of improvement, but too many people are still indifferent to the problem. It takes financial support, political pressure—we'd like to stir up some enthusiasm for both." Kaine hesitated a moment, then went on. "I was asked to coordinate the effort because of my own experience. My blindness was caused by an automobile accident—the boy driving the other vehicle was drunk."

He said it calmly and matter-of-factly, obviously expecting no response. "I suppose I should warn you, Jennifer," he continued with a smile, "that you would probably have to put in quite a few weekends and evenings. But I'd make it up to you. You could have time off through the week every now and then. By the way, do you like to jock? Would you want a show of your own?"

"Actually, that's one of my favorite parts of the business," Jennifer admitted quickly, growing more and more interested in the job.

"Well, you could have your choice right now between two shows. I need someone for a live talk show in the evening, or you could have a three-hour drive in the afternoon."

Jennifer was hooked. "I think I'd really like the job, Mr. Kaine."

"The name's *Dan,* OK? You've got a dynamite voice, Jennifer, you know that? Should be great on the air."

Before she could reply, Kaine went on in his slow, soothing drawl. "Can I ask you about something else? Gabe filled me in on most of your background, but I've got to admit that I'm curious about how you went from studying opera in Rome to a radio station in West Virginia."

Jennifer was deliberately evasive, hoping he wouldn't press her for details. "I—well, it's kind of a long story."

"That's all right," Kaine said agreeably, as if he had all the time in the world.

Jennifer swallowed with difficulty, feeling her stomach knot with tension. The memories were still painful—too painful to discuss with a stranger, even one who seemed as kind as Daniel Kaine. "Mr. Kaine—Dan—I don't think it's relevant. And it is . . . personal."

He looked surprised but recovered quickly. Obviously, he had no intention of retreating from the subject. "Your sheet said you'd studied voice for a long time. Two years in Rome with some famous *maestro,* right? Then you came home, went to O.U. for a degree in communications, and worked in a radio station on the side." He paused, but only for an instant. "You were interested in a stage career in opera?"

"I . . . was at one time, yes."

"Why did you change directions?"

After a noticeable hesitation, Jennifer answered quietly, her tone flat and unemotional. "Because I wasn't good enough to do what I had originally hoped to do."

Kaine tapped his long, blunt fingers lightly on the desk. "Who said?"

Jennifer made a weak attempt at lightness. "One of the best voice coaches in Europe. He said it very kindly, of course."

Picking up a pencil, he twirled it back and forth between the thumb and two fingers of one hand. "That's rough. Is that what you had always wanted, to have an operatic career?"

Jennifer blinked furiously against the hot wetness burning her eyes. Impatient with herself and unsettled by his apparent determi-

Storm at Daybreak

nation to press the issue, she remained silent, even though he was obviously waiting for some sort of reply from her.

After an awkward silence, he went on. "The pain's still pretty fresh, is it, Jennifer?" he questioned softly.

If she admitted the truth she would feel foolish. It sounded so petty in contrast to the enormity of Daniel Kaine's problem. Her own loss suddenly seemed pathetically insignificant as she studied him. She wondered at his air of self-assurance, his apparent tranquility. It had to be a front, she told herself defensively. No one with that kind of disability could possibly be as emotionally . . . *together* as he appeared to be. No, she concluded abruptly, either this man was some sort of a rare spiritual giant or he had simply erected one of the most impressive facades she had ever encountered. Her instincts suspected the latter. At any rate, she felt a grudging touch of respect for him.

Once more Kaine met her silence with the same easygoing, pleasant tone of voice. "So this job is what? An alternative?"

"Yes," Jennifer replied tersely. "An alternative."

To her surprise, he smiled. "You want it just for the money?"

Jennifer had always found it impossible to be less than honest. "That's the biggest reason, yes. My father mortgaged almost everything we have to send me to Italy. I have two younger brothers, one who just got married and another . . . in a private school. It's time I paid my own way."

"I can understand that," Kaine said agreeably, still smiling. "What about moving? Would that present a problem for you?"

So he hadn't written her off after all! "No, it wouldn't," Jennifer said immediately. "My only ties are my family—and I wouldn't be all that far away from them. And, Mr. Kaine—*Dan*—what I said about the job being an alternative . . . I'd still do my best for you, I honestly would."

His smile grew even warmer, and his voice held a note of inter-

18

est when he spoke again. "You're not intimidated by me—by my blindness—are you?"

"I—" She stopped, considering his question. "No. No, I don't think I am."

With one last tap of his fingers on the desk, he rose from his chair and walked slowly around to her, extending his hand. "I thought not. Well, we need to see about finding an apartment for you. Will you need a furnished or unfurnished place?"

He was offering her the job! Just like that. Jennifer stood up, shook his hand, and smiled brightly. "Furnished. And cheap," she added.

Kaine grinned. "We'll get Gabe and my sister, Lyss, to help us with that. Lyss is coming over to go to lunch with us in a while; we can talk to her about it then. How soon do you think you could start, once we find you a place to live?"

"Two weeks?"

"Great. I'll call Gabe in a minute and see if Lyss is here yet."

For an instant, he appeared to consider something. Then, his expression briefly uncertain, he dipped his head down. "Jennifer?" His voice was soft and halting. "I wonder—would you mind if I . . . looked at you? With my hands?"

Something caught and tightened in Jennifer's throat, but she ignored it. "No—I mean, I don't mind at all."

It was an unsettling experience. She hadn't expected such gentleness, not from such a big man. He rested his hands lightly on her shoulders for just an instant before moving to trace the oval of her face, hesitantly at first, then with more confidence. He molded her face between his large hands, shaping every feature with light but firm strokes.

"You're tall. What . . . five-seven?"

"Eight," Jennifer said tightly, clearing her throat. "Five-eight, actually."

Kaine nodded and smiled thoughtfully. "That's good. Short

women make me a little crazy. I never seem to be able to find them, you know? Never know how far down they are."

Jennifer stared blankly into his face, then laughed, but only for a moment. So unexpectedly intense was her response to his touch that she had to close her eyes against it. His fingertips were heavily calloused, and she fleetingly wondered what sort of work a blind man might do to cause calluses. His hands explored slowly, brushing over her high forehead, lightly winging out from her eyes, barely touching her closed eyelids, seeming to take note of her eyelashes before moving down over her cheekbones and the hollows beneath. He allowed his thumbs to touch the outside corners of her mouth only briefly, but long enough for her to catch a sharp, uneven breath before he fanned his fingertips gently along her jawline.

"I don't think you eat very much, Jennifer," he said softly, smiling as though he had discovered a small secret.

"My youngest brother calls me Bones, if that tells you anything," Jennifer volunteered. Her voice sounded terribly unnatural. She thought she would choke when he touched the dimple in the middle of her chin, then slid his hands slowly outward to scan the length of her hair. He murmured something she didn't catch, then asked, "What color is your hair?"

"Uh . . . it's dark brown. With some red—auburn, I guess you'd call it." She hoped he wouldn't detect the slight tremor in her voice.

"Must take forever to dry," he commented with a small, thoughtful smile. He moved one finger back to the scar just in front of her right ear. "What happened here?"

Jennifer could hardly believe the sensitivity of his hands. That scar was barely noticeable, even to her. "I fell off a horse at a girlfriend's farm when I was twelve. A piece of barbed-wire fence got in my way."

"Tomboy, huh?" he chuckled softly.

"I'm afraid so." She wondered if the jelly sensation in her knees was due to lack of sleep or his touch.

His hands quickly framed her face once more, very gently, then dropped away. "Thank you, Jennifer, for understanding my need to do that." His features softened even more. "Gabe told me you were lovely," he said quietly, with a nod of agreement. Then he grinned. *"Bones,* huh? Sounds like something I'd say to *my* sister."

Though she was trim and fit, the name "Bones" hardly described Alyssa Kaine. A physical education teacher at the Christian school that she, Dan, and Gabe Denton had once attended, Lyss had the same athletic build as her brother. As the four of them laughed and talked over lunch at a nearby restaurant, Jennifer knew she had already made her first friends in Shepherd Valley.

"Papa Joe" Como, the proprietor of the restaurant, also owned some rental property in town. As soon as he learned that Jennifer was going to be working at the radio station, he insisted on showing her a house that would be "perfect" for her use.

Jennifer fell in love with the quaint three-room bungalow and its white wicker furniture almost immediately. And "Papa Joe," who seemed far more interested in finding a tenant who would take care of his property than in charging an exorbitant rent, quoted a monthly rate well within her reach. They finalized the arrangement with a down payment and a handshake.

When she was finally ready to leave, Dan walked her to her car, accompanied by Sunny. After she was settled behind the steering wheel, he leaned down to her window. Jennifer again had the disturbing sensation that he was looking directly into her eyes.

"Well . . . hurry back, Jennifer," he said softly in a tone that sounded almost wistful. He touched her shoulder lightly, then straightened. "We'll have a welcome party for you once you get settled."

Jennifer watched him from her rearview mirror for as long as possible—this tall, dark, enigma of a man with his golden companion standing quietly at his side. For the first time in years, she felt a trace of hopeful anticipation. She was surprised to realize that she wanted the next two weeks to pass quickly. *Very* quickly.

THREE

D AN pulled a fisherman's sweater over his head as he walked into the kitchen. Suddenly, he stopped and stood listening, his hands in the back pockets of his jeans.

He heard nothing, but for the first time in almost five years, he was engulfed by the same blood-chilling sensation that had plagued him during the early months of his blindness. That oppressive, menacing feeling that he was being watched—like a bug under glass. Isolated. Vulnerable. Helpless.

Perspiration started on the palms of his hands, and he felt the beginning of a tremor in his arms and legs. His heart pumped harder, and he braced one hand on the counter to steady himself. He tried to swallow but couldn't. All he could do was wait until it passed.

The rehabilitation counselor in Pittsburgh had warned him that he could expect occasional anxiety attacks indefinitely, but he had hoped that was all behind him. *It's these crazy phone calls,* he told himself. They were coming nearly every night now, and sometimes through the day at the station. Rarely did the man say anything; usually the line remained ominously silent. Last night the phone had rung long after midnight. When Dan answered, he heard nothing but the sound of ragged breathing.

He caught his breath now, aware that his heartbeat was gradually leveling off. Feeling weak, he wiped his hands on his jeans

and lowered himself to one of the stools at the counter to wait
for his head to clear.

He knew he should tell someone about the calls. But he also
knew what it would mean if he did. Everyone would start hovering over him again, watching him, *protecting* him. His mother.
Gabe. Lyss. Even his dad. It would be like before, during the
weeks following the accident. He would lose his freedom, his independence again.

No way. Not yet. He would say nothing until he absolutely
had to.

What good would it do anyway? What could he tell them?
That some crazy man seemed bent on driving him over the edge?
Even though he had sensed the sick anger and something akin to
hatred behind the voice on the phone, the man had made no real
threat.

So far.

The dream was coming more often now, too. It was different—more demanding, more harrowing than ever before.
There was nothing he could do to prevent it. His subconscious
seemed to have a will of its own, though he'd tried everything
he could think of to avoid a repeat of the nightmare. It was
always the same.

He would sleep uneasily, a sleep with no real peace, then would
suddenly find himself on that same winding mountain road again.
He would hang the corkscrew curve near the top of the hill only
to be met by two blazing halos of light looming toward him
through the fog. He would feel himself suspended, weightless, for
a brief spark of eternity. Then the mushrooming headlights of the
oncoming truck, like two furious, malevolent eyes, would explode
into his face. Terror would grip him by the throat as metal
rammed metal, while glass shattered and blew to pieces in a slow-
motion kaleidoscope of horror.

And then he would hear someone scream, not realizing it was

his own voice until the smoking chamber of the car echoed the sound of it over and over again before tossing it out into the night. Finally, he would gape through shock-glazed eyes at the last thing he would ever see in his lifetime—a face behind the windshield of the truck, a face fragmented and distorted by broken glass and a heavy shroud of mist. The face of fear, a macabre rictus, frozen in an endless, silent scream. . . .

And then the nightmare would end. Always at the same point, always in the same way, always incomplete. He would awaken, at first in a storm of panic, then weary and drained with the reality that it was only a dream, that it was over . . . but that he was, indeed, blind. He would lie quietly, sweating, trembling, forcing himself to think about the dream—for there was always something unfinished about it, something he could never quite remember.

He supposed the telephone calls could somehow be triggering the old anxieties. He wondered, too, if the calls might possibly be connected to the upcoming radiothon. The station had recently begun to highlight the nationwide campaign with hourly announcements, many by Dan himself. It wouldn't be the first time someone who was already a little unhinged went off the deep end because he didn't like what he heard on the air.

With a resigned sigh, Dan straightened his shoulders and hauled himself to his feet. This was *not* the best frame of mind for the coming evening. He forced himself to shake off the melancholy that had threatened to engulf his emotions most of the day, like a low-hanging cloud that refused to move.

Jennifer—and half the town, he reminded himself wryly— would be here within minutes. *Jennifer.* He said her name to himself, quietly, with a touch of a smile, relishing the sound of it on his lips. *I'm in trouble, all right. But maybe not the kind I've been worried about. The real trouble, I suspect, has a lot more to do* with a certain lady who always smells like a vanilla-scented candle and has a voice like warm, thick honey. The same lady who, according to Gabe, has exactly four freckles on her nose and looks like a model for an aerobics advertisement.

The lady also happened to be the guest of honor at the party he would be hosting in a few minutes.

Dan tried to shove his attention back to more mundane matters, but the thought of Jennifer's presence in his home—an entire evening to simply be close to her, to hear that sensational laugh of hers, to fill his senses with the sunshine-warm fragrance of her hair at his shoulder—made his smile break even wider across his face. He tried to push aside his own adolescent foolishness, but the glow of his smile lingered.

With a self-mocking shrug, he pursed his lips in a soft whistle, palmed a few pretzels from a bowl on the snack-heaped harvest table in the dining area, and walked into the living room. He stopped in front of the fireplace, where flames were rising and crackling cheerfully.

Sunny padded in and lay down at his side. Dan stooped down and began to stroke the golden retriever. He knew her favorite rubber ducky was resting snugly between her two front paws. After feeding her a pretzel from his hand, he muttered a reminder to himself that "you must never spoil a guide dog, Mr. Kaine." *Absolutely.*

He stood, flexed his shoulders, and began to pace the length of the room. In truth, it was an unbroken flow of rooms with no walls, furnished with primitive accent pieces and early West Virginia carpentry. When he reached the "music room" at the far end of the first floor, he stopped to insert a CD into a player on the bookcase shelf. Jerking the volume control well past the comfort level, he shoved his hands into his pockets and breaking into a satisfied smile, began to sing along with a contemporary Christian band.

Sunny reluctantly stirred. Dan could imagine the retriever turning a long-suffering, mildly censuring look at him, as though to make the observation that he was becoming more and more peculiar lately.

Jennifer changed clothes for the third time and took a long, disgruntled look at herself in the mirror. "What is *wrong* with me tonight?" she muttered to herself. "You'd think I had a date at the governor's mansion."

Rummaging through several boxes, she found the leather boots she had bought on sale the winter before and hurriedly pulled them on. She frowned at herself again in the full-length mirror on the bedroom door, deciding too late that the casual slacks and oversized jacket made her look even thinner than she was. She buttoned one large button, considered the effect, then immediately unbuttoned it. She had skipped too many meals during the hectic days of packing and moving, and it showed.

She raked a brush through her hair, then paused, her hand suspended above her head, as she realized that the one person she was so anxious to impress couldn't even see the result of her efforts!

"Brilliant, Jennifer," she said under her breath, grabbing her shoulder bag and slinging it over her arm. "Absolutely brilliant."

She shrugged quickly into her coat and began to fish for her car keys as she raced out the door. Tripping on the front step, she choked with exasperation when she dropped her purse upside down, spilling its contents all over the small cement porch. She scrambled to pick up the clutter, shoving a collection of eight or nine pens and pencils back to the bottom of the bag, along with her wallet, her pocket organizer, half a dozen stamps, two Hershey bars—but no keys.

Fuming, she walked into the carport. A quick glance through

the window of the Honda confirmed that the keys were still in the ignition. She tried the door and discovered with relief that she hadn't locked it.

She had to stop living this way. She had to get organized, take control of her life. She really did.

She drove with extreme caution, deliberately holding in check what her dad called her "lead foot." The streets were little more than mounds of drifted snow and thin layers of ice. The road crews apparently hadn't been able to keep up with the fast-falling, wind-driven snow that had begun in the afternoon, even though it seemed to have finally stopped.

In spite of some faint apprehension about meeting so many new people all at once—the list Dan's secretary had shown her earlier in the week looked as though most of Shepherd Valley would be there tonight—she was looking forward to the evening. She was curious about the way Dan lived and was eager to see his home. At first she had been surprised to learn that he lived alone and wondered how he could manage, even with Sunny to help. But after three weeks of daily contact with the man, she no longer questioned Daniel Kaine's ability to manage anything.

The light she had been waiting for changed, and Jennifer moved through the intersection slowly, her mind still filled with thoughts of her enigmatic boss. There was no denying the attraction the man held for her, though she had scolded herself more than once for allowing him to occupy such a prominent place among her thoughts. Still, he was an intriguing, complex personality, far different from anyone Jennifer had ever known. As for the way her emotions ran riot every time he came near—well, he was simply a very *compelling* man.

He was also a strangely *intimate* man. This trait might have put her off in someone without Dan's innate kindness and acute sensitivity. But Jennifer had quickly grown comfortable with his eagerness to know, to understand, to "see" through the eyes of others what he could no longer see for himself.

It was now routine for her to give him at least a sketchy idea of what she was wearing, especially color, or to casually describe their surroundings when they were driving. She told him of any significant change in another employee's appearance and fell into the habit of describing little things that caught her attention whenever they were together.

She had come to understand that he drew heavily upon his memories and considered himself fortunate in having been sighted most of his life. He was still able to project images onto the screen of his mind, he had explained to her, whereas those who had been blind from birth had to depend upon the observations of someone else, plus whatever they could glean from their other senses, to help them form mental pictures.

Jennifer hadn't said anything, but she was more than a little skeptical about his positive attitude. She found it almost impossible to see even the smallest grain of "blessing" in the tragedy of Dan's blindness. So far, however, she had seen no trace of anything that might hint of false courage or shallow optimism.

It would be difficult *not* to be drawn to the man, she assured herself once more as she turned slowly onto Keystone Drive. In addition to his commanding physical presence and multifaceted personality, he bore his disability with an incredible aplomb. Dan obviously relished his independence, yet he didn't hesitate to ask for assistance when he needed it. There was a definite aura of strength about him, even though a touching vulnerability would occasionally surface when least expected, as had been the case earlier in the afternoon. Jennifer had walked into Dan's office and found him standing at the large window behind his desk, his face and one hand pressed to the glass as though he were staring outside. As usual, his dark hair had fallen over his forehead, barely brushing the pale vertical scar at his eyebrow. He had been dressed in a white crew-neck pullover with a quilted front and gray cotton trousers with worn knees. He wore the casual outfit as he wore everything else—with the natural grace of an athlete comfortable with his own body. But there had been a sadness imprinted on his features that tugged at Jennifer's heart. She had felt a sudden intense need to say or do something that would bring a smile to his face.

She hadn't spoken, feeling awkward about intruding upon what was obviously an unprotected, private moment. But he had known she was there.

"Jennifer?" he questioned softly, without moving.

"Yes. I can come back—"

"No, it's all right," he assured her quickly, motioning her closer. "Come in."

She went to stand by him, seeing the vapor his warm breath had made on the cold windowpane.

"Katharine said it was snowing," he said quietly.

"Yes, it is. It started about an hour ago."

He rubbed his fingers gently against the glass, as though he could touch the scene outside. "I used to love to stand here and look down on the valley when it was snowing." His expression was pensive. "Do you like it—the snow?"

"Oh, yes. I love it! I always have."

He was quiet for a moment. Then he touched her lightly on the shoulder. "Help me see it again, Jennifer. Tell me what it looks like."

The wistful note in his appeal had thrown Jennifer off guard for just an instant. She glanced from Dan's profile to the winter scene outside, forcing her voice into an even, conversational tone when she spoke.

"Well, let's see . . . it's dark, almost like evening. The street lights are on all the way down the hill—lots of houses are lit up, too. And most of the cars have their headlights on. It looks as if traffic's having a hard time already. I can see at least four or five cars stalled halfway up Rainbow Drive."

She stopped, moving closer to him to peer out the window. "It's a heavy snow. The branches on that old blue spruce by the walk are really drooping." Then she added, as much to herself as to Dan, "The snowflakes are the big, fat squishy ones, the kind that are fun to catch with your mouth open."

She looked up at him. The melancholy that had darkened his features only moments before had now lifted and brightened to a tender smile of remembrance. When he reached for her, fumbling to find her hand, Jennifer linked her fingers with his without thinking.

"Did your mom ever yell at you for messing up her window like this?" Dan asked. He blew against the window, then took her hand and pressed her index finger against the cold, wet glass. *"J-e-n-n-i-f-e-r."*

"My turn." Still smiling, he transferred his hand from on top of hers to trace his finger in the fog on the glass.

"Wait a minute—we ran out of steam," Jennifer told him, laughing. "Breathe."

"I am breathing."

"On the *window*, Dan. We need more steam."

"Right. More steam." He opened his mouth to blow on the glass, then stopped. "Ah . . . tell me there's no one else in the room, Jennifer."

"Just us."

He leaned his forehead lightly against the glass, quickly steaming up more of the window, and Jennifer helped him write his name beneath hers.

"This is a very symbolic thing we've done here today, Jennifer," he said gravely. "You realize that, don't you?"

"Symbolic?"

"Absolutely." He dabbed his wet, cold finger on the end of her nose. "Once you write your name in a man's breath, you become a part of his life."

Even now, remembering the moment set Jennifer's heart racing. She had better get a grip, and soon. *He wasn't serious,* she reminded herself. *It was a joke. Nothing more.*

Jennifer forced her thoughts back to the present as she killed the motor of the car. Leaning back with a relieved sigh, she studied the "Kaine barn," Dan's home. She had already heard a great deal about it. It was as unconventional and as unique as its owner. It truly *was* a barn—a large, restored early American barn attached to a small clapboard house, which, as Dan had explained to her, now housed his indoor pool. Structurally spectacular, it had a sturdy, rustic appearance—dark oak siding, seamed metal roof, and varied styles and sizes of windows. It was tucked into the hillside and looked down on an absolutely breathtaking view of the valley.

She dragged in a deep, steadying sigh as she slid out from under the steering wheel and began to trudge up the snow-covered walk to the house. "Speaking of breathtaking views," she muttered softly to herself.

She stopped to stare for a long moment at Daniel Kaine, who had just thrown open the door and stood waiting for her with a smile that made her heart go into an unexpected tailspin.

FOUR

DAN dropped his hands lightly onto Jennifer's shoulders as he helped her shrug out of her coat.

"Relax, kid. Mountaineers are very friendly folks. You don't need to get tensed up about being in a room full of them."

Jennifer shook her head, marveling at his uncanny ability to sense her emotional barometer. "Nobody's ever given a party for me before. I'm a little nervous."

He squeezed her shoulders reassuringly and was just turning to hang up her coat when Lyss walked up and took it from him. Jennifer stared at the two of them together, Lyss and Dan, struck again by how much they resembled each other. Lyss was as striking in her own way as Dan, with the same penetrating blue eyes and dusky hair that appeared to be trademarks of the Kaines.

Naturally, it wasn't long before Gabe joined them. Jennifer had observed that wherever Lyss was, Gabe was sure to follow. The two were engaged—and had been, Dan had informed her, for nearly two years. Apparently Lyss was the holdout, insisting they have a down payment for a house before they married.

The four of them started toward the kitchen, only to be stopped on the way by a small boy with silver-blond hair and apple cheeks. He came bounding up, with Sunny at his heels. Dan grinned tolerantly and hoisted the boy up to his shoulder in one easy motion. "Did you and Jim give Sunny her dinner like I asked?"

"We put some good stuff in with her dog food, Dan. Hamburger and eggs." The boy gave Dan a hug and Jennifer a bashful smile.

Jennifer grinned at him. She had already met Jason Lyle at church. The small eight-year-old with the enormous brown eyes was an orphan—mentally limited, but only slightly—who lived at the county children's home. Both of his parents had been killed in a motorcycle accident when he was only a few months old. Dan had first become acquainted with the boy through the Friend-to-Friend Association, a countywide mutual aid ministry for the disabled that Dan and some of the people at his church had helped to establish. The Kaines and Gabe took turns seeing that Jason got to church and Sunday school each week.

He was an incredibly beautiful child, Jennifer thought, so physically perfect that it was difficult to realize he might never exceed the mental capacity he had already attained. She couldn't be near the boy without feeling a stab of resentment at the cruel blow that had been dealt to him. How could God give a child such remarkable appeal and then cripple his mind?

Jason never failed to remind her of her younger brother Loren—gifted with an unusually fine mind but an imperfect body. To Jennifer's thinking, Loren and Jason were only two among many examples of divine injustice.

She watched Dan swing the boy over his head and then set him lightly on his feet. There was an obvious flow of affection between the two of them. It was no secret around the station that Dan would like to adopt his little friend but was reluctant to do so because he wanted more for Jason than what he thought he could offer as a blind, single parent.

"Go get Jim and the two of you take Sunny outside for a few minutes," Dan instructed Jason. "And bundle up good, you hear?"

Jennifer watched the small boy trot off to the kitchen and begin to tug eagerly on Jim Arbegunst's sleeve. Jim, the tall, sad-eyed teenager she had first seen in the studio on the day of her interview, was helping Papa Joe with the food. Jennifer had been immediately drawn to this boy with his uncertain smile and haunted eyes. He worked part-time at the station after school and on weekends. Gabe often referred to Jim, who followed Dan around with undisguised devotion, as "another one of Kaine's kids."

A quiet, noticeably unhappy youth, Jim was the only son of a farmer who lived on a small plot of land just outside of town—a piece of ground Dan described as too anemic to yield anything more than a token crop of vegetables. According to Dan, Caleb Arbegunst supplemented his income by running a temporary shelter for delinquent boys, a kind of stopping-off place where the court sent youngsters until more permanent arrangements could be made.

Apparently, some residents of the community had mixed emotions about the shelter. From time to time, questions were raised about the advisability of placing so many teens in the care of a man with Arbegunst's reputation. He was rumored to be an alcoholic with a fiery temper, and some believed that his wife, who had deserted Caleb and Jim when the boy was still a toddler, had left because she could no longer deal with her husband's cruelty.

Dan's voice pulled Jennifer's attention back to him. "My folks sent their best wishes—and their regrets that they couldn't be here." He moved Jennifer's hand to his forearm and covered it with his own as they began to walk through the house. "They won't be back from the convention until late tomorrow night. But they want you to come to lunch Sunday after church."

Jennifer had already been to the Kaines' twice for dinner and would have jumped at any invitation to enjoy Pauline Kaine's cooking again. "You're sure I won't wear out my welcome?"

"No chance. However, I *do* have an ulterior motive for getting you invited."

"Oh?"

"Mm-hm. I was wondering if you'd be willing to drive me up to the farm afterward. I should warn you, I suppose, that I'd like to take Jason along, too." He stopped walking and turned toward her.

"The farm?" Jennifer was distracted by the music room at the far end of the house. Her glance traveled over an ebony grand piano occupying an enormous amount of space, two sophisticated-looking keyboards, a drum set, and a number of smaller stringed instruments. On either side, tall bookshelves held an impressive stereo component system.

"Helping Hand," Dan went on. "The summer camp for disabled kids I told you about." Located about sixty miles from Shepherd Valley, the Helping Hand had once been a conventional farm. For the last three years, Dan and Gabe had been working hard to turn it into a large camp that could accommodate children with a variety of physical and emotional challenges.

"Oh—sure, I can go. No problem." Jennifer expelled a quick breath of surprise. "You never told me you were a musician!"

He gave a deprecating shrug. "I just play around with the keyboards some. It relaxes me. Mostly I use all this with my teen group. I like to have them out here to practice instead of rehearsing in the church basement. You'd be surprised at the cooperation I get when I promise a swimming party in exchange for a good rehearsal."

"I've heard a lot about your teen choir. How big is it?"

He grinned. "Don't ever let them hear you call them a *choir,* Jennifer. They're an *ensemble,* or a *group,* or even a *bunch*—but never, ever a *choir.* We usually have about fifteen. Ask me on a bad night, and I'd say fifty."

"And he loves every minute of it," added Lyss, who, along with Gabe, had followed them from the great room. "He and his drummer."

"His drummer?"

"In person," Gabe said, poking his head over Lyss's shoulder. "The kids call me *Sticks.*"

"That's for your legs, man, not your drumming," Dan cracked.

"Uh, huh . . . well, you don't want to know what they call you, old buddy," Gabe retorted dryly.

The three of them insisted on showing Jennifer the pool house, Dan's special pride and joy. By the time they returned to the main living area, the house was filled with guests milling about.

Jennifer spent the next half hour meeting people, then went upstairs to the loft with Lyss and Jason. The boy had had an accident with his fruit punch and was in need of a quick cleanup.

"This is where I sleep when I spend the night with Dan. I even keep some of my clothes here," Jason told her proudly as they entered the large bedroom.

For an instant, Jennifer had the peculiar sensation that she had just stepped onto a nineteenth-century ship. The room held a variety of nautical items, including a splendid teak-and-brass binnacle and a hand-rubbed ship's wheel. The massive bureau was topped by a model of a clipper ship, and the wall shelves were lined with such artifacts as a whaling harpoon, different kinds of lanterns, an antique compass, and a bell clock. The only things not directly related to the sea were the huge half-tester bed, covered with a colorful quilt, and a stone fireplace with an old, broad-bottom rocking chair in front of it.

Jennifer breathed a long, appreciative sigh. "What a *wonderful* room! Dan must love the sea!"

Lyss nodded as she scooped a clean shirt from a bureau drawer and helped Jason change. "He does. He and Gabe were always building ship models when they were kids. Before the accident, they used to run white water on the Cheat River every chance they got. Dan has always been crazy about water—anything from the ocean to a swimming pool." With a smile, she gave Jason an affectionate swat on the bottom and sent him on his way. The boy flashed Jennifer a mischievous grin as he raced by her and headed for the steps.

"The loft used to be just one big room," Lyss explained, gesturing to an open doorway opposite the bureau. "But Dan started doing so much counseling a couple of years ago that we partitioned off enough space to make a guest room for visitors."

"Counseling?"

Lyss took a moment to run a comb through her dark hair, glancing over her shoulder in the mirror at Jennifer. "Every now and then one of the therapists from the rehab center in Pittsburgh sends someone down here to stay a few days, someone who's having a hard time emotionally."

"I don't know how he does it," Jennifer said, shaking her head. "How does he keep up with everything? He must never have a moment for himself!"

"Well, he likes to keep busy. Sometimes I think he takes on a little too much, but—" She shrugged, leaving the thought incomplete.

"Lyss—how long did it take? For Dan to get over the accident?"

Lyss turned, pushed up the sleeves of her bright red sweater, and walked to a nearby window, glancing out for a moment. When she turned back to Jennifer, her expression was grave. "I'm not sure anyone ever really gets over something like that."

Feeling rebuked, Jennifer nodded. "It's just that he's so . . ." She groped for a word, finding none.

"I know." Lyss smiled a little and went to sit down on the bed, motioning for Jennifer to do the same. "It was difficult—horribly difficult—for a long time. Sometimes I didn't think he would ever be himself again," she said quietly. For a moment her attention seemed to drift away, and she sat plucking idly at the bed quilt.

"It's hard to imagine Dan ever being different than he is now," Jennifer said. "He has to be the most amazing man I've ever met."

Still not looking up, Lyss nodded and continued to smile. "He's pretty terrific." She ran her hand through her short, casually styled hair, then glanced across the bed at Jennifer. "He was such a great athlete. Did you know he took a gold at the Olympics? He's a marvelous swimmer! Of course, he's always excelled at anything he attempted—"

She stopped short and laughed. "Listen to me—I'm sorry. I'm afraid I'm not always very humble where my big brother is concerned."

"No, I understand," Jennifer protested. "You have every right to be proud of him."

"I *am* proud of him. I think he's wonderful," Lyss declared almost fiercely. "It was a nightmare, seeing him lose so much, watching him fight so desperately to hold on to his dignity—and his sanity. He had to start all over again, just like a child—" Her bright blue eyes glistened with unshed tears, and Jennifer impulsively reached across the bed to squeeze her hand with understanding.

"That's what was hardest for me," Lyss explained in a quieter voice. "Seeing him so . . . defeated, so helpless. Dan's always been my hero. With six years between us, he spoiled me terribly the whole time I was growing up."

She was obviously remembering things she would rather forget. "It was *awful,* seeing him like that, reduced to almost total helplessness. Watching him trip, bump into walls, stumble, having to stand by while he tried to feed himself without spilling—" She stopped, her voice again shaky. But after a moment her expression cleared, and she went on. "Of course, that was all before his rehabilitation, and Sunny. After he came back from Seeing Eye, he hired a therapist to give him special mobility training. It was amazing to see what Dan learned in such a short time—how to arrange his clothing, code his money, organize the kitchen. The therapist even gave him a crash course in self-defense."

Lyss got to her feet and walked around the bed toward Jennifer, who also stood. "Without a doubt, Dan's determination to be independent is one of the things that kept him going after the accident." She attempted a smile. "Of course, that unbearable stubbornness of his may have been a factor, too. But over the long haul, it had to be his faith in God that helped him survive."

Jennifer's reply was faint. "I wonder how he did it." She glanced at Lyss. "How he managed to . . . go on trusting, under the circumstances?"

Lyss studied Jennifer, her gaze questioning but patient. "I don't think anyone but Dan could explain that," she answered.

"Can I ask you one more thing—about the accident? What actually happened?"

"Oh, I thought maybe Gabe had told you, or even Dan. He'll talk about it, you know; you don't have to avoid the subject with him. Actually, what made the whole thing even worse for me was that Dan was on his way back from visiting me at the university the night it happened."

Her face contorted briefly with the pain of remembrance. "It was my birthday, but I had finals and couldn't come home. So Dan drove down to deliver my birthday presents. He did that a lot," she said, smiling a little as she continued. "He would just show up, without warning, always bringing me something—a new book or clothes or money." Her voice softened. "He was forever bringing me money. I always seemed to be broke when I was in college."

"And the accident happened on his way home?" Jennifer prompted gently.

Lyss nodded, leaning wearily against the doorframe. "It was late, and there was a heavy fog. It was a head-on collision."

"The other driver—he was killed, wasn't he?"

Again Lyss's eyes misted. "Yes. He was only sixteen. Apparently he was drunk—at least he'd been drinking a lot. The state police told us they found an empty bottle at his feet, and his clothes reeked of liquor. They said the boy had probably died instantly from a broken neck, even though Caleb ran for help as soon as he was able."

"Caleb?"

"Caleb Arbegunst. Jim's father. You see, it was his truck. The boy who was driving was one of the boys from the shelter. Caleb was taking him to the detention center, but he got sleepy and let the boy drive. Evidently he started drinking as soon as Caleb fell asleep. Caleb didn't know the boy had alcohol with him."

Lyss's mouth twisted with disgust. "At least he *said* he didn't know. For my part, I don't believe much of anything Caleb Arbegunst says."

"You know, I don't think I've heard a good word about that man since I came to Shepherd Valley," Jennifer said.

"And it's not likely that you will, because no one can find anything good to say," Lyss told her, still frowning. "Anyway, Caleb was thrown from the truck and was unconscious for a long time. When he came to, he went to a nearby farmhouse to call the state police. They found the boy dead and Dan unconscious."

An involuntary shudder gripped Jennifer for an instant. "And when Dan woke up . . ."

"He was blind."

They were both silent for a long moment. Finally, Lyss gave a long sigh, then smiled. "Let's get you back downstairs. You're supposed to be the guest of honor at this shindig, remember?"

Later in the evening, about the time Jennifer would have expected the party to break up, people began urging Dan and Gabe down to the music room. Lyss went along, making her way to one of the keyboards while Gabe sat down at the drums.

Jennifer watched the three with delighted surprise, her mouth dropping open when Dan crashed into a thunderous cadence at the piano, then unexpectedly broke away to the driving beat of a top Christian contemporary number. Gabe immediately backed him up on the drums, and after the first few measures Lyss added the keyboard—and her voice. She and Dan blended together in a tight, professional harmony. Almost instantly, everyone in the room became a part of the music, clapping their hands or singing along through a number of contemporary and traditional gospel songs.

Jennifer continued to gape with amazement at Dan. So he "played around with the keyboards some," huh? A warmth enveloped her heart as she watched him. He could probably do anything he wanted at a keyboard, she speculated, and his voice was more than adequate. The man never seemed to run out of surprises!

The noise level in the room skyrocketed as Gabe plopped a green baseball cap onto Dan's head and strapped an old flattop guitar around his neck. When Gabe reached back into the corner for a fiddle for himself, Lyss picked up a banjo—and everyone went crazy.

For the next twenty minutes, the trio indulged themselves in a bluegrass demonstration that left Jennifer wide-eyed and open-mouthed. She was astonished at the way Gabe could grind the fiddle, even more fascinated by Dan and his guitar as he turned it from a mournful, whining freight train one minute into a flashy, frenzied blaze of superior "pickin'" the next. Now she knew why his fingertips were so calloused.

At one point, she was caught short by an unexpected—and unwelcome—pang of yearning. "This group could use a singer with a little class," Gabe jokingly called out to her. For one precarious moment Jennifer was tempted.

It had been a long, difficult road, burying the desire to sing, a desire that at one time had been more powerful for Jennifer than the craving for food. But bury it she had. Or so she had thought. Now here it was again, that aching, all-too-familiar pulsing in her veins that cried for an outlet. The need to create, to communicate, to celebrate—

No! With a determination that bordered on anger, she slammed the door of her mind, shook her head at Gabe, and forced her attention back to the music. The three of them continued to ham it up to the hilt until Lyss gave up her banjo in defeat, collapsing in a fit of laughter at the slapstick antics of Gabe and her brother. Finally, Dan tipped his baseball cap to the crowd, then tossed his arm around Gabe's shoulder.

Jennifer stared at Dan, once again puzzling over his apparent enjoyment of life. Not for the first time, she wondered if the peace that seemed to emanate from him could actually be genuine. She found it increasingly difficult to doubt what she saw in him, yet in some inexplicable way Dan's strength and contentment stirred a sense of uneasiness in her own spirit that she found herself unwilling to face—as well as a longing that bordered on envy, envy for whatever it was that gave his life such a unique, shining quality.

For Dan was a man who lived his life in darkness—or, as he had once corrected her, in "grayness." Because of his blindness, he walked among shadows, his steps guided only by his own personal faith. Yet he managed to shed a gentle, steady light on his surroundings wherever he went.

Was it possible that she even *resented* his boundless passion for living, his inconceivable serenity and strength? Perhaps his strength evoked in her some nameless guilt for her own lack of spiritual maturity. The very idea made Jennifer wonder what kind of person she had become.

Almost irritably, she also wondered why she should be spending so much time and energy thinking of Dan at all.

But that was another question for which she had no answer.

The truck was well hidden in the thick grove of pine trees at the side of Kaine's house. He had parked just high enough on the first rise of the hill so he could watch without being seen.

He could see everyone leaving now, laughing, calling back and forth to one another as they half walked and half slid to their cars. He had been waiting for over two hours. It hadn't been so bad at first. As long as everyone was inside, he could run the engine and keep the heater going. But when they started coming out, he was afraid someone would hear the truck, so he'd killed the motor. Now he was shaking with the cold. He crossed his arms over his chest and hugged them to his body as tightly as he could, shivering even as his anger heated.

Kaine must have had half the town in there. You wouldn't think a blind man would be throwing parties. But Kaine wanted everybody to think he was no different from anyone else.

Like the way he'd come on to the woman. He had seen the two of them before tonight, smiling at each other, just as though they were a normal couple, like they belonged together. Was that grinning ape really dumb enough to think she liked him?

Everyone was gone now, everyone except for Kaine and the woman. He watched them come out of the house, the dog at Kaine's side. He was far enough out that the dog shouldn't notice the truck, but he squirmed, ready to pull out in an instant if he had to.

Kaine walked the woman to the car. *As if he'd be any protection to her.*

The man sneered and rubbed his hands together to warm them. Even with gloves, they were stiff from the cold. It wouldn't be long now, though. The woman was leaving.

He cracked the window on his side just enough to listen. The light, steady wind carried their voices. . . .

"What would it take to get you to sing again?"

Jennifer stared up at him. "Dan, I told you—"

"I know what you told me, Jennifer," he interrupted agreeably. "I'm just asking if there's any chance I could change your mind."

"None," she said without hesitating. "Why?"

Dan shrugged. "I'm going to combine the adult worship choir at church with my teen group at Easter for a musical. Having a trained voice to sing the part of Mary Magdalene would be a real plus."

"You've never heard me sing," Jennifer reminded him.

"You hum around the station all the time, didn't you know that? I recognize quality when I hear it."

"I—no. I'm sorry, Dan, but I can't."

He nodded as if he understood. "I don't suppose you'd want to listen to it before you give me a definite no, would you?"

"Dan, please—"

He tilted his head toward her as though he might continue to press. But then he smiled and touched her lightly on the arm. "OK. Listen, you be careful on the hill. It's a lot worse going down than coming up when it's this icy."

The man in the truck grimaced when he saw the woman place her hand over Kaine's just before she opened the car door. "I'll be fine," he heard her assure him. "Dan—thank you for tonight. No one's ever done anything like this for me before."

Kaine dropped the retriever's harness, ordered the dog to stay, then placed his hands on her shoulders.

She shouldn't let him touch her like that . . . she probably feels sorry for him . . . or aims to keep her job by playin' up to him. . . ."

The man licked his lips, wishing he could hear what they were saying. But they were talking softer now, and the wind had shifted.

Is he going to kiss her?

No, she was getting in the car, starting the engine. Finally she pulled away and began to ease the car down the hill, leaving Kaine alone with the dog.

Suddenly the dog raised its head and turned toward the truck, lifting its ears as a menacing growl started in its throat. Kaine jerked his head around, too, and for an instant the man in the truck froze.

Then he remembered. Kaine couldn't see him. Kaine couldn't see anything.

He grinned as he suddenly brought the truck's engine to life with a thunderous roar. He cackled to himself and came charging out from the grove of pine trees, heading straight for the blind man and his dog.

He saw Kaine's mouth drop open, saw panic wash over his face, and he laughed even harder. He floored the accelerator and crushed the heel of his hand against the horn, skidding away from the blind man at the last possible minute, only seconds before he would have leveled him. The dog went crazy, snarling and barking like a wild thing.

That'll give him something to think about until I decide what I want to do next. . . .

FIVE

EVER since her welcome party three weeks before, Jennifer had been living in overdrive. She didn't mind; in fact, she thrived on it. The only thing that worried her was the amount of time she seemed to be spending with Dan—more specifically, how much she *enjoyed* the time she spent with Dan.

In addition to all the hours she was putting in on the radiothon, she now had the afternoon drive time each weekday. She jocked her own show, consisting mostly of contemporary and gospel music, public service announcements, and top-of-the-hour news. It was informal, fast-paced, and fun.

She was learning a lot, but she still had a lot more to learn. Because most of the station's procedures had been adapted to Dan's blindness, she had to take a slightly different approach to things she had once considered routine. With other tasks, she had to start from scratch.

She had recently mastered his Braillewriter and could now type messages directly into Braille. Gabe had taught her how to make up the special, raised version of the "hot clock" he had designed for Dan—a clever variation of the pie-chart broadcasting schedule used by sighted disc jockeys. By now she had met most of the station's major advertisers, covered an assortment of community events, learned her way around town, and done a fifteen-minute feature on Helping Hand Farm after her visit with Dan and Jason.

One of the things she enjoyed most was something for which she received no salary. Along with several other volunteers from the station and the community, she donated a few hours each week as a reader for the closed-circuit radio service the station operated. The service provided over twenty hours of weekly broadcasting for the blind, furnishing receivers free of charge to those who couldn't afford to rent them.

In her spare time, she unpacked a box here and there. She was proud of the fact that after living in her little bungalow only six weeks, she had no more than four or five boxes left to empty.

She was also making lists. Jennifer had decided that she needed a strategy for organizing her life. She had bought a book on time management at the bookstore in the mall and was following it chapter by chapter, line by line. She was going to take this seriously, she promised herself. If she was going to be an efficient assistant, she needed to get organized.

At the moment, however, she was down on her hands and knees, burrowing in the bottom of her credenza. She was almost absolutely *positive* she had put the entire stack of Braille scheduling charts for the radiothon in there. But she had been so busy over the last few days, she had taken to tossing everything that didn't require immediate attention onto the same shelf. Now the charts were missing—if they had ever been there in the first place.

She grumbled to herself, then scrambled to her feet and turned around to—"Dan! Don't *do* that!"

He stood by her desk, looking mildly offended. "What exactly did I do?"

"You—*appeared*. You're so incredibly quiet. Clear your throat or something when my back is turned—" She grimaced. "Oh dear. I keep *doing* it! Of course, you don't know when my back is turned."

"Is your face red, Jennifer?"

"It certainly is. And so are my knees. I've been trying to find those schedules for the radiothon—the ones I typed on the Braillewriter for you."

"They're on my desk."

"Why are they on *your* desk?"

"Didn't you say you typed them for me?"

"Yes, but I put them in my office—"

"No you didn't. You put them on my desk." He shook his head sadly. "The mind is the first thing to go, kid."

"Not in my case. It's in better shape than my back."

"I have to go to the grocery story today." He said it with all the enthusiasm of a man facing an IRS audit.

Jennifer perched on the edge of her desk and grinned at him. She found Dan's strong dislike for grocery shopping both interesting and amusing. He had been known to resort to trickery, even bribery, to wheedle someone else into doing it for him. He had successfully used his routine on Jennifer two or three times. *But not today, Daniel,* she thought impishly. *Not today.*

"Fine," she said evenly. "I'll be happy to go along and help, if you like."

He had been expecting just that response, obviously, and jumped on it. "You sure you have the time?" Dan was a master of the thoughtful, concerned frown.

"Mm. No problem."

"I'm really pushed this afternoon. If you're sure you have time, I'll just give you my list. It's only half a dozen items or so." If a man's smile could be relieved, smug, and victorious all at the same time, Dan's was.

"No."

He looked surprised. "No, *what?*"

"No, I'm not doing your shopping. I did it last week—twice. I said I'd *help*. Today, we go together."

He pulled his mouth to one side as if considering his choices. "Why together? It would be more efficient for only one of us to go, wouldn't it? It would certainly save some time." He arched one heavy brow in his best "I'm trying to be reasonable" expression.

"For you, maybe. Not for me. It'll be faster for me if you go along," Jennifer said brightly. "You say you need half a dozen items. Fine—I'll pick up three, you get the other three. We'll be back at the station in twenty minutes flat."

He slumped but accepted defeat graciously. "You want to go now?"

"After lunch."

"I suppose I'm buying."

"Why, what a nice idea, Dan! I'll be ready in five minutes."

After a quick lunch at Papa Joe's, they headed for the shopping center. A few minutes later Jennifer pulled off the road into the parking lot, splashing through an enormous puddle. She squinted her eyes, peering through the rain-swept windshield.

"What is this, monsoon season?" she grumbled. "Isn't there ever a happy medium in West Virginia's weather? Something a little less severe than blizzards and cloudbursts?"

Dan shrugged. "We'll have snow again by the end of the week. Maybe sooner."

She glanced over at him. "And that's our radar weather exclusive for today, folks. News at eleven."

"I'm as accurate as that guy on cable, the one who rhymes all his forecasts."

"True. But he's a great-looking guy."

"I would hope, Jennifer, that you're beyond being impressed by a handsome face."

"No woman can resist a true poet, Daniel."

"You actually watch that man?"

"Every evening at six. Faithfully."

He shook his head. "That's disgusting."

She grinned. "I'm going to let you and Sunny out at the door while I park. Otherwise, you'll both drown."

She waited until Sunny had guided Dan through the entrance of the supermarket before pulling away to look for a parking place. Finding nothing nearby, she nervously began to scout some of the rows farther out. It probably wasn't a good idea to leave Dan alone in the market too long, even with Sunny. He truly *did* get a little strange about shopping. She suspected he felt slightly less confident in stores than he liked to admit. Still, he had Sunny, so he'd be fine. . . .

A few minutes later, Jennifer rushed into the supermarket wringing water out of her drenched hair. She stood near the checkout lanes and scanned the front of the store for a glimpse of Dan and Sunny, finally locating them at a nearby produce bin. She started toward them but stopped a few feet away, intrigued by the curious scene taking place.

Dan, a somewhat grim smile on his face, was attempting to separate one flimsy plastic sack from another. With a soft grunt of frustration, he finally dropped Sunny's harness, pulled open the sack, and began to sort through the oranges in the case, squeezing them lightly before dropping one into the plastic bag.

Jennifer was about to move and offer her help when a short block of a woman with square shoulders and white hair done up in sausage-link curls walked up to Dan. She squinted up at him belligerently.

From her military stance at his right side, her head came only two or three inches above his waist. With a stern thrust of her chin, she gave a tug to her serviceable black raincoat and bellowed up at him in a voice that would have done a drill sergeant proud. "You shouldn't squeeze them oranges!"

Dan, his hand suddenly suspended in midair over an orange, cocked his head to one side quizzically, then bent down toward her voice. "Ma'am?"

His small, polite smile faded when she repeated her warning, with some elaboration. "You'll bruise 'em! You pick good oranges by their color, not by the way they squeeze. Here, let me show you."

With no further fuss, she tucked her red umbrella under one arm and planted herself firmly next to Dan as she began to sort efficiently through the oranges. "Hmph! Men! Reckon your wife's at work."

Too surprised to resort to his usual sense of humor, Dan simply stood alongside her, his mouth slightly agape. "Uh . . . ma'am—"

"Sent you to do the shopping, did she? Well, you'd best go along with her a few times and learn how to do it proper! I wouldn't have turned my man—God rest his soul—loose at the market alone, not for anything. Look here, now!" She thrust a slightly mottled-looking orange directly upward to within an inch of Dan's nose. "See all those green places that're pushed in? You don't want that, no sir!"

Giving him no opportunity to react, she removed the bruised orange, trading it for a healthy one. "Here's a good one now. Well, open your *bag!*" Shaking her head with impatience, she plopped the large, perfect orange into the plastic sack still dangling from Dan's fingers. His mouth dropped open a little wider, but he said nothing.

Jennifer chewed the knuckles of her fist in a noble attempt to choke off a giggle, willfully choosing to ignore the small voice that prompted her to interrupt.

"Well, are you gonna finish gettin' what you want out of that bin, young man? I have some shopping of my *own* to tend to!" She hurled a withering look of disapproval at Dan.

"Oh—sure . . . yes, ma'am!" In his haste to oblige, Dan knocked one of the oranges from its fixed place on top of the rows. Twenty other round, ripe oranges promptly tumbled down and over the produce bin onto the floor.

Jennifer swallowed a groan of dismay and took a step forward, stopping again when Dan's accuser dropped quickly to her knees, hiking up her coat and dress enough to allow freedom of movement. Dan stood numbly mute, looking positively stricken.

"I swan, I don't know how some folks find their way home," the woman muttered, clucking her tongue in exasperation. With deft movements, she rolled a few oranges up onto her arm, then proceeded to bob up and down like a tightly compressed jack-in-the-box until she had replaced all the fruit in the bin. Waiting, Dan scratched his head, looked embarrassed, and reached for Sunny's harness.

Jennifer knew it was time to make an entrance. She fixed her face into what she hoped was a sober expression and approached the two of them. "Can I help?"

A quick look at Dan's scowling face confirmed what she feared—he had heard the snap of amusement in her voice. In a tone thick with menace, he leaned over and growled at her. "Where did you park—Cincinnati?"

"This your woman?" The fruit expert eyeballed Jennifer with disdain. "I'd handle the marketing myself, if I were you."

Jennifer swallowed almost painfully, halting the explosion of laughter that she knew would ruin her. "Ah . . . yes. Yes, I suppose I should," she said agreeably, meeting the woman's frown with a smile.

After this exchange, Dan squared his shoulders with dignity, cuddled the plastic sack of oranges to his chest, and pretended to glance innocently around at his surroundings.

"He's slow, is he?" The woman lowered her voice to a grating whisper.

"Slow?" Jennifer looked up into Dan's face, which was a classic study in self-control. "Well . . ."

The woman appraised Dan once more, without emotion, expelling a small grunt of sympathy for Jennifer. "I expect he's a handful, big boy like that." And with that sage pronouncement, she walked away.

It was Jennifer who finally broke the silence, dredging up every shred of self-control available to her in an effort to sound reasonably serious. "Well, Daniel, what else would you like besides oranges?"

"How long have you been standing there, Jennifer?" he asked in a deceptively mild voice, holding out the plastic sack to her as though it might be contaminated.

Jennifer meekly took the bag. "How long? Oh—well, you see, Dan, I had to look for a parking place. I was hurrying—I know how much you hate being alone in the supermarket—when I saw this elderly lady trying to juggle her cane and umbrella in the parking lot. She had dropped her sack, and her groceries were spilling out into a puddle. I had to help her, of course. I couldn't just leave her there like that. I thought you'd be all right, since Sunny was with you."

"That's good, kid. Very good," he said in a nasty tone of voice. "Go on. I can't *wait* to hear the rest of this."

"Daniel, it's *true,* honestly, I'm telling you—"

"How long, Jennifer?"

She took a deep breath, prepared for his wrath—which, she had to admit, was deserved. "I don't think I missed too much, actually." She bit her bottom lip and waited expectantly. "Are you angry with me?"

"Angry?" he repeated smoothly, flinging an arm around her shoulder and giving her a rather rough hug. "Oh, I don't get angry, Jennifer—"

"I just get even," she echoed in unison with him.

"You're doing better, though," he said.

"What?"

"Well, I was expecting you to tear into that poor little old lady with your standard lecture on how to treat the disabled." He gave her a tolerant smile. "I think it's actually a healthy sign that you were able to stand there and enjoy my misery, Jennifer."

He laughed at her small, disgruntled sound of self-defense. "C'mon, kid. I'll show you how to handpick the finest apples in the county."

Before they left the shopping center, Jennifer coaxed Dan into a quick visit to the pet shop. He did everything he could to talk her into taking home a cross-eyed Siamese kitten that stole her heart as soon as she walked up to its cage, but she reluctantly left it there.

"I don't know if I can have pets or not. It didn't even occur to me to ask when I rented the house." She glanced behind her as they went out the door.

"Well, why don't you find out? Joe Como is so taken with you, he'd let you stock your own ark if it made you happy."

Once inside the car, Jennifer stared out at the dismal afternoon and the cold rain still falling steadily. "Another few hours of this, and the ark might be a real possibility."

It was only a little after three, but the slate gray sky and the downpour made it look more like evening. Jennifer drove with the headlights on dim and the windshield wipers on high.

Dan contentedly helped himself to a half-pound bag of chocolate-covered peanuts. "Want some?"

Jennifer glanced at the candy with longing. "They make me hyper," she said ruefully, scooping out a handful.

"What doesn't?"

Ignoring him, she turned off the main highway onto the two-lane county road that provided a shortcut to the radio station. "I don't know . . . maybe I should have stayed on the Drive. Visibility is zilch, and I hate this road."

"It's getting colder, too," Dan said. "Better watch the bridge—it might be slick."

Jennifer glanced in the rearview mirror. There wasn't another car in sight. "Looks like everyone else had sense enough to stay home today."

They lapsed into silence for the next few minutes, listening to the station and munching peanuts. The new disc jockey was doing part of Jennifer's show in her absence.

"He's not nearly as good as you are, you know," Dan finally said, breaking the quiet.

"Why, Daniel—and I thought you hadn't noticed." Jennifer attempted to cover the warm rush of pleasure she felt at his compliment.

"Mm. I notice more than you think. Our advertising has increased quite a bit for that afternoon drivetime. Started about a week after you took the show."

"Aha! *That's* why you noticed. Money talks."

He shrugged. "You're good. You've got a lot of class on the air. You're easy on the ears, witty—" He paused. "Your voice . . . grabs people. Holds them. I think they hear the same thing in it I do."

"What?"

"The smile in your voice," Dan replied simply. "Were you smiling just now?"

"Yes," answered Jennifer slowly. "How did you know?"

"I can hear it. I don't have to see your smile to feel it. And I think our listeners feel it, too."

Flustered, Jennifer tried to pass the moment off lightly. She looked at him out of the corner of her eye. "Your shopping is done, so that's not your game. What are you up to, boss?"

Dan closed the candy sack and stashed it between them on the console. "There *is* something I'd like to talk about."

Instantly alert to the gravity of his tone, Jennifer nodded. "I knew it."

She glanced sideways to see him lace his fingers together and crack his knuckles, an uncommon gesture for Daniel. "Jennifer . . . how would you feel about . . . going out with me?"

"Going out with you?" Jennifer parroted his words, trying to concentrate on the highway, which was beginning to reflect a suspicious-looking glaze. It was sleeting. She moaned aloud.

"Sorry—it was just an idea." Dan's face went immediately slack.

"What—oh, no! I didn't mean—"

"It's OK," he said quickly. "I don't always read signals right. My mistake."

"*Dan*—" Jennifer reached out to touch his arm—"I was groaning because it's *sleeting* and the road is horrendous. Not because you asked me out!"

He said nothing. Jennifer looked over at him again, bewildered by the unmistakable tension lining his face. He looked as if he were about to jump from the car.

Daniel Kaine? *Insecure?*

Understanding finally dawned. "You're asking me for a date, is that it?"

"In my own inimitable way," Daniel said dryly after a noticeable hesitation.

"Oh." Jennifer bit her lower lip.

Well, why not? A date was only a date, after all. She spent most of her waking hours with him as it was. What would be so different about a date?

An alarm sounded somewhere in Jennifer's head. She was already too attracted to Dan and spent far too much time with him. An honest-to-goodness date would only intensify an already treacherous situation, and she really shouldn't. It would definitely not be a smart thing to do.

"Of course I'll go out with you, Dan," she said softly. "I'd like that very much."

He cracked his knuckles again. "Look, you don't have to say yes just because you work for me. I wouldn't—"

"I didn't."

"Didn't what?"

"Say yes just because I work for you."

"Well, there *are* drawbacks, Jennifer. I'm not exactly your conventional date."

"I don't know that that's necessarily a drawback, Dan."

"You'd have to pick me up, you know."

"That's hardly a problem."

"And Sunny goes with me."

"Sunny and I are pals. What evening did you have in mind?"

"We could ask Gabe and Lyss to come along. That way you wouldn't have to drive—"

"I enjoy driving. When?"

"Look, Jennifer, I want to be sure you understand that—"

"*When,* Daniel?"

He grinned, relaxed his hands, and drew a long breath. "My mother does that."

"Your mother does what?" Jennifer asked impatiently.

"Calls me *Daniel* in that tone of voice when she gets impatient with me. How about tomorrow night?"

"It's a weeknight."

He was instantly wary. "You're busy?"

"Not unless you make me work overtime again, I'm not. Fine. Tomorrow night. But only if I can leave the station by five."

"Four, if you like."

"Deal. Just to satisfy my curiosity, why were you so uptight about asking me for a date?"

"I wasn't uptight. What makes you think I was uptight?"

"Your lips turned blue and you broke the knuckles on both hands."

"I always do that. It doesn't mean I'm uptight."

Jennifer waited.

His expression sobered. "I just wasn't sure if you would want to. The employer-employee thing." He turned his face toward the window on his side. "And the blindness," he added, his voice lower. "There's not exactly a waiting list of women wanting to go out with a blind man. I'm sure you can imagine some of the possible complications."

Jennifer remained silent for a moment. "Well, I think I can handle most of those . . . complications by now, don't you?" she asked evenly. "Since we're together so much?"

He turned toward her. "You're really comfortable with the idea?"

Jennifer considered her reply. There were times when she felt distinctly *uncomfortable* with Dan. Unsettled. Even disturbed. But she knew it had nothing to do with his blindness. It had more to do, she suspected uneasily, with some new and unfamiliar emotions that wouldn't seem to give her any peace these days.

She hoped she didn't sound evasive. "I'd say so. I—" She swallowed the rest of her words as she glanced out the side mirror. A pickup truck was moving up rapidly behind them. Too rapidly. She saw him skid on the slippery road once. Then again. But he continued to close in on them. Jennifer's hands tensed on the steering wheel.

"What's wrong?" Dan asked, immediately alert to the tension in her.

"I *hate* it when people do that! There's a pickup truck right on my bumper."

"Maybe if you slow down he'll go around."

Jennifer glanced down at the speedometer and eased up on the gas pedal. When she looked in the mirror again, the truck had slowed down, too. He was staying right with her.

She slowed even more. So did the truck.

"Is he still tailgating you?"

"Yes. And he's making me extremely nervous. There's ice on the road, and it's not safe—"

"Pull off, why don't you? Let him pass."

"I think I will. He's getting a little too close." She turned on her right blinker and slowed even more, easing the car over to the shoulder of the road.

By the time Dan heard the sound of the truck's engine, it was too late. It was the same truck, he was certain of it. There was the choppy, distinctive miss of a blown head gasket and the additional loud whirring of something loose or broken under the hood. The sound he had heard the night of Jennifer's party. The sound of the truck that had tried to run him down—or at least had tried to make him *think* it was going to run him down.

"Jennifer, watch out—"

The warning came a second too late. He felt the jolt, the sudden push from the rear on Jennifer's side of the car, heard the loud crunch of metal. The car went pitching off the pavement and into a ditch. He snaked out one hand to help her steady the wheel and cried out a sharp warning. "Don't brake! Go with it!"

He heard her ragged breathing, heard her gasp for air, but he could tell by the way she was gripping the wheel that she hadn't panicked. The sudden, careening stop knocked his arm sharply against hers, but they were all right.

He heard the truck go on by, heard the sound of the motor gradually fade as it roared on down the road. His hands were shaking as he released his seat belt and reached for her.

"Jennifer—"

"Oh, Dan—are you all right?"

"I'm fine. What about you?" he asked gruffly, gripping her hand.

For a second, they both sat speechless and stunned. Then Jennifer unlocked her seat belt and fought for a couple of deep breaths. Without a second thought, Dan ignored the console and reached across the seat, gathering her into his arms.

Jennifer's tenuous self-control shattered, and she choked on a ragged sob. Dan felt his own hands tremble as he tried to calm her. He held her for a long time, pressing her face against his shoulder, murmuring soft sounds of comfort against her hair.

"It's OK, now. We're fine, honey, we're just fine."

"But it must be awful for you." Her voice sounded strangled against his shoulder. "Another car accident after what happened before. . . ."

Dan shushed her gently, smiling to think that, after what had just happened, her primary concern was for him. He cradled her tightly against his chest, rocking her back and forth as he would a child.

"I'm perfectly fine," he assured her. "Gabe has given me a couple of much bigger scares in his old T-bird. Don't even think about it."

"But, Dan, that was *deliberate!* That truck intentionally rammed into us!"

"Are you sure, Jennifer?" But he knew the answer to his own question. *He might have really hurt someone this time,* he thought. A cold trickle of fear iced the back of his neck as he realized that *someone* could have been Jennifer. What was he going to do about this nut? He couldn't just let it go on.

"Did you get a good look at the truck?" he asked her. "License number, anything?"

"No," she said. "It was an old pickup, that's all I noticed. A Ford, I think."

He had known it was a truck, had known by the sound of it that night when the guy came barreling over the hill at him. But another Ford? He swallowed hard. *Just a weird coincidence, that's all. There must be hundreds of Ford pickups in this county.*

He cupped the back of her head again. "Shh . . . there's nothing we can do about it now. He's long gone. We'd better get back on the road. Are you OK to drive?"

Drawing away from him, Jennifer sniffed a few times. He heard her fishing for a tissue. She blew her nose, then expelled a long breath. "Yes, I'm all right. We're in a ditch, but I think I can get out. It's not that deep."

She moved away from him, and he heard the click of her seat belt. After several minutes of rocking the car from reverse to drive, they were out of the ditch and back on the road.

In the silence on the way back to the station, Dan could hear Jennifer's anxious breathing. Twice he heard her seat creak as she turned to look back over her shoulder. And he understood. If he hadn't been blind, he would have been looking over *his* shoulder, too.

SIX

D URING the next few days Jennifer found
herself growing increasingly concerned about
Dan's peculiar quietness. He was pensive,
unusually serious—even moody, she thought. Two or three
times she had walked into his office and found him sitting
at his desk, raking his hands through his beard in a gesture
of weariness and frowning as if he were worried about
something. When she tried to get him to talk about it, he
pretended he didn't know what she meant and quickly
changed the subject.

The only times Jennifer had been with him over the past
week had been during work hours at the station or on a work-
related project. Objectively, she knew that shouldn't concern
her. Still, she couldn't help but wonder why he had suddenly
become so distant.

Today had been no different. They had been on the church bus
for over half an hour on their way to a youth rally in Clarksburg,
and he had spoken no more than two or three sentences the
entire time. She had helped him enough with the ensemble to
know he was usually buoyant and full of fun when he was with
the teens. At the moment, however, he seemed distracted and
almost lethargic.

"Does Gabe always drive the bus?" she asked, making yet
another attempt at conversation.

For a moment, she thought he hadn't heard her. But he finally answered. "Most of the time," he said.

Something about his hands caught Jennifer's attention. They were clenched tightly in his lap, and every now and then he would squeeze them together as though they ached.

Her gaze moved back to his face. "Jason is having a great time up there with Jim Arbegunst and the other fellows. Do you usually bring him with you to these rallies?"

Dan nodded. "When we can. He likes being with the teens. They give him a lot of attention."

"The ensemble is providing all the music tonight?"

"Mm-hm."

Another long interval of silence followed. Jennifer glanced across the aisle to the other window, staring out with no real interest at the rugged, mountainous landscape. It had turned cold again, and the contoured hillsides were snow-covered against a deep gray winter's sky.

"I think it's going to snow again."

Dan made no reply. Finally Jennifer decided she'd had enough. "Dan, are you upset about something?" she demanded bluntly.

That seemed to get his attention. He relaxed his hands as if he had only then noticed what he was doing and turned his face toward her. He looked surprised.

"Upset?"

"You're awfully quiet. In fact, you've been quiet all week. Is something wrong?"

He frowned and shook his head. "No. I'm sorry, I guess I've just had a lot on my mind."

"Are you angry with me?"

His look of surprise returned. "Why would I be angry with you?"

"I don't know." Jennifer thought for a moment. "I did nag you about calling the police last week, after that truck ran us off the road. I still don't understand why you wouldn't report it."

"I told you why," he said tightly. "It wouldn't have done any good."

Dan immediately regretted his shortness with her. He softened his voice. "We didn't even have a license number, remember? There are a lot of Ford pickup trucks in this county."

"Well, I still think we should have told the police."

Dan could hear the slight edge in her voice and knew she didn't understand. Why should she? More to the point, how *could* she?

He wasn't even sure *he* understood. None of it made any sense. He was beginning to feel like a marked man. Ever since the incident with the truck last week, the phone calls had been coming more frequently, almost regularly. And each time he had had the peculiar sensation that the caller was angrier and more disturbed than ever. Worse still, he'd had the distinct feeling at least twice this week that someone was watching the house. He had tried to tell himself he was just going through another round of anxiety attacks. But he wondered.

The man called the house every night, sometimes more than once. Occasionally, he spoke; more often he didn't. He had begun calling the station almost daily. But he never came right out and explained what he was up to. Over and over, Dan had asked himself whether the caller actually meant him harm, or whether he was simply trying to frighten him. Or, even more likely, if he was just a loose cannon looking for a target.

He also wondered if there was any significance to the fact that as the radiothon drew nearer, the harassment seemed to intensify. A connection seemed unlikely, yet he was beginning to suspect that there might be one. Could the idea of the radiothon possibly be so abhorrent to someone that he would go to this length to stop it?

He found that hard to believe. Yet he couldn't shake the feeling that in some way the radiothon was at the heart of this siege of madness.

If he were right, he knew he would have to tell someone soon, no matter how odious he found the idea. Too many people were involved in the radiothon. He couldn't let his own stubborn independence overshadow common sense. If he waited too long and this turned out to be more than a scare tactic, he might put someone else in jeopardy.

Someone like Jennifer.

The thought stabbed him in the heart.

He reached over and covered her hand with his. "I'm sorry. I guess I *have* been preoccupied," he said softly, turning toward her. "You have to understand. There's this lady in my life who's messing up my head. I seem to have a lot of trouble thinking of anything else but her these days."

"You needn't apologize," she murmured. "I know you're busy."

He squeezed her hand. "Am I forgiven?"

She pressed her fingers against his but said nothing.

Jennifer and Dan started through the entrance of the host church while Jim took Sunny for a pit stop. Distracted for an instant when Gabe yelled a question at them from the bus, Jennifer turned back to Dan, only to see him narrowly miss being hit in the face by the swinging church door.

She started to cry out a warning, but it died on her lips as he pivoted smoothly away from the door, narrowly avoiding its impact.

"How did you do that?"

"Do what?" Dan waited for her to guide him down the hall to

the auditorium. "I wish Jim would bring Sunny on back. I could use her for a while."

"You've done it before," Jennifer said, bending over to pick up some music she'd dropped. She tucked her free hand under his arm and began to walk with him. "You avoid collisions as if you could see them coming."

"I have facial vision," he replied.

Just then, Jim and the retriever came through the door, and Jennifer waited while Dan put Sunny's harness on.

"What's facial vision?"

"Radar," Dan said shortly, allowing Sunny to lead him up the steps to the platform.

Jennifer stared at him for a moment, then followed. "Figures," she muttered dryly. "Batman and Robin together again."

"Great team," he answered cheerfully. "Jim, if you're going back to the bus, tell Gabe I need him in here as soon as possible to help set up the sound.

"It really is a kind of radar," he went on to explain to Jennifer. "Bats have it. When objects—or people—move, they send out sound waves. If you really work at it, you get to the point where you can estimate the size of an object. It's helped to save my head a number of times."

He stood unmoving for a moment, as if trying to get his bearings. "Give me the layout of the platform, would you? I haven't been here for over a year. I don't especially want to provide any unexpected entertainment for all these teenagers by falling on my face."

"You're at the front right now." Jennifer glanced around them. "There's nothing up here except a grand piano and a console organ a few feet to your left. And there's a podium at the far left front. Of course, we haven't got any of our stuff in place yet." She opened his music case and searched until she found the program for the evening, which she had typed into Braille for him.

Jason came bounding up the steps just then, screeching to a sudden halt in front of Dan. He started to pet Sunny, then stopped.

"Dan, can I take Sunny off her harness and keep her with me?"

"No. Remember what I told you about that, Jason," Dan said firmly, squatting down on one knee by the retriever. "Sunny has a job to do, and she expects to take her orders from me. When the harness is on, that means she's working and can't play. When I take it off, she knows it's all right to have fun."

"Oh yeah . . . I forgot. You're her boss."

"Something like that." Dan stood, hooking his thumb in the harness.

"And you're Jennifer's boss, too." A frown ridged Jason's forehead. "How does *she* know when it's all right to play?"

Dan lifted one dark eyebrow in obvious amusement. "Ah . . . right. Well, you see, Jason, Jennifer likes her work so much she's always having fun." He turned around with a smug grin. "Isn't that right, Jennifer?"

Jennifer crossed her arms over her ski jacket and weighed her answer carefully. "That's exactly right, Jason," she declared, watching Dan incline his head in anticipation. "That's why I work so much overtime. It's strictly for *fun.*"

"*Dan—*" Jason shifted impatiently from one foot to the other.

"All right, all right. Take her and go." Dan removed Sunny's harness and hustled the dog and the boy off with a grin. "But stay close to Jim."

The boy hesitated. "Will you be OK, Dan? Without Sunny?"

"I'll be just fine, sport," Dan said with a smile. "Jennifer will be my eyes for now."

As Jason and the retriever took off, Dan turned slightly, raising his chin in the alert, listening expression he often wore. "So— what do you think of my little buddy?"

"Oh, he's adorable! It's just too bad. . . ."

Dan's smile faded. "Too bad?"

"You know—that he's the way he is." Jennifer had heard the tone of his voice change and glanced up at him.

"Retarded, you mean?"

Jennifer wondered at the somber expression on his face. "Dan? Did I say something wrong?"

"No. Not really." His smile was strained and quickly gone. "I'll be honest with you. That phrase—*it's too bad*—has been a pet peeve of mine ever since the accident. I understand it bothers a lot of people with disabilities. It's . . . a little like someone raking long fingernails across a blackboard, you know?"

She saw him clench and unclench his right hand as he went on. "A quadriplegic I met through Friend-to-Friend told me it always made him think of a gaggle of mourners standing over a coffin and clucking their tongues over the body."

Embarrassed, Jennifer bit her lower lip nervously. "I'm so sorry. I didn't know."

His mouth softened to a more natural smile. "You couldn't. Don't worry about it. Sometimes I overreact. But what you said about Jason . . ." He hesitated, took a deep breath, then exhaled slowly.

"Dan, I didn't mean to—"

He dismissed her protest with a wave of his hand. "I understand what you meant. But I don't agree with you. I guess I don't think about Jason as being—deprived. Just special."

"Are you saying it doesn't bother you that Jason is so . . . *limited?*" she asked incredulously.

He shrugged. "You tell me, Jennifer—is Jason really so much worse off than other kids? Than *normal* kids?"

"But he's such a beautiful little boy!" Jennifer countered sharply. "Doesn't it make you angry, Daniel, seeing the unfairness of his life? Doesn't it hurt you, knowing he's—trapped like that?"

"Trapped?" Something flickered in his eyes—the eyes that usually held only tenderness or laughter or concern—and his chin lifted just a fraction.

"Well," she stammered uncertainly, "he's never going to be able to lead a normal life."

Dan's jaw tensed even more. "You see Jason as a tragedy, do you?"

"I—no! That's not what I meant, I—"

"No? What, then?"

She heard the accusation in his voice, saw a muscle tighten at the corner of his mouth. The conversation had suddenly gone wrong, and she hurried to end it.

"I think it's so unfair, that's all," she murmured. "I don't understand why God allows some of the things he allows—"

Dan moved just a step closer to her and straightened his shoulders. Then, unexpectedly, his expression began to gentle and his mouth curved into a thoughtful smile. "And you'd like to correct a few of his mistakes, wouldn't you?" he asked quietly.

"What?"

"Let's forget it," he suggested abruptly, still smiling.

"Not until you explain that last remark." Jennifer dug in, not about to budge.

He remained silent for a moment. Then a familiar glint of amusement crossed his face. "You're such a rebel," he said mildly, reaching out to entwine a strand of her hair around his finger. "In the sixties, you would have spent most of your time at sit-ins and protest marches, I'll bet." With a small nod of his head, he added, "Instead, you're stuck with an exasperating blind man and a mentally limited little boy. No real challenge for a gal with a burning heart."

"At least you didn't say *bleeding* heart," she muttered grudgingly.

"Now you're angry with me." Suddenly he looked extremely vulnerable.

"No." Jennifer found it next to impossible to be genuinely

angry with Dan, even though he *could* be the most exasperating man at times. But for now, she could feel her petulance fading as she studied him.

His face was so . . . *endearing,* she thought. It was the face of a man who had known great pain and enormous loss, yet had miraculously retained the ability to laugh deeply and live—even love—fully. Shadows had marched across that face, but they had been powerless to destroy the light of the man. A quiet flame glowed from within, the subtle blending of gentleness and strength, humor and kindness, that made him Daniel Kaine.

"Jennifer, I wasn't criticizing you." He spread his hands with apology. "We just look at things differently. You see Jason as trapped. I don't. If I did, I'd have to see myself the same way . . . and I don't dare.

"That boy," he continued quietly, "has a precious gift of wonder. He appreciates all the little ordinary things that other people never even notice. To Jason, a colored rock is a special gift. A seashell is magic. A butterfly is a friend. And life is . . . pure, unqualified joy."

The warmth in his tone deepened, and tenderness filled his smile. "He has a faith that you and I can only envy. He *knows* the Father. He holds God's hand, talks to him about every little thing in his life—frogs and rainbows and ladybugs, the dream he had last night, the scrape on his knee, the hurt in his heart." Dan shook his head in a knowing gesture of affection.

"I believe that Jason says 'I love you' to the Lord with every breath he takes. He has an enormous capacity—and a tremendous need—for love. Just like all of us," he added quietly.

Jennifer lowered her eyes to stare at the floor. She suddenly felt terribly young and insensitive.

"Do you really think," he asked, his voice deep with emotion, "that's what it's like to be trapped?"

"I'm sorry, Dan," Jennifer choked out. "Obviously, I don't know what I'm talking about."

"You *are* upset with me. Don't be," he urged her. "I hate it when your voice loses its smile."

She looked away from him, feeling a sudden need to hide her agitation, even though she knew he couldn't see her face. "No. Really, I'm not!" she protested, trying to force a note of brightness into her words.

He stood unmoving, as though he were attempting to search her mind, to probe the corners of her heart. Neither of them spoke for a long time.

Suddenly she felt his hands on her shoulders, a light, uncertain touch. Then he tipped her chin upward, forcing her to face him. Jennifer caught her breath. The tenderness in his expression made her heart ache.

"Jennifer," he said very quietly, his hands tightening on her shoulders, "I wish I could find a way to convince you to let go of your anger."

"Anger?" Again she looked away, unable to endure the depth of feeling that had settled over his features.

He nodded sadly. "Anger. That's what it is, you know. You're angry with God. About your singing career. My blindness. Jason. So many things.

"You think God is unfair. So you beat your fists against his will." His expression was gentle, his tone firm but not censuring. "It doesn't work, Jennifer. I can tell you from experience that being angry with God doesn't work." He brushed her cheek lightly with one finger. "He's not your enemy, Jennifer."

Jennifer tensed under his hands. She didn't want to argue with him. She didn't want to explain herself or try to defend herself. Dan was right about the anger, but she didn't want him to know the extent of it. She didn't want to expose the barrenness of her spirit to a man whose faith seemed to scale mountains and soar with the eagles.

Ridiculously, she almost wished him less than he was, a weaker man, because suddenly she wanted desperately to be big enough for him, to be *good* enough for him.

She knew that any woman who would love this man would have to have wings on her faith, wings that would enable her to rise above the shadows and fly beyond the darkness.

Unfortunately, the wings of *her* faith were pitifully weak. Perhaps even irreparably broken.

SEVEN

W HEN they stepped outside three hours later, they were met by an angry blast of wind and swirling snow. Obviously, the snow had been falling for some time; the ground was already covered.

"I simply love this weather," Jennifer muttered.

"Might as well get used to it," Dan said. He slung one arm around her shoulder as he held Sunny's harness with the other hand.

Jennifer wrinkled her nose and squinted her eyes against the pelting snow. Ahead of them, Gabe was hustling everyone onto the bus, growling out orders to speed up the loading of equipment. The teens, trying to meet his demands, were running back and forth from the bus to the auditorium, sliding and skating on the pavement as they tugged their instruments up the steps of the bus.

Jennifer brushed snow from her hair and face as she followed Dan and Sunny down the aisle. On the way, she exchanged wisecracks with the teens who were already on board. She stopped long enough to settle Jason into a seat beside Jim before going on to the rear of the bus to sit with Dan.

He waited until she scooted in next to the window, then coiled his long frame into the seat beside her, with Sunny settling herself in the aisle by his side. "This may be a long ride," he said, opening the cover of his Braille watch and touching its face. "We'll be lucky to get home by one if the roads are as bad as Gabe thinks they're going to be."

The words were no more out of his mouth than Gabe stood up from the driver's seat and turned to face his passengers, giving the zipper of his coat a sharp tug. His voice was unusually serious and authoritative. "People, I want you to do your driver a big favor. Just lean back, relax—and sack out! Beginning now. This is *not* a good night for giving old Gabe a hard time. In fact, I strongly recommend that you don't even breathe too heavy."

The request was unnecessary. Most of the teens, already drowsy from the late hour and the rich food they had eaten after the rally, fell asleep within minutes.

Lulled by the warmth from the heater and the monotonous roar of the tires on the snow-covered road, Jennifer felt her eyes growing heavy. Even so, she made an attempt to carry on a conversation with Dan.

"You look tired, Daniel."

"I am." With a large, contented yawn, he leaned his head back against the seat, turning his face to Jennifer. "You?" He reached for her, wrapping her slender hand snugly inside the warmth of his larger one.

"Because my speech is slurred and my eyes won't focus? Of course not. Comatose, maybe, but not tired."

He laughed softly. "I'll lend you a shoulder if you want to take a nap."

"Mm . . . you're tempting me, Dan, you really are." Jennifer's voice thickened as she fought to keep her eyes open.

"My pleasure," he assured her in a whisper, his free hand gently coaxing her head onto the broad warmth of his shoulder.

"I probably can't sleep, you know," Jennifer protested with a huge yawn, trying hard to ignore the crazy flip-flop of her heart.

She glanced uneasily over her shoulder at the icy window beside her. Snow was pelting the bus, driven by a moaning, angry wind.

Shivering, she nestled a little closer to Dan's warmth. "Bad weather always makes me nervous."

"Anything you can't fix makes you nervous, rebel. Go to sleep. The Lord can handle this one without your help."

Too tired to protest, Jennifer yawned again. "Mm-hmm . . . I s'pose. . . ."

Dan smiled with enormous pleasure, leaning closer to accommodate Jennifer's head on his shoulder. He felt like a king as she leaned contentedly against him. He touched his cheek to her hair, and the soft fragrance made him almost dizzy.

It occurred to him that this was probably one of the few times Jennifer wasn't actively protesting . . . *something* . . . and he smiled.

She moved her hand, bringing it to lie against his chest as she stirred in her sleep. He covered it with his own, curling her slender fingers under his as though he were sheltering a small dove beneath his palm.

Please, Lord, let it be her . . . after all these years of waiting, being afraid to hope and being afraid not *to . . . please, let her be the one.*

Within moments, he closed his eyes and fell asleep.

Jennifer awoke to the engine drone that had soothed her to sleep. She looked up at Dan from under heavy-lidded eyes, her heartbeat quickening when she saw the tender way he had locked her hand in his. A warm blanket of sweetness enfolded her as she gazed up into his sleeping face. His silken charcoal hair was ruffled from sleep, falling away from his face instead of forward as it usually did.

In the rare vulnerability of the moment, she thought she could detect just a glimpse of the boy he had once been. A tendril of sadness coiled around her heart as she studied him. What was it like for him when he woke up morning after morning to the same gray void—always the same, whether he was awake or asleep? How did he face day after day of getting up in the dark . . . going to bed with no moonlight creeping through his window, no stars to wish on? How did he live, knowing it would never again be daylight for him?

Such a good, kind man, Lord, she thought sadly, unaware for a moment that she was praying. *Why did this have to happen to him? With all the cruel, wicked people in this world—people who bring nothing but misery to others—why did such a terrible thing have to happen to Dan?*

A familiar well of bitterness bubbled up in her again, and her thoughts turned even more resentful. *Why Daniel . . . or Loren . . . or my mother . . . or little Jason? Not one of them ever did a mean thing in their lives.*

A random thought of her own personal hurt insinuated itself among the others—her dream, her special, bright, shining dream. The focus of her life had been to sing, to bring people to their feet in awe of the music, the glorious music. . . .

I won't think about it. I promised myself I'd never think about it.

She looked up at Dan again. Odd, how in such a short time she had come to count on this man, to trust him and believe in him when she couldn't seem to believe in much of anything else. She thought she could literally throw her life into his hands with complete confidence. What a strange, inexplicable way to feel about—a blind man.

Suddenly, an old, bittersweet memory drifted into her mind, a memory touched with pain and poignant with love. She saw her mother's face, frail and white and drawn in the last remaining days of her life. She heard the strained voice, once so melodious and resonant, now drained of its rich, vibrant strength. And she saw herself, a frightened, angry teenager, fighting to hold on to her mother. To the end, she had gone on fighting. . . .

It was one of the last times they had prayed together, and Jennifer had had to force herself to keep her head bowed and her thoughts turned to God. She was so terribly angry by then. And afraid. Afraid of what was coming, the suffering her small mother would yet endure, the desperate loneliness her father would have to bear, the adolescent Paul's confusion, and poor little Loren's bewilderment. Loren had been unable to understand, at only eight years old, why his irritable, anxious older sister was suddenly doing all the things for him his mommy had once done.

In spite of her weakness, her mother's voice had been surprisingly strong that day.

". . . Jennifer is such a good girl, Father, a strong girl. She will need a strong man, Lord. I know that even now you are preparing such a man for her, just as you're preparing Jennifer for her future husband. I pray that he will be a very special man, Father . . . very special indeed, for Jennifer is special, too."

She had opened her eyes then and looked directly into Jennifer's gaze, her frail hand clasping her daughter's even tighter. "You must be sure to wait, Jennifer. Wait for God's man."

Unhappy, sick with pity and worry for her mother, Jennifer had only managed a disinterested mumble. "Yes, Mother. I will."

Her mother had smiled then, her eyes brimming with love and certainty. "He'll be . . . different, I imagine; no ordinary man. The Lord knows you need a strong, different kind of man to help you harness that independent spirit of yours and bring it into line for God's work." She had moved her hand to Jennifer's cheek, still smiling into her daughter's eyes. "You wait and see, Jennifer. He'll be a very special man. . . ."

Suddenly, Jennifer looked up at Dan and felt a need to touch him. She reached out to smooth a dark wisp of hair away from his forehead, and he slowly opened his eyes. He squeezed her hand, his slow, gentle smile enveloping her in its warmth.

"I didn't mean to wake you," Jennifer murmured. She thought she should probably move away, but she felt a sudden sense of loss at the very thought.

Had her mind not been so thick with fatigue and clouded with memories, she might have felt a trace of amazement at how easy it was, how right it felt, to be almost in his arms. Indeed, she *was* in his arms, she suddenly realized, with one hand against his chest, still tucked inside his, and his other arm now coming to rest securely around her shoulders. But she felt not even the slightest inclination to move away.

"Is it still snowing?" he asked softly.

"Are you admitting a radar failure?" she teased in a whisper. Glancing out of the corner of her eye—as much effort as she could bring herself to make at the moment—she shuddered at the lack of visibility. "It's *awful!* I can't see anything."

He gently cupped her shoulder with his hand, moving her closer to him until her face was almost touching his. "Then don't look," he said softly, smiling the irresistible slow smile she had grown to cherish so very much.

Jennifer was unable to look away from his face. They were so close, their lips almost brushing. But still they didn't touch. She sensed that he was waiting, wondering, and she felt herself dropping deeper into the dark stillness wrapped around them.

"Is the gang still asleep?" he finally whispered, moving his hand from her shoulder to lift and comb gently through the tousled waves of her hair.

"I think so. Hard to believe so many teenagers can all conk out at once, isn't it?" Jennifer felt an irrational urge to start babbling, to chatter away the sweet intensity of the moment.

"No one's awake but us?" His voice was low, so low it made her catch her breath.

"Just . . . us," she answered weakly. "And Gabe, I hope." Her words stuck in her throat when he began, with an achingly gentle touch, to trace the pattern of her face. His rough fingertips traveled over her smooth skin, lingering on her lips. "Why?" she choked out.

"Because . . . " The word was no more than a whisper as his thumb tenderly rubbed across her dimpled chin. "I don't especially want an audience the first time I kiss you."

Jennifer saw his eyelashes flutter uncertainly against the upper ridge of his cheekbones. His hands framed her face as he lowered his head. At last he found her lips, touching them with his own in a kiss as light as a whisper.

Jennifer's heart seemed to melt like a low-burning candle when Dan breathed her name, just once, against the softness of her cheek. She could hear her pulse pound in her ears, the only sound around them in the darkness.

He gathered her as close as the seat would allow, kissing her once more, a longer kiss of tenderness and searching and meaning. When he finally put her gently away from him, Jennifer heard him sigh as though it made him very sad.

"Ah, Jennifer," he whispered against her cheek, "you are such a gift . . . such a precious gift."

"Daniel—" She reached up to touch the textured velvet of his bearded cheek, and he quickly covered her hand with his own.

"So fine," he murmured. "Everything about you is so . . . *fine . . . so beautiful* . . . and you don't even know it. You have no idea how very precious you are . . . especially to me."

Jennifer's head suddenly began to pound. *It can't be Daniel, Lord . . . it can't be him, can it? He's strong—but he's too strong. Far too strong for me. I could never be what he needs, what he deserves. Never. I don't understand this man, I don't understand his strength or his obedience to you or his peace. It can't be Daniel . . . that wouldn't work at all, Lord . . . it just wouldn't work at all.*

She buried her head in the warmth of Dan's shoulder, ignoring—for the moment at least—how very different they were from each other and the thought of how impossible it would ever be to reconcile those differences.

EIGHT

THE man leaned back as far as possible against the torn seat of the truck. The streetlight wasn't shining directly on him, but it was shedding enough of a glow to make him nervous.

He chewed his lower lip anxiously with his teeth, then sneered at his own skittishness. No one was paying any attention to the truck. Kaine couldn't see anything, and the woman wasn't looking anywhere but at Kaine. The other two, that blabbermouth Denton and Kaine's sister, were looking in the window of the music store next to the restaurant.

He narrowed his eyes as he stared at the guide dog walking beside the blind man. Frowning, he stroked the deep vertical line that edged one side of his mouth. That dog could be a problem. He might have to take care of the dog first.

He watched the four of them, laughing and horsing around like a bunch of kids as they got into Denton's T-bird and pulled away from the curb.

Kaine was all lit up tonight, a stupid grin plastered all over his face. If he wasn't such a Sunday do-gooder, a body might think he'd lifted a few.

His mouth curled into a contemptuous smile. It was the woman; that's why Kaine was glowing like a Christmas tree. He had been watching them for over two weeks now. They were almost always together. Sometimes they'd go to her house and eat, then she'd take him up the hill to his place. They went to Como's restaurant a lot, too. Sure, Kaine could afford that. He had to be loaded, the way he was always throwing his money around.

Yeah, they were getting real thick. He'd been watching. He liked to watch the woman. She almost always closed her drapes over the sheer curtains in her living room, but there was enough of a gap at the side of the window that he could still see in. When Kaine wasn't there, she'd curl up on the couch with a pencil tucked behind her ear and read or listen to music.

She was a pretty woman. Too good-looking for a man who couldn't even see her. She had a nice voice, too. Sometimes he listened to her on the radio. But once in a while Kaine would be on the air with her, and then he'd turn them off. He wouldn't listen to them talk to each other on the radio. You could hear her get all smiley when they were together. You could hear in her voice that she liked that big hairy ape.

It didn't matter. Kaine wasn't going to be around much longer. As soon as he tormented him some more, made him pay for the misery he'd brought on him, he'd turn him off for good.

The thought made him snicker out loud. He waited a minute, then pulled out and followed the Thunderbird, staying well behind.

Just as he had hoped, they went to the Terry woman's house. He slowed down almost to a stop and watched as Denton let Kaine and the woman out, then took off with Kaine's sister.

Good. That meant he'd have time to pay a visit to the blind man's empty house.

He pressed the gas pedal a little harder and took off. He felt anxious and excited. With a chuckle of elation, he reached into the deep pocket of his hunting jacket, removed a small flask, and took a quick swig of its contents. After two more gulps he stuck the flask back in his pocket. That was better. He felt warmer now. Ready to deliver his little surprise to the Kaine residence.

He wiped his mouth with the back of one hand, glancing down at the floor on the passenger's side of the truck. His anticipation flared as he looked at the gallon bucket and the crowbar lying beside it.

You like games, Kaine. You been playing games with me for a long time, making me wait, worrying me half-crazy . . . now I'm gonna have the fun. It's my game now, blind man. And you're gonna be the loser.

A sudden unpleasant thought sliced through the thick haze of his mind, causing his laughter to die abruptly. *The woman . . . what if Kaine has told the woman?*

The two were always together. All you had to do was watch them and you could see they had something going. Kaine had kept quiet all these years—probably just biding his time, planning to ruin him eventually—but he hadn't had a girlfriend until now. Wouldn't he likely tell his woman?

The slight tremor in his hands turned to an almost violent shake as he fought to keep a grip on the steering wheel. He began to nod his head up and down, pulling his mouth into a furious snarl. *Maybe he's already told her . . . maybe she already knows.*

He didn't want to hurt the woman. Not yet. He had plans for her, once Kaine was out of the way. Still, he ought to find out what she knew, if anything.

He glanced down once more at the floor of the truck before turning up the hill to Kaine's place. He'd make his little delivery, then go back down to the woman's house and see what he could find out.

He had eavesdropped on them before. Standing outside by the living-room window, he could hear them pretty well. That's what he'd do. There was time. Plenty of time. This was his game now. He'd call the plays.

He smiled. And he'd name the players. The woman was just another part of the game, after all.

NINE

DAN set his empty pie plate on the table beside the couch. Then he stretched, locked his hands behind his head, and leaned comfortably back against the plump cushion, smiling with obvious contentment.

"Well, Jennifer, your banana cream pie more than makes up for your coffee," he said lazily.

Jennifer returned from the kitchen with a fresh cup of coffee for herself and a second glass of milk for him. "I think you should know, Daniel, that no one else has ever complained about my coffee."

He continued to smile, and her heart turned over. It occurred to her that Dan always looked larger in her tiny living room. It also occurred to her that he looked entirely too handsome in that ivory silk shirt.

"Your mustache is white," she told him dryly as he took a big gulp of milk.

Sunny stirred restlessly, raising her head to glance at them, then around the room. Dan stroked her ears, and she soon settled down again. "Have you noticed how much more relaxed Sunny has been tonight?" Jennifer asked. "I think she's finally getting used to the house. Remember how restless she was last week when you had dinner here?"

He nodded. "A lot of things affect her. Even the weather. She's probably hoping for a reward if she's especially good tonight. Like her own piece of banana cream pie, maybe."

"And she just may get it, too. By the way, Daniel," she said with exaggerated emphasis, sitting down beside him. "I read the article in this morning's paper about the award you're getting. I can't believe you didn't tell anyone about it before now."

The local paper had carried a front page announcement that a well-known national organization would be presenting their annual humanitarian award to Dan in recognition of his continuing efforts for the disabled, specifically his work with Helping Hand Farm and the Friend-to-Friend Association.

He shrugged and set his glass down by his plate, dabbing the milk from his mustache with his napkin.

"You're going to be a folk hero if you get any more awards, Daniel," Jennifer teased, thinking of the impressive array of plaques and medallions already decorating his office.

He smiled a little. "It seems to me that the real heroes are the ones who don't get any awards." He rolled up the sleeves of his shirt, then leaned over to give Sunny a pat on the head.

"Dan, you deserve that award," Jennifer protested.

"The ones who really deserve the awards," he went on as if he hadn't heard her, "are the families and friends of the disabled. Sometimes it's even tougher on them than it is on us, but I'm not so sure anyone realizes what *they* go through."

Jennifer collected their dishes and took them into the kitchen, watching him across the counter as she loaded the dishwasher.

"When something happens—like what happened to me," he went on, "we get so caught up in *surviving* that we're often too absorbed in ourselves to realize what's happening in the lives of the people who love us.

"We become so involved in the rehabilitation that we tend to lose touch with what our families are going through. To some extent, we can vent our frustration in the process of rebuilding our lives. But the ones who have to stand by us . . ." His voice drifted, and he waited until Jennifer returned and sat down next to him before going on.

Finally, he leaned forward and rested his elbows on his knees, lacing his fingers together. "I know my family—and Gabe, too— have kept as much of their own pain away from me as possible." His smile was touched with sadness. "But they've suffered right along with me. A lot."

"Your family," Jennifer said sincerely, "is nothing short of wonderful."

"They are, aren't they?" Dan agreed, his tone distracted. Jennifer knew he was remembering.

He remembered that the first sound he had heard, waking up from the nightmare to an even worse reality, had been his mother's soft weeping from across the room. Once she realized he was awake, though, the sobbing had stopped. There had been only her cool hand brushing his hair away from his forehead as she attempted to give him what was left of her own strength. Even now Dan could feel her soft, fragrant cheek pressed against his, as though she could somehow absorb a part of his pain into herself.

And his dad . . . kneeling by the hospital bed, gripping Dan's hand, holding onto him as he prayed unceasingly. Those skillful, highly trained physician's hands that for years had strived to heal the pain and illnesses of others had suddenly been helpless to heal the agony of his only son. Even so, his father had forced him to fight, to reject self-pity and discouragement, in favor of sheer grit and determination. Lucas Kaine had shed his tears alone, so his son need not be wounded even more by his grief.

Lyss had been there, too, of course. Dan could still remember lying there, listening to her pace back and forth in her long-legged, smooth, athletic stride. The soft scent of the baby powder she always used had been strangely comforting in its familiar freshness. Sweet Lyss, trying to be so strong and cheerful and encouraging . . . never letting on how desperately frightened she was for her big brother.

And Gabe . . . faithful friend and brother of his heart. Gabe, who for years had made the story of David and Jonathan come alive for Dan. It had been Gabe who had restrained Dan and made him face what he was doing to those who loved him that awful day—or was it night—when he learned the final verdict, the sentence that had threatened to destroy his hope . . . and his sanity. . . .

He had reached up to push Gabe away, out of his life, along with everyone else. But then he felt the dampness of his friend's tears, and finally they had wept together for Dan's loss. . . .

"Dan?" Jennifer reached out to touch his shoulder, then hesitated.

He lifted his face, and slowly his features cleared. "Sorry." He smiled, a smile again tinged with sorrow. "I was thinking about heroes."

He slipped his arm around Jennifer's shoulders, and she leaned back against him, thinking how quickly she had grown to feel comfortable and strangely secure with this big, gentle man.

"Tell me about your family, Jennifer," he said casually.

After a moment's hesitation, Jennifer began to speak of her father and her brothers. She told him about Paul first, who at twenty-four had a new wife and a new job as a park ranger. "To Paul, there's nothing worse than a city apartment or a crowded room," she said, smiling. "He would make a wonderful hermit."

Her tone sobered as she told him about Loren, just recently turned nineteen. A victim of cerebral palsy, Jennifer's younger brother spent his days in a wheelchair. "Loren is so special," she said softly. "I don't think he has ever been bored, not once. He has this incredible thirst for learning. He would be—he could have been—a marvelous teacher."

She let her words trail off, then shifted her attention back to Dan. "He and Dad want to meet you. They're both *very* impressed that I'm working for an Olympic star."

"Your dad must be a pretty impressive guy himself," Dan commented. "The last few years couldn't have been easy for him—without your mother."

"Actually," Jennifer replied, tilting her head so she could look up at him, "Dad is a lot like you."

"Oh? Is that good or bad?"

Jennifer studied his face, then replied as truthfully as she could. "Dad is . . . very strong. Nothing shakes him. He simply—copes. He's a rock." She sighed deeply. "He loves people, too—like you. Dad always finds the best in everyone, and he never seems to take time for his own concerns because he's too busy helping everybody else with theirs."

She was surprised to see that Dan appeared strangely flustered by her words. His voice was almost gruff. "Thank you, Jennifer."

"For what?"

"For comparing me with a man like that." He turned his face away slightly, but not before Jennifer saw a shadow pass across his features. "I'm afraid," he added quietly, "your observation isn't all that accurate. But I'm still flattered."

Neither of them spoke for several minutes. Finally Dan broke the silence. "Your mother died of cancer, you told me?"

"Yes," Jennifer replied tightly. "When I was sixteen."

His hand tightened on her shoulder, and he rubbed his chin lightly across the top of her head. "That must have been tough for all of you. Was she ill a long time?"

"Two years."

He nodded. "You've had a lot of pain in your life already."

Surprised, Jennifer looked up at him. "Nothing compared to the pain *you've* had."

"Pain is pain, Jennifer," he said gently. "When you lose something or someone precious to you, it leaves a hole in your life."

A hole in her life. That's exactly how Jennifer felt sometimes. As if somewhere, deep inside her spirit, there was a huge, gaping vacuum. An emptiness.

Dan pulled her a little closer. "Jennifer . . . tell me why you won't sing anymore."

"I can't," Jennifer said without explanation.

"Can't—or *won't?*" he parried quietly.

"Is this a counseling session, Daniel?" Jennifer's tone was sharper than she'd intended.

"Not unless you want it to be," he replied agreeably, squeezing her shoulder. "I think I know a little about what it's like. It feels as though there's a *deadness* inside of you. Like there's nothing where the music used to be except a kind of—silence."

Jennifer stiffened at his incredibly incisive perception, then slumped her shoulders. "Yes," she whispered, not trusting herself to say more.

"I understand that."

She squeezed her eyes shut in response to the note of tenderness in his voice.

"I know that emptiness, Jennifer," he went on, his tone infinitely gentle. "The 'vacuum of despair,' it's called. I suppose I could describe in detail how you feel. But I can also tell you that it doesn't have to last forever."

His fingers lifted a strand of her hair as he went on, obviously choosing his words with a great deal of care.

"Losing hurts. And so we grieve. There's nothing wrong with that. We *need* to grieve. Grief is a vital part of being healed. It doesn't pay to try to shortcut the process. You have to just . . . go through it, experience it, be engulfed by it. At least for a time."

His arm around her tightened protectively. "But sooner or later you have to face the pain. You have to admit that you can't handle it alone. At that point, you have only two real choices. You can accept the circumstance, whatever it is, and lay it down at the feet of the Lord. To do that, you have to believe that God has a reason for allowing even suffering. Whatever the pain, you can be sure that God will work in and through it for your good—and for his glory."

His voice grew even quieter. "Or, you can fight it. You can throw your spiritual fists up and refuse to surrender. If you choose to fight—" he hesitated a fraction of a second, then continued—"you leave that hole in your heart unhealed, and it just keeps getting bigger. The emptiness keeps on growing until it finally swallows you up, until your entire life is absorbed into that gaping, empty abyss . . . and there's nothing left except pain and anger and misery."

"I *have* accepted it," Jennifer murmured dully. "I'm not fighting . . . not anymore."

He sighed deeply as he reached to tip her chin up toward his face. "I don't think so, Jennifer. I think what you've done is *resign* yourself. There's a difference—a critical difference—between resignation and acceptance." He held her tightly, but with exquisite tenderness.

"Resignation doesn't leave any room for hope or joy," he said. "It's a closed door. And sometimes a lot of anger and resentment are trapped behind that door. But acceptance leaves the door open for God to work his will." He paused for a long moment, then added, "What I hear in your voice, Jennifer, is *resignation.*"

As though anticipating her protest, he stopped her words by gently touching a finger to her lips. "When we're children, trust comes naturally to us. We accept—because we still see God as a loving Father. But when we grow up, well, we seem to find resignation easier than acceptance.

"We grow older, and we learn about things like cancer and war and famine and AIDS. Sometimes we start to think that God has changed, and we lose our hope, or we assume he was never what we believed him to be in the first place—and we lose our trust. As our world gets bigger and wider, we discover that a lot of it is ugly and filled with injustice and pain. But what we forget," he said, his voice dropping until it was scarcely more than a whisper, "is that the God of our childhood is still bigger than the world and all the suffering it can bring us."

He coaxed her head against his chest and held her for a long time. Jennifer somehow sensed that Dan had just thrown her a lifeline—if only she could make herself grab hold of it. She heard the truth and the wisdom of his words. But she wasn't anything like Dan. What was easy for him might well be impossible for her.

In contrast to his maturity, strength, and wisdom, she was full of confusion and bitterness and rebellion. Regrettably, she feared that no amount of understanding or caring or even love could ever close the gap between them.

As if he could sense the turmoil going on inside her, Dan put her gently away from him for a moment and pulled something out of his shirt pocket. "Here—I brought you something."

Jennifer looked at him.

He pressed an unlabeled cassette tape into her hand. "It's the demo for *Daybreak*. I thought you might want to listen to it. Sorry I don't have a book—all I had at home was my Braille score." He paused a beat and said quietly but pointedly, "You just say the word, and I'll get a book for you."

"Dan, please don't—"

"I want you to listen to the tape," he insisted. "That's all. The music—and the lyrics—are special to me." His smile made something warm and infinitely tender wrap itself around Jennifer's aching heart. "All I'm trying to do is share something that's special to me with someone . . . who's also very special to me."

Jennifer took the tape.

Abruptly, Dan stood and pulled her to her feet. As if to shift the mood to a more comfortable lightness, he informed her he was now ready for his second piece of pie. "Before old Gabe shows up and does me out of it."

"Right, boss," Jennifer agreed, grateful for the change in mood.

They headed for the kitchen, with Sunny padding along behind them. "I suppose you want another glass of—"

Jennifer stopped dead as she saw the face staring in the window of the back door. Dan crashed solidly into her from behind, the sudden thrust of his weight nearly knocking her off balance.

"Whoa! Your turn signal's out, lady!" he said, laughing as he caught her shoulders with both hands.

At the same time, Sunny muttered a low growl and charged the rest of the way into the kitchen. She hit the back door full force, barking and snarling, looking back at Dan as if to reassure herself that he was safe.

"Daniel . . ." Jennifer's throat felt like sandpaper. An icy rope of fear snaked the entire length of her body.

Dan stood unmoving, obviously tense. "What's wrong?"

The skull-like face at the window was gone. He had turned to flee as soon as he'd seen Jennifer approaching. But she was still unable to move, riveted in place by the memory of that spectral face peering in at them.

"Jennifer?" Dan pressed more insistently. "What is it?"

"Daniel, someone was out there—watching us."

Dan tightened his hold on her shoulders. "What do you mean? Where?" His voice was suddenly rough.

"Outside—at the kitchen door. He ran as soon as he saw me." Jennifer's voice was trembling as violently as her hands.

Dan heard the tremor in her voice, even above the din Sunny was making. He silenced the retriever with an abrupt command, calling her to his side. He stood unmoving, holding Jennifer to him as he tried to think.

After a moment, she slipped out of his grasp. "I'm going to look out the side window," she whispered.

"Be careful," Dan cautioned her, feeling a wave of anger and frustration rise at his own helplessness. "Do you see anything?"

"No, nothing. I'm sure he's gone. I probably scared him as much as he scared me," Jennifer said, her voice still unsteady.

"What's Sunny doing? Is she still watching the door?"

"No. She's watching you."

Dan gave a nod. "Then he must be gone. But stay away from the door. And turn out the lights." He hesitated. "If there are any curtains or drapes open, close them."

Dan listened to her moving around in the living room, flipping switches and drawing drapes. The sound he was waiting for came within seconds—the familiar sound of a pickup truck pulling away. His stomach knotted when he heard the faint rattle and the recognizable miss as the noise of the motor faded into the night.

Jennifer returned, touching his shoulder. He wrapped an arm around her. "This just infuriates me," she grumbled. "I haven't had a Peeping Tom since I was in college. You'd think—" She stopped suddenly. "Dan—what's wrong? You're pale as a ghost!"

Instinctively, Dan gathered Jennifer even more tightly against him.

"Dan? What is it?"

Dan's mind was reeling. *It had to be the same truck . . . the same man.* The realization chilled him. Had the man been watching *him* . . . or Jennifer?

Guilt stabbed at him as he realized that his silence about the phone calls and threats might have endangered her. If his obsession about his precious independence had jeopardized Jennifer in any way, he would never be able to forgive himself.

"*Daniel*—"

"It's all right—he's gone."

"Yes, I heard the car leave, too, but why—"

"It's not a car, it's a truck."

"Oh—you can tell just by hearing the engine? I don't know how you—"

"It's the same truck that ran us off the road," he said shortly.

"Are you sure?" She sounded skeptical.

"I'm sure," he said, not explaining. "You can turn on the lights now. And call Gabe. Then we'll call the police."

"The police?"

Dan heard the confusion in her voice. "He could come back," he said. "Just . . . call Gabe, would you? I'd like him to be here when the police come. He'll still be at Lyss's apartment. Have him bring her, too. You can go back to her place to spend the night."

"No, I don't need to do that—"

"*Jennifer*—would you just do what I ask!" He felt her tense at his sharpness, and he quickly gentled his tone. "Please. I'll explain later."

Silently, she moved out of his embrace and made the calls.

TEN

G ABE and Lyss were no more than three or four minutes ahead of the police.

Within minutes, both officers had come back inside from checking the area to report they had found nothing except some footprints and tire tracks.

"You were right, Miss Terry," said the taller of the two policemen. "Apparently, he'd been standing close to the front window, as well as on the back porch. You can track him through the snow."

Jennifer offered coffee to both officers, and they drank it in the living room while Dan gave them an accounting of his anonymous phone calls and the incidents with the pickup truck. He also revealed his suspicion that someone had been watching his house at night—probably the same man Jennifer had seen at the kitchen door. He kept to himself—for the moment at least—his hunch about a possible connection between the harassment and the upcoming radiothon. Nor did he reveal the depth of rage and sick hatred he had sensed in his tormentor.

When he had finished his tale, he waited. Even though he couldn't see their faces, he sensed that Gabe and Lyss—and probably Jennifer—were more than a little upset with him.

Lyss wasted no time in confirming his assumption. "I can't *believe* you've kept all this to yourself, Dan! *Why?*"

Jennifer was quick to jump in with her two cents worth. "Dan, how *could* you? You could have been hurt—or even worse—and none of us would have even known you were in danger!"

Surprisingly, Gabe waited until the women had vented their outrage before pointing out to Dan that he should have at least told *him*. "I have been known, on occasion, to keep my mouth shut if it's absolutely necessary, you know. This wasn't one of your brighter moves, pal."

Dan nodded his agreement to every charge they hurled at him, making no attempt to defend himself. "If you're all finished, I think the officers have a few questions they want to ask me," he said quietly.

An embarrassed hush fell over the room as Lyss and Jennifer muttered hasty apologies.

"Dan, do you have *any* idea who might be doing this?" asked Rick Hill, one of the policemen.

Dan pushed his hands down into his pockets and shook his head. "No, I don't, Rick. It could be anyone." Hesitating, he made a quick decision, then added, "But I've got a hunch the radiothon may be yanking this fellow's chain."

"Why do you think that, sir?" asked the other officer, a rookie Dan hadn't met before tonight.

"Because the phone calls and all the rest of it started when we first began to advertise the radiothon on the air," Dan explained. "He's made several cracks about me 'minding my own business' or 'sticking my nose in where I don't belong.'"

Neither policeman spoke for a few seconds. Finally, Rick Hill began to question Jennifer. "Miss Terry? Is there a man who might be upset with you or Dan? An ex-boyfriend, maybe?"

Dan heard the puzzlement in Jennifer's voice. "There's no one like that," she said. "Besides, as I told you, I didn't recognize the man I saw at the door."

Again she described the face she had seen, shuddering at the memory. "I think he was middle-aged—or older. Very thin . . . extremely thin. He looked almost—"

When she stopped, the younger of the two officers gently prompted her. "Yes, ma'am?"

"It sounds ridiculous," Jennifer went on, "but he had a face like a—a corpse. Bony, sunken—and very pale."

Dan heard the policeman's pen scrape the paper as he made a note of her words. "Well, there's not a whole lot we can do tonight," said Rick Hill. "But one thing's for sure, Dan—you shouldn't be by yourself until we find out what's going on. You're entirely too—" He let his sentence drift off, obviously feeling awkward.

"Helpless?" Dan supplied, with a slight lift of his chin.

"Well—not that, but certainly . . . vulnerable."

"He won't be alone," Gabe said flatly.

Dan jerked his head in Gabe's direction, a sharp retort on his tongue. Instead, he bit back his protest and said nothing.

It was starting, just as he had known it would.

As they all made ready to leave, Dan was surprised when Jennifer drew him into the kitchen. "Dan," she said, holding tightly to his arm, "I want you to know . . . if I seemed angry a few minutes ago, I wasn't. It's just that I'm so afraid for you. And I hate it that you've been going through all this alone."

Before Dan could reply, she added, "What I'm trying to say is that, even though I wish you'd told us, I think I understand why you didn't."

A wave of gratitude, almost painful in its sweet intensity, swelled deep inside Dan. Jennifer tightened her grasp on his arm as she went on. "I think I know what your freedom—your independence—means to you, Dan." Her voice sounded small and unsteady. "I also know that the only reason you finally told us the truth is because you were concerned for *me*. Please promise me you'll let Gabe stay with you until this is over. I need to know you won't be alone."

Dan nodded in resignation. Somehow, the realization that she understood made everything a little easier, a little more bearable. But that shouldn't surprise him. Jennifer had her own special way of making everything she touched just a little bit better . . . at least for him.

ELEVEN

GABE—I want your word that you won't say anything about this yet to my folks."

The two of them were sitting at the counter in Dan's kitchen, drinking coffee and talking. It was almost eleven, but Dan was too tense to sleep, and he could tell by Gabe's voice that his friend's nerves were stretched as tightly as his own.

Gabe uttered a small grunt of skepticism. "You don't really think Lyss is going to keep quiet about this, do you?"

"She will," Dan said meaningfully, "if you ask her to and explain why you agree with me."

"Buddy, you overestimate my influence with your sister," Gabe grumbled. "But I'll give it a try. I'd better call her yet tonight before she has a chance to get on the phone with your mother."

Dan nodded with relief. "While you talk to Lyss, I'm going to do a few laps. I've got to loosen up if I'm going to get any sleep." He stood and walked across the kitchen to the door that opened into the pool area. "Come on in and join me when you get off the phone."

Gabe's voice was laced with exaggerated disgust. "You know I believe in total sloth after seven P.M. No, you run along and play, Daniel. I'll talk to the lovely Alyssa and then take Sunny outside for her bedtime thing. Maybe by then you'll have come to your senses."

Dan grinned and shook his head, then went on to the pool,

flipping on the light in case Gabe decided to follow after all. For a moment, he thought he caught a whiff of an unfamiliar odor. He frowned, shrugged, then went on to the small dressing room on the east wall and changed.

He dove into the pool quickly, plunging himself immediately under the water. He was eager for the quiet comfort, the soothing blanket of calm that he knew would soon wash over him.

But something was wrong. A slight difference in the rhythm of the water, a barely discernible sluggishness, made him suspect a problem with the filtering system. Curious, he surfaced and gasped for air.

The strange, unfamiliar smell he had noticed on entering the pool area assaulted him full force. At the same time, he felt a thick, sticky mass thread its way down his face and begin to spread over his shoulders. He shook his head violently back and forth in an attempt to throw off whatever it was. When it didn't budge, he treaded water and began to pull his fingers through his hair and over his beard. The stuff was like liquid glue. He turned a few inches in the water, and when he did, the same viscous muck slapped relentlessly at his upper arms and torso.

For the first time in his life, Dan panicked in the water. An unholy dread assailed him, and his heart seemed to stop. In desperation he scissored himself and plunged beneath the water, trying to wash away the revolting substance from his body. But when he broke above the water again, he knew instantly he had done himself no good. The stuff was like tentacles, and there seemed to be no shaking it.

He fought to put down the paralyzing grip of panic. He forced himself to swim, shouting wildly for Gabe as he hurtled through the water.

At the side of the pool, he struggled to pull himself out of the water. He heard Gabe cry out and at the same time slipped and lost his balance. Totally disoriented now, he groped wildly for something to hang onto. He cracked his elbow, then hit his head on the wall of the pool before Gabe was finally able to grasp him firmly under the arms and haul him out of the water.

The room suddenly became a surreal chamber of Gabe's shouts and Dan's labored gasps for air. He felt himself losing consciousness and wondered if he was going to die. Gabe was gripping his shoulders so hard that pain shot down his back. Lights flashed on and off in his head. The smell grew stronger.

Gabe sounded furious, desperate. "Dan! *Dan!* Can you hear me? It's all right, buddy, it's all right . . . it's only paint . . . it's red paint, man, that's all . . . just paint."

Gabe kept yelling at him, crying his name. He was panicky, too. Dan could hear it in his voice.

"I thought it was blood. . . . I heard you shout and I saw you coming up out of that water . . . covered with that red mess. I thought it was blood . . . I thought you were bleeding . . . I thought you were dying, man!"

Dan finally caught a breath, then slumped in Gabe's arms.

Humiliation was no stranger to Dan. In five years of being blind, he had suffered his share of indignities and had survived any number of embarrassing moments. He had handled most of them without completely losing his sense of humor.

He reminded himself that no one but his best friend had witnessed the scene in the swimming pool. But for some reason he still felt like a fool.

He sat on a chair in the large bathroom off the pool, docilely allowing Gabe to wash paint off him. The entire bathroom—especially himself, he thought with a disgusted sniff—reeked of turpentine.

He was aware that Gabe was doing his best to snap him out of his black mood. "Don't get within ten feet of an open flame for the next few days, buddy. You don't want to be responsible for the big boom all on your own."

When Dan made no reply, Gabe tried a different tack. "Does Jennifer like your beard?"

"What?"

"Your beard, man. Does she like it?"

"How do I know if she—" Dan thought for a moment, then sighed. "She's never complained about it."

"So you'd like it saved, I suppose."

"Saved?"

"It would be easier if the beard went," Gabe said carefully. "Along with an inch or two of your hair, my friend."

Dan made no attempt to match Gabe's humor. "I've had a beard ever since the accident. It's a lot easier than shaving in the dark."

"Right," Gabe said quickly. "We'll just soak it in turpentine."

Neither made any further attempt at conversation for a long time. Finally, as if he were unable to stand the silence any longer, Gabe said, "You all right, buddy?"

"I'm fine," Dan answered wearily. "Just tired."

"The police are coming out again first thing in the morning," Gabe told him.

"Why? They weren't able to find anything when they were here tonight."

"It won't hurt to check around again when it's daylight. The guy might have dropped something they missed in the dark."

"Did he break the pool-house door when he jimmied it?" Dan asked.

"No. The lock is sprung, but the door wasn't even splintered. We'll get a deadbolt put on there tomorrow."

"I'm glad Jennifer went home with Lyss. I'm worried sick that this nut will try something with her." Dan's pulse hammered at the thought.

"I still can't believe he pulled a stunt like this," Gabe grated out. "I'm telling you, Dan, we've got to watch you every minute until they catch this guy. He's a real sicko."

"Nobody's going to watch me every *minute!*" Dan spat furiously. "I had enough of that before!"

Gabe halted his ministration to Dan's face. "I know," he said quietly. "But the alternative could be a lot worse. Dan, this is no practical joker we're dealing with here. Someone out there wants your skin. Whoever he is, whatever his reasons, he's out to get you. This guy is a *nut case,* Dan!"

Dan swallowed hard and slumped a little lower in the chair. "It's Jennifer I'm worried about."

"Well, that balances out, old buddy," Gabe said lightly. "Because it's *you* Jennifer's worried about. As for me, I'd kinda like to lock both of you up for a while."

The nightmare came again that night. Dan fought it, as always, sensing even in the labyrinth of his subconscious that this time might be the time he didn't survive the terror. But it burrowed through his defenses, through the tunnel of his sleep, just as the headlights had cut through the mountains that foggy night. . . .

He felt the car bumping and weaving on the narrow, potholed road . . . heard the soft background music of the radio, turned to his own station . . . smelled the new-leather scent of the Buick . . . tasted the dank humidity of the night. He even saw his own eyes in the rearview mirror as he lightly tapped his fingers on the steering wheel in time to the music. . . .

But this time the nightmare didn't end as it usually did. This time there was something different about it. It went on, past the headlights and the deafening crunch of metal and his own scream of terrified denial. A flash of color suddenly zigzagged in front of him, a spray of red and black—

And then it was over, and he was awake. He sat bolt upright in bed, drenched in perspiration and gripped by a new, almost irrational fear. Tonight he felt more terrorized than ever before. He could have screamed with his desperation to banish the horror from his mind once and for all.

Instead, he faced the sickening, inescapable conviction that it would simply go on and on, through countless nights of his life, until he finally discovered whatever it was that waited for him at the end.

At least he hadn't wakened screaming this time. He expelled a shaky breath and kicked the blankets off, then got up and made his way to the bathroom to splash cold water on his face. Sunny padded quietly along behind him, waited, then returned to the bedroom with him—as though she, too, sensed the need to watch over him more cautiously than ever.

His head was still pounding. He figured his blood pressure must peak at stroke level every time he had the nightmare, and tonight had been even worse.

For a long time, he sat on the side of the bed and rested his head on his hands, thinking . . . and finally praying. . . .

Oh, Lord, please forgive me for my selfishness of these past weeks, for staying silent about the phone calls and everything else. I know it was nothing but pride. Lord, help me to get past this stubborn need to handle everything on my own. Just look at what I've done. . . . If Jennifer had been hurt, I think I'd die, Lord. I couldn't live with knowing I'd hurt her by my own foolish pride. . . .

After a while he stretched out on the bed, reached to give Sunny a reassuring pat, and then lay, eyes open, for another hour or more. Occasionally he thought about Jennifer and managed to smile. Once he wept. Finally, he fell into a restless, troubled sleep.

TWELVE

J ENNIFER spent the next few days in an agony of suspense and dread, but the time was surprisingly uneventful. Even the phone calls to Dan had stopped. No more uninvited visitors at her bungalow, no more hair-raising attacks by the pickup truck, no more terrorizing pranks like the episode in Dan's swimming pool. Unfortunately, no new leads had developed in the police investigation either.

Dan had had a professional service drain, clean, and refill the pool. It had taken most of the week. By Sunday, Jennifer's routine had also returned to normal. She could almost relax and pretend that everything was as it should be. But there was no denying the undercurrent of foreboding that never quite went away. Dan had revealed enough about *his* suspicions to trigger her own anxiety, and she lived with an underlying apprehension that affected her every waking hour.

Her enthusiasm for the radiothon had ebbed, the initial excitement changing to dread. She had suggested to Dan that he cancel, or at least postpone, the whole event. But she might as well have saved her breath. A stubborn thrust of his chin and a firm shake of his head were his only reply.

He was obviously determined to go through with the radiothon, and that was that. The best they could hope for was that the police would soon turn up a clue that would lead to the end of this sick campaign of terror.

Jennifer could scarcely bear to think about the incident with the paint in Dan's swimming pool. He finally seemed to be snapping out of the despondency that had settled over him after that awful night. But this cruel wave of torment was taking its toll on him. His step lacked its usual spring these days. His smile faded a little more quickly, and his voice held a note of hesitancy that hadn't been there before. It was as though small pieces of his confidence were being hacked away, one chip at a time. He seemed to have to work much harder these days at maintaining his sense of humor. Still, he managed to surprise her in the most unexpected ways.

Like this afternoon's phone call.

"Sledding? No, Daniel, I am not coming up to go sledding with you and Jason. I am *tired.* Can you say *tired,* Daniel?"

Jennifer shifted the telephone receiver to her other ear as she edged the kitchen curtains back to look outside. An unexpected spring snowfall brightened the late afternoon gloom. It *was* beautiful. . . .

But, no. Definitely not. She was going to bed early tonight, just as she had been promising herself for several days now.

"You may function very well on nothing but adrenaline," she said to Dan, "but we weaker mortals need something called *sleep.* "

She could almost believe the apologetic note in his voice was genuine when he answered. "I'm really sorry, Jennifer. I *have* kept you too busy the last few days, haven't I?"

"You might say that," Jennifer agreed dryly.

"I understand. I'll explain to the boys. Jim Arbegunst is here, too, so he can help Jason with his sled. Mom will be disappointed, though. She wanted us to come to dinner afterward. Pork roast and dressing." He paused, then added, "And fudge cake."

Jennifer glanced down woefully at her half-eaten peanut butter and pickle sandwich—her Sunday dinner. "That's bribery, Daniel."

"It is, isn't it?" he admitted cheerfully.

"Well," she waffled. "I'd have to eat and run. Your mother might be offended." With a frown of distaste, she dropped the remainder of her sandwich into the trash can by the refrigerator.

"She knows how swamped we are," Dan put in. "She'd probably even send some dessert home with you, if you couldn't stay."

"You think?"

"I'll see to it. You'll come, then?"

"I suppose. But I *am* leaving early, Daniel."

"Oh, absolutely."

Suddenly another thought occurred to Jennifer. "What about Gabe? He *is* still staying with you at night, isn't he?"

"Not tonight. He drove over to Clarksburg to cover the concert at First Baptist, remember?"

"*Dan*—you promised you wouldn't stay alone at night until—"

"It's already taken care of." Jennifer heard the forced patience in his tone. "That's why Jim is here. He's staying over tonight."

"Jim is only a teenager, Daniel—"

"Jim is nearly six feet tall," Dan pointed out, "and perfectly capable of providing exactly what I need—a person in the house who can see what I can't."

Jennifer didn't like it. But he had used his "don't push me" tone of voice. And maybe he was right, after all. The important thing was that he have someone in the house with him who could see.

Not that he seemed to require a lot of assistance. Jennifer didn't even stop to wonder how Dan would manage sledding.

Radar, how else? she thought with a wry smile, slipping into a pair of thermal underwear and her oldest jeans.

Dan and the boys were already outside when Jennifer pulled into the driveway. Jason, out of breath with excitement, met her at the car.

"Are you going to ride on my sled, Jennifer?"

Jennifer rumpled his hair and, taking his hand, walked with him up the driveway toward Dan and Jim. "Is that shiny red sled yours, Jason?"

His head bobbed up and down. "Dan gave it to me for Christmas!"

"Well, since red is one of my favorite colors," Jennifer said, grinning at him, "I am definitely going to ride on your sled."

She walked up to Dan and gave his hand a quick squeeze. "Is it dinnertime yet?"

He shot her a cryptic smile as he zipped up his gray snowmobile jacket. "You have to earn your dinner, Jennifer."

Jennifer glanced warily from Sunny—who was off her harness and obviously ready for fun—to Jason. "Oh, no," she groaned. "This looks suspiciously like a three-on-a-sled deal to me!"

Dan's arm went around her shoulders companionably. "You catch on fast."

Jennifer turned to Jim. "Why do I get myself into these situations?"

The boy turned his haunted eyes on Jennifer, as if infinitely grateful for her attention. "Don't worry, Miss Terry. I'll take Jason and Sunny with me."

"You're a brave boy, Jim," Dan said with a chuckle. "And I'm not even going to argue with you. All right, gang, let's get going!"

"You're really going to ride with me?" Dan pulled their sled with one hand as Jennifer took his other arm. Sunny had already bolted ahead with the boys.

"Only if you promise no belly-whoppin'," Jennifer warned him.

"Well . . . it might be better if you steer," he suggested after a second or two.

"Actually, Daniel, I had already thought of that."

By the time they reached the top of the hill, they met Jim and Jason on their first trip down. Jason was squealing with delight and hanging tightly onto Sunny, who was tucked securely between the two boys.

Jennifer almost gave up before they even got started. Trying to fit on a sled in front of Dan was next to impossible. "You need a two-seater," she ranted, eyeing his long legs hopelessly.

Laughing, Dan enfolded her as tightly as possible inside his arms, tucked his legs precariously outside hers, pulled her snugly back against his chest, and yelled, *"Geronimo!"*

Their first slide down was surprisingly smooth. In fact, by their third downhill run, they agreed they made quite a pair and that there was really nothing to it except skill and lightning-fast reflexes.

But on their fourth trip down, Dan leaned too far to the left, causing them to lose control. Before either of them knew what had happened, they found themselves tumbled together in the middle of an enormous snowdrift.

Jennifer scrambled awkwardly to her knees, staring open-mouthed at Dan, who was laughing so hard he choked on a spray of snow.

Rolling onto his side, he caught his breath and molded a sizable snowball, which he proceeded to toss at Jennifer with surprising accuracy.

Jennifer scrambled toward him. Wiping the snow from her face, she began to pummel him with her mittened fists. This only made him collapse into helpless laughter. Finally he hauled himself onto his knees and caught her by the wrists. "Don't you beat on *me,* slugger!" he warned, still laughing. *"You're* supposed to be the navigator here, remember? I'm just along for the ride."

"Ohhh! Just let me up! Get away, Daniel! I mean it, now! Let me up, I'm going to—"

"You're going to *what?"* he drawled, balancing on his knees. "You're all right, aren't you, hon?" he asked with a phony expression of concern. "Here—I've got something for you."

"What?" Jennifer narrowed her eyes.

"Just open your mouth."

"Daniel Kaine, don't you *dare*—" Her last words got swallowed up by the handful of snow he pushed at her face.

Yanking herself free, Jennifer then let go with a few snowballs of her own. But within seconds, she gave up. Dan, as if sensing her surrender, poised on his knees and smiled a slow, lazy smile, then dipped his head in search of her face. Jennifer ducked, deliberately twisting back and forth so he couldn't find her, then breaking up in laughter at the determined smirk on his face.

"Stop that, woman," he ordered sternly, finally catching her chin in his hand and holding her steady. "You're fouling up my radar." His expression suddenly sobered. He whispered her name as if savoring the sound of it, then covered her mouth very gently with his own.

Something infinitely tender and achingly sweet squeezed Jennifer's heart. She watched him from a soft haze, wondering at the small sigh he uttered as he released her, then brushed her cheek with a fleeting touch of his gloved fingertips.

Both of them remained silent, unmoving, like two statues in the snow, Jennifer searching Dan's face. Slowly, he removed his gloves, tossed them to one side, and framed her face between his hands. He held her gently but firmly for a long moment before touching his lips to her temple. "Jennifer . . . I love you."

THIRTEEN

T HE incredible power of emotion behind his words made Jennifer lose her breath. She stared up at Dan's love-softened face, involuntarily reaching out a hand to caress his bearded cheek. Her breath, when she finally found it again, was as ragged and uneven as his.

Dan slipped his arms around her and gathered her to him, cradling her against his chest and rocking her slowly back and forth in the snow. Jennifer thought her heart would break and shatter into a thousand pieces when she heard his anguished whisper against her forehead. "Ah, Jennifer . . . what I would give to look at you, to see you—really *see* you—just once."

Those achingly honest words opened her heart and her senses as nothing else could have. All her fears about being wrong for him, all her doubts about being good for him, were swept away for one wonderful, unforgettable moment.

She pulled her gloves off and cupped his face between her hands, pulling his head gently down to her. "Oh, Daniel, you *have* seen me," she murmured just before touching her lips to his. "You've seen my heart."

His hands trembled on her shoulders. "I know I have the most colossal gall in the world to say this to you. And I may be way out of line, but I have to say it now because I might not ever have the courage again."

Jennifer held her breath, half afraid of what she was about to hear.

He turned her slightly in his arms so he could rest his hands more firmly on her shoulders, keeping her close, yet holding her just far enough away from him that she could see his breath in the cold air. Gone now was his earlier expression of uncertainty and the faltering note of doubt in his voice. Instead he wore a look of decision, the expression of a man who has met his destiny and is about to surrender to it.

"I am head-over-heels, hopelessly in love with you, my sweet rebel." The tenderness that settled over his face caught Jennifer's heart by surprise and held it captive. "I think," Dan added softly, "I was as good as totaled the first day you walked into the station, when I found you stumbling around with your eyes closed so you'd know how it felt to be blind."

He gave a slow nod, and Jennifer saw a fleeting gleam of insight dart across his features. "You've changed my life, love. For the first time in years, I feel like a whole man again. Jennifer . . . I'm asking you . . . if you'll marry me."

Jennifer could do nothing but stare at him, as limp beneath his hands as a rag doll. She hadn't expected this. Of course she had known he cared for her . . . but *love? Marriage?* Impossible. She was light-years away from this man in every way that mattered.

"I know I can't offer you anything but broken pieces," he was saying quietly, "but I'll love you more than any woman has ever been loved by a man. I can promise you that much, at least."

Jennifer looked at him with dismay. She swallowed, cleared her throat, still unable to face the growing uncertainty now settling over Dan's face. "Dan . . . I don't know. I'm not sure, that is— what to say. . . ."

He smiled, though his voice was unsteady when he answered. "How about something like, 'I can't live without you, Daniel' for starters? I could be content with that. For a while, anyway."

"Oh, Dan—I *do* care for you, but—"

"How much?" His hands tightened on her shoulders.

"What?"

"How much do you care for me?"

"Well, I can't put my feelings into words, exactly. I can't just—"

"Try."

Jennifer gaped at him, her mind suddenly reeling at this whole impossible situation. "Well, I care a *lot,* I suppose, but—"

"Do you love me, Jennifer?"

"Daniel, you don't just answer a question like that in the middle of a snowdrift! Besides—we really haven't known each other long enough to—"

"Do you *love* me, Jennifer?"

He reached for her hands and enfolded them between his own. With an expression of great patience, he waited.

"Now, Daniel . . . you know we're nothing alike. In fact, we're total opposites."

He nodded agreeably.

"Oh, we may have a few things in common," she conceded, "but basically we're like—"

"Oil and water?" he supplied helpfully.

Jennifer blinked. "Well—that may be a bit extreme. But certainly we don't see things the same way at all. You're very patient, and I'm not."

"Mm. That's true."

Jennifer looked at him. "You're very—accepting. And tolerant. And we *both* know I'm not."

He nodded his head sagely. "I'm afraid that's also true."

"Nothing seems to bother you. You're just a very mellow, easygoing man."

"Granted."

"You're—philosophical. I'm analytical. You're careful and precise. I'm impetuous and completely unorganized. And tense. I'm very tense. I'll probably have ulcers by the time I'm thirty."

"Marry me and have kids instead." He raised both her hands to his lips and skimmed a gentle kiss over her knuckles.

"And we never agree on anything, besides—" Jennifer glanced up at the lazy smile on his face. "What did you say?"

"I think I just proposed again," he said, still smiling.

The soft touch of amusement in his voice faded to a more serious tone. "Tell me something, Jennifer. Does my blindness have anything to do with the way you're evading the question?"

Jennifer gasped, appalled that he could think such a thing about her after all this time. "Of course not!"

As she watched, a subtle look of relief crossed Dan's face. "Forgive me. I had to ask. You, more than anyone else, know the problems that will accompany me into marriage."

"Oh, Daniel," she murmured, the words breaking her heart even as she spoke them. "It has nothing to do with your being blind! You're—a *wonderful* man! You're sweet, and you're strong, and you're thoughtful—a woman couldn't hope for a finer man than you! But you deserve someone who's . . . more *like* you, not someone like me."

He seemed to wince at her words. "Jennifer . . . my love, I'd do anything to make you see the truth about me." He clasped her hands tightly in his. "Don't you understand, Jennifer? There's nothing special or unique about me! If I were as strong as you think I am, I'd get out of your life today. No, love—I'm just a man, a very ordinary man who wants the same things any other ordinary man wants. All I want," he said, his voice almost a whisper, "is a woman to love, a home to share with her, and maybe some children to call me Daddy."

He hesitated, then asked her again, "Jennifer . . . do you love me?" Jennifer held her breath. She saw his hopeful expression change to a stricken look of defeat. Without quite knowing what she was doing, she moved more closely into his arms. "Yes," she said in a voice so faint it was nearly lost in the wind, "I'm afraid I do."

She looked up into his face then, and she thought the expression of relief and happiness settling over him was the most beautiful sight she had ever seen in her life.

He wrapped her snugly in his arms and whispered against the hollow of her cheek. "Don't be afraid, Jennifer. Don't ever be afraid to love me. I'll never hurt you. Don't you know by now that I'd die before I'd ever hurt you?"

They remained silent for a long moment, locked in each other's embrace.

Jennifer finally broke the silence. "Dan—I *do* love you. But that doesn't mean I'm ready to talk about marriage yet."

"I'm really sorry to hear you say that, Jennifer," he said with mock disapproval, "because if your intentions are anything other than honorable, this relationship will never work."

"Stop that!" she scolded, poking a finger into his chest. "This is very serious, Daniel."

"Uh . . . can I say just one thing, love?"

"What?" she snapped.

"I hear the happy sound of children's laughter. Could we possibly continue this conversation inside, where it's a little warmer and a whole lot more private?"

Startled, Jennifer peered over his shoulder. Sure enough, Jim and Jason and Sunny were barreling over the slope of the hill, only a few feet away from them. "We may be able to manage the warmth by going inside to the fire, Daniel. But privacy?" She shook her head. "Don't count on it."

Later, after everyone had changed into dry clothes and warmed up with hot cocoa, Dan agreed to let the boys use the pool. "But we'll have to leave here no later than five if we don't want to miss dinner. So when I say it's time, you guys will have to move."

Sunny, obviously determined not to miss the fun, squeezed through the door with the two boys as they left the kitchen.

"It's odd how well they get along together, considering the age difference," Jennifer commented. She was sitting on one side of the kitchen counter, noting Dan's easy but precise movements as he placed their cups in the dishwasher and wiped off the sink with a sponge.

"Jim is absolutely starved for attention, for someone to care about him."

Surprised, Jennifer looked at him. "But what about his father?"

Dan gave a sigh and dried his hands. "Jim is a lonely, unhappy boy," he said with a troubled frown. "I'm afraid his father's idea of attention is a strong rod."

Jennifer puzzled over his words, but he didn't explain. Instead, he walked around to her side of the counter and tugged lightly at a damp strand of hair. "So," he said, changing the subject, "have you listened to the tape I gave you yet?"

"No, I haven't listened to the tape you gave me yet," Jennifer retorted glibly. "When exactly do you think I would have had time?"

"I seem to remember you having a cassette deck in your car," he countered. "Why are you putting it off?"

"I'm *not* putting it off."

A knowing smile curved his mouth, but he said nothing.

"I really *haven't* had time, Daniel! And we know whose fault that is."

He shrugged agreeably. "It's just as well, maybe. There's something else I probably should have given you first."

He walked to the large rolltop desk that sat between the dining area and the living room, returning with a loose-leaf notebook.

"What's this?" Jennifer asked as he laid the notebook on the counter in front of her.

"Actually, it's a kind of journal," he said quietly.

Jennifer glanced curiously from him to the notebook. "A journal?"

Dan nodded. "It's something I started not too long after the accident."

He went into the living room and bent down to stir up the fire. Then he straightened, turning back to her. With his hands in his pockets, he stood, saying nothing as he scuffed the toe of his shoe against the floor.

His attention abruptly shifted back to Jennifer. "I'm sure it'll be hard to read," he said, gesturing to the notebook. "My handwriting was pretty bad even when I could see. Katharine didn't start typing my notes until later."

He lifted his chin, his expression uncertain. "I just thought it might help you with some of the questions you seem to have," he said carefully. "I thought—" He choked off a sound of frustration. "I don't know *what* I thought. I'm sorry, Jennifer, I know I don't have any right to push my opinions onto you." He turned away from her to face the fireplace.

Jennifer stared at his back for a moment, then glanced down at the notebook. She opened it and began to leaf through it, her eyes drawn to the words on the first few dog-eared pages. There seemed to be page after page of Dan's own words, miscellaneous quotes, and Scripture verses, scrawled unevenly but still legible.

Something sad and poignantly tender wafted through her as the significance of what she held in her hands finally registered. Before her were months of Dan's most personal, excruciating agony . . . hundreds of his heartrending, soul-searching thoughts and discoveries. He was opening his deepest, innermost feelings to her.

She got up very slowly and walked to him. When she reached his side, she laid her hand gently on his shoulder and waited for him to face her. "Daniel," she said softly, "are you sure you want me to read this?"

He nodded but didn't answer right away. "Yes. I do," he finally said, his voice quiet. "And not entirely because I'm hoping you'll find something in it—to help you. Some of my reasons are selfish, I admit."

His tone was gentle but steady as he explained. "I think I'm selfish enough to want you to understand what it was like—after the accident—and coward enough not to want to tell you."

Jennifer stared up at him, then shook her head slowly from side to side. "No—" Her voice broke and she hesitated. "I don't think so. I don't believe you have a selfish or cowardly bone in your body, Daniel Kaine."

He frowned at her words. "That's another reason I think you need to read that journal, Jennifer. Sooner or later, you're going to realize I'm not the man you think I am. We'll both be better off if you know it now, not later."

Saying nothing, Jennifer studied him carefully for a long time. Finally, she dropped her hand from his shoulder and hugged the notebook tightly against her heart. "Will you just tell me one thing, Dan? Why are you so determined that I . . . learn to accept life the way you do? Why does it matter so much to you?"

He didn't respond right away. Finally, he reached for her hand and, going to the couch, sat down with her beside him. "Jennifer, I love you too much to ignore your hurt, the pain I hear in your voice," he said quietly, still clasping her hand. "With all my heart, I want you to be able to surrender that pain to the Lord."

He drew her closer. "I just want to help you see that once you stop fighting God, at that very point you win," he said. "Jennifer, the Lord will never, ever give you less than his best. Even when life brings loss or suffering or a broken heart, God knows exactly what he's doing. He can redeem anything and turn it to good."

Jennifer studied his strong, kind face, wishing she could simply take what he seemed so determined to give, at the same time

knowing it could never be that easy for her. "Daniel . . . how can
I possibly accept what I don't even *understand?*"

Dan moved closer, gently coaxing her head onto his shoulder.
"That's your problem, love," he said quietly, stroking her hair.
"You try to *understand* first. The fact is, though, that understanding
isn't the issue. There will always be things that are beyond our understanding. That's why it's absolutely vital that we take God on
faith and just trust his love—for ourselves, and for others."

He seemed to choose his next words with great care. "We see
today, Jennifer, but God sees eternity. We yearn for our comforts,
but he wants our maturity, even if that maturity entails pain. In
our search for happiness, we live for ourselves. But God says, 'Die
to yourself. Live for *me.*'"

Silence hung between them for several minutes as Jennifer
searched her heart for a response, only to find none. "Daniel . . .
it isn't that I don't want—what you have. I *do* want it! I want it
with all my heart. I've been a Christian for most of my life, but I
still don't have the kind of faith you're talking about. It seems so
easy for you. But it's not easy for me, Daniel! Not at all."

He went on stroking her hair. "Jennifer, whatever faith I have
was a gift. God gave it to me only after I stopped ramming my
head against his will."

He paused, then went on. "This may not make much sense to
you, but I can tell you truthfully that I never knew the meaning
of peace until after the accident—after I lost my sight."

He must have felt Jennifer tense in his arms, because he nodded and smiled. "It's true. The Lord used that time to teach me
something I might never have learned otherwise. Oddly enough,"
he said, "I found my personal key to faith in the book of the
Bible I was named after—the book of Daniel.

"Remember when King Nebuchadnezzar warned Shadrach,
Meshach, and Abednego that unless they worshiped the golden
image, he would toss them into the fire? I had read that story for

years," he said, smiling faintly, "without ever paying much attention to their answer. But once their words really sank into my heart, I knew that I had discovered an entirely different kind of faith than I'd ever known existed. They told the king that their God 'was able to deliver' them out of the fiery furnace—but that even if he *didn't,* they weren't going to stop worshiping God and start bowing down to an idol."

Jennifer moved in his arms just enough that she could more clearly see his face. When she did, she wondered at the expression of almost youthful enthusiasm that now lined his features. "It was like being struck by lightning," he said. "I had accepted Christ as my Savior when I was just a boy. But I had never let him be sovereign in my life—I had always stopped short of allowing him to be my Lord and Master. What I finally came to realize, after the accident, was that Christ has the right to either deliver me or *not* deliver me." He paused. "But I *don't* have the right to base my love for him and my trust in him on what he does for *me.* He's already given his life for me. *That's* what I base my faith on—the Cross. Nothing else."

Something deep within Jennifer's spirit began to stir ever so slightly. Dan's words had struck a distant chord, and now she thought she could almost catch a glimpse of a light she had thought extinguished, a hope she had lost sight of long ago.

She still didn't understand. But somehow she knew he was talking about a kind of peace that would change her life. Slowly, she lifted her head to study him. "Daniel," she said finally, "will you pray for me?"

His smile was immediate and wonderfully tender. "Love of my heart," he said in a voice rough with emotion, "I have been praying for you since that first day you crashed into my life. Why would I stop now?"

FOURTEEN

L ATE Wednesday afternoon, everyone at the station
      was racing against the clock in preparation for the
      radiothon on Friday. Jennifer and Dan had been
swamped all day, trying to clear up last-minute details between
their spots on the air, advertising meetings, and eleventh-hour
instructions to other members of the staff.

They were about to finish up the afternoon drivetime. Dan
had volunteered to help Jennifer jock her show so she could
move in and out of the studio to work on other projects as necessary.

"I put that cart you wanted Jay to use this evening right on
top," Jennifer said as the last selection came to an end. "And an
extra copy of tomorrow's log so he can double-check it."

Dan nodded, waited a few seconds, then opened his mike for
the last spot of the afternoon.

". . . Just a quick reminder about the weekend radiothon." He
spoke into the microphone in his slow and easy drawl. "Beginning Friday night at eight o'clock, we're going to furnish you
with thirty-six straight hours of your favorite Christian music,
some guests you won't want to miss, and, of course, our own Jennifer Terry, doing her incomparable imitation of Mighty Minnie
Mouth. . . ."

Grinning, he took a good-natured stab at Gabe, then turned
serious. "On the sober side, people—" Jennifer groaned at his

unintended pun—"if you turn the station on even a few minutes a day, you already know what we're doing this weekend. We're hoping for a flood of phone calls, letters, and donations to help us put some serious pressure on the people who make this country's drunk driving laws."

He paused for only an instant, long enough for his tone to turn grave. "Most of you know me, so you know that I'm a victim of a drunk driver—one victim among thousands of others. I'm blind because of someone else's lack of judgment and disregard for human life. But, friends, I'm one of the *lucky* ones."

Jennifer caught her breath, fascinated by what she was hearing. She had heard some very straight talk from Dan since he'd begun to advertise the radiothon, but not like this. The expression on his face was steady and calm, but she knew him well enough to know that he disliked any mention of his disability over the air. He was always extremely careful not to exploit his blindness. He wouldn't consider a "personal pitch," as he referred to it, unless he was convinced it would benefit someone else.

"I'm more fortunate than many others," he continued. "I survived. I'm *alive*. A lot of victims of drunk drivers don't live to protest. I did. And quite frankly, I don't like what happened to me. I had something very precious taken away, and I had absolutely nothing to say about it. But thousands of people every year— many of them not yet old enough to vote—lose their *lives*. That's what this weekend is all about. I'm asking you to stay with us for those thirty-six hours and listen to some of the things we hope to achieve with these nationwide radiothons, then do your part to help. Please."

After a moment, he closed his mike, took off his headset, and walked slowly out of the studio as if he had just completed a routine broadcast. Jennifer followed him, tears in her eyes and an enormous lump in her throat. She was so proud of him she could have wept, yet so angry at what had been done to him she would have lashed out in fury had there been somewhere to strike.

Two hours later, she was still in her office, sorting through programming schedules for the weekend, checking the log, and trying to get as many details as possible buttoned down for Gabe. She was bone-tired. She had planned on leaving before five today, but there had simply been too much to do.

Dan had promised her three days off after the radiothon, and she knew she was going to need the break. Even though she was reluctant to leave with everything that had been happening, she was still looking forward to going home.

She decided to quit for the day. She stacked the file folders on the credenza behind her desk, then left her office for Dan's.

"Dan, do you want that guest schedule tonight, or can it wait until—" She stopped just inside Dan's office when she saw Gabe and Dan with their heads together over some papers on the desk.

Gabe glanced up and gestured for her to come on in. "We're finished, Jenn."

Gabe started for the door, and Dan got to his feet. "Why don't you go on home?" he said to Jennifer. "You sound exhausted. We can finish up the rest of the schedules tomorrow."

"You don't have to coax me," Jennifer said. She turned to leave, then stopped. "You're taking Dan home?" she asked Gabe.

He nodded. "After I take him to Sager's for a chili dog."

Dan groaned and made a face, then waved Jennifer off.

In the lobby, she noticed a brown-paper package about the size of a shoe box on top of the receptionist's desk. She stopped to look, and, seeing that it was addressed to Dan, tucked it under her arm and started back down the hall.

Gabe had gone back to his office, and Dan was just putting Sunny's harness on her when Jennifer told him about the package. "Go ahead and open it for me," he said.

"Might be the new postal scale I ordered," Jennifer said, slicing through the sealing tape with a letter opener. "Nope. It's a shoe box."

Dan straightened and came back to his desk. "I didn't order any shoes. What's in it?"

Jennifer put her purse down and pulled the lid off the box. For a moment she could do nothing but stare in horror at the contents. Her sharp cry of disgust brought an answering bark from Sunny. In an instant, Dan was at her side. Jennifer struck out at the box, pushing it away.

"Jennifer? What's wrong?"

Dan caught her arm, and Jennifer turned toward him. At the same moment, Gabe came striding back into the office, stopping when he saw Jennifer's face. "What's going on?"

Jennifer motioned to the shoe box on the desk, her gaze following Gabe's as he picked up the box and looked inside.

Gabe's reaction to the three dead mice with their eyes gouged out was as vehement as Jennifer's had been. He turned to Jennifer, his face ashen.

"Is anybody going to tell me what's wrong?"

Dan's harsh question broke the silence. Jennifer looked at him, then at Gabe, whose eyes blazed with a mixture of anger and revulsion. "This is sick," he choked out. "Really sick."

Dan waited only another second or two before stepping around the desk and fumbling for the shoe box. Gabe stopped him just in time, grabbing his arm. *"Don't! Don't . . . touch it!"*

Slowly, Dan pulled his hand away. "What?" he said quietly. "What's in the box?"

It was Gabe who finally told him, his voice as hard as stone. "Field mice. Dead field mice."

Dan went pale. "Field mice?" he repeated.

"Three of them," Gabe told him. He stopped, glanced at Jennifer, then added, "Their eyes . . . they have no eyes."

Jennifer reached for Dan's hand, watching him closely.

He looked stunned. His mouth went slack, then tightened. "No eyes?" he repeated softly. Then he gave a slow nod. "Three . . . blind . . . mice."

Jennifer gripped his hand even tighter. "Kind of a weird way to make a point, isn't it?" Dan said, trying to smile, not quite managing it. His voice was low and none too steady.

Gabe pulled a piece of paper from beneath the dead mice with an expression of distaste. "There's a note," he said, his voice tight and furious.

"Read it," Dan said evenly.

Gabe read it to himself first, glanced at Jennifer, then cast a worried look at Dan.

"Read it, Gabe," Dan said again.

A muscle at the side of Gabe's mouth twitched as he cleared his throat. "It says—*This is no bluff, blind man.*"

Jennifer saw Gabe's eyes cloud dangerously. She sensed that he was close to exploding. He held up the note and began to ball his hand into a fist, as though to crumple the paper.

"Gabe—no!" Jennifer cried quickly. "Don't! We have to show it to the police!"

He stopped, looking from her to the note. "I'll call them," he said shortly, pitching the note onto the desk.

He moved toward the phone, then stopped, turning to Dan. "This is a real psycho, Dan. He isn't just out to scare you. He means to *hurt* you." Then he picked up the phone and dialed 9-1-1.

Jennifer didn't realize how tightly she had been gripping Dan's hand until he gently pried her fingers loose and tucked her hand securely inside the crook of his arm. "You all right?" he asked quietly.

She stared up at him. "I'm frightened," she said simply. "Really frightened."

He squeezed her hand reassuringly. "It'll be all right. He may just be hoping to make us drop the radiothon."

"Oh, Dan, it's more than that, I'm sure of it! But maybe we *should* postpone the radiothon, at least until—"

He gave a deep sigh. "Jennifer . . . I can't cancel it now. Think of all the time and work and money we've sunk into it. We *have* to go ahead. If I let every kook who didn't like my choice of programming dictate what I do or don't do, I'd soon be off the air for good!"

Jennifer studied him, wondering how much of his composure was genuine. "How can you *not* be afraid, Daniel? Don't you see the significance of—this?" She pushed the shoe box farther down the table.

He pulled her a little closer. "Let's not jump to any conclusions until we talk to the police, OK? Let's see what they have to say."

The police judged the threat real enough that Daniel should have round-the-clock protection. The problem was, they simply didn't have the manpower to provide it. But they promised to work out some kind of coverage, at least throughout the radiothon.

Dan rebelled at the idea, just as Jennifer and Gabe had expected him to. But in the end, the firm, commonsense demands of the police stopped his protests. It was decided that Gabe would spend the night at Dan's house with an officer stationed outside.

When one of the policemen stated that a man would also be placed outside Jennifer's house, Dan turned sharply in the direction of the officer's voice. "You think she's in danger, too?"

The young patrolman hesitated before answering, darting a quick glance at Jennifer. "I think we don't want to take any chances, Mr. Kaine. We don't know what kind of nut case we're dealing with, and someone *was* outside Miss Terry's house the other night."

Jennifer felt a cold trickle of fear snake down her spine, but she was far too frightened for Dan to get bogged down in worry for herself.

"Gabe," she suggested, "couldn't the two of you stay at Dan's parents—just for tonight?"

"No." Dan's retort was curt and sharp.

Gabe looked at him thoughtfully. "That might not be such a bad idea, Dan—"

"And it's not a good one, either," he responded shortly. "We're not bringing my folks into this. We're not going to tell them anything about it, Gabe. Forget it."

Gabe rolled his eyes at Jennifer and shrugged. "You're the boss," he said grudgingly. "OK. Why don't we get out of here so everyone can get some rest?"

It had been years since Jennifer had spent a totally sleepless night. Not since her last week in Rome, after her hopes had been crushed by the blunt pronouncement of Maestro Paulo, had she sat in a darkened room and watched the long, tedious hours of the night plod wearily toward dawn.

Tonight seemed even more endless. The presence of the unmarked patrol car gave her no comfort. She could only think of Dan.

Finally, because she knew she might go mad by morning if she didn't find something to help her pass the hours, she placed the *Daybreak* demo tape in her tape player and lay facedown on the bed to listen. At one point, she remembered the notebook Dan had given her, but she was too keyed up to read.

An hour later, she played the tape over again. It was quite simply one of the most powerful musical scores she had ever heard. It was a musical journey, a journey through the darkness of despair—as detailed by the blind man Jesus had healed; a journey through the darkness of sin—Mary Magdalene's account; and a journey through the darkness of unbelief—a Roman soldier's experience. Each of them was searching for an end to their personal darkness.

And each of them found the Light of the World in God's gift of his Son, Jesus Christ.

It was beautiful. It was unique. And Jennifer knew it contained the power to change lives. No wonder Dan was so taken with it.

For one brief moment, she ached to try the songs of Mary Magdalene. She knew in her heart that her voice was right for the music. But just as quickly, she reminded herself that her voice wasn't the problem. It was her *spirit* that could no longer sing.

FIFTEEN

O N Friday evening, fifteen minutes before the beginning of the radiothon, Jennifer sat in the lounge, staring vacantly outside.

It had been what Dan called a "mizzling" day. The morning had been dreary and oppressively humid, the rest of the day even gloomier. A fine drizzle of rain was now beginning to dampen the evening—and Jennifer's mood.

She would have given almost anything for a few hours of untroubled sleep and an entire day of peace and quiet, a day in which she had to do nothing but simply *think*.

Certainly, she had a few things to think about. But the one thing she really *wanted* to think about—*needed* to think about— had to be pushed onto the back burner of her mind, at least for now. How could she hope to be objective about the fact that a man had recently declared he loved her—and had asked her to marry him—when she was in the midst of a thirty-six hour physical and emotional blitz; when her daily routine consisted of Peeping Toms and pickup truck assaults; and when the man she loved was being hounded by a psychopath?

With a heavy sigh, she turned her attention back to the moment. Her top priority for now was just to get through this weekend, though try as she might, she couldn't shake the chilling premonition that somewhere a bomb was ticking madly away—a bomb that could explode at any second.

Although she dreaded leaving Dan—especially since the incident with the dead mice in the shoe box—she felt she *had* to go home for a few days. She hadn't seen her dad or Loren for weeks, and then only for one day; their disappointment had been painfully obvious when she had left after only a few hours.

There was also no denying the fact that she needed time away from the station—time away from *Dan*. Time to think.

Glancing out the window again, Jennifer saw a patrol car park in the station's lot and a policeman approach the sidewalk leading to the front door. The police had promised that an officer would be at the station throughout the weekend. The protection should have been reassuring, but at the moment it didn't seem to help very much.

Jennifer drained the last of her coffee and rubbed the back of her neck. With a grim smile, she decided she was beginning to feel a little like a character in an old science fiction story—a man who had been imprisoned in a room with walls slowly moving inward and a tide of water gradually seeping up through the floor. The man knew he would eventually be crushed by the walls or drown in the water; his dilemma was deciding which way he preferred to die.

Dan and Sunny came into the lounge just then. Dan looked disgustingly fresh, except for his red-rimmed eyes. As always, his clothes were neatly pressed, his grooming impeccable.

Jennifer glanced down at her own outfit, a hasty, last-minute selection she'd had to settle on this afternoon when she realized that most of her clothes were in the laundry basket. Her sweater was a size too big and tended to hang in a lopsided slouch over her waist, and her slacks could have done with a good pressing.

"Jennifer?" Dan stopped a few yards from her chair.

"Be with you in a minute. As soon as I finish sticking pins in my arm to see if I'm still alive."

His smile was affectionate. "You didn't sleep either?" He was to have napped on the couch in his office while Jennifer rested at home for a few hours that afternoon. But from the looks of his eyes, he hadn't slept all that much.

"Not really. But why is it that I look like a bag lady while you look as if you've been posing for TV commercials?"

"What kind of commercials?"

"Oh, you know the ones—the guy has perfect hair and perfect teeth, and he's leaning back on a fencepost with his face lifted to the wind while he watches a gorgeous white stallion gallop through the heather on the hill."

"You didn't say anything about a perfect nose."

"You noticed, huh?"

She studied his face, unable to stop a tug of tenderness that made her heart turn over. "So—how are you, boss?" she asked him softly.

He shrugged. "OK. I rested a little."

"Good thing, since we have the first shift. Speaking of which, we'd better be getting to the studio."

Dan yawned deeply and followed her out the door. "Katharine said she put a fresh pot of coffee and cups in the studio. We must look pretty bad."

"Nah. Batman and Robin, in charge as usual. Come on, let's go wake up Shepherd Valley."

"I think we'd better wake each other up first."

Dan and Jennifer stayed on the air until eleven that night, then yielded to Gabe and Jay Regan for three hours. As they walked down the hall from the studio, Dan told Jennifer about a phone call he had received that afternoon.

The supervisor at the county children's home, Mrs. Grayson, had called to tell him that a couple had recently inquired into adopting a special child. They were interested in an older child, not an infant, and specifically wanted a boy.

They stopped at the door of Jennifer's office, and she studied him with concern. "Are they considering Jason?"

He nodded. "Mrs. Grayson said she'd like to talk to me about it before she interviews the couple. She wanted me to come in today or tomorrow, but when I explained about the radiothon, she offered to come up to the house Sunday afternoon."

Jennifer could tell that he was shaken by this unexpected news. "You're upset, aren't you?"

He bent down to release Sunny from her harness, then stood and leaned against the doorframe of Jennifer's office.

"To tell you the truth, I'm not exactly sure *how* I feel about it." He crossed his arms over his chest, saying nothing for a moment. "I just want whatever's best for Jason," he finally said. "And I've never been convinced that living with me would be the best thing for him. A single parent—who's also blind . . ." He shrugged. "I used to think that he might be just as well off at the children's home. I hadn't thought much about someone wanting to adopt him, though I suppose I should have realized it might happen."

A faint, sad smile touched his lips, then faded. "Can I ask you something? Just supposing you might agree to marry me—how would you feel about a . . . ready-made family?" As if he sensed her surprise, he quickly added, "Does Jason still make you uncomfortable?"

"I don't—it isn't that he makes me uncomfortable," Jennifer said carefully. "I just feel so *sorry* for him! Dan, we can't talk about this right now—"

"I know," he assured her quickly. "I'm not being fair to you. One crisis at a time is enough, right?" His smile was tender as he reached out to touch her hair. "Tired?"

"Mm. Not me. I'm past fatigue. I'm now into the zonk stage."

"The what?"

"Zonk. Total collapse. The mind shuts down but the mouth goes on."

"Oh. Kind of like the way Gabe is all the time."

"Exactly."

He nodded and started to turn away. "I'll have someone call you in about three hours."

"Gently, Daniel. Tell them to be sure and call me very, very gently, otherwise—" A distant rumble interrupted her in midsentence. "What was that?"

"What was *what?*"

"That noise."

"That noise?" he asked right after another low growl of thunder echoed far away. "I believe," he said sagely, "that's the sound of an approaching storm."

"A *thunderstorm?* At this time of year? We had snow a few days ago!"

"You're in the mountains now, love. The temperature can move up—as it has over the past few hours—or down with no warning. It's not unusual for us to have some nifty storms this time of year, once it starts to warm up."

"Oh." Jennifer shivered.

"What's wrong?"

"Nothing," she said quickly, her voice a half-tone higher than usual.

"No," he drawled softly. "I don't believe it. Not you."

"What?"

"You're afraid of storms?"

"Who said I'm afraid of storms? Did I say I'm afraid of storms?"

"You *are,* aren't you?" He brushed the knuckles of one hand lightly under her chin.

Jennifer shrugged, trying to keep her voice light. "I don't

exactly *like* storms, I suppose, but I wouldn't say I'm *afraid* of them."

"I see." He grinned down at her and tapped her lightly under the chin once more. "What *would* you say?"

"Terrified," she said after a second. "I'd probably say terrified."

He shook his head in disbelief. "Well, somehow I think that once you hit that couch, you'll forget all about the storm." He tousled her hair affectionately. "Now go on—sack out while you can."

Dan's last thought before drifting off to sleep was that he might have been wrong after all. Maybe the radiothon wasn't going to bring his psycho caller out from under his rock. Maybe nothing would happen. Maybe he needn't worry about the rest of the weekend. . . .

And then he was on the mountain road again . . . but this time it was different, totally different. The nightmare propelled him at a dizzying speed past the headlights, past the crunch of metal, past his own terrified scream. He saw the flashes of color again, like last time. He knew he was dreaming, but he couldn't stop it, couldn't stop the car or the dream or even slow things down. He was slammed against the wheel, tossed back and forth against the seat, then against the wheel again. And the truck just kept right on coming, closer, closer, faster than ever before. There was a face—no, it was only an open mouth, no face—just someone screaming at him in anger . . . or in fear . . . and then he was back at the beginning. It was starting all over again, and he knew what was going to happen . . . he would feel the pain and the mind-freezing terror again. He had to stop the nightmare or it was going to kill him this time . . . the truck wasn't going to take his sight, it was going to take his life, and he had to stop it. . . .

He *couldn't* stop it; there was something he had to see, something he'd forgotten, and it was desperately important that he remember . . . now, right now. He had to go a little closer, even let himself be hurt, so this time he'd remember, this time he would know. . . .

"Dan! Daniel! Wake up! Dan!" Jennifer was shaking him gently, framing his perspiration-soaked face between her hands. "It's all right," she murmured. "You're just dreaming, Dan. It's all right, I'm here . . . it's all right now."

Dan threw an arm over his face to shield himself from the pain, to stop the truck.

"Jennifer?"

"Yes." Her voice was shaky, and he knew he must have frightened her. "Are you all right, Dan?" She wrapped her arms around him, burying her face against his shoulder. "You must have had an awful nightmare."

Dan couldn't answer her yet, couldn't quite focus his mind. Jennifer was with him, but where were they? He blinked his eyes once, then again. It was still dark. He couldn't see.

Then he remembered. And the memory hit him with the cold thud of sick reality, just as it had every morning for over five years. He couldn't see because he was blind. He wasn't ever going to see again.

He let Jennifer hold him, secretly drawing what calm he could from her, allowing himself to be soothed by her. He was always alone after the nightmare. There was never anyone to comfort him, to ease the terror. With grateful relief, he let Jennifer hold him now and murmur softly to him until he could face the darkness again.

SIXTEEN

BY Saturday night Dan knew what he had to do. Even though there hadn't been so much as a minor incident during the radiothon, which would end tomorrow morning, all his instincts told him something was going to happen and that this weekend would somehow trigger whatever it was.

He had decided to go on the offensive. If at all possible, he wanted to put an end to this madness while Jennifer was safely out of harm's way. She would leave by noon tomorrow to visit her family in Athens. That meant he had two days to take the initiative, to provoke his tormentor to make a move.

He thought he knew how to go about it. But he would have to wait. First, he intended to make certain that Jennifer was gone.

The man in the pickup truck sat staring at the back of the radio station, his view distorted by the rain slashing the windshield. Occasionally, his eyes would flick back and forth in rhythm with the halting, noisy scrape of the windshield wipers. Mostly he stared straight ahead.

Anticipation quickened his breathing. He rolled down the window a few inches and tossed a half-smoked cigarette outside onto the saturated ground, immediately pulling another from the pack in his jacket pocket. Squeezing it tightly between his nicotine-stained fingers, he squinted as the smoke from the match burned his eyes.

It was late, but the radio station was only dimly lighted. No more than half a dozen cars were in the parking lot, including the black Cherokee that belonged to the station, the Terry woman's Honda, and Denton's Thunderbird. And a police cruiser.

He curled his lip as he stared at the patrol car. He hadn't counted on the police staying this late. He had waited all evening, his pickup safely hidden behind the brush and pine trees on the hill. But the cruiser was still there.

His chest tightened painfully, and the sour taste in his mouth grew even more rancid. He might just as well go home for the night.

He fiddled with the radio dial. Even this close, the station was laced with static, the night sparked with electricity. A gospel song came over the air, and he turned it off with a snap.

Kaine hadn't been on the air for a long time. He wondered what he was doing in there. Not that it mattered. He wasn't going to be able to finish him tonight anyway. He'd have to wait till tomorrow. But that was all right. Kaine would be worn out by then. And he wouldn't be surrounded by so many people. Maybe it would be even better, easier to take care of him at home. Alone.

By seven Sunday morning, Dan knew he could delay no longer. The radiothon would end in an hour. Jennifer was down the hall, briefing Jay Regan and Gabe, who would be handling the regular Sunday broadcasting; she wouldn't hear him on the air. He opened his mike, took a deep, steadying breath, and began to speak. "And now a word for my friend in the noisy pickup truck." He paused, then went on. "I got your package. And your messages. Now I've got a message for *you*." He kept his voice level as he spoke softly into the mike.

"I know who you are. And I know what you're doing, and why. So let's stop playing games. I've known what you want for a long time now. And after this weekend is over, the police will know everything *I* know." He hesitated for an instant, then added, *"The blind man is calling your bluff, pal."*

He turned off his mike, quickly cued up another song, and said a brief, silent prayer.

You and I both know it's me who's bluffing, Lord. I don't have a clue who this nut is, but I've got to make him show himself while Jennifer's gone. I have this sick feeling that he might try to get at me through her. I don't know what else to do, Lord. I can't shake the thought that I'm running out of time, that he's closing in. I have to force his hand now, before someone besides me gets hurt. . . .

The man hurled his coffee cup across the room, his eyes blazing as the pieces shattered on the wall and fell to the floor.

Big-mouthed ape! Who did he think he was, anyway? Talking to the whole town like that!

His eyes were watering, and he wiped them on a dirty sleeve, then slumped down onto the torn plastic seat of a kitchen chair. So, he'd been right all along. Kaine *did* know. But he must not have known too long. Otherwise, he would have done something about it before now.

Well, it was a good thing he'd already planned to get rid of him. Once Kaine blabbed to the police, it would be too late.

They'd never believe me, not against that blind self-righteous hypocrite! The whole town thinks he's some kind of a saint or something. Who's going to take my word against his?

Well, after today he wouldn't have to worry anymore. With Kaine out of the picture, no one would ever know the truth. He'd be safe. Finally safe.

SEVENTEEN

D AN missed her already, and it was only one o'clock. Jennifer hadn't even been gone three hours yet, but her absence was like a hole in his heart.

If it hurt this much when she left him for two days, how would he live with it if she refused to marry him, if he had to settle for living on the outside fringes of her life forever? She was as important to him as breathing by now. Without her, he'd just be taking up space.

Oh, Lord, you know how much I love her. I've let myself believe that you brought her into my life for me to love, to marry. But what if I'm wrong? What if I'm wrong?

Would she talk to her father and brother about him? Would they try to discourage her from getting involved with a blind man? With a stab of apprehension, he realized he couldn't blame them if they did. If Jennifer were his daughter, he might do the same. How many fathers would encourage their daughters to marry a person with his disability?

He sank down onto the piano bench, letting his fingers run idly over the keys with no purpose other than to fill the emptiness of his house with sound . . . any sound. It seemed strange to be alone. Of course, it wouldn't last. But he was glad for it now, at least.

He had tried to put Gabe's mind at rest about leaving him alone for the afternoon, insisting it was more important that Gabe be at the station the rest of the day. Gabe had agreed only after Dan promised to have Lyss or his dad pick him up as soon as his appointment with Mrs. Grayson was finished.

Dan had already called the police and told them they needn't keep an eye on the house this afternoon, that he'd be leaving shortly. Now he had nothing to do but wait for Mrs. Grayson. He had every intention of leaving the house as soon as she did.

Earlier he had almost decided to spend the afternoon alone, waiting for his psychotic friend to make a move. But he had finally admitted to himself that he wasn't that brave. Or that stupid.

He was beginning to think his scheme to lure his unknown adversary into the open had been full of holes from the beginning. Because he'd been so determined to force his assailant's hand during Jennifer's absence, he had ignored the fact that, if this nut came after him while he was alone, there was very little he could do to stop him. Even Sunny would be little help in a situation like that.

Besides, while his first thought had been to protect Jennifer, he didn't want anyone *else* getting hurt either.

Preoccupied by his thoughts when the doorbell rang, he misstepped on his way to answer it and stubbed his toe against the rolltop desk. He opened the door, appalled to discover that Jason was with Mrs. Grayson.

"I hope you don't mind my bringing him along, Dan," the superintendent said as they entered. "But he's missed you terribly the last few days, and I thought it might be good for the two of you to spend a few minutes together."

Dan hesitated, then replied, "Sure. That's fine. Jason, you can play with Sunny while I talk with Mrs. Grayson."

In truth, he was disturbed that Jason had come. He was tense and edgy enough without having to worry about something happening to the boy. But he managed a smile and a playful cuff on the chin before sending him off with Sunny to the loft.

"I'm sorry I haven't been able to spend any time with him this week," Dan said as they sat down in the living room. "I explained about the radiothon—"

"I understand," Mrs. Grayson assured him. "But the child has become terribly attached to you, Daniel, and he's unhappy when he's away from you for any length of time. That's what I wanted to talk about."

Dan remained silent while she told him about the inquiry she had received from the prospective adoptive couple. "I just wanted to be completely sure you weren't interested in adopting Jason yourself before going any further."

Surprised, Dan hesitated for a moment before answering. "I *would* be interested—very interested—if I weren't blind . . . and single."

"I understand that. But I've seen you and the boy together, Daniel, and quite frankly I have my doubts that a physically perfect couple can meet Jason's needs any better than you can—if as well."

Caught off guard by her words, Dan was uncertain how to reply. "There would be problems," he began.

"There are *always* problems when you become a parent," she said, and Dan could hear the smile in her voice. "But I've worked with children and adoptive parents for years, and I've seen some otherwise insurmountable problems overcome by plenty of love and common sense."

"I *do* love the boy," Dan said thoughtfully. "And I'd jump at the chance to have him with me if I thought I wouldn't be cheating him."

"How could *loving* the boy possibly be *cheating* him?" Mrs. Grayson gave Dan no time to respond. "If you should decide to pursue the idea, it might be advisable for you to fill out a preliminary application. It wouldn't bind you to anything," she assured him quickly. "But it would let us get started on a home study and reference check. And it would allow me to place you in the file for consideration as a prospective parent. In addition to others, of course."

Dan rubbed one hand over his chin, then gave a small nod of his head and smiled. "There's someone I'd like to discuss this with, Mrs. Grayson. Would I be hurting my chances if I waited until the middle of the week to turn in an application?"

After encouraging Dan to take his time and consider his decision carefully, Mrs. Grayson rose to leave.

They called Jason and Sunny downstairs, but the boy begged Dan to let him stay. "Just while Mrs. Grayson does her errands, Dan. Please? I'll be real quiet."

Dan was uncomfortable about being alone at the house with Jason right now, but he couldn't explain that to the boy. Finally, he agreed that Jason could stay, but only until Mrs. Grayson returned from her errands.

Jason and Sunny trooped off to play in the yard while Dan walked Mrs. Grayson to her car. The superintendent advised him not to say anything to Jason that would give him false hope, but did suggest that the two of them might at least discuss the possibility of adoption.

After her car pulled away, Dan called Jason to him. "Let's give Sunny a few minutes to run, now that the rain has stopped," he told the boy. "She's been cooped up inside the station with me all weekend."

The afternoon was heavy with a thick humidity. Dan let Sunny romp off, knowing she'd return to check on them now and then. Besides, Jason liked the idea of guiding Dan around the yard, and they usually made a game of it.

"There's something I'd like to talk about, sport," Dan said, taking Jason by the hand.

"What, Dan?" The boy's tone was distracted. Obviously, his attention was more on Sunny than the conversation.

Dan proceeded to tell the child, simply and sincerely, how he felt about him. "You're very special to me, Jason. I like being with you, and I love you very much. In fact, you're like my own little boy. That's how much I care about you. Do you understand that?"

They stopped walking, and Dan felt Jason clasp his hand even tighter. "I love you, too, Dan," the boy said. He surprised Dan with his immediate, sober response and his perception. "And I wish you were my daddy."

Dan felt a little tug at his heart when he heard how small and serious Jason sounded. "Why, Jason?" he prompted. "Why would you want me to be your daddy?"

"So I could stay with you forever."

After a pause, Dan asked, "You'd like that, would you? To stay with me, even though you might never have a mother?"

Jason considered that for a moment. "I'd like to have a mother, too. But I wouldn't be sad without one if you were my daddy." Then something else occurred to him. "Maybe Jennifer would like to be my mother. I think she likes me. And I *know* she likes you!"

Dan's grin was a quick flash of pleasure at Jason's words. "You think so, huh?" Laughing, he picked the boy up and swung him to his shoulder, then set him lightly to his feet.

The retriever bounded over at the sound of laughter, eager to be included. Suddenly she stopped, alert to a sound the others had missed.

Her instinct, born of long, intensive training, years of experience—and immeasurable love—was to immediately ignore her own desire to play, even to ignore the fact that she wasn't on her harness. Moving like a fireball, she hurled herself directly at her master.

The dog took the first bullet in her side and yelped. The boy, thinking the retriever wanted to play, jumped toward her. He caught the second bullet.

Dan heard Sunny's shriek of pain, then heard Jason go down with a surprised cry. In one lightning-fast instant, he realized what he had heard—and knew the shots had missed their intended target.

With the third explosion, he reacted by raw instinct, pitching to the ground in an attempt to remove himself as a target. After another second or two, he choked out Jason's name, then called for Sunny.

No sound broke the deadly quiet on the mountain. He could hear nothing but the pounding of his heart as he lay, silently waiting. He forced himself to lie perfectly still, hoping the sniper would think he'd been hit.

He'll eventually come to make sure he got me. The thought froze him with panic. He felt his skin grow cold and wet with perspiration, and he thought he might be sick. He swallowed hard against the hot taste of bile rising in his throat. He wanted desperately to reach out and grope for Sunny or Jason, but he didn't dare.

He was totally helpless, a sitting duck. There was nothing he could do, no way he could help Jason and Sunny.

He didn't even know for certain where they were. They might still be alive, but they would bleed to death if he didn't get help for them.

Help me . . . merciful God, help me. . . .

He stiffened, held his breath, and suddenly his entire body began to tremble. He heard an engine, someone coming up the driveway. He clenched his teeth together until the tension hurt his jaw, forcing himself not to move, not to cry out. Was it a truck? He tensed even more, then melted with relief. No. Closer now, he knew it was a car. It couldn't be Mrs. Grayson coming back; it was too soon. But the car was familiar.

His dad's Lincoln! *Thank you . . . oh, my dear Lord, thank you. . . .*

Then he realized he had to warn his dad. He couldn't let his father pull in the driveway and get out of the car without knowing—he had to warn him.

He waited until the solid, powerful sound of the big engine slowed as it turned into the driveway, waited until the exact instant the ignition died before pushing himself to his knees and hauling himself upright to wave his hands and shout a warning.

EIGHTEEN

THE steady downpour of rain had been with her since she left Athens, turning the road outside her windshield into an eerie, distorted rivulet. But Jennifer had cried so hard since her frantic departure that she no longer knew whether it was her tears or the rainstorm obscuring the road.

Lyss's call that evening had come only hours after Jennifer's arrival at home. She had been so badly shaken by the news that her dad begged her to stay overnight and leave in the morning. But she couldn't possibly have waited, had instead thrown her things back into her suitcase and, kissing her father and Loren good-bye, had started for West Virginia.

The ache at the back of her neck was nothing compared to the ache in her heart as she remembered her conversation with Lyss. "Dan told me not to call you, Jennifer, but Gabe said I should."

Lyss's voice had been frightened and strained as she relayed the bad news about Jason and Sunny. She had gone on to explain that, according to the police, the shots had been fired from a high-powered hunting rifle, probably from the upper side of the hill behind Dan's house. The sniper's getaway would have been easy and quick.

Jason had still been unconscious when Lyss called Jennifer. Fortunately, the shot had just grazed him—but the boy must have hit his head on a rock when he fell, causing a concussion. Lyss's father had indicated it might be several hours before they had a clearer picture of the child's condition.

As for Sunny, apparently she had been hit in the side. The vet seemed to think she would be all right, but it was too soon to be sure.

Jennifer couldn't bear to think what this had done to Daniel, although Lyss had been painfully honest about her concern for her brother.

"Physically, Dan is fine," she had assured Jennifer. But as she'd gone on, Jennifer had realized that she was weeping quietly, even as they spoke. "He's so . . . *shattered,* Jennifer! And he's blaming himself for the whole thing!"

Lyss explained then how Dan had deliberately tried to bait his tormentor into making a move while Jennifer was gone.

Dismayed that he would have endangered himself on her behalf, Jennifer remained silent while Lyss continued.

"You're not going to find the same Dan you left, Jennifer," she had warned. "I haven't seen him this way since the accident."

Now Jennifer wiped at her eyes, squinting against the monotonous swipe of the windshield wipers. Lyss's final words evoked the memory of what her father had said upon learning of her love for Dan—and his proposal—before they'd heard about the shootings.

"You know, Jenny—" no one but her father ever called her Jenny—"I think the secret of your Daniel's remarkable spirit is that he's placed it in the hands of a loving God, a God who is far, far wiser than any of us. Daniel has allowed God to work his will in whatever way he chooses, even through a tragedy like blindness."

Steven Terry's dark brown eyes had studied Jennifer for a long time. "That's how it was with your mother, too. Even in those last few days at the hospital, just before she died, she allowed the Lord to use her illness—to use *her*—to make a difference for others."

His eyes had misted and his voice had been unsteady as he explained. "You need to know, Jenny, that there are at least half a dozen lives somewhere out there that might never have been changed if it hadn't been for your mother's faith." He had paused a moment before going on. "I believe with all my heart that, if she could, your mother would tell you to look for the glory in things, not the grief."

Jennifer was trying, but at the moment she was finding it almost impossible to see any glory.

Well after eleven, she drove into town, the rain coming down so hard she could just barely make out the red lights of the radio tower on the hill. For some inexplicable reason, the sight of the tower saddened her. Dan's life revolved around that station—he ate, lived, and breathed it. It was that way with Jason and Sunny, too—they had become such an essential part of Dan's life.

She felt a wrench of dismay as she realized that it almost seemed as though Dan were being cut off from everything that mattered most to him.

The thought made her press the gas pedal a little harder. Suddenly it seemed absolutely vital that she get to Dan as quickly as possible.

She found him at the hospital with Lyss and Gabe. She stopped short for a moment when she got off the elevator on the second floor. She could see the three of them sitting in the small lounge at the far end of the hall. Taking a deep breath to steady herself, she began walking down the corridor toward them.

Gabe stood as soon as he saw her and gave her a weak smile. Lyss also got to her feet, glancing from Jennifer to Dan, who sat woodenly, his head buried in both hands.

He raised his head when he heard her approaching steps. Jennifer thought uneasily that his features registered no real surprise or pleasure, only a kind of sullenness.

"Jennifer?" His tone was as wooden as his expression.

Now that she was close enough to get a good look at him, Jennifer felt almost ill with dismay. She found it difficult to respond to Lyss's welcoming hug or Gabe's quick squeeze of her hand. Instead, she could only stare with concern at Dan. His hair needed combing, his blue sweatshirt was spotted with what appeared to be grass stains and blood, and his face was haggard, engraved with stark, grim lines of fatigue and worry. Other than voicing her name, he made no move to acknowledge her presence.

She took a deep breath, then forced herself to stoop down beside him. "Dan—are you all right?" She covered his hands with her own, but he held himself rigid, unmoving, offering only a small nod to her question.

"Jason—how is he?"

When Dan didn't answer, Jennifer looked up at Gabe and then Lyss, who shook her head. "No change. He's still unconscious."

Returning her attention to Dan, Jennifer studied him, still hoping for some sign of welcome. Finally he spoke. "Who called you?"

"Lyss. She knew I'd want to be here."

"She told you what happened then," he said heavily.

"Yes. Oh, Dan . . . I'm so sorry. I know how much they both mean to you." She paused, then tried to reassure him. "They're going to be all right, Dan."

He slumped back against the chair. "Even now," he said thickly, "we still don't know who he is."

"But we'll find out," Jennifer insisted, getting to her feet. She turned to Gabe. "Haven't the police learned anything yet?"

With a look of abject frustration, Gabe shook his head. "Not a clue."

Just then Lucas Kaine, a big, silver-haired model of his son, walked out of a room a few doors down and approached them. Jennifer thought Lucas appeared to be as exhausted as Dan. But his eyes lighted when he saw her standing there, and he managed a smile for her.

"Jennifer, I'm so glad you're here." He darted a quick glance at his son. "There's no change, Dan. I just checked Jason again."

His gaze took in everyone at once. "I think all of you should go home now and get some rest." He held up a restraining hand when Lyss started to object. "Jason will be monitored throughout the night. That's all we can do right now." He hesitated, then added sternly, "You look terrible—every one of you. You're not doing anyone any good this way."

He then turned a meaningful look on Gabe. "I want Dan to stay with us tonight. Will you take him out to the house? I'm going to stick around here for another hour or so."

Gabe hesitated and looked uneasily at Dan, who simply gave a brief shake of his head. "I'm staying with Jason. In case he wakes up."

With an uncertain glance at Lucas, Gabe closed the distance between himself and Dan. "Dan, you're not going to accomplish anything except to wear yourself out," he told his friend.

"I'm staying," Dan said flatly.

With a tired sigh, Lucas met Gabe's eyes and shrugged. "All right. If that's what you want, son."

"Take me to the room, please, Gabe," Dan said dully.

Gabe looked at Dan with surprise, as if he'd just become aware of Sunny's absence. He reached out tentatively to take Dan's arm. "Sure, buddy. This way."

Surprised and disturbed, Jennifer watched as Dan docilely allowed Gabe to lead him down the hall to Jason's room. He hadn't even told her goodnight. She had to fight back tears of pain and rejection as she watched the two of them walk away. Dan's shoulders were slumped, his steps uncertain and shuffling.

For the first time since she'd met him, Jennifer thought with sick despair, Dan actually looked . . . blind.

NINETEEN

O VER the next few days Jennifer saw all too clearly what Lyss had meant about Dan not being the same.

On the surface, he seemed to go about his usual routine. He went to work. He went home—although "home" had temporarily become his parents' house. He went to visit Jason at the hospital and Sunny at the vet's. Although Jason remained unresponsive, the doctors were still hopeful that his condition would improve. As for Sunny, she seemed to be recovering nicely. She recognized her visitors and nuzzled Dan's hand lovingly when he approached.

Somehow, it was Dan who seemed to be the most wounded of the three. He had become an empty reflection of his former self. His sustaining sense of humor, his upbeat disposition—even his warmth—had all but vanished. He came to the station but stayed out of the studio, remaining in his office to work behind closed doors. He ate most of his meals alone at his desk, and Jennifer knew that much of his food ended up in the trash can. If he happened to venture into the lounge when others were present, he sat quietly drinking his coffee, never really participating in the conversation. Even to Jennifer, he was merely courteous, but impersonal and distant.

He had taken to walking with a cane and wearing dark glasses, both of which had come as a shock to Jennifer. The first time she saw him with the unfamiliar gear she wanted to weep for him and, at the same time, shake him.

As if he had sensed her surprise—and possibly her disappointment—he made a lame effort to explain. "Without Sunny, I'm a bit of a menace," he said. "I stumble easily, bump into things. The cane helps me to avoid breaking my neck. That and the dark glasses let others know I'm blind."

When Jennifer offered the cautious observation that Sunny's absence was only temporary—a few days at the most—he said nothing, but merely went on down the hall, the cane tapping in front of him on the way.

Gabe hated the cane and the glasses as much as Jennifer did. "When Dan came back from Seeing Eye with Sunny," he told her, "he said he'd *never* use that 'despicable cane' again. Those were his exact words." He went on to explain that, although the cane and dark glasses were perfectly acceptable props, it bothered him that Dan had come to rely on them again. "I can't help but think it's just another indication of how depressed he really is."

Jennifer made every effort to return their relationship to what it had been, all to no avail. Her attempts at humor bombed hopelessly; her not-so-subtle hints that he was avoiding her seemed to fall on deaf ears. Dan had shut her out, along with everyone else. And there seemed to be nothing she could do about it.

By Wednesday evening, she was physically and emotionally exhausted. Combined with Dan's bewildering and painful rejection was her continual concern for Jason and Sunny—not to mention the grim reality that somewhere out there a lunatic was still loose, and more than likely still bent on hurting Dan.

At the moment, she could think of nothing else but Dan. She had left the station earlier than usual, bogged down in a black mood that was growing worse by the minute. Driven by sheer desperation to find something—anything—that would help her understand what Dan was going through, she now sat at her kitchen table, hunched intently over his journal. She didn't know what she was looking for—perhaps some kind of magic key that would unlock the secrets of his heart so she could help him to get through this awful time.

Before tonight, she had scanned a few pages of the journal but had been reluctant to plumb the depths of emotion and insight she suspected the pages might contain. This evening, however, she began on page one, stopping only when her attention was captured, a few pages later, by something in Dan's notes, an observation that reminded her of one of the musical selections from *Daybreak*.

At the same time, a splash of color tucked in the back lining of the notebook caught her eye, and she pulled out what appeared to be a book jacket. She studied it curiously for a moment, then drew in a sharp breath of astonishment. What she held in her hands was the cover to the published musical score of *Daybreak*. It clearly identified Daniel Kaine as the composer of both lyrics and music.

Jennifer stared at the cover for several minutes, her gaze locked on Dan's name. Finally, she reached behind her to the portable tape player on the counter. The demo for *Daybreak* was still in place, and she pushed the play button to start it. Then she returned to the journal.

For the next few hours, she was held captive by this extraordinarily personal, penetrating glimpse of the mind and heart of a man she was only now beginning to understand. It was an intensely painful process. Her eyes often blurred by tears, Jennifer followed the spiritual and emotional journey of a man groping his way toward the reality of a loving God, a man seeking sanity in the midst of a nightmare, hope in the midst of despair, and faith in the midst of destruction. Long after the last light of evening had turned to darkness, she continued to trace Dan's steps, to walk with him through the long and dreary midnight of his soul.

She even found herself praying with him—not the quick, routine type of prayer her devotions had degenerated to over the past few years, but the plea of an injured child in the first throes of recognizing her own need for healing.

She was there with him, beside his hospital bed years before, when his horror-stricken brain refused to acknowledge reality but continued to anesthetize itself to time and place. *In dark places he has made me dwell,* she read, *like those who have long been dead. . . .*

She sat by the bed and watched him fight his way through the maze of pain and shock and denial, felt his sickening awareness of being violated, mutilated, and humiliated. *I am the man who has seen affliction. He has driven me and made me walk in darkness and not in light. He has besieged and encompassed me with bitterness and hardship. . . .*

She smelled his fear and tasted his tears, shared his anger and suffered his defeat, until she thought she could no longer bear the haunted labyrinth of his heart. *He has made me desolate . . . my soul has been rejected from peace; I have forgotten happiness. My strength has perished, and so has my hope from the Lord. . . .*

But she couldn't leave him. By now she was his partner in agony as she saw him fumble his way past utter despair and finally get to his knees, then stand and begin to fight. *I have called you by name; you are mine! When you pass through the waters, I will be with you; and through the rivers, they will not overflow you. When you walk through the fire, you will not be scorched, nor will the flame burn you. . . .*

She echoed his anguished questions during those first weeks after he left the hospital, as he suffered the frustration and humiliation of dependency. *Oh, that I knew where I might find him. . . . I would present my case before him and fill my mouth with arguments. It is God who has made my heart faint, and the Almighty who has dismayed me, but I am not silenced by the darkness, nor the deep gloom which covers me. . . .*

Then, slowly and reluctantly, she began to listen with him throughout the weary days and weeks and months of searching, as God spoke and challenged and thundered his truth from the pages of his Word. *I am the Lord, and there is no other, the one forming light and creating darkness . . . I am the Lord who does all these. Who has given to me that I should repay him? Whatever is under the whole heaven is mine. . . .*

Weakly, she knelt with him in the garden of his final battle, waiting and watching as he finally admitted his humanness, his weakness, and his sin. *Who are you, O man, who answers back to God? The thing molded will not say to the molder, "Why did you make me like this," will it? Or does not the potter have a right over the clay? Behold, like the clay in the potter's hand, so are you in my hand. Woe to the one who quarrels with his maker. . . .*

She fell facedown with him in the dust and ashes of his pride as his broken, shattered spirit once and for all acknowledged the truth of his Creator, the sovereignty of his Savior, and the infinite love of his Redeemer. *My spirit is broken. I have declared that which I did not understand, things too wonderful for me, which I did not know. Shall we accept good from God and not accept adversity? I know that my Redeemer lives. . . . Though he slay me, I will hope in him. . . .*

And finally, Jennifer realized, as Daniel had, that he had been weak until the Lord made him strong . . . that he had been frightened until the Lord made him brave . . . that he had been rebellious and angry until the Lord made him gentle and kind . . . that he was no more than what his Lord had made him, and the best of what he now was had come out of the fire of affliction.

On these pages born of his pain, she saw his pride, his stubbornness, his rebellion, his fury, his fear, his denial, his doubt, and his weakness. She watched him come to the end of his own resources, humble himself, and acknowledge the majesty and sovereignty of his God. She witnessed a man broken by grief and pain transformed into a restored, whole man of God. *And the Lord*

blessed the latter days of Job more than his beginning . . . the Lord gave
and the Lord has taken away. Blessed be the name of the Lord.

And then Jennifer knelt and allowed the Lord to begin the
same healing and renewing process in her own life, knowing this
was what Daniel had meant. This was what he had wanted for her.

She wept and prayed for what seemed like hours, giving God
her anger and rebellion, her confusion and resentment and hopelessness. She gave God her fractured ego, her shattered dreams, her
broken heart.

And finally, she knew her healing had begun.

While still on her knees, Jennifer caught a new, incisive glimpse
of truth about the man she loved more than life, a truth Dan himself had already tried to convey to her. He was no giant, no spiritual colossus. He was only a man, human and imperfect and
subject to the same faults and frailties as she was. He was a
wounded hero who had fought on the battleground of his faith—
and overcome. Through his loss, he had won; in his weakness, he
had become strong; and in his surrender, he had been made much
more than a conqueror.

Jennifer had long wondered at the secret of Dan's peace. Now,
ever so slowly, that secret began to come to light in the shadows
of her mind. Daniel had realized—and acknowledged—God's
absolute right to do with his creation as he willed. And then he
had learned to trust the Lord's love enough to surrender his own
broken heart and his searching soul to that love. In the abyss of
his pain, he had finally thrown himself upon the mercy of his
God . . . and God had taken the bitter dust of blindness and
breathed a new life of faith into being. This was the light that
glowed from Daniel Kaine, the light at which others warmed
their hearts.

But now his light was flickering and threatening to go out. He
was giving in to defeat and guilt and despair. Jennifer sensed in
him a weariness, a hopelessness that simply refused to fight

another battle. And she understood, even sympathized with, his inclination to retreat. Once more the humiliation and despair of dependency had been thrust upon him. Added to that was his loss of pride and sense of helplessness at being unable to protect those he loved.

Jennifer ached for him. But she couldn't allow him the crutch of guilt or the comfort of self-pity. Somehow she must make him remember what he had tried so desperately to teach *her.*

In her heart, she knew she might well be the only one who could give him the will to stand and fight again.

TWENTY

B Y Friday evening, Jennifer knew it was time to confront Dan.

It was another odd, unseasonably warm night. The atmosphere was almost oppressive with electricity. Thunder drummed faintly in the distance, and thick, ink-black clouds hung ominously above the valley. Jennifer gripped the steering wheel, shuddering when the sky suddenly blazed with lightning.

She saw with relief that Dan's house was bathed with light, inside and out. The security light by the garage was on, as were the carriage lights on either side of the front door. Inside, the lower level was aglow throughout. The apprehension she had felt upon learning from Dan's mother that he'd returned to his house for the weekend faded when she saw a police cruiser parked on one side of the driveway.

Shepherd Valley was small enough that the police force always seemed to be short of manpower. But ever since the shooting incident with Jason and Sunny, the department had made certain that a patrolman was nearby whenever Dan had to be alone for any length of time.

According to Dan's mother, he had been extremely restless and depressed all evening. Finally, he had insisted on going home, and Gabe had driven him.

Pauline Kaine had sounded worried. "Gabe is going back to

stay the night at Dan's, but first he and Lyss are dropping by to check on Jason. I wish Dan had gone with them."

Jennifer cut the engine and got out of the car. She tucked Dan's journal under her arm, then covered it with her raincoat before hurrying up the driveway to the porch.

Rick Hill, the same patrolman who had been at her house the night of the Peeping Tom incident, unlocked the door, leaving the security chain on until he saw Jennifer. He was in uniform, and Jennifer noted uneasily that his hand was touching his holstered service revolver when he opened the door for her to enter.

"Good to see you, Miss Terry," he said politely. "Mrs. Kaine called to tell me you were coming."

Jennifer tossed her yellow slicker over a dining-room chair, holding on to the journal.

"Dan's in there," the policeman said, gesturing toward the door that led from the kitchen into the pool area. "Sounds like it's cooking up a storm outside."

Jennifer nodded. "Something's headed this way, I'm afraid."

She pushed up the sleeves on her sweater and started toward the pool area, opening the door slowly and quietly. She stopped just inside. Dan was in the water; obviously, he hadn't heard her enter. Jennifer stood watching him with fascination, remembering Dr. Rodaven's words when he had first told her about Dan's blindness: "Kaine was a real powerhouse in the water."

He still is, Jennifer thought. But she sensed that the power now emanating from him as he thudded through the water in a perfectly executed front crawl was at least partly born of anger and frustration.

She expelled a sharp breath of appreciation as Dan reached the far end of the pool, did a lightning-fast flip turn, then roared through the water again. He was approaching her now, and she could see the mixture of anguish and rage contorting his features.

As he turned and did another lap, Jennifer glanced from the

man in the water to the two photos on the pool wall—photos which, according to Dan, his mother had insisted on hanging. They had been taken at the Olympics the year he won the gold medal for the United States. A younger, beardless Dan was standing in the middle of a beaming huddle consisting of his parents, Gabe, and Lyss. He looked pleased and flushed with victory.

Jennifer's eyes misted as she turned her gaze back to the pool. Dan had stopped in the middle of a stroke and was treading water. The strong emotions that had been playing on his features only a moment before had relaxed to a look of weary resignation.

"Dan—" Jennifer walked around to the side of the pool and stopped, waiting.

He jerked with surprise, bobbing up and down in the water a few times before making his way to the side of the pool. "Jennifer?" He hauled himself up out of the water and sat down on the edge of the pool, fumbling for a white terry cloth robe lying nearby. Jennifer stooped to hand it to him.

"Do you see my towel anywhere?" he asked, shrugging into his robe.

Saying nothing, Jennifer retrieved the towel off a nearby aluminum chair and pressed it into his hands.

"What are you doing here?" Dan's guarded tone stopped just short of being rude.

"I—thought perhaps we could talk."

His eyes narrowed as he began to towel-dry his hair. "Something wrong?"

"No," Jennifer said quickly, hesitating before going on. "But . . . I thought it was time I gave you an answer." At his puzzled expression, she added, "To your proposal."

He froze, his arms suspended above his head. An expression very much like anger settled over his features, but he remained stonily silent.

Jennifer cleared her throat and continued. "You asked me," she

said as evenly as possible, "to marry you. Remember?" She held
her breath, watching him.

Dan's face darkened, and for a moment he looked uncertain.
Then, unbelievably, he began to dry his hair again with slow,
steady motions.

"Go home, Jennifer," he said quietly but not unkindly. "Don't
do this. Not now."

"Don't do what?" Jennifer clenched her hands at her sides.
"Don't you want my answer?"

"Just . . . don't." His voice was hard with warning. But Jennifer
instinctively understood his reaction. He thought she had come
out of pity.

She had to remind herself that this was Dan. Not as she had
learned to know him and not as she had grown to love him . . .
but Dan, nevertheless.

"I see," she said quietly. "You weren't serious, then . . . when
you asked me to marry you? When you told me you loved me?"

She knew she had hit a nerve. He actually flinched and stopped
that inane, monotonous toweling of his hair. "Things are different
now. I don't have to tell you that." He dropped the towel onto
the chair beside him, letting his hands dangle loosely at his sides.

It struck Jennifer suddenly that he had lost weight. And she was
certain there were lines fanning out from his eyes that hadn't
been there a few days ago. Suppressing the pity that threatened to
unnerve her, she went on. "What exactly has changed, Dan? Your
feelings about me?"

He turned away from her, but before he did, Jennifer saw his
face glaze with pain. "Listen," he bit out, "You don't owe me an
answer. You don't owe me anything. Just go home. Please."

"No."

He pivoted around in surprise.

*Please, Lord, let me get through to him. Let me reach him, help him
. . . please. . . .*

"Daniel, you said you loved me. Has that changed so quickly?"

"What are you *doing* here?" His voice sounded strangled.

"Humiliating myself, apparently," Jennifer replied in a small voice, determined not to cry.

"Jennifer—don't . . ."

"I came to tell you that my answer is *yes*, Daniel. I want to marry you." She could hear her own weakness in her tremulous words. "Unless, of course, you *have* changed your mind. About us."

She felt a quick stab of hope when she saw a parade of conflicting emotions begin to march across his face. But abruptly he shook his head, lifting a restraining hand as though to stop her from going any further.

"Jennifer, don't do this to me, don't—"

"And if you're thinking," Jennifer pressed on, determined to hold what small edge of advantage she had gained, "that this has anything to do with my feeling sorry for you, forget it." She deliberately sharpened her tone.

He started to reply, but she moved in even harder. "I don't feel sorry for you at all," she said firmly. "In fact, Daniel, if you want the truth, I think I'm angry with you."

His dark brows knit together in a confused frown. "What—"

"I read your journal," she said matter-of-factly. "And I have to tell you that it seems to me you've forgotten a few things."

"Now, *listen*—"

He was angry. Good. At least he was feeling *something*.

Jennifer slammed the journal down on the aluminum table near the pool. "What you wrote on those pages, Daniel," she said carefully, knowing she was treading on shaky ground, "and the glorious piece of music that came out of it, is life-changing." She paused. "I know it's changed *my* life."

The angry set of his mouth relaxed only slightly. "What are you talking about?"

"I can't help wondering, though, about some of the things you wrote in your journal. If they were true five years ago, aren't they true today?" She took a deep breath, then decided that after going this far, she couldn't quit now. "Has God changed in the meantime?"

She was amazed at her own insolence. She prayed she wasn't going beyond the point of forgiveness.

"What exactly are you getting at?" The anger he was so obviously fighting to control was like a physical blow to Jennifer. Thunder, much closer now, rolled and slammed against the house, a fitting accompaniment to the fury blazing in Dan's eyes. Jennifer shivered involuntarily when lightning cracked and lighted the darkness outside the floor-to-ceiling glass windows.

Unexpectedly, her thoughts rioted, and an enormous wave of guilt washed over her. Who did she think she was, violating his privacy like this? She had come here, intent on trying to shock Dan out of his depression. But she had never intended to hurt him. He had been hurt enough. Certainly she didn't want to be the one to inflict even more.

Her eyes began to sting, and she suddenly wished she had never begun any of this. She felt as though she were losing an already tenuous grip on something very fragile, but very, very precious.

"Dan—" She heard the uncertainty in her voice. And so, apparently, had he.

"Don't stop now, Jennifer." His face could have been carved in stone.

Jennifer took a deep breath, then spilled the words out in one jumbled rush. "Everything you tried to tell me . . . it was all true."

Still he remained motionless, an impassive statue.

"You were right—about all of it."

He gave a small shake of his head and frowned. "What *are* you talking about?"

She squeezed her eyes shut for an instant, then opened them

again. Through her tears, she was relieved to see that his anger appeared to be ebbing. Now he simply looked confused.

"Your journal, Dan. The things you wrote . . ."

His frown deepened. "What about it?"

"Oh, Daniel . . . it broke my heart! And that's exactly what had to happen! I had to be broken—completely broken—before God could put the pieces back together the way he wanted them. You can't mend something that isn't *broken!*"

Her words spun between them, churning into an echo that bounced across the hollow recesses of the pool house. Hesitantly, Jennifer took a step, then another, until she had closed the distance between them. Her heart was in her throat, her pulse thundering. She hadn't realized until that instant just how tightly she had been holding herself together.

Finally, when she was close enough to touch him, she stopped and stood perfectly still, raising her eyes to study with infinite caring his strong, firmly molded features. A look that was at once forlorn and hopeful now gentled his smoldering expression of moments before.

Unable to help herself, she lifted an unsteady hand and lightly touched her fingertips to his face. "Daniel . . . I understand now. What you've been trying to tell me all along. About having faith enough to trust God's love, his right to work his will in our lives . . . even when it seems that he's being unfair or that he's only doling out punishment." She paused. Perhaps it no longer made any difference, but she had to tell him everything. She had to share the life-changing explosion that had occurred in her spirit.

"In your journal," she went on, "toward the end, you wrote out Romans 8:28. 'And we know that God causes all things to work together for good to those who love God. . . .' That's the message of *Daybreak,* too, isn't it, Daniel? That God took the ugliest, most shameful symbol ever known—the cross—and turned it into glory. That what seemed to be the most awful event in history was changed into the most *important* event in history."

Even in the face of his passivity, Jennifer couldn't control her newfound joy. "Oh, Dan, don't you understand? I'm *free* now! I don't have to fight God anymore! I don't have to be angry anymore! You knew it long before I did, but I had to find it out for myself! And I did! Because of *you!* It was all there, in your journal—and in your musical, *Daybreak.*"

For a long moment, it was as though he would never move again, and Jennifer dropped her hand away from his face, letting it fall to her side in reluctant defeat.

"Maybe it doesn't matter anymore," she said in a near whisper, agony straining her voice. "But I just had to tell you." Her final words were nearly lost in the repeated blows of thunder that shook the windows of the house.

Dan's sightless eyes slowly filled with tears, and he tried to turn away from her. But Jennifer saw and grasped his shoulders with both hands, holding him. "No—don't turn away from me, Dan! Don't shut me out, please."

Had she caused the grief that washed across his face when he turned back to her? "Jennifer . . . I can't—" He swallowed with obvious difficulty. "You deserve so much more than I can give you."

"I don't *want* anything more than you can give me!" Jennifer cried. "I just want *you.*" She studied him, her heart filled with love and determination. "I want to be your wife, Dan."

"Jennifer, don't you understand?" he said, misery lacing his words. "I can't look after you the way a man should." His despair was almost tangible. "I couldn't even protect an innocent little boy . . . or my own dog. That could have been *you* that day! You could have taken the bullets meant for me—and I wouldn't even have known you were in danger!"

The words exploded from him, a harsh, agonized cry that stunned Jennifer into momentary silence.

She stared at him, understanding finally dawning. "Is *that* what's wrong?"

He didn't answer.

"It *is*, isn't it? You're punishing yourself! Because you tried to bait this lunatic to come after you in order to protect me. And then Jason and Sunny got hurt—"

He grabbed her arm in an almost painful vise. *"Yes!* And *I* caused it! It was my stupid pride, my stubbornness!" Abruptly, as though he realized he might be hurting her, he gentled his grasp on her arm.

"I thought I could manage it," he said harshly. "That's always been my way. To manage things on my own."

His jaw tensed and he shook his head at Jennifer's small cry of protest. "I thought, after the accident, that I'd finally gotten rid of that insufferable pride of mine. I even reached the point where I could actually accept help from people." He gave a nasty, short laugh. "You'd expect me to have a healthy dose of humility after I had to learn to eat and brush my teeth all over again, wouldn't you?"

Tears trickled slowly down Jennifer's cheeks as, outside, the sky finally released its pent-up deluge amid the growling thunder and flashing lightning.

"Then you came along." Dan's gentle smile of wonder—the first sign of his former tenderness Jennifer had seen in days—nearly broke her heart. "And suddenly I needed my pride back all over again." He reached out a tenuous hand to lightly graze one side of her face. "I wanted to be . . . enough for you, don't you understand? I wanted to be everything you thought I was—a giant."

Jennifer blanched. It was true. That's exactly what she had made of him in her mind. A giant of a man . . . even a spiritual giant.

His smile now turned bitter. "I may have made a halfhearted attempt to convince you I wasn't the man you thought I was. But the truth of the matter was that I enjoyed your fantasy. I wanted to be *exactly* what you thought I was. Strong. Capable. In charge. It didn't take too long for the old stubborn pride to rear its head again. I was determined to have a—*normal* relationship with you. Love. Marriage. A family. I wanted it all. I wanted to be everything you wanted me to be. And all the while, I knew I was asking for the impossible."

Jennifer closed her eyes. When she could finally bring herself to look at him again, her heart wrenched to see that tears were now falling freely down his face.

"Oh, Dan," she murmured with dismay, "you *are* everything I want, can't you understand that? *I want you* . . . exactly as you are. You say you couldn't protect a little boy or your own dog. But Dan . . . I'm *neither.* I'm a grown woman. You don't have to watch over me. I can watch over *myself.* Daniel—I don't need you to *protect* me. I need you to *love* me!"

Somehow she made her way into his arms. She felt his strong shoulders slump. He leaned against her, burying his face in her hair . . . and he wept.

Jennifer now fully understood his former pain and his near-ruin, the hopelessness that had very nearly defeated and destroyed him five years before. Her face was soaked with his tears and her own, and she was blind now, too, her vision blurred by their mingled tears. Outside, the night sky wept with them, and the mountain roared as though in its own agony. But Jennifer knew nothing except the man whose hurt she now tried to absorb into her own soul. She held him as tenderly as she would have a child, promising him silently that he would never again bear his pain alone.

And she knew then, as she could never have known before, how it must have been for him after the accident. She saw with a startling clarity how incredibly wrong she had been about the man who now wept in her arms. She saw how weak he must have been, and she realized for the first time the infinite amount of strength the Lord had given him, the awesome quality of faith

God had woven from that weakness. She saw how very far her beloved had actually come . . . such a long, hard way.

"Jennifer . . . I need you. . . ."

She nodded, and murmured softly against his bearded cheek.

"You make me whole . . . you make me a man again. . . ."

"I love you, Daniel. . . ."

"You really will marry me?"

"Oh, yes, love, of course I'll marry you."

"Soon . . . ?"

"Whenever you say. . . ."

The fury outside the house muted the shrill ringing of the telephone. "Dan—the phone—"

Ever so slowly, he lifted his head and wiped the dampness from his eyes with the back of his arm. "Would you get it?"

Moving reluctantly out of his embrace, Jennifer walked to the wall phone and lifted the receiver.

It was Pauline. As soon as Jennifer answered, Dan's mother exploded with the good news. "Jennifer—Jason is conscious! He's asking for Dan! Lucas just called. Tell Dan that Jason is going to be all right!"

The excitement in her voice carried across to Dan. Jennifer saw him whisper, *"Thank you . . . thank you, Father."*

"Yes, of course, I'll drive him to the hospital," Jennifer said into the receiver as she watched Dan begin to nod. "Yes, we'll go right away!"

By the time she hung up, Dan was beside her, his arms around her. He kissed her lightly, saying, "I'll get dressed. While I change, why don't you tell Rick he can go, that we're going to leave? There's no point in his staying here without us."

Dan smiled—his old smile, the one Jennifer loved to distraction—and she knew that everything was going to be all right. It really was.

TWENTY-ONE

JENNIFER leaned out the door to watch the patrol car pull out of the driveway. The wind-driven rain sprayed her face, and she was about to duck back inside when something caught her attention.

The headlights of the patrol car flashed across the east side of the house, momentarily illuminating the dense grove of pine trees only yards away. Jennifer stuck her head out even farther, ignoring the rain. She had seen something, she was sure of it, out there among the trees. Craning her neck as far as possible, she squinted into the darkness. But the lights from the patrol car were gone now, and she could see nothing but rain-swept shadows.

Still, she waited uneasily, trying for another glimpse of whatever she thought she had seen. Suddenly, an eerie blue-white glow framed the entire lot, followed by a roll of insistent thunderclaps. Jennifer winced, hunching her shoulders and squeezing her eyes shut—and missing the opportunity to get another look at the lightning-illumined field.

She shook her head in self-disgust as she jumped back inside and shut the door behind her. If she wanted to see anything, she had to keep her eyes *open*.

She stood there for a moment, her back against the door, trying to shake off her fear of the storm. Finally, she turned and started back toward the pool house.

She had just begun to breathe a little easier when a dazzling bolt of lightning nailed the ground outside the window to her right. She stopped dead, riveted by the iridescent explosion, then screamed at the boom of thunder that shook the mountain and plunged the house into total darkness.

Jennifer's blood froze. For one breathless moment, she could do nothing but stand motionless, rigid with fear.

The darkness around her was as thick as ink. She felt light-headed and hoped she wasn't going to pass out. She had to get back to Dan, to tell him about the lights going out.

But it wouldn't matter to Dan that the lights were out, she thought fleetingly. It would only matter to *her.*

She pushed a fist against her mouth, then dropped it, and clenched her hands tightly together. After a moment, she began to grope her way toward the open door of the pool house. She stumbled in the darkness, grazing her hip against the kitchen counter and kicking Sunny's food bowl across the floor.

Finally she grabbed the doorframe and stopped just inside the entrance, peering down the length of the pool.

"Dan?" She squinted into the warm dampness of the room. "Dan, the power's out. Should I call—"

The question died on her lips. She halted in midstep, her heart hammering with a vengeance. Lightning streaked, over and over again, revealing two shadows close to the door of the dressing room. On the other wall, the outside door stood open, an ominous, gaping black hole. Jennifer realized that one of the shadows—the larger one—was Dan. He appeared to be facing the wall, while the other shadow pushed against him.

Disoriented, Jennifer struggled to take in the scene in front of her. Another flash of lightning illuminated the pool house, and now she realized that Dan was pinned against the wall, with a man holding a gun at his back!

Too terrified to be cautious, she screamed. The gun-wielding man whirled toward her, his corpselike face illuminated for a dazzling instant, framed for all time in her memory. It was the same cadaverous face she had seen peering in her kitchen window!

She lunged forward, intent only on helping Dan. The man waved the gun, took a wild shot at her, and Jennifer dropped to the floor. She lay there, panicked, watching as Dan pivoted around and snaked his foot out in a low kick that knocked his assailant off-balance and sent him sprawling, arms waving, into the pool. The gun sailed out of his hand and went bouncing over the tiled floor, echoing loudly all the way down the room.

Jennifer clambered to her knees and lunged toward Dan. But she stopped dead when he shouted, *"Jennifer—get the gun!"*

Jennifer's gaze scanned the floor in search of the gun. She saw it, lying only inches from the rim of the pool. Glancing back at Dan, she saw him shrug out of his robe and slide smoothly into the water. He was going after his assailant!

Her mind felt numb. She couldn't think. A tight thread of hysteria threatened to snap somewhere inside her, and she was able to hold onto her reason only by sheer force of will—and the awareness that Daniel was alone in the pool with a madman.

"Daniel, what are you *doing?* I'm coming in, too! You can't see where he—"

"No!" he shouted over his shoulder. "I can't keep track of him *and* you! Just stay quiet so I can hear—and *get the gun!"*

Still Jennifer hesitated. Finally, her stomach clenching with panic, she forced herself to pick up the gun. She held it extended from her body as far as possible, staring at it as though it were something alive and extremely deadly.

Dan felt the water enfold him like a warm blanket as he pushed himself away from the side of the pool and began to quietly bob up and down, listening and waiting. Within seconds he had a fix

on his assailant's location, the man must have panicked. There was
no time to waste; the other might regain his senses any moment.

Dan went under the water with one smooth scissor motion
and began to push forward slowly but confidently. The pressure in
his ears and on his lungs was nothing in comparison to the
weight of desperation closing in on him.

Who *was* this lunatic, anyway? Someone he knew? What had
he ever done to evoke this kind of hatred in the man?

The muffled exclamations above the surface of the water were
much louder now. Dan began to feel the current lapping against
his face from the other's thrashing movements. He knew he was
close. Very close.

He also knew he had all the advantages for a few more seconds, at least. The sensation was rare, but exhilarating. For years he
had lived with the feeling of always being at a disadvantage. He
liked the idea of being in control for a change. There was also the
fact that the other man was fully clothed, while he was still in his
swim trunks. The weight of his assailant's soggy clothing would
go against him.

Best of all, Dan thought, the power was out. His adversary
would be as much in the dark as *he* was. And he had smelled alcohol on the man. If his reflexes were diminished, that would only
give Dan even more of an advantage.

He swam quietly, feeling a change in the ripples as he went.
Apparently, the man had begun to move away. His cries sounded
farther out, and the current from the churning of the water had
also begun to drift off. Dan followed the movement and the
sound as closely as he dared, staying under the water and remaining totally quiet.

Until at last he knew he had him.

Dan roared up through the water in one explosive motion,
grappling for his assailant. He took him from behind, raising his
arms directly above the man's head and pushing him down into

the water. The man tried to wave his arms. He cursed and shrieked, striking Dan in the face several times before catching him in the midriff with his elbow.

But Dan was much bigger and in far better condition. Every move the other made was in vain. Finally, with one large, powerful shove, Dan plunged him under the water and followed him down.

The man tried to fight, but was quickly pulled to the bottom by the weight of his clothes and his own panic. Dan refused to let him go. He followed him to the bottom and efficiently locked an iron forearm around his neck in a relentless hold.

As her eyes adjusted to the darkness, Jennifer stood by the side of the pool, staring with terror into the water. She could make out dark shadows of movement beneath the surface, but nothing else. Trembling, she gripped the gun, steadying it with her other hand.

They had been below for what seemed like hours. She waited, scarcely breathing. She should call the police, but she couldn't move until she knew that Dan was all right. If they didn't come up in the next few seconds, she was going in. She even kicked her tennis shoes off in preparation.

How much longer should she wait? How long could they stay down?

She screamed and nearly dropped the gun when a wave of water sprayed her in the face as both men suddenly broke above the surface. Weak with relief, she saw Dan swim to the side of the pool, dragging the other man along with him. When he reached the pool wall, Dan hauled himself partly up out of the water, holding his assailant securely with one arm until he could pull him the rest of the way out.

"Jennifer—"

She was already beside him. "Daniel! Are you all right?"

She stopped when light flared as the electricity suddenly returned. "Dan, the lights!" she exclaimed. "The lights are back on!"

Dan was panting heavily with exertion. "Good! Take a look at this guy. Who is he anyway? Do you recognize him?"

Jennifer was still shaking. "I don't know his name, but he's the same man who was at my door the other night."

Dan nodded as if he weren't surprised. Flipping the still unconscious man over onto his back, he knelt beside him and lowered his head to listen to his chest. "He swallowed most of the pool. I'm going to have to pump him out."

He raised the man's head and checked his airway, then flipped him—none too gently, Jennifer noticed—onto his stomach and began applying firm pressure on his back to pump the water from his lungs.

"Jennifer, you'd better call the police."

Jennifer carefully placed the gun on the table, then ran to the poolside phone to dial the police. Once she had delivered her message, practically screaming into the receiver, she hurried back to Dan, going to her knees to see if she could help. But the man was already gulping and coughing up water.

"Check his pockets, Jennifer. I want to know who he is," Dan told her as he continued to knead the man's back.

Jennifer pulled a soaked, ruined billfold out of the back pocket of the man's khaki work pants and opened it. The contents were soaked and her hands were trembling, but she finally managed to separate the driver's license from the other papers. "OK," she muttered, "here's his license. Let's see—" Jennifer stared down at the wet, laminated card and made a strangled sound of disbelief.

TWENTY-TWO

D ANIEL—it's *Caleb Arbegunst!* Jim's father!"
Dan froze in midmotion. Beneath his hands, the
man spewed out water and coughed convulsively.
"Caleb? Are you sure?"

"That's what it says!" Jennifer continued to stare down at the
license for a moment, then scanned the other papers in his wallet.
"Yes—here's a credit card. And . . . here's some kind of social ser-
vices I.D. They all say the same thing. But *why,* Dan? What does
Caleb Arbegunst have against *you?"*

He shook his head. "I hardly even know the man! I had only
seen him once before the accident, and I haven't talked to him
since."

Jennifer had nearly forgotten that Caleb Arbegunst had been
with the teenage boy who hit Dan's car and caused his blindness.
Still, what possible reason could he have for trying to kill Dan?

"It doesn't make any sense," Dan said, his voice puzzled as he
rolled Arbegunst over onto his back. "The man is a virtual
stranger to me. I—"

Suddenly he stopped, and Jennifer watched in horror as his
face contorted in pain. "Dan! What is it? What's wrong?"

He seemed riveted in place, his face frozen in a look of
anguish. He started to tremble, and Jennifer almost panicked,
afraid he might be going into shock.

Seeing the robe he had tossed by the side of the pool, she

scrambled to her feet and went after it. She returned, draping it around Dan's shoulders.

She knelt down beside him, watching him closely. Finally the tremor racking his body began to subside. He shook his head back and forth as if trying to clear his mind. "Something—about the nightmare," he said, then stopped. His shoulders slumped, and he frowned as he grazed the fingers of one hand over the scar at his eyebrow. "I can't think. . . ." His voice drifted off.

They both jumped in surprise when the man between them stirred and twisted, then began to flail his arms. His bloodshot eyes were wild and disoriented, his soaked clothing plastered to his emaciated body.

Dan quickly pinned him to the floor and held him there. Arbegunst thrashed, twisting his head from side to side as he tried to free himself from Dan's grip. He cursed and shrieked at them as he struggled to break free.

Jennifer's stomach knotted as she watched them. When she saw Dan begin to shake again, she laid her hand on his forearm, thinking to steady him. He didn't seem to be hurt, but he was obviously in the grip of some kind of emotional storm she couldn't comprehend.

Suddenly the insane babbling from the man on the floor penetrated her consciousness.

". . . should have killed you the first time . . . knew it. Knew you'd cause trouble. . . ."

Dan choked off an exclamation and frowned, listening.

"What trouble, Caleb? What kind of trouble?" he prompted.

Arbegunst went on muttering in a crazed monotone. "Just waitin' on me, weren't you . . . just bidin' your time to ruin me, so you could take my kid . . . thought you'd drive me nuts, didn't you, then you could have my boy. . . ."

Jennifer looked at Dan and saw his jaw tighten even more as he bent low over Caleb Arbegunst.

"Daniel—what is he talking about?"

Dan waved off her words. "Waiting on *what,* Caleb?"

"All these years, you knew . . . just waitin' to tell, tryin' to make me crazy, tryin' to take my boy. Well, you ain't gonna get him. I'll shut you up for good this time, Kaine. . . ."

Dan pressed him harder to the floor. "Tell what, Caleb? What is it you think I'm going to tell?"

Jennifer framed her face with both hands in sick horror and bewilderment. She looked from Dan, whose face was a mask of self-control, down to Arbegunst, shaking and thrashing in weak futility.

"You saw me . . . you knew I was drivin' that night. They said you couldn't remember anything, but I knew better. Your memory came back a long time ago, you were just waitin' to tell. You waited so you could get my boy, didn't you? You went and gave him that job, coddled him, took him places, let him swim in your big, fancy pool. . . ."

"Driving?" Daniel echoed hoarsely. *"You* were driving . . . the night of the accident? Not the boy?"

Arbegunst uttered an ugly snort, and Jennifer felt suddenly nauseous, as much from the stench of alcohol as the emotional maelstrom.

"I wouldn't let one of those no-good punks drive my truck," Arbegunst snorted. "He wanted to . . . said I was drunk. I wasn't drunk, never been drunk on the road . . . I'd had a few beers waiting for him, that was all. Wasn't drunk. . . ."

Jennifer heard no more, the rest of his words lost to her as she reached out to grasp Dan's arm. She felt dazed and sickened by what she'd just heard. The man was admitting what he thought Dan already knew. But Jennifer took one look at Dan's face and realized that Dan *didn't* know. He had *never* known!

"Dan . . . does he mean what I think he does?"

Her question fell between them, dying quickly in the silence.

Even the storm outside was subsiding, nothing left of it except a few weak spurts of lightning and the sound of muffled thunder moving off into the distance. The earlier torrential rain had turned to a gentle, rhythmic patter, almost hypnotic in its steady thrum against the metal roof.

Jennifer continued to watch Dan, fearful of what he might do. His grasp on Arbegunst never faltered. He was like a kneeling statue, frozen in place. The erratic rhythm of his breathing, the thin line of perspiration that had begun to drape itself along the ridge above his dark brows, the sudden, uncharacteristic paleness that settled over his face were the only hints of the storm that might be gathering in his soul.

"You were driving the truck, Caleb?" His voice was ominously quiet. "Not the boy?"

Jennifer had never had such an urge to lash out and strike a man as she did when she heard the high-pitched explosion of laughter that ripped from Caleb Arbegunst's mouth.

"Dumb kid, tried to grab the wheel from me . . . coulda got us both killed. . . ."

Dan's face contorted into a thunderous mask of rage. He moved his hands from Arbegunst's shoulders to his neck, and Jennifer gasped when she saw his fingers clench and unclench. "Dan—"

"The boy *was* killed, you drunken—" Suddenly Dan stopped, shook himself almost violently, and Jennifer saw his hands tighten once, then again, before dropping back to Caleb Arbegunst's shoulders.

"You put the boy under the wheel—after the crash." He made it a statement, not a question.

"Yeah . . . you were out cold . . . you didn't see me, nobody saw me. He was just a scrawny kid; I pushed him right under the wheel. Nobody ever knew. Even poured whiskey on him so they'd think he was drunk. They didn't even check me out.

Nobody saw. Nobody knew . . ." His red-rimmed, watery eyes cleared and focused on Dan. "Except you."

Jennifer watched Dan, afraid of what he might do. His features were unreadable. "No, Caleb," he said, his voice chillingly quiet. "I never knew. No one knew but you. Until now."

Slowly, little by little, the man on the floor quieted, the insanity temporarily stilled. He stared up at Dan, as if unable to grasp or accept the truth of what he had heard.

"You're lyin'! You knew—you always knew! You wanted to make me crazy . . . you wanted my boy. . . ."

Dan shook his head in a sad, hopeless gesture. "You poor fool," he murmured softly. "You sold out your whole life—even your own son—for a bottle of temporary escape and a soul full of guilt."

Still holding Arbegunst to the floor, Dan looked like a man coming out from under a long sleep.

"I never knew," he said again. "I had nothing to go on except a nightmare. A bad dream that never seemed to end. Your secret would probably have been safe for a lifetime."

Arbegunst twisted his head back and forth in violent denial. "No, you knew . . . you always knew. You even said on the radio you knew who I was. . . ."

Dan didn't answer right away. When he did, his tone held a note of surprise. "I wasn't talking about the accident. I was just trying to bait you, draw you out into the open so you'd make a move. And then I nearly caused Jason and Sunny to get killed. No," he said once more, very softly. "You were the only one who knew the truth, Caleb."

They heard the sirens then, wailing up the mountain. Jennifer drew her first long breath in what seemed like hours and rose trembling to her feet to open the front door for the police.

But Gabe was already through the door, using the key he always carried. He blasted through the entrance to the pool house, nearly knocking Jennifer to the floor in his effort to reach Dan. "What happened—what's going on? The police chased me all the way up here!"

Jennifer saw with relief that there was a ghost of a smile on Dan's face when he answered. "Relax, buddy—everything's under control."

At that moment, two police officers brandishing revolvers charged in behind Gabe. Dan hauled himself to his feet and, after turning Caleb Arbegunst over to the police, slipped into his robe.

Almost at once, Gabe began shooting questions at Dan, who gave him a few brief but concise answers, then held up a restraining hand. "I need a minute. Take everyone into the house and leave me alone, would you?"

Jennifer thought he sounded—and looked—extremely weary. Gabe darted a questioning look at her, and she managed a weak but reassuring smile.

Dan pulled in a long breath, then said again, "I need to be alone . . . just for a few minutes. Please?" He paused, then added, "Then if someone will take me, I want to go to Jason."

"Isn't anyone going to tell me what's happened?" Gabe's voice was decidedly testy.

"Jennifer," said Dan, "talk to the man, would you? I'm going to change into some dry clothes."

Jennifer stood with Gabe and watched Dan as he turned and began walking slowly toward the dressing room. She thought with admiration that Daniel Kaine was the only man she had ever known who could wear a terry cloth beach wrap with as much style as a royal robe.

He went on walking, her stricken prince, and she saw his slumped shoulders gradually lift and finally straighten in the familiar mantle of determined strength he wore so easily and so well.

Abruptly, he stopped beside the aluminum table near the pool and after a slight hesitation picked up the cane he had left there. For a moment he stood unmoving, as if he were making a decision. Then, with a jaunty flick of his wrist, he tossed the cane lightly into the air, caught it easily on its descent, and sent it sailing smoothly into the deepest part of the pool.

Jennifer couldn't see his face, only his back. But she knew beyond a doubt he was wearing the vagabond grin she had grown to love so well.

Daniel felt the warmth, the excitement, and the special hush of hope in the sanctuary unique to Easter Sunday. He heard the choir stir slightly, readying themselves for the finale of *Daybreak*.

As Jennifer began the solo, he wondered if he would ever find it possible to separate that rich and glorious singing voice of hers from the low, endearing speaking voice of the woman he loved.

Just as it had during rehearsals, her voice once again moved him to worship. He realized anew that one of the miracles of her gift, one of the wonders of her voice, was the way the Lord seemed to lift it, temporarily, above human things, using it to bring people to their knees in simple worship. For the next few moments, she would no longer be his Jennifer, his beloved, but instead, an instrument of praise.

With that thought, he straightened his shoulders and readied himself for what he knew he and the entire congregation were about to experience. He smiled to himself in anticipation and silently thanked his Lord for all the doors that had been closed . . . and all the new doors that had been opened . . . to lead Jennifer to this place—to *him,* to the music, and to her new peace of spirit.

Dan gave thanks, as he so often had, that her voice, deemed less than enough for operatic stage, was so wonderfully perfect for the Lord's purposes. And then he simply listened and let his own spirit soar along with the voice and the music. . . .

Slowly, Jennifer returned from the place the music had taken her. She opened her eyes and saw Dan standing there, smiling to himself, yet smiling at her, too, and she knew once more that, even though he couldn't see her face, he was seeing her heart. He was looking deep inside her, seeing what was there and loving what he saw.

As she held the last note and heard it echo and fade into the hushed sanctuary, she thanked her God for the light he had poured into her heart, into her spirit . . . and into their love, hers and Daniel's.

She smiled a little when the choir breathed a collective sigh with the congregation, and Lyss, standing next to her, squeezed her hand. At the end of the row, Gabe gave her an uncommonly serious nod of affirmation.

She watched the effect of the music gradually lift away from the congregation, seeing many of them dry their eyes before flinging themselves to their feet in a combined accolade to their God, to the choir—and to Daniel.

She saw the proud, happy faces of her dad and Loren smiling up at her. And she watched little Jason—her future son—grin from ear to ear as he waved eagerly to her. She smiled at Jim Arbegunst, seated between Dan's parents, who now had temporary custody of the boy. She thought it was the first time she had ever seen Jim looking happy and healthy and unafraid.

Her eyes filled when she saw Dan finally relax his shoulders from the monumental effort into which he had poured so much of his heart and soul. He wiped a handkerchief across his forehead and dabbed at his cheeks. Then he turned around to the congregation and raised one hand in a sweeping motion of tribute to the choir and the large wooden cross that stood behind them. Finally, he turned back to the choir, gently smiling in Jennifer's direction . . . and her spirit started to sing all over again.

As the choir began to leave the platform, she waited for Dan. Together the two of them, along with Sunny, walked down the aisle, following the choir out while the congregation waited. When they were almost to the door, Dan took her hand and placed it snugly on his forearm, covering it with his own.

"Is the sun shining this morning, love?"

Jennifer glanced up at his smiling face, then down at her hand and the diamond solitaire gleaming there. The ring captured a sunbeam, a rainbow of light streaking in through the stained-glass window nearby.

"Oh, yes, Daniel," she replied, glancing from her ring up to him. "The sun is definitely shining this morning."

The Captive Voice

The Captive Voice

B. J. Hoff

Tyndale House Publishers, Inc.
WHEATON, ILLINOIS

Published in 1987 as *The Domino Image* by Accent Books

Scripture quotations are taken from the *Holy Bible,* New International Version®. Copyright
1973, 1978, 1984 by International Bible Society. Used by permission of Zondervan Publishing
House. All rights reserved. The "NIV" and "New International Version" trademarks are registered in the United States Patent and Trademark Office by International Bible Society. Use of
either trademark requires permission of International Bible Society.

Library of Congress Cataloging-in-Publication Data

Hoff, B. J. (Brenda Jane)
  [Domino image]
  The captive voice / B. J. Hoff.
    p. cm. — (Daybreak mysteries ; 2)
  Previously published: The domino image. Elgin, Ill. : Accent Books, 1987.
  ISBN 0-8423-7193-1 (softcover)
  I. Title. II. Series: Hoff, B. J. (Brenda Jane). Daybreak mysteries ; 2.
  PS3558.034395D66   1996
  813'.54—dc20   96-12927

Printed in the United States of America

01 00 99 98 97 96
7   6   5   4   3   2   1

AUTHOR'S NOTE

My sincere thanks to Cedar Point Marketing Department Sandusky, Ohio, for questions so graciously answered and information so generously supplied.

> *Crowds may praise*
> *And nations cheer,*
> *The whole world may applaud . . .*
> *But above the noise,*
> *His own will hear*
> *The still, small voice of God.*

> *B. J. Hoff*
> *From "Voices"*

The man on the beach tugged at the zipper of his navy jacket, then shoved his hands into the pockets of his jeans. He stared for a moment more at the small dollhouse-like cottage he had been watching for over an hour, then turned and walked away.

She hadn't come out of the cottage tonight. Last night and the evening before, she had gone walking. But not tonight. He could see a soft glow of light behind the drapes, and once the door had opened just enough to admit a small gray-and-white cat. But he hadn't caught even a glimpse of her before she disappeared behind the closed door.

The man stopped walking and looked toward the pier. His gaze fastened on the white lighthouse just beyond, its red light blinking through the gathering dusk. The air off Lake Erie was damp, unusually cool for July.

After a few seconds he ran a hand through his hair, passed it over the back of his neck, then resumed his long-legged, uneven stride. He hurried down a narrow lane between two rows of cottages, crossed an alley, and turned into a dark, isolated street. Unlocking the door of a dusty black car, he glanced around, then quickly slid behind the steering wheel, his head brushing the roof of the car. He punched the key into the ignition and immediately pressed the power door lock. His hands trembled slightly on the steering wheel as he waited for the engine to warm up.

He glanced at his watch, then pulled a small penlight from the glove compartment. Focusing a stream of light on the seat beside him, he flipped through the pages of a black ring binder until he found what he wanted. He stared for a long time at a newspaper photo beneath a transparent sheet protector. Finally his gaze moved to the article beneath the picture. Lowering the penlight, he scanned the brief article, clipped from the *Nashville Banner* three years earlier.

Vali Tremayne continues to be unavailable for comment regarding her career plans. The top female vocalist in the contemporary Christian music industry for over two years, Miss Tremayne is said to be recovering from an emotional collapse following the recent tragic death of her fiancé, composer and recording artist Paul Alexander, in an airplane crash over the Appalachian Mountains.

Joanne Seldon, Miss Tremayne's agent, has also refused to discuss her client's future plans. Sources say, however, that Miss Tremayne has "retired" from the music industry and is presently recuperating at a lakefront resort in northern Ohio, near the family of Paul Alexander.

The deceased musician's mother, renowned novelist and literary award winner Leda Alexander, resides in Sandusky, Ohio. His twin brother, Dr. Graham Alexander, is a well-known and highly respected research scientist who founded Alexander Center, one of the largest and most influential research centers in the country. The Center is located in northern Ohio, and Dr. Alexander makes his home in Port Clinton. . . .

The man looked up from the news article and pushed a cassette tape into the car player. For several moments he sat unmoving, staring straight ahead, his fingers on the steering wheel

drumming a mindless accompaniment to the rich female voice
on the tape.

He finally switched off the penlight and eased out of the parking place, then turned up the volume on the voice of Vali
Tremayne.

Vali had seen him again tonight. Or at least she thought she had.
This was the third straight evening she had felt as if someone was
watching her, waiting. But whenever she looked for him, she saw
little more than a vague silhouette beyond the seawall.

A shadow, that's all it was. She wouldn't bother Graham with it.
There was no need to raise more questions. . . .

With an uneasy frown, she dropped the corner of the drapes and
turned from the window. Her gaze swept the living room, usually a
cheerful splash of color with its lemon walls and floral chintz, but
now steeped in shadows from the dim light of a table lamp. After a
moment, she walked across the room and picked up a framed photograph from the bookshelf. A dark-haired man laughed out at her.
Gently, she touched the glass with her index finger, rubbing the surface as if she could evoke a response. *Paul* . . .

Almost guiltily, she set the frame back in place. Graham had
wanted her to put his brother's photograph away long ago. At first,
he had only suggested that she remove this last memento of her
relationship with Paul. Later, suggestion had strengthened to
request, but even though Vali was reluctant to hurt Graham, she
couldn't bring herself to let go of this last image of the man she
had loved with all her heart.

She stood staring at the photo, remembering the day it had
been taken. Paul had laughed about his agent's insistence that he
should adopt a more serious, thoughtful expression for his publicity photos. . . .

"I'm supposed to look more—*intense,*" he had told Vali, drawing his face into a ridiculous caricature of stern piety. The expres-

sion lasted only a second before he broke into his irrepressible grin.

Paul, with his laughing heart and smiling eyes . . . always so happy, so confident, so hopeful. Until all the bright and wonderful things that endeared him were destroyed in a burning plane.

Vali pressed the fingertips of one hand to her temple, where a subtle pulse of pain was beginning to throb. It was always that way when she let herself remember, when she allowed her thoughts to drift back to the time they'd had together, the things they had shared. . . .

No. Don't try to remember. Graham was right. She mustn't think about the past. She mustn't try to remember. Yesterday was dead. It was meant to be buried. Buried with Paul.

Reluctantly she turned away from the photograph and went back to the window, again nudging a corner of the drapes aside to look out. No one was there.

At last she turned and after checking the locks on both the front and back doors, took her pill, then settled down on the couch to read Leda Alexander's latest novel.

ONE
September

O H, Daniel—I wish you could see the beach! It
looks exactly the way I remember it." Jennifer
tugged at Dan's hand to pull him along beside her,
then stopped to allow Sunny, Dan's golden retriever guide dog, to
do her job.

Her husband of exactly one week smiled at her excitement.
"I'll see it through your eyes, love. But let me take off my shoes
first, OK? I never could walk in sand with my shoes on."

Jennifer plopped down beside him on the warm sand and
pulled off her own tennis shoes, then sat looking out over Lake
Erie. Even though it was warm for September, the beach was dot-
ted with only a few people. The Labor Day weekend was over,
bringing an end to the annual vacation season. The few tenants
and cottage owners still in the area would now be occupied with
readying their cottages for winter. Most of them would be gone
by the end of the month.

"Glad we came?" Dan asked, pulling her to her feet with one
hand.

"It means the world to me," Jennifer said, her voice soft. "The
Smokies were wonderful, but this place is so special to me, Daniel.
My family brought us up here every summer until the year
before Mother died." She took his tennis shoes and carried them
with her own so he could hold Sunny's harness and still walk arm
in arm with her.

"There's a pier not too far away from us—with a lighthouse at the end," she told him. "When I was a kid, I used to fish there with my dad."

It was second nature for her to help Dan see things through her eyes. Several months ago, he had hired her as his executive assistant at the Christian radio station he owned in West Virginia. By now Jennifer had grown accustomed to keeping up a continual flow of observation so Dan would always be aware of his surroundings.

He had been blind for more than five years. But in spite of his disability, Dan was the most fascinating, and often the most baffling, man Jennifer had ever met. He was almost overwhelming in size. He topped Jennifer's five-eight by more than half a foot, and he had the athletic physique of a former Olympic swimming champion. Yet he was easily the gentlest, kindest man she had ever known.

In Jennifer's eyes, her husband was a remarkable man—and she loved him more than life. She flooded Dan's world with affection, and he, in turn, openly adored her, cherished her, and made her—she was certain—the happiest woman on earth.

She was also an acutely *curious* woman. At the sight of a sprawling stone bi-level house standing at least a hundred yards away from its nearest neighbor, Jennifer came to an abrupt halt. The house was secluded almost to the point of obscurity by enormous trees and a high seawall. Nevertheless, it presented a friendly, inviting appearance, with early fall flowers blooming all across the front and pale yellow curtains blowing at the open windows.

"I've *got* to get a closer look at this place!" she said, abruptly tugging at Dan's arm. "Come on, Daniel."

"Jennifer, don't—" Too late, Dan swerved, the retriever stopped, and Jennifer whirled around to correct her mistake. All three collided.

"Uh-oh," Jennifer muttered, looking up at Dan's face. "I did it again, didn't I?"

Dan's reply was an exaggerated wince of pain as he gingerly touched one rib.

Immediately concerned, Jennifer drew in a sharp breath of dismay. "Did I *hurt* you? Oh, Daniel, I'm *sorry!* I wasn't thinking—I was staring at this wonderful house! I'm *really* sorry. . . ."

As if he could no longer contain it, he flashed a roguish grin. "That's OK, darlin'," he said mildly. "I don't suppose I can complain about your running into me when that's what brought us together in the first place."

Jennifer gave the afflicted rib a gentle shove. "I didn't run into *you* that day, Daniel Kaine. You ran into *me.*"

Still grinning, he shrugged. "Whatever. It worked."

"Come *on,* Daniel! I want to get a closer look at this house."

"What's so great about it?" he asked, looking a little disgruntled at being led by both his wife and his dog. He stumbled over a stone and stopped where he was. "If you two are going to work as a team, I wish you'd get your act together."

"This place is *not* your typical lakeside cottage," Jennifer said distractedly, urging him on. "It's all stone, and it goes on forever. And it's so mysterious looking."

"Mysterious looking," Dan repeated dryly. "What's that mean?"

Slowing her stride, Jennifer gripped his arm a little tighter, then started up a narrow walkway that led from the end of the seawall to the front door of the house. "It has a certain . . . presence," she told him. "It looks like a house with secrets."

When Dan mumbled something inaudible, Jennifer ignored him and kept on going.

She started toward the side of the house, but Daniel hesitated. "Do you hear that?" he said, stopping to listen.

The sound of music came pouring from the house. It sounded like a full-sized band, but Jennifer recognized a state-of-the-art keyboard when she heard one. She also knew enough music to spot the technique of a professional.

"It's coming from this side of the house," Jennifer said, abruptly leading off to the right. "Let's go around where we can hear better."

Dan dug in his heels. "Jennifer . . . am I right in assuming that we're tramping around on private property?"

Jennifer looked at him. "We're not going to bother anyone, Daniel." Again she tried to get him to move. This time Sunny gave Jennifer a look of mild exasperation as if to convey the point that she needed no help in doing her job.

Dan sighed but resumed walking. "I'm totally dominated by two females."

"And you love it. Now come on."

A large casement window was open at the front of the house, and Jennifer headed resolutely toward it. They stopped only a few feet away. The brilliantly executed instrumental music reverberating from the house was now joined by an incredibly smooth, powerful female voice—a voice with tremendous range and perfect control.

Dan reached for Jennifer's hand and squeezed it as they stood listening.

It was a wonderful song, the lyrics a powerful testimony to the grace and glory of God. And Jennifer had never heard it before. Within the course of a week's broadcasting at the station, she heard all the current CCM pop and traditional chart-toppers, as well as any promising new recordings. If this song had been out there, she would have known it. This one was brand new, she was sure—and a natural hit.

But it wasn't only the song that held her captive. It was the voice.

Dan, too, seemed riveted by the singer. "Jennifer . . . do you recognize that voice?" he asked in a low murmur.

"I know I should; it's awfully familiar. . . ." Jennifer drew in a sudden sharp breath. *"Daniel* . . . that almost sounds like . . . but, no, it couldn't be—"

"Tremayne," Dan said softly, shaking his head in wonder. "Vali Tremayne. It has to be her."

"But it *can't* be," Jennifer protested stubbornly. "Vali Tremayne hasn't sung for years. Besides, what in the world would she be doing up here?"

"I think Paul Alexander was from somewhere in this area. Wasn't there some speculation after he died that Vali Tremayne came up here to live so she could be close to his family?"

"I don't remember anything like that. But I *do* remember that she quit singing."

"I'm telling you, that's her," Dan insisted.

Jennifer knew it was unlikely that he was mistaken. Still, she found it difficult, if not impossible, to believe that they were standing outside a beach house listening to one of the Christian music industry's most popular singers.

A thought struck Jennifer. "Didn't Vali Tremayne have some sort of nervous breakdown after Paul Alexander was killed?"

Dan was paying far more attention to the music than to Jennifer. He nodded vaguely. "I heard something like that, but . . ." He paused. "Weird . . ."

"Weird? What's weird?"

He shook his head. "Nothing. It was just a feeling I had for a minute. Listen to that keyboard. Someone sure knows their stuff, huh?"

"Well, I'm going to find out who's in there," Jennifer said briskly.

"Jennifer, we can't just go to the door."

Jennifer was already moving toward the front of the house. "Of course we can, Daniel," she said. "Don't worry, I won't embarrass you. We'll simply introduce ourselves and find out who—"

Her voice faltered, then caught. She stopped dead when she

saw the front door open. *"Daniel—,"* she hissed furtively—"somebody's coming out! Let's go back around to the side so they won't think we're snooping."

"We *are* snooping, Jennifer," Dan said testily. "Where are you, anyway?"

"Wait!" Jennifer caught his arm, restraining him while she peered around the corner of the house.

The man stepping off the small concrete porch into the yard was tall—nearly as tall as Daniel, Jennifer thought. And like Daniel, he also wore a beard, though his was more closely trimmed. There, however, the resemblance ended.

Where Daniel's frame was powerful and muscled from years of disciplined training as a swimmer, this man looked lean and wiry, almost gaunt. His hair was an odd tawny shade, generously threaded with silver—in direct contrast to his darker beard. His skin was deeply tanned, and as he walked out into the yard Jennifer could see that he had a slight but noticeable limp, as if his right leg were somewhat stiff.

It was his voice, however, that made her eyes widen with curiosity. He spoke in a hoarse, strained whisper as he turned to the open doorway.

"Vali, I don't see her anywhere. Maybe we'd better go look."

Both Jennifer and Daniel jumped, reacting not only to the strange whisper of the voice but to the name the voice had spoken. Jennifer's eyes followed the direction of the stranger's gaze, and she expelled a soft sound of amazement.

Framed in the doorway of the house stood a slight young woman with a lovely patrician face, a face as familiar to most Christian music fans as her voice.

Too stunned with excitement to be discreet, she blurted out, "Dan—it's *her!* It's Vali Tremayne!" She flushed with embarrassment as both the woman in the doorway and the light-haired man whirled around in surprise.

TWO

U H . . . hello," Jennifer stammered weakly, feeling
decidedly foolish.

There was no reply. Vali Tremayne's expression
wasn't hostile, only curious. But the man appraised the Kaines
with a speculative, none-too-friendly stare that added a touch of
uneasiness to Jennifer's embarrassment.

Obviously, the present circumstances called for an explanation.
Just as obviously, Daniel had no intention of offering that explanation.

"We were just . . . uh . . . taking a walk." Jennifer paused,
waited, and tried again. "I noticed your house and wanted to get
a closer look at it. There aren't many places along the beach
nearly as nice as this. . . . That's why it caught my attention. You
see, I used to come up here all the time with my family, so I
remember things pretty well. But I can't remember seeing this
place before."

The blond man's skeptical stare unnerved Jennifer as much as
Daniel's deliberate silence irritated her. Her words spilled out
even faster. "I was telling Daniel—this is Daniel—," she
explained, tugging at his arm to coax him closer, "how attractive
your home is. Oh, by the way, I'm Jennifer Terry. I mean, Jennifer
Kaine. We're on our honeymoon, you see. We've been married a
week now."

She glanced at Daniel and saw that he appeared to be cringing.

"I'm terribly sorry," she said, determined to redeem herself. She felt a flicker of hope when a ghost of a smile touched Vali Tremayne's lips. "I suppose you think we're trespassing—actually, we *are* trespassing, I know. But we couldn't resist your music. Daniel owns a radio station—a Christian station—and he recognized your voice, Miss Tremayne. I told him it couldn't be you, but . . ."

"Jennifer . . ." Daniel's voice was pleasantly soft, unmistakably firm, and enormously welcome. Jennifer breathed a long sigh of relief. He would take charge now. She smiled at Vali Tremayne, then at the tall, tense-looking man who had gone to stand a little closer to the singer. The man made no effort to return her smile.

"It's my fault, I'm afraid," Daniel said with great charm. As he spoke, Sunny sat calmly but alertly beside him, staring at the two strangers as if to emphasize the fact that her owner was her personal responsibility. "I'm probably one of your most faithful fans, Miss Tremayne, and I simply had to find out for myself if that incomparable voice was real or recorded."

He took a few steps and thrust his right hand forward as if he knew exactly where the others were standing. "As my wife said, I'm Daniel Kaine. And this is a real pleasure."

Jennifer watched him closely, suppressing the desire to roll her eyes. Her gaze then moved to the other man. She watched as his dark gray eyes darted from Daniel to Sunny, then back again to Daniel's face. Apparently he had just realized that Daniel was blind. His expression gradually relaxed, and the look of suspicion faded as he quickly stepped toward Dan, his hand extended.

At the same time, Vali Tremayne ran a slender hand through her hair—her incredible *mahogany* hair, Jennifer thought with admiration—and smiled uncertainly with what appeared to be a touch of shyness.

"I'm David Nathan Keye." The man's odd, whispering voice drew Jennifer's attention away from Vali. He was studying Dan's face with keen interest as they shook hands. "And I believe you already know that this is Vali Tremayne," he added, nodding his head in the singer's direction.

Jennifer had a fleeting impression of something slightly off balance in the man's face, then realized that his left eye had a faint droop, as if it were heavier than the right. She sensed a kind of melancholy about him, an odd contrast with what looked to be a glint of mischief in his eyes. He was attractive enough, she supposed. The light hair was a surprising accent to his dark skin, and his features were strong and pleasant. In spite of his appeal, however, Jennifer felt a certain ambiguity in the man that instinctively put her on guard.

His next words surprised her. "You're not by any chance a composer?" he asked Dan.

Hesitating for an instant, Dan answered, "I run a Christian radio station. But *you're* a composer," he quickly added. "And an impressive one. I know your music."

Keye looked surprised but continued to study Dan. "There's a Daniel Kaine who wrote an absolutely wonderful piece of music called *Daybreak*," he said in his peculiar voice. "I believe he's . . . blind also. That's why I asked if you're a composer. I thought perhaps . . ."

Unable to contain herself any longer, Jennifer exclaimed with pride, "That's Daniel! He wrote *Daybreak!*"

Keye's facial expression brightened to a look of genuine admiration. Without hesitating, he gripped Daniel's hand again, this time shaking it more vigorously. "I've wanted to meet you since the first time I heard the score of *Daybreak,* just to tell you I think it's the most powerful piece of contemporary Christian music I've ever heard."

When Keye again turned his attention to Jennifer, she was surprised to see that there was a faint glow of warmth in his eyes. "And are you a musician, too, Mrs. Kaine?"

"Goodness, no! I'm—"

"A fantastic singer . . . and a terrific wife," Daniel finished for her.

"I'm *not*," Jennifer quickly protested. When Dan laughed, she glanced from him to Keye. "I mean, I hope I'm a good wife," she said, flustered, "but don't listen to anything else he says."

"Why don't we go inside and have some coffee?" the composer suggested. "Vali and I were just about to take a break when we noticed Trouble had disappeared again."

"Trouble?" Jennifer repeated blankly.

The singer spoke for the first time since their encounter, explaining softly, "My cat. Her name is Trouble."

"For good reason," Keye added sardonically. "Come on in," he offered, starting toward the porch.

"David, if they're on their honeymoon," Vali said uncertainly, "perhaps they'd rather not. . . ."

The composer looked from Vali to Jennifer. "Sorry," he said with an unexpectedly boyish grin. Reaching into the pocket of his striped shirt, he pulled out a stick of gum. The guarded cynicism so evident in his expression a few minutes before seemed to have totally vanished. He tucked the gum into his mouth, still smiling at Vali. When he looked at the small young woman standing next to him, a hint of an emotion that could only be tenderness filled his eyes. "I wasn't thinking."

"But we'd love to come in," Jennifer said quickly. "Wouldn't we, Daniel?"

Dan opened his mouth to say something but seemed to change his mind. With a knowing smile, he nodded. "Sure. Is this your home?" he asked Keye.

"I rent it." The composer took Vali's arm as they stepped back onto the porch and held the door for Dan and Jennifer.

"Do you mind my dog?" Dan asked him.

"Not at all," Keye assured him. "What's his name?"

"*Her* name," Daniel corrected. "Her name is Sunny." He

pursed his lips. "We'd better put our shoes on, Jennifer, before we go inside."

"Not necessary," Keye said with a smile. "My place is ever so humble. Just come as you are."

He waited for Sunny to guide Daniel through the doorway, then followed the others into a large, comfortably furnished living room dominated by a walnut grand piano and a bank of digital keyboards. The room was clean but cluttered. Stacks of music manuscripts were everywhere, and an empty coffee cup seemed to be on every table.

The composer crossed the room and took an indifferent swipe at the heap of manuscript paper and magazines on a table in front of the couch. "The place is messy but rat free," he said over his shoulder. "Let's go into the kitchen. It's probably cleaner, since I seldom use it. Say, you didn't see a slightly weird-looking cat anywhere, did you? Looks a bit like a confused, overweight rabbit with stubby ears?"

"I'm afraid not," Jennifer said, laughing at him.

"David keeps hoping she'll just vanish," Vali told them with a scolding glance at the composer. "The two of them have been at war since the first day they met."

"That was no meeting," Keye said archly. "That was a *blitzkrieg.*"

"She's only a kitten," Vali protested.

"With the heart of a cheetah," Keye returned, leading the way into a large, country kitchen with an adjoining glassed-in sunroom.

Watching the two of them, Jennifer wondered about the relationship between Vali Tremayne and David Nathan Keye. Like Daniel, she had recognized the composer's name right away. Not only had he written many of the recent hit songs on the Christian music charts, but he was a well-known keyboard artist as well. And he was obviously, her romantic spirit suggested, quite taken with the young singer standing at the kitchen counter pouring coffee. Remembering the tragic death of Vali's fiancé, Paul Alexander, and the numerous references to her inconsolable grief, Jennifer found herself hoping that Vali had indeed found someone else.

In a surprisingly brief time, the four of them fell into an easy, companionable conversation, sitting around the small oval table in the spacious kitchen, drinking coffee, and talking as casually as if they had known each other for years.

Jennifer could hear the respect in Dan's voice when he spoke to Keye. "You've got music all over the charts right now, David. You must write in your sleep."

The composer took a tray of cookies from Vali and brought it to the table, then straddled a chair. "Sometimes I wish I could. My music is actually my ministry, you see." He stopped, then added, "Obviously, this isn't the voice of a preacher. So I write music. Vali says I'm a workaholic." His smile was gentle as he watched the singer pull up a chair beside him.

"He doesn't know when to quit," Vali explained, glancing at Jennifer. "But if I could write music like David's, I probably wouldn't want to stop, either."

Jennifer stared at her, struck by Vali's flawless features. She remembered seeing pictures of her from years past. But she now realized the publicity photos hadn't even begun to reveal the singer's ethereal loveliness.

Her skin had a translucent quality, and her jade-colored eyes dominated her face with a haunting sadness that made it difficult to look away from her. Her hair—*that wonderful, incredible hair,* Jennifer thought—was an untamed cloud that formed a swirling, dramatic contrast to the delicate perfection of her face. Even dressed casually, in jeans and a striped rugby shirt, she looked like an exiled princess. Keye had even referred to her as "Princess" a couple of times during their conversation, and Jennifer had smiled at the appropriateness of the pet name.

Suddenly aware that she was staring, Jennifer turned her attention to Daniel, who was asking Vali Tremayne about her career. "Are you recording again, Miss Tremayne?"

The singer stared at him, her expression unmistakably troubled. "Please . . . call me Vali," she said quietly. "I . . . I don't know, about recording, I mean. It's been . . . a long time. David has been working with me on some arrangements, but I haven't . . . made any real decision yet."

She had a peculiar, static way of speaking that communicated a kind of uncertainty, a reluctance to assert herself. Combined with the faint hint of bewilderment in her eyes, she gave off an aura of skittishness, much like a young animal about to bolt.

"What Vali is much too polite to tell you," Keye quickly inserted, "is that her agent more or less strong-armed her into working with me. You see, a lot of people—myself foremost among them—want to see Vali back in the industry. My producer and I are trying to sell her on the idea of using my music as her return vehicle."

Vali went on staring at the table as Keye spoke.

"Well, that sounds like a great idea to me," Daniel said lightly, as if he could sense the tension in the room.

Keye continued to study Vali intently as Dan went on. "You've been doing keyboards for a number of artists, haven't you? In addition to your own composing?"

"Actually, that's what gave me my start when I moved from the West Coast," Keye replied, finally dragging his gaze away from Vali. "Some people in Nashville knew my work and got me a few jobs. Eventually I was able to get a couple of my own numbers recorded."

"You're from California, then?" Daniel asked.

"For the most part." The composer flashed a brief smile, then let the conversation drop for a moment as he poured himself another cup of coffee. "Until October, at least, I'm a Buckeye. My rent is paid until then."

"Jennifer's a Buckeye," Dan said, smiling in her direction. "A transplanted one, that is. She's learning to become a Mountaineer now."

"A Mountaineer? That's West Virginia, isn't it?" the composer asked.

"Shepherd Valley," Dan replied with a nod. "Just a little town at the foot of some great mountains."

"And you own a Christian radio station? That means you're one of the fellows who can help make or break my career."

Dan laughed easily. "I'm afraid we don't have that kind of influence. But you don't have anything to worry about—you're well on your way."

"That may depend on whether or not I can get Vali to sing my music," Keye said, turning to look at the singer.

His remark disturbed Jennifer; it sounded as if the composer intended to use Vali. She knew it was none of her business, but something about the quiet young singer inspired her protective instincts.

Unexpectedly, Vali smiled at him. "David, you make it sound as if I had to be forced to work with you."

Keye shrugged, but the smile he gave her was gentle. "My rent's only paid until October, Princess. I'm running out of time to come up with that one special number you simply can't resist."

"Well, you'll certainly be doing all of us a big favor," Daniel said to Keye, "if you can get her back into a recording studio."

The composer nodded. "There's a host of people out there who agree with you, Daniel." His gaze darted to the kitchen window. "However," he said, "you're about to meet someone who *doesn't.*"

His whispered comment was sharply punctuated by a loud, demanding knock on the side door. Sunny roused from her place by Dan's chair with a warning growl, then stood waiting alertly at his side. Dan reached to gentle her with his hand and a soft word of reassurance.

Before the last thud died away, a big, dark-haired man pushed through the door, charging into the kitchen as if he needed no invitation. He stood staring at the four of them through narrowed eyes, his expression questioning and seemingly hostile.

Without getting up, David gave the man a thin smile. "Won't you come in, Graham?"

Jennifer couldn't take her eyes off the other man. His handsome features seemed vaguely familiar. Not quite as tall as Daniel, he looked to be about twenty pounds heavier. She would guess him to be in his early to mid-thirties. His well-tailored gray suit looked decidedly out of place in these casual lakefront surroundings. The impression was that of a somewhat arrogant, imperious personality.

He flicked a sharp glance at David, then frowned at Vali. "You might let me know when you're going to be away from your cottage for such a long time, Vali. I've been trying to call you for well over two hours now." His voice was refined, clipped, almost British in nuance.

Jennifer flinched in surprise when Vali stood, pushing her chair back so abruptly it almost toppled.

"Oh, Graham—I'm so sorry! David and I were working on some new numbers . . . and then we met Daniel and Jennifer—" She stopped, glanced for an instant at Jennifer, then turned back to the man now towering over her. "I suppose I didn't think. . . ."

The man called "Graham" cast a withering look at Keye, then raked both Jennifer and Daniel with a look of impatience before returning his attention to Vali. "That's becoming somewhat of a habit with you these days, isn't it, dear?" he asked icily. "Not thinking."

Vali colored and began wringing her hands. "I . . . should have called you. I forgot."

"I would think by now you'd know how I worry about you, Vali."

"Yes . . . I do know, Graham. . . ." Vali's voice had softened until it was almost as much of a whisper as Keye's.

The composer now stood, his eyes glinting with an unpleasant look of challenge. "It was my fault, Graham—as usual," he rasped. "When I'm working with Vali, I'm afraid I have a tendency to forget everything else but . . . the music."

In the face of the other's cold silence, Keye continued. "Let me introduce you to Daniel and Jennifer Kaine. Fellow musicians— and new friends. Daniel, Jennifer—this is Graham Alexander. A very . . . close friend of Vali's."

THREE

JENNIFER almost choked. *Graham Alexander.* The twin brother of Vali's deceased fiancé. There had been a lot of publicity at the time of Paul Alexander's death, including a number of references to his brother, a research scientist, and his mother, an internationally known novelist. Staring hard at the big man with the chilling eyes, Jennifer was surprised she hadn't seen the resemblance immediately. The man standing across the table from her looked enough like his dead brother to be mistaken for him, except for the extra pounds he was carrying. Or was it the lack of Paul Alexander's trademark smile that made the difference?

Graham Alexander offered only a grudging nod in acknowledgment of the introduction before turning to Vali. "You *did* remember that we're meeting Mother at the Twine House for dinner?"

"Of course, Graham," she replied. "I wouldn't forget something like that. I'm looking forward to it."

Graham Alexander's gaze swept over Vali, and Jennifer felt a pang of sympathy for the lovely young singer, who was clearly ill at ease. "You'll be changing into something more suitable, I imagine?" Alexander said, an edge still in his voice.

Vali looked at him blankly, then glanced down at her jeans. "Oh . . . yes. This isn't . . . I was planning to change."

David crossed his arms over his chest and stared at Graham

17

Alexander. "I didn't realize the Twine House is formal," he said, lifting a hand to his face in a mock gesture of dismay. "And to think I went there in *my* jeans last night. It's a wonder they didn't toss me out."

The scientist settled a look of contempt on Keye, his silent glare making a statement of its own.

David shrugged, "Ah, well . . . what would you expect from a beach-bum musician. Right, Graham?"

If his intention was to annoy Alexander, it seemed to work. He scowled, adjusted the knot of his silk tie, and turned to Vali. "I'll pick you up at six. We're to meet Mother at six-fifteen." Without waiting for an answer, he pecked her lightly on the cheek, turned one more scathing look at David Nathan Keye, then turned and walked out the door, slamming it behind him.

It was quiet in the kitchen for a long, awkward moment after he left. Vali was obviously embarrassed, and Jennifer could sense the tension in David as well.

Daniel finally broke the silence. "We should be going, Jennifer," he said, standing and reaching for her hand. "We haven't even unpacked all our things yet."

Keye and Vali followed them outside, where they stood talking for a few more moments. Dan started to shake hands with the composer, then stopped suddenly. "I wonder . . . would the two of you mind if I looked at you? With my hands?" He smiled ingenuously. "To tell you the truth, it's a little more than a blind man's curiosity. I thought it would be something to tell my kids someday."

Jennifer was surprised when Vali stepped up to him without hesitating. "Your children probably won't know who you're talking about, Daniel," she said softly, "but go right ahead."

As Dan explored the lovely face at his fingertips, Jennifer smiled, remembering his gentleness the first time he had "looked" at her.

After he dropped his hands back to his side, Daniel turned toward David. "I'll just bet you're not that pretty."

The composer's eyes narrowed for an instant as he studied Dan. Jennifer thought she sensed a fleeting look of anxiety in his expression, but he covered it with a brief smile. "A keenly accurate assumption, Daniel." His whispery laugh sounded forced and nervous, but he bore Dan's examination of his face with seeming good humor.

Jennifer was puzzled by her husband's questioning frown as he finally let his hands drop away from Keye's face. "It's always interesting to me when I finally put a face with a voice," Dan said casually. "You surprised me, David. I pictured you without a beard—and a little heavier."

Keye lifted one eyebrow skeptically. "What? Not Quasimodo?" Dan frowned in earnest.

The composer laughed. "The voice. People react to it in different ways."

"What caused it?" Dan asked him directly.

Keye shrugged. "Accident. My vocal chords were crushed." He paused, then added, "I read about what happened to you in some of the news releases for *Daybreak*. A drunk driver, wasn't it?"

Dan nodded slowly, and Jennifer knew he was about to ask Keye something else. Instead, he stooped to pat Sunny on the head, then straightened and shook hands with Keye. After a few more good-byes, they parted. Both Vali and David stood in the doorway, waving as Jennifer and Dan started down the walk and turned toward their own cottage.

Later that night, Jennifer and Daniel walked hand in hand along the shore, allowing Sunny to run free. The air was still warm, holding no hint of the approaching autumn that usually came early to northern Ohio. It was the kind of night made for hushed voices, soft music, and quiet laughter.

"What do you think of our new acquaintances?" Daniel asked as they walked along.

Jennifer didn't answer right away. "I'm not sure," she finally said. "They're . . . a little different. Nice," she added, "but different."

"How old would you guess David to be?" Dan said.

Jennifer thought for a moment. "Early thirties, at least. He has a good bit of gray in his hair, but it's mixed in with blond, so you don't really notice it at first." She paused. "What did you think of him?"

Daniel shrugged. "I'm not sure. For some reason, I found him difficult to visualize." After a moment he added, "There's something . . . peculiar about his skin."

Jennifer looked at him. "Peculiar? What do you mean?"

"It's . . . too supple for a man his age." Dan gave a short laugh. "I know it sounds odd, but he has the skin of a teenager. And around his hairline . . ." He didn't finish.

"His hairline?"

Again Dan laughed and shook his head. "I must be losing my touch."

Jennifer groaned. "If that was a pun, you've done better, Daniel."

He grinned. "Humor me." He said nothing else for a moment. "You're sure he's in his thirties?" he finally asked, still sounding puzzled.

"Definitely."

"Hm. His left eye droops a little, doesn't it?"

Jennifer glanced up at him. "You don't miss much, do you? Yes, as a matter of fact, his eye *does* droop. Just a little, enough to make him look rather . . . cunning."

"Cunning? That's a detective-story word, Jennifer. What do you mean?"

She considered. "Smart. A little devious, I think. But nice." She hesitated. "That's the strange thing about him—overall, he seems to be very nice, good-natured, charming. Definitely intelligent. But there's something else that doesn't quite fit, and I'm not sure what it is. He's—"

"Tense," Dan finished. "Explosive. Like a volcano about to erupt."

"What?" Jennifer was only half listening. "Let's stop here a minute, Daniel. I've got a stone or something in my sandal."

"I'd say he's under a great deal of stress," Dan mused.

"Mmm. He limps . . . did I tell you?" She pulled a small stone from the toe of her sandal. "Like his leg is stiff."

Sunny came bounding up to them, and Dan stooped to rub her ears, then straightened. "And the lovely Vali is like . . . a frightened fawn," he remarked.

Jennifer drew in a sharp breath. "That's *exactly* what she makes me think of! I couldn't have been any more surprised by her, Daniel. You hear her sing, and you get this fantastic sense of power and control. But in person, she's actually . . . *shy,* I think. Even insecure."

They started walking again. "What about Graham Alexander?" Jennifer said, linking her arm with Dan's. "Do you suppose they're engaged? I didn't see a ring."

"He certainly seems to have some sort of hold on her, doesn't he?"

"I thought he was insufferable. What kind of vibes did *you* get about him?"

He grimaced. "I don't get *vibes,* Jennifer. I'm blind, not psychic."

"Ooh, touchy." She grinned at him, savoring the way the soft puffs of wind off the lake lifted strands of his hair, ruffling it and tossing it gently over his forehead. "But what did you think of him?"

His tone was puzzled when he answered. "I'm not sure. They're an interesting trio, aren't they?"

"Well, I can tell you one thing," Jennifer said decisively. "David is in love with Vali."

Dan came to an abrupt halt, and a ghost of a smile flickered across his face. "And Daniel," he said softly as he gathered her into his arms, "is in love with Jennifer." Without warning, he lowered his head to kiss her lightly. Then again, this time not so lightly.

"Daniel . . ." Jennifer's protest was halfhearted as she returned his kiss. "There are people on the beach."

"Then what we need to do," he murmured against her hair, "is get off the beach."

FOUR

T HE man was almost asleep when the demanding shrill of the bedside phone shattered the
silence. He bolted upright in the darkness and
reached for the receiver.

"Who are they?"

Groggy, he was slow to react to the impatient voice on the
other end of the line. "They?"

"The blind man and the woman—who are they?"

He looked at the digital clock on the nightstand. Twenty minutes after midnight. "Kaine. Daniel and Jennifer Kaine. There's no
problem with them—they'll be gone in a few days."

"Anyone new could be a problem at this time."

"I hardly think we need to feel threatened by a blind man and
his wife." The man's voice dripped sarcasm.

There was silence for a moment. "Only the singer is a threat.
And, as you've so confidently assured us, the solution to that particular problem is forthcoming." The caller's voice grew even
more harsh. "May I ask again . . . *when?*"

The man sighed, trying for patience. "Soon. I need a few more
weeks, I told you."

"No. One week, no more. You've already wasted far too much time."

"Everything is working out exactly as I planned. She remem-
bers nothing, and I've become very important to her. The rest is a
matter of time."

"No, my friend. Either you have a definite solution, a commitment, within the next week, or we eliminate her." The caller hesitated, then added, "Which is what we should have done in the first place."

"That is, and always has been, an extremely foolish idea!" the man snapped. "She's far too well known, and it would simply be too much of a coincidence after the airplane crash. No," he said firmly, "my way is better. You'll see."

"Well . . . we shall hope that you are right. In the meantime, we'll be helping you however we can."

"What do you mean?"

"Simply that the more disoriented and confused she grows, the more dependent upon you she will become."

"I can handle this alone," the man said sharply.

"Of course you can. But we're in this together, are we not? The least I can do is to lend you a bit of assistance."

"I'm warning you," he grated, "if you do something to spoil what I've accomplished so far—"

"Do not warn me of *anything*, my friend." The voice was soft, the threat implicit, the click of the phone final.

Only after he replaced the receiver did the man finally switch on the lamp. He sat on the side of the bed for a few more minutes, then stood. With a scowling glance at the telephone, he threw on a bathrobe. One week. Not nearly long enough.

But he knew there would be no more time, no more delays. Somehow, he would have to move everything up.

FIVE

I REALLY respect your courage, darlin'," Dan said with a wondering shake of his head. "But doesn't the idea of me in an amusement park remind you of Daniel in the lions' den?"

Jennifer poured him a second cup of coffee and refilled her own cup before sitting down at the table beside him. "As I recall," she said pointedly, "*that* Daniel got out without a scratch."

"Besides, amusement parks close after Labor Day," he said mildly, reaching for his third doughnut.

"But Cedar Point is open for two weekends *after* Labor Day. And this happens to be the last weekend. Come on, Daniel, I really want to go. It'll be fun."

"Fun for who?"

"Fun for *whom*. Will you go?"

"Absolutely not."

She sighed. "I've wanted to go back to Cedar Point for years." Her voice was soft, intentionally plaintive. "It would make this week even more special."

"Ah . . . sentimentality. Nice touch, Jennifer. But I'm still not going."

She poked him.

"Jennifer, you wouldn't want me to think that the success of our honeymoon depends on me making a fool of myself at an amusement park, would you?" He took a bite of the chocolate-covered doughnut.

"Since when are you intimidated by a new adventure?" she challenged. "Daniel, I can still remember how amazed I was—and impressed—when I first started working with you and discovered how different you were from what I had expected."

He finished his doughnut, wiped the chocolate from his mouth, and leaned back in his chair. Crossing his arms comfortably over his chest, he smiled—a wide, knowing smile that plainly said he knew what was coming but wanted to hear it anyway.

"Why, I distinctly remember, Daniel, being totally dumbfounded at the way you handled things. I mean, I'd always had the idea that people with disabilities are somewhat . . . insecure."

He nodded wisely.

"But you were so extroverted and authoritative, so confident and willing to try new things—you shattered every preconceived notion I'd ever had."

He made a brief, self-deprecating gesture with his hand. "Aw shucks, honey."

"In fact," she went on, ignoring him, *"you* made *me* feel inhibited sometimes; you were so willing to take a chance, eager to try new experiences. . . ."

Laughing, he put up a restraining hand. "This is good, darlin'—not one of your better routines, but still good."

She studied his face hopefully. "Are you thinking about it, Daniel?"

"Mm. Maybe."

When he began to drum his fingers on the table, Jennifer was pretty sure she'd won.

"Does this place have a roller coaster?" he suddenly asked, stopping his rhythmic tapping.

"Does it have—Daniel, Cedar Point probably has more roller coasters than any other amusement park in the country," she announced smugly, then paused. "But you wouldn't want to ride a roller coaster, would you? I mean, wouldn't that be kind of scary when you can't see anything?"

He grinned wickedly. "It's what you *can* see that terrifies you on a roller coaster. OK," he said decisively. "We'll go. *And*—we will ride all the roller coasters in the park. Together." He crossed his arms over his chest again, his smile daring her to refuse.

"I . . . ah . . . actually, I've never been on a roller coaster, Daniel."

His grin became a full-scale smirk. "Jennifer," he drawled, sitting forward on his chair and rubbing his hands together with obvious glee, "this is going to be an unforgettable day."

The day couldn't have been more perfect for their plans. The temperature was in the low seventies, the air was dry, and the sky looked like frosted blue glass.

"It's going to be *extremely* crowded," Jennifer remarked as she craned her neck to study the long lines waiting at the entry gates. "There must be dozens of people ahead of us."

"Just don't lose me in the crowd," Dan said.

Hearing what sounded like a touch of anxiety in his voice, Jennifer glanced up at him. "Does it bother you a lot, being without Sunny? I didn't think we'd be able to go on the rides if she came with us."

"I don't especially like crowds, even with Sunny," he admitted. "It's too easy to get confused."

Jennifer frowned, annoyed at her thoughtlessness. "Oh, Daniel, I'm sorry! I was so intent on having my own way I didn't even stop to think how difficult this might be for you. Listen, we don't have to go in—we'll leave right now."

He covered her hand on his forearm with his own. "No way, darlin'. If you think I'm going to miss a chance to ride all those roller coasters, think again."

She thought his smile might be a little forced. "Daniel, are you sure?"

"Absolutely. I can't wait to—"

Jennifer and Dan both whirled around in surprise when they heard a rasping voice call their names. Standing off to one side was Vali Tremayne, accompanied by David Nathan Keye, who smiled and waved what looked like a handful of passes.

"I can get all of us in on these," he said. "Let me treat, OK?"

Without waiting for a reply, he and Vali walked over. Keye touched Dan lightly on the shoulder in a friendly gesture, then linked arms with both Jennifer and Vali as he began to move around the line and up to the entry gate. Jennifer held Dan's hand tightly so they wouldn't get separated.

Once through the gate, after thanking Keye for their free admission, Jennifer turned to Vali and said, "So you decided to take advantage of this last weekend, too?"

"I twisted her arm," David said with a grin. "I love amusement parks. And I figured if this one is so great that I heard about it in California, it must really be something."

"You won't be disappointed, David," Jennifer told him, glancing around. "Oh, look—here comes the clown band!"

A parade of wildly dressed, zany clowns came strutting down a nearby lane, playing a variety of instruments and shouting among themselves.

After they passed, David took Vali by the hand and looked thoughtfully from Dan to Jennifer. "Say, you two wouldn't want to pair up with us for the day, would you?"

"David," Vali quickly objected, "they're on their honeymoon, remember?"

"Oh—right. Sorry; of course you'd rather be alone—"

Jennifer elbowed Dan, who flinched, then responded to his cue. "No, that sounds good to us. Jennifer?"

She nodded her head eagerly. "We'd love to!"

Vali searched Jennifer's eyes. "Are you sure? We'd understand if you'd rather not."

"No, really—it'll be fun."

"Well, then, what are we waiting for?" David studied Dan for a moment, then asked matter-of-factly, "What's easiest for you, Dan? Walking on the outside or in between?"

Daniel replied without hesitating. "The outside, with Jennifer guiding me. She's not as good as Sunny," he added dryly, "but I guess I can't be particular today." Jennifer dug him lightly in the ribs, and they started off.

Over the next two hours, they rode the train, ate french fries; rode the log ride, ate hot dogs; rode the Tilt-A-Whirl, ate cotton candy; rode the bumper cars, and ate pizza.

"I'm going to be sick," David groaned, rubbing at a dab of tomato sauce on the front of his striped shirt.

"You deserve to be," Vali told him.

Jennifer didn't miss Vali's faint blush—of pleasure, she thought—when David hugged her to his side and said, "Have a little pity, Princess. I'm turning green."

"What we need," Daniel announced, "is a change of pace. A nice leisurely ride that won't stir up or dislocate anything."

"Wise counsel, Daniel." The composer adjusted his sunglasses with one finger.

They started walking again. "We'll have to bring Jason up here next year," Dan said.

"He'd love it," Jennifer agreed.

"Jason?" Vali gave them a questioning look.

"Our son."

David threw them a somewhat startled glance.

"We have an adopted son," Jennifer explained. "Well, almost adopted. It won't be final for a few months yet. Dan was planning to adopt Jason before we got married, so now we're finalizing it in both our names."

"How old is he?" asked Vali.

"Almost nine," Jennifer answered. "And he's absolutely adorable." Jason was staying with Dan's parents for the duration of the honeymoon, and already Jennifer found herself missing the small towhead who had so quickly charmed his way into her heart.

"Well, Daniel, what nice, leisurely ride do you recommend for us?" David asked as they started walking again.

Dan considered. "The Ferris wheel, I think."

"Oh, no!" Jennifer said, a little too quickly.

"Oh, no?" repeated her husband.

"It's too . . . high."

"Are you afraid of heights, Jennifer?" Vali looked genuinely concerned.

"She won't admit it, but she is," Dan told them.

"I wouldn't say I'm *afraid,* exactly."

Dan gave her a smug look. "I thought you believed in confronting your fears."

"There's no fear to confront here, Daniel," she countered. "I simply don't want to get on an airborne Tinkertoy with my stomach feeling like a cement mixer. Not all of us," she said pointedly, "have steel tubing for a digestive tract."

His grin broadened. "From what you've told me, it'll come in real handy when I have to start eating your cooking."

Jennifer muttered under her breath, then said reluctantly, "Oh, all right. We'll ride the Ferris wheel. But don't say I didn't warn you."

Vali stood waiting in line, vaguely wishing Jennifer hadn't agreed to "confront her fears." Actually, she didn't much like this ride either. But she found herself more likely to keep quiet about her own fears—surely far more numerous than Jennifer Kaine's—when she was with David. For some inexplicable reason,

she didn't want him seeing what Graham called her *neuroses*.
David obviously thought well of her. Lately she'd been surprised
by how much she wanted to keep his respect.

They had become good friends in these past few weeks of
working together. At least, *she* counted *him* as a friend. For David's
part, he made her a little uncomfortable sometimes by hinting—
strongly—that he was attracted to her as a woman, not only as a
friend. He was recklessly candid about it, too—even around Graham. In fact, he sometimes seemed intent on deliberately *goading*
Graham.

Last night, after learning that Graham would be in Cleveland
for two days, David had become disconcertingly blunt about his
feelings.

"You're not engaged to the man, right?" he had asked Vali
directly.

"Not exactly, but—"

"I don't see a ring, Vali."

"He's asked me to marry him."

"And have you given him an answer?"

"Well, I have to be . . . sure."

"And you're not?"

"I—almost . . ."

"Almost doesn't count, Princess."

"David—"

They had been sitting beside each other on the piano bench,
and he had flashed that impish grin of his and cuffed her lightly
on the chin with a gentle fist. But suddenly his dark gray eyes had
lost their glint of mischief, darkening to an expression that made
Vali's heart lurch and threaten to betray her loyalty to Graham.
He had taken her gently by the shoulders and held her captive
with his searching look. "Vali, surely you know that you've
become very important to me. Give me a chance, Princess . . .
that's all I'm asking . . . just a chance."

Without understanding why, Vali had become almost angry with him. She resented the ease with which he threatened her orderly lifestyle. She had pushed him away. "I won't work with you if you're going to act like this!"

He had apologized at once—but only for upsetting her. Not for being interested in her. And he still looked at her . . . that way . . . the way that said he cared about her. Deeply.

David unnerved her, exasperated her, at times almost frightened her with his intensity. And yet she trusted him. Why was that, she wondered? How could she trust such a troublesome, stubborn, impudent man? A man so different from Graham. Graham was so strong, so dependable, so . . . in control.

"Penny for them, Princess," David whispered at her side.

Vali jumped, then locked gazes with him, caught off guard, as always, by the affection in his eyes.

With a small laugh, she told him, "I'm afraid I was wishing Jennifer weren't so brave . . . about facing her fears."

His expression quickly sobered. "We don't have to go on this thing if you'd rather not."

"No—I'm just . . . a little jittery, I suppose." Vali brightened and smiled at him. "We came to do it all, remember?"

He slipped one long arm around her shoulders to move her through the gate. "Here we go, then."

Vali stepped into the gondola, uncomfortably aware that the operator was staring curiously at her. After getting into the seat, she glanced up at the man's face, unsettled by what appeared to be a glint of amusement in his darkly shadowed eyes. Quickly she looked away.

Dan and Jennifer were in the car just above them, and Vali could hear them laughing as the car began to move. *What a special pair they are,* she thought with a smile. That wonderful, incredible blind man somehow gave others a sense of security in his presence—and so did his lovely Jennifer, with her laughing dark eyes, ready wit, and totally unselfish interest in others.

"I love to see you smile like that," David said. He still had his arm around Vali, and he gently squeezed her shoulder. "But I'm almost jealous because I don't know why you're smiling."

"The Kaines," she said simply, looking out over the park. "I was thinking about how special they are."

"Ah, there goes my ego again. I was hoping you were thinking of me."

"David, you're impossible," Vali scolded, captured by the smile in his eyes when she turned to look at him.

Disturbed by her own feelings, she quickly looked away to scan the crowd below. As they began to ascend, she caught sight of what she thought was a familiar face.

A man, completely bald, stood motionless in the throng of people at the base of the ride. Vali was certain he was staring up at her. Not tall, but square and somewhat heavy, he had the thick, overmuscled appearance of a boxer past his prime. In a conservative dark suit, he looked grossly out of place in his surroundings.

The sight of him unnerved her, for she felt a slight sense of recognition as she looked at him. Yet she was positive she had never seen him before. David said something to her just then, and by the time she glanced back into the crowd, the man had disappeared.

Vali was still trying to identify the stranger in her memory as they climbed to the top. Suddenly a loud *crunch* threw her against the safety bar, and the ride came to an abrupt stop.

SIX

V ALI heard Jennifer cry out above. At the same time, the nervous laughter and uneasy mutterings of the other riders increased around them.

David had pulled her back away from the safety bar when the car lurched, but Vali desperately wished they weren't so near the top of the ride. There was just enough breeze to make the car rock gently back and forth, and she swallowed hard a couple of times against the sick wrenching of her stomach.

David tightened his protective hold on her and gently coaxed her face against his shoulder. "OK?" he whispered.

Vali nodded, grateful for his warm closeness. "Is something wrong, do you think?"

"I'm not sure."

She glanced up, and his troubled expression unsettled her even more. She tried to laugh. "Well, whatever it is, I wish it could have gone wrong when we were a little closer to the ground."

He squeezed her shoulder. "It's all right. Probably just a new operator learning his job at our expense." With his free hand, he tugged lightly on a wave of Vali's hair. "Actually, I paid him to keep us up here for a bit. Got you at my mercy now, pretty lady."

Vali kept her face burrowed against his shoulder, unwilling to move for fear of making the car sway even more. "Don't make fun, David. I don't like this."

He rested his chin lightly on the top of her head. "We're all right, Princess," he whispered hoarsely into her hair. "Don't you know by now I wouldn't let anything hurt you?"

Vali looked up at him, feeling her heart turn over when she saw the way he was caressing her with his gaze.

They remained that way for a long moment before a shutter seemed to close in his eyes, and he looked away. He continued to hold her, but now there was nothing more than an awkward silence between them.

Fifteen minutes passed; the voices of riders in the other cars gradually grew more agitated. When David tapped her lightly on the shoulder and pointed to the ground, Vali looked, then sighed with relief. The ride operator was helping two young girls out of the car closest to the ground. Then he began to lower the wheel so that each car could empty its passengers. Slowly and methodically every gondola was lowered and emptied until it was David and Vali's turn.

Without knowing why, Vali jerked her hand away when the operator reached out to help her. Saying nothing, the young man raked a thin wisp of blond hair away from his forehead, staring hard at her as David got out.

"Was there a problem?" he asked the operator.

At the sound of David's whisper-voice, the man shot him a questioning look. "No big deal," he muttered. "Slight problem on the axle. Sorry for the delay."

Vali saw David give the man a long, studying look before leading her to the gate, where Dan and Jennifer stood waiting.

"So much for your idea of a nice, leisurely ride, Daniel!" Jennifer was teasing him as Vali and David approached.

Dan wore a sheepish grin. "You have to admit, it gave you a good chance to confront your fears."

"That was *not* a confrontation, Daniel," asserted his wife. "That was an *assault.*"

"I think we owe Jennifer the ride of her choice about now," David offered, and everyone quickly agreed.

Somehow the ride of Jennifer's choice got postponed. As the four of them walked by the *Magnum* roller coaster, David mumbled something to Daniel, and the two stopped near the crowd waiting to get on.

"It's a conspiracy." Jennifer turned to Vali. "Are you going on?"

Vali looked at her, then at David, who grinned and gave her a thumbs-up sign.

"Yes," the singer replied, much to Jennifer's surprise and dismay. "I think I will."

Jennifer swallowed. "Then so will I."

Dan looked suspiciously gratified.

Once they arrived at the end of the line, however, Jennifer's resolve began to flag.

"Oh dear . . ." She attempted a weak laugh. "I am *so* disappointed . . . but it looks as though I won't be able to do this after all."

"Why not?" Dan asked her skeptically.

"Well, you see, there's a sign here that says you have to be *this* tall in order to go on the ride, and I'm afraid I don't measure up. I'll just go sit down on a bench and wait."

Dan held her hand with an iron grip. "Nice try, Jennifer. Now, come on."

Jennifer eyed the wicked-looking coaster one more time, swallowed hard, then moved, with all the enthusiasm of a condemned prisoner en route to the execution chamber, to take her place in line. Somewhere behind them, she heard someone mention, in an awestruck voice, the fact that you could see the "first hill" from anywhere in the park.

Feeling a little sick, she stopped to tie her tennis shoe. As she straightened, a rather odd-looking man just off to her right caught her attention. Unnerved by his pale-eyed stare, she suddenly realized that it was Vali who was the focus of his attention, not herself.

She watched him closely. His dark suit and tie were peculiarly out of place in the amusement park, especially on such a warm day. Involuntarily, Jennifer shuddered. Something about the man seemed strangely sinister. She glanced away for just a second, then looked again, disturbed to find his eyes now riveted on her. Jennifer turned her back on him, but it seemed that she could still feel his malevolent stare burning into her. *Probably just some oddball voyeur,* she thought with distaste.

"What's it look like, Jennifer?" Daniel asked, suddenly breaking into her unsettled thoughts.

Jennifer stared up at the coaster, then froze. The twisting, convoluted tracks just ahead rose to an inconceivable height—a *deadly* height! She swallowed down a soft sob of denial.

"Jennifer? What does it look like?"

She looked from the *Magnum* to her husband. "Like my worst nightmare," she said thickly. "Daniel . . . you don't want to do this. Trust me."

He rubbed his hands together gleefully. "My kind of coaster."

"Be quiet, Daniel. I'm praying."

"Jennifer—"

"I'm *serious,* Daniel. I *am* praying."

"Boy-oh-boy." He grinned with pleasure. "This is going to be good!"

When the car started up the first incline, Jennifer decided with guarded relief that maybe it wouldn't be so bad after all. She didn't care for the clanking and grinding and lurching, and the hill seemed to go on forever. Still, the safety bar seemed secure, and Daniel's large, solid frame next to her gave her what she hoped wasn't a false sense of protection.

It was the first drop that jolted her with the blood-freezing reality of just how wrong she had been. It was a terrible feeling, a stomach-crushing, mind-exploding feeling.

"Daniel!" she screamed. "We're going to fall out!"

"People don't fall out of roller coasters, Jennifer!" he shouted back. "It's got something to do with centrifugal force!"

Centrifugal force! Was that all that was holding them in place? "I *hate* this, Daniel!"

"No, you don't!" he yelled with assurance above the din of screaming people and banging clatter. "You're having fun, Jennifer!"

Jennifer somehow managed to open her eyes long enough to turn and look at her husband. With disbelief she saw his upraised arms, the look of pure pleasure on his face, and for heaven's sake, the crazy man was *laughing out loud!*

"It doesn't go any faster, does it, Daniel?" she screamed in terror, unable to hear her own voice as they hugged a death-defying loop.

"Right, honey! It'll go a *lot* faster! You'll love it!" He waved his arms a little more. "Man, this is a *good* one!"

The wind slapped Jennifer's face. The noise shattered her eardrums. The creaking, clanging metal tracks rose and fell. People screamed. Daniel laughed. Jennifer whimpered.

"Are your hands up, Jennifer?"

"My entire body is paralyzed, Daniel Kaine! The only thing up is my blood pressure!"

"I told you you'd love it, didn't I?"

"Daniel, don't you *hear* me?!"

Then she knew. They were going to plummet off the track. The whole chain of cars was simply going to topple off and go flying into the crowd. She felt the car lean, felt herself being lifted from the seat, then pushed back into place. She looked down, over the side, into the trees. She saw the lake . . . and screamed. Terrorized, she twisted and threw her arms around Daniel's middle, pushing her head under his upraised arm. Again she screamed, this time into the hard, safe warmth of his ribs.

As she stepped out of the car, her entire body shaking, Jennifer silently promised herself that she would never—absolutely *never*—let him talk her into anything ever again.

The carousel was their final stop before leaving the park, each of them declaring that Jennifer, good sport that she'd been, deserved at least one quiet, *safe* ride.

It was a beautiful carousel with ornate cornices, vivid panels, elegant chariots, and a choice of gallopers, jumpers, and flying horses. The calliope music was loud and happy.

Jennifer and Vali chose two proud-looking jumpers, with the men opting for flying horses on the outside.

"Now this is more like it," Jennifer declared as Dan gave her a hand up to her mount before getting on his own somewhat wild-looking stallion. "I love these things," she told him. "When I was a little girl, I used to ride them over and over again, pretending I was an Indian princess or a lady in King Arthur's court."

Dan grinned as he settled onto his horse. Directly in front of them, Vali and David talked in hushed, serious tones, making Jennifer smile at their obvious attraction for each other.

She couldn't help but wonder who would be best for Vali—David Keye or Graham Alexander. Not that it was any of her business, she reminded herself, but she wasn't sure that she actually approved of either man.

Perhaps she was being unfair to Graham Alexander. The scientist obviously cared about the lovely young singer. And while David's interest might be just as genuine, it might *not* be as good for Vali. Certainly he was a more disturbing kind of man than Alexander appeared to be. Clever and witty and outrageously unconventional one moment, he could turn suddenly quiet and withdrawn the next.

Ah, well, she thought with a tender glance at her husband sitting quietly next to her, *not every man can be a Daniel.*

She looked around the platform, taking in the horses and the people astride them. At the operator's stand, a small, red-haired young man with glasses was talking with a dark, lanky youth. She saw the redhead move to start the ride, then stop at something the other boy said. He looked at his wristwatch, then jumped from the platform, leaving his companion to operate the carousel.

Impatient, Jennifer turned to look at the crowd of bystanders. She drew in a sharp breath of surprise when she caught a glimpse of a familiar face. Standing well behind a line of observers was the same man she had seen earlier at the *Magnum,* the bald man in the dark business suit.

Jennifer's gaze locked with the man's pale, hard stare. He narrowed his eyes, then glanced from her to Vali before backing out of the crowd and walking off. The ride began to move. Jennifer tried to keep track of him as they circled, but he disappeared.

Perhaps her uneasiness was foolish, but this second appearance of the peculiar-acting stranger troubled her. She was sure she had never seen him before, yet something about him made her feel threatened. More specifically, she realized, he made her feel frightened for Vali.

Abruptly, Jennifer tried to shake off her feelings, determined that nothing was going to spoil this ride. She glanced over at Dan, relishing the sight of his strong, bronzed profile as he sat smiling on the flying horse.

The sun was just beginning to fade below the horizon. It had been a magical day. Jennifer smiled fondly at the memory of the young girl who had once ridden this same carousel, her head filled with wonderful, romantic dreams. Now she had her very own prince, and he was stronger and more handsome than any of the leading men of her schoolgirl dreams. She was in love, she was happy, and life was good.

Caught up in her temporary euphoria, the gradual change in the calliope's volume and the slight shift in rotation of the platform escaped her notice until Dan called out to her. "Jennifer?" His voice was sharp with concern. "What's going on?"

At the same time, Jennifer saw Vali dart a worried look at David, who in turn cast a measuring look at the carousel's machinery.

The speed was still increasing, the music growing continually louder. Jennifer heard children begin to cry and saw several people move in closer as they watched. She could hear a growing buzz of alarm among the crowd, and she felt her heart lurch, then race even faster than the music.

Like a macabre dream, the platform whirled faster and faster, horses flying, chariots thumping, the grinding calliope now loud and ugly and distorted.

Jennifer cried out to Dan, who slid off his mount and moved in beside her to wrap a steadying arm around her waist. David jumped from his horse and went to Vali.

With his free hand, Daniel covered Jennifer's white-knuckled grip on the carousel rod. "Can you see anything?" he asked her. "The ride operator? Where is he?"

They were flying now, faces outside the fence whirling by in a dizzying kaleidoscope.

"I can't see anything!" Jennifer cried hoarsely. "Daniel, don't let go of me!"

In answer, he tightened his grip protectively on her waist.

Suddenly, just when it seemed that the entire carousel would snap and break apart like a child's toy, the music began to slow, then the platform . . . and, finally, Jennifer's heart.

As unexpectedly as it had begun, it was over. David and Vali, white-faced, turned to Jennifer and Dan. The four of them stayed frozen in place for seconds after everything had come to a halt, not speaking, barely breathing.

It was Vali who finally broke the strained silence. "Please . . . let's get out of here."

The sound of her voice roused the others into action. Dan helped Jennifer slide from her horse, pulling her against him for a moment. Gently, he touched her cheek. "Are you OK?" he whispered into her tangled hair. "You're not hurt?"

"I'm . . . fine," Jennifer said, her voice trembling. "I just want to get off, Daniel."

She clung to him as they left the ride and walked into the midst of the curious, stunned bystanders who stood murmuring among themselves.

Vali waited with them while David and one of the other riders questioned the red-haired carousel operator. When David finally returned, his face was ashen and taut with controlled anger. "He says he has no idea what happened. Someone sent a message that he was to come to the office. The fellow who brought him the message offered to stay until he got back. But he was gone by the time the ride operator returned."

Dan's expression was skeptical, but he said nothing.

On the way to the exit, the day now spoiled, Jennifer's mind raced. She couldn't shake the feeling that there was a connection between the strange-looking man in the dark suit and the malfunction of the carousel.

Vali hadn't said a word since leaving the ride. She continued to lean heavily on David, her face chalk white. With a worried aside, Jennifer suggested to Dan that they follow the other couple to their car before going to their own.

When they reached David's sleek black Corvette, the composer turned to them, releasing Vali long enough to shake hands with Daniel. "Thanks for sharing your day with us—I hope it wasn't a total loss for you." His face was granite hard with tension.

"We enjoyed being with you," Dan assured him. "Vali, are you all right?" he asked after a slight pause.

Vali didn't answer but simply hugged her arms a little more tightly to herself. David's eyes never left her face as he slipped an arm back around her shoulder.

Before they parted, Jennifer decided to tell the others about the man she'd seen at the *Magnum* and then again at the carousel.

"He kept staring at Vali," Jennifer continued. "And it was . . . an unpleasant look. Almost a . . . frightening look."

David's face paled. "What did he look like?" His mouth thinned to a hard, tight line, and his whispering voice sounded harsher than usual.

As Jennifer went on to describe the worrisome stranger, she saw Vali lift her head with an astonished look. For a moment the singer seemed about to say something, but finally she dropped her gaze away, remaining silent.

David, too, had a peculiar, stricken expression on his face. As soon as Jennifer ended her description, he said a hurried good-bye and helped Vali into the passenger's seat, then hurried to the driver's side and slid behind the wheel.

Jennifer had the impression that the enigmatic composer could hardly wait to leave the parking lot. Neither he nor Vali looked back as he drove away.

Shivering, she reached for Dan, urging him to hurry as they started for their own car.

SEVEN

EARLY the next morning, Dan sat on the porch of their cottage in a lawn chair, enjoying the cool air and the sounds coming in off the lake. He could tell by the slapping of the waves that it was choppy this morning, and he found himself wishing he could see again, could stand along the shore and watch the sea gulls play over the breakers. From somewhere down the beach a dog barked, and beside him, Sunny made a low, answering growl of her own.

Hearing footsteps, Dan sat up a little straighter. Sunny stirred and uttered a perfunctory little bark.

"Morning, Daniel. If you're not the picture of a contented, happy man, I never saw one."

"Hi, David, you're out and about early."

"I like to walk the beach when it's like this. You can almost smell fall in the air."

At Dan's invitation, David sat down on the porch step. "I thought I'd stop and make sure you and Jennifer are both all right. I know your day at Cedar Point wasn't exactly what you'd hoped for."

"We're fine," Dan said easily. "Jennifer is inside getting dressed. Her hair dryer went on the fritz this morning, so we're going to try to track down a discount store later."

He reached over to rub Sunny's ears, and the retriever gradually settled back into her comfortable slouch again.

"How's Vali?" Dan asked. "Have you talked with her this morning?"

"Only by phone. I'm going to stop by for a few minutes before I leave. Actually, that's another reason I wanted to see you. I was wondering if I could ask a small favor of you and Jennifer. I hate to keep imposing, but—"

Dan made a quick dismissing motion with his hand. "You're not imposing. Did you say you're leaving?" He took a sip of coffee, then set his cup on the table beside him. "Would you like some coffee? There's plenty."

"No, thanks. I'm sure I'll have more than my limit later on today," he said. "I have a meeting with a producer and some other people in Nashville this evening. I plan to be back early tomorrow, but I'm a little concerned about Vali. I was wondering if you and Jennifer would mind giving her a call later today—just to check on her."

"Sure, we'd be glad to. You think she's still upset about yesterday?"

David didn't answer right away.

"Jennifer was afraid she might have made things worse for Vali by describing the man she saw at the rides," Dan ventured.

"I don't know," the composer replied. "Vali isn't . . . very strong. Emotionally, I mean. She's had . . . some problems."

"I hoped that was all behind her," Dan said carefully. "I had heard that she had a difficult time after Paul Alexander's death, but that was three years ago."

Dan heard the frustration in David's deep sigh as he shifted restlessly on the step. "Most of the time Vali seems all right. But it doesn't take much to shake her. She was badly frightened last night. I couldn't get her to talk to me at all until this morning. Now she's trying to laugh it off, but I'm not all that comfortable with leaving her alone today."

"Vali said Graham was out of town, too. Is he still gone?"

"Yes," David rasped shortly. "He won't be back until sometime tomorrow."

"Well, we'll be happy to check on her. Jennifer will be glad for a chance to say hello."

"Thanks, Dan—I really appreciate it." David paused. "Your Jennifer is a very special lady."

Dan smiled. "Yes, she surely is."

"Have you known each other for a long time?"

"Not really. I hired her as my exec at the radio station the first of the year and proceeded to fall head over heels in love with her." He hesitated. "What about you, David? Do you have someone special in your life?"

The musician didn't answer for a moment. When he did, his whisper-voice was softer than ever. "Not . . . exactly." After a slight pause, he added, "Just . . . high hopes."

"Vali?"

"It's that obvious?"

"Jennifer is always on the lookout for romance. She's hard to fool." Dan couldn't stop a smile at the thought of his wife's quick mind and inquisitive nature.

"Well . . . the competition is pretty tough, I'm afraid."

"Graham Alexander?"

"He's a rather formidable opponent."

"They're not engaged, are they? Jennifer said she didn't notice Vali wearing a ring."

"Not yet. But Graham is giving it his best shot."

Dan shrugged and lifted his eyebrows. "Until she's wearing a ring—until the wedding itself, in fact—you've still got a chance."

"Not much of one, I'm afraid." David sounded discouraged. "Graham has a definite edge on me. You see, Vali feels enormously indebted to him."

Dan frowned. "Why is that?"

"You know that Graham is Paul Alexander's twin?"

Dan nodded.

"Well, after his brother died, Graham more or less made himself responsible for Vali's welfare. You see, Vali had a complete breakdown after Paul's death."

Dan heard David get up and step down off the porch.

"All I know is what I've been told by others," he continued, "but it's common knowledge that Vali fell apart emotionally. She wouldn't sing, wouldn't eat, wouldn't see anyone—wouldn't even go out of the house, I understand."

"She's obviously better." Dan reached for his coffee cup, then felt for the pot to pour himself a refill.

"Oh, yes, she definitely is," David quickly agreed. "Though I'd like to see her a lot . . . stronger. More secure about herself, at least. At any rate," he continued, "she attributes her present . . . well-being . . . to Graham."

"I don't understand."

The composer hesitated. "Apparently Graham and his mother brought Vali up here after her . . . breakdown. They saw to it that she got excellent care in a mental health center for several months. After that, she lived with Leda—that's Graham's mother—for a few weeks until she moved into her own place here on the beach. Both Leda and Graham seem to have appointed themselves her guardians—not in the legal sense, but certainly in every other way. Graham in particular keeps a very watchful eye on Vali."

Dan could hear the undercurrent of resentment in David's words. "It sounds as if he might have been fond of her when she was still engaged to his brother," he said thoughtfully.

"No, not at all," David replied. "From what Vali's told me, she and Graham barely knew one another until after the airplane crash. She and Leda had spent some time together, and I think they became close right from the beginning. But that wasn't the case with her and Graham. Anyway," he went on, "all that changed after Paul died. Now Vali seems to feel an extraordinary sense of gratitude toward Graham. In fact—" he paused for an instant— "I suppose this will sound like nothing more than jealousy, but I get the feeling that Graham Alexander has fostered a kind of unhealthy dependency in Vali."

"A dependency on *him,* you mean."

"Yes. I think he has managed to convince Vali that she can't function without him, that she's . . . helpless . . . on her own."

Dan had his doubts about the musician's theory, but he kept them to himself. "Why would someone with Vali Tremayne's talent and reputation get involved in a relationship like that?"

"It's just a hunch," said David, "but I think Graham somehow discovered Vali's weakness and capitalized on it. You see, she has this incredibly distorted sense of her own worth. At some time in her life, her self-image was virtually destroyed—or maybe it never developed. As illogical as it may seem, considering who she is— and how special she is—Vali has absolutely no self-confidence. I think she's probably the most insecure person I've ever known."

Troubled, Dan thought about this as he traced the rim of his coffee cup with his thumb. "Yet, Vali's a Christian."

"Vali was also an orphan," David replied. "Apparently she was tossed around from one foster home to another for years. I'm convinced that's at the heart of her problems. She loves the Lord with all her heart, and in her own way she has a close walk with him. But she has no real understanding of God's love for *her,* as an individual." He paused, then added, "I imagine we both know Christians who have been spiritually crippled because they're unable either to understand or to accept their own worth in God's eyes. With Vali, I'm afraid it's become a severe emotional problem."

Dan was quiet for a long time. "She must trust you a great deal to confide in you as she has," he finally said.

"A lot of what I know about Vali I learned from other people," David explained. "But, yes, she *has* shared some things about her past with me. The rest . . . well, I care so much about her, I think I just somehow sense her feelings."

"Does she know you're in love with her?" Dan asked gently.

"I'm afraid I haven't done very well at hiding it."

"It could be that you're just what she needs to break this . . . *dependency* . . . on Graham Alexander."

"Naturally, I'd like to think so." David gave a small, harsh laugh. "But I don't have much time left, I'm afraid."

"Why? Because of your other contracts?"

"Other contracts?" David repeated. "Oh—well, yes. The agreement was that Vali and I would work together for a few weeks, then she'd make a decision about returning to her career. But in the meantime, I have recording commitments of my own to honor, and soon I'll have to go back to Nashville to stay. My time is running out."

"But you could still see her—"

"If I can't convince Vali to pick up the pieces of her career while I'm cloistered with her for hours every day, I certainly can't hope to when I'm hundreds of miles away from her." He stopped. "Yet I can't let Graham Alexander win!"

"That almost sounds like a war," Dan said mildly.

The composer was silent for a long time. Dan could hear the strain in his whisper-voice when he finally replied. "In a way, it is. But I happen to believe it's a war worth fighting."

"In a war, David, someone always gets hurt," Dan pointed out gently. "And someone always loses."

"Yes, I know," the musician whispered. "But I can promise you this, Daniel. Whatever happens, I intend to make sure that Vali isn't the one who gets hurt."

After the composer had walked away, Dan bent forward in his chair and propped his elbows on his knees. He thought about everything David had told him, puzzled by his conflicting impressions of the man.

Being blind made it difficult to "read" another person, although he had become reasonably adept at gauging the emotional barometers of those around him. It suddenly occurred to him, however, that even if he could see David's face, he quite possibly wouldn't know any more about the enigmatic musician than he already did. A deep-seated but growing doubt about the man made Dan wonder if anyone had ever seen the true face of David Nathan Keye.

EIGHT

T HE man shifted his tall frame inside the phone booth, keeping one eye on the highway a few feet away.

"That fiasco at Cedar Point was incredibly stupid! What in the world possessed you? And to go yourself—"

The voice on the other end of the phone sighed with exaggerated patience. "I believe I've already explained that we simply meant to assist you with your plan. It was all quite safe."

"It was foolish, not safe!" the man snarled. "The only thing you accomplished was to make the Kaine woman suspicious."

"What do you mean?" The voice hardened.

"She *saw* you, that's what I mean. She saw you *twice,* as a matter of fact. And when I talked to Vali this morning, she was more on edge than ever."

"Then the day was a success. You need her disoriented, do you not?"

"I don't need her watching her shadow!"

"You're allowing your anxiety to distract you from the fact that all this is working to our advantage."

The man pulled at his shirt collar. "Listen to me. I know what I'm doing. If you'll just stay out of it and give me the time I need, I can tie up all the loose ends once and for all."

The voice sighed again. "Time is becoming of extreme importance, my friend. We've been patient with your infatuation with the Tremayne woman and your insistence that you can effectively silence her. But the truth is—"

"I told you—"

"The truth is," the voice interrupted with an icy note of warning, "that you're not much further along with your plan today than you were when we started. Now, we both know there's a good possibility that the singer could put us—and a number of other people, important people—behind bars for the rest of our natural lives. In addition," he pressed on in an even, cold tone, "the unfortunate return of her memory of certain events could prove disastrous to a project it has taken years to implement. That cannot be allowed. The Tremayne woman is to be neutralized. Your way, if you can accomplish it within five more days." He paused, drew a deep breath, and added quietly, *"Our* way, if not. Is that clear?"

"Perfectly clear," the man grated resentfully. "What about the others?"

"Don't give the other couple—the Kaines, is it?—a second thought. If they should turn out to be a problem or complicate our plans in any way, they're entirely expendable. We'll take care of them."

NINE

THE evening was warm, the lake calm, the breeze gentle. Dan and Jennifer strolled leisurely along the beach, his right arm resting lightly around her shoulders, his other hand gripping Sunny's harness. They walked in contented silence, Daniel smiling softly to himself as he allowed his thoughts free rein. In his usual manner, he prayed as he walked, sometimes silently, sometimes in a soft murmur.

He knew it would surprise most people to learn that he counted himself a peaceful, happy man. The reason for his peace was his relationship with a God of unconditional love and endless mercies. The reason for his happiness was the woman walking closely at his side.

How she had changed his life . . . sweetened it, enriched it, given it a meaning and an ongoing joy he would have once not dared to hope for. And these days at the beach had been glorious. . . .

Abruptly, his smile faded as an unbidden memory surfaced, bringing with it a wrenching pain. All too clearly he remembered another evening walk along a beach, this one in Florida. It hadn't been a happy time, that summer after the automobile accident that had blinded him. In truth, it had been one of the most difficult times of his life. Gabe Denton, his closest friend, had insisted that Dan put the radio station under temporary management and get away—away from home, from work, and from as many of the painful memories as possible. Dan had reluctantly given in to Gabe's urging, and together they had spent two months in a rented house on a private beach near Fort Myers.

Loneliness had tormented him like a viper that summer, poisoning him with discouragement and fear . . . the fear that he would spend the rest of his life without sight, without love, without hope . . . that he would grow old alone, never knowing the companionship or joy of having a wife and family. One particular evening, he and Gabe had walked for hours in silence along the deserted beach, neither of them able to voice each other's private dread. For one brief, desolate moment, Dan had felt an almost overwhelming urge to simply walk into the sea and let it take him.

Even years after he had finally made peace with God about the blindness, the awful loneliness had still lingered, sometimes threatening to break him. Too many times he had experienced the unsighted person's dilemma of feeling alone in the midst of a crowd, even among his own family—cut off, isolated, a solitary man in a lonely world.

But then . . . then Jennifer had come sweeping into his life, into his heart. Jennifer, his sweet, gate-crashing rebel, with her wild, wonderful mane of hair that smelled like sunshine and her honeyed voice that warmed his soul. Jennifer, with the laugh that shattered his doubts, the touch that melted his senses, and the love that had vanquished his fear of loneliness and set him free—free to love her.

Oh, my Lord . . . my loving, gracious Lord, how can I ever, ever thank you enough for her?

Hearing Daniel's soft murmur of praise, Jennifer smiled up at his profile. "What are you thinking about?"

"Just counting my blessings, darlin' . . . again," he said with the love-touched smile that was reserved for her alone.

She wrapped her arm around his waist and hugged him tightly. "We have a lot of them to count, don't we, Daniel?"

"Indeed we do, love. Indeed we do."

"Do you ever feel . . . almost guilty? Because we're so happy and other people aren't?"

"No," Dan replied without hesitation. "Just extremely grateful." He paused. "What prompted that question?"

"Oh, I don't know." She poked at a mound of sand with the toes of her bare foot. "When I see someone like Vali Tremayne, I feel almost ashamed that I can be so happy when she's so miserable."

Dan stopped. "Do you really think she's that unhappy?"

"Yes," Jennifer replied without hesitation. "I think she's *terribly* unhappy, Daniel. And I wish there were something we could do about it."

"I'm afraid all we can do right now is what David asked us to do," he said, gently squeezing her shoulder. "Let's walk over to Vali's cottage and make sure she's OK. The rest we'll have to leave to the Lord."

≈≈≈

Vali called the cat one more time, then turned to leave the beach and go inside. She stopped when she saw Dan and Jennifer approaching from the other direction, waved, and waited as they drew near.

She was genuinely glad to see them. She liked Jennifer Kaine more than any other woman she had ever met—except for Leda, perhaps. And she thought Jennifer liked *her,* too.

Vali had never had a close woman friend, even in college. She had been far too shy back then to make any gesture of friendship on her own. Later, after she and Paul had become successful as a team in the Christian music industry, she hadn't felt the need for anyone in her life except him. Paul had often encouraged her to make friends with some of the other young women they met in their profession, but Vali had never been comfortable initiating any kind of relationship.

After Paul's death, she hadn't wanted anyone. Leda had been there, of course, and Vali owed the older woman a great deal. But Leda was more a mother figure than a friend, more a source of strength than someone to share with on a mutual level.

Now, as she saw the open friendliness on Jennifer's face, she wished there could be more time to get to know her—and Daniel, too. They made her feel wanted, and they made her feel . . . special. For the most part, she was unacquainted with both feelings.

"Hi, Vali!" Jennifer called warmly. "You going for a walk, too?"

"I've already been. Actually, I've been trying to find my runaway cat again."

Daniel laughed. "Does Trouble ever stay home where she belongs?"

"Not very often, I'm afraid. At least, I seem to spend an awful lot of time trying to track her down."

"Are you worried about her?" Jennifer asked.

"Oh, no," Vali said, waving off the suggestion. "She'll show up before long, once she realizes it's past dinnertime." She glanced from Jennifer to Dan. "You two look like you got some sun today."

"And a few new freckles," Jennifer said, rubbing the tip of her nose. "We spent most of the day on the beach. Daniel, of course, just keeps turning darker and darker, but I feel a little pink in places."

"It was a good day to get a burn," Vali agreed, "but I hope it doesn't stay this warm all night. My air conditioner isn't working right, and I haven't been able to get a repairman yet this week."

After a few more minutes of exchanging small talk, Dan and Jennifer left her and walked on down the beach. Vali called

Trouble one more time, then gave up and went inside. She had
left a table light on before going on her search, and now she went
to turn on the hanging lamp behind the piano as well.

She had drawn the drapes long before dark. Vali had always
hated the darkness. Even after she went to bed she always left a
lamp burning in the cottage. It had been Paul who had finally
helped her understand her fear, which Vali knew bordered on
nyctophobia. Alice Carter, one of the many foster "mothers" in
her past, had often "disciplined" Vali by locking her in a small,
dark, and mildewy basement under the kitchen. When her behavior was deemed particularly unacceptable, Vali had been made to
stay there, alone and terrified, throughout the night.

Vali found herself wondering if her own fear of the dark had in
any way contributed to her empathy for Daniel Kaine and his
blindness. She shuddered at the thought of what Daniel must
endure every day of his life.

Sinking down onto the sofa, she reached for the newspaper,
then decided to fix some iced tea before settling in for the evening.

On the way through the small dinette between the living room
and the kitchen, she stooped to retrieve one of Trouble's yarn
balls. As she straightened, she caught a glimpse of something not
quite right in the direction of the kitchen. She took a step, then
froze. Holding her breath, she stared into the gaping blackness of
the open back door.

The skin on her forearms tightened as she fought to control
her fear. *Someone had been in her cottage.* She was positive she had
locked the door before going outside. Someone had come into
her home, boldly leaving the door open behind him.

Where was he now?

An involuntary image flashed through her mind, rocking her
with panic. *The man at the Ferris wheel.* The man Jennifer had seen

at the roller coaster and again at the carousel. The man with the cold, malevolent eyes.

She shook her head to banish his face from her mind. What had made her think of him?

Had he been the one watching her cottage earlier in the summer? Vali tensed even more, remembering the faceless figure who had stood outside in the darkness several weeks ago, never revealing himself, never approaching her. Simply . . . watching. She had convinced herself it was only her imagination. But what if . . .

What if he were here, inside the cottage?

Don't panic. Breathe . . . take a deep breath . . . stay calm.

No. If anyone was inside the house, he would have shown up before now. She was being childish. She was alone in the cottage; she was sure of it.

She had to shut the back door. Finally, carefully, she forced herself to take one tentative step at a time until she was standing in the middle of the kitchen.

Should she turn on the light? Her instincts told her to flood the room with brightness; still she hesitated.

Vali stared at the door for what seemed an interminable length of time before she could finally bring herself to slam it shut and throw the bolt.

Shaking, she leaned against the door, bracing her hand against the wood as she drew a long, steadying breath.

Now what?

Slowly, reluctantly, she turned around. She knew she had to search the cottage.

If only David hadn't gone away . . . or if Graham were here.

Startled by the realization that she'd thought of David first, Vali quickly turned her thoughts away from him. *Graham . . . it's Graham I need, Graham I want, not David.*

But Graham wasn't here. He was still in Cleveland. And David had gone to Nashville.

She had to do *something*. With one more deep breath, she began fumbling along the wall for the light switch. Finding it, she flipped on the light, blinked, and waited.

There was no sound, no sign of movement. Nothing.

She had to search the rest of the cottage. The living room was safe; she had just come from there. That left only her bedroom and the small bath.

On impulse, Vali opened the silverware drawer and took out a butcher knife. It could be used against her by an intruder lurking somewhere in the darkness, but it made her feel more secure.

Gripping the handle, she crossed the narrow hallway to her bedroom. The room was dark, shadowed, oppressively quiet. She took a step, heard something, backed off, and waited.

Silence.

Once again she took a hesitant step into the room, then another. Unable to stand the darkness any longer, she groped her way toward the nightstand by the bed and with trembling fingers switched on the lamp.

The lively garden colors and splashes of floral prints scattered throughout the room sprang to life, giving her a reassuring sense of normalcy. She swallowed against the sour taste of fear in her mouth. So far so good. But if someone were hiding in here, where would he be?

Under the bed, her mind answered. *Or in the closet.*

Gripping the knife, Vali dropped down on all fours and flipped back the bedspread. Her heart pounded wildly as she peered into the dim recesses under the bed.

Nothing. Nothing but a few dust bunnies and one of Trouble's yarn balls.

She breathed a sigh of relief and got to her feet.

Then she heard the noise again—behind her, in the closet. She whirled around.

A soft *thud,* then another. Vali's hand went up to her mouth, clenching into a tight, defensive fist.

Someone was in the closet. What if she hadn't heard the noise until later? She would have come into the room, undressed for her shower, gone into the adjoining bathroom, and then . . .

She had to get out of the cottage!

But what was he waiting for? He'd had any number of opportunities to grab her by now.

What did he want?

Vali suddenly remembered the knife in her hand. She glanced at it, then raised her eyes to the door of the closet.

She began to walk. Carefully, quietly, slowly.

She stopped once, then went on.

Something scraped at the door, louder now, more insistent.

He was baiting her, teasing her, playing games with her. . . .

She reached for the doorknob, paused, then yanked the door open, jumping back as it slammed against the wall.

Finally she stepped closer, the knife held high as she peered into the darkness of the closet. Her eyes searched the shadows between the clothes, up to the shelves, then down at the floor.

Suddenly something lunged at her with a screech, and Vali screamed.

TEN

ORROR gave way to incredulous relief as Vali
stared down at the small gray-and-white ball of fur
now wrapping itself eagerly around her ankles,
humming in a low, welcoming purr.

"Trouble!"

The knife fell from her hand, clattering onto the wooden floor.
The cat jumped, darted an accusing look at her owner, then raced
from the room.

Vali didn't know whether to laugh or cry. Relief continued to
pour over her as she stood shaking, as much from a sense of her
own foolishness as from her earlier panic.

She went into the living room, where she found Trouble huddled under the piano bench, watching her. "Bad kitty!" Vali
scolded, but only halfheartedly. She was too relieved to be angry
with her small companion.

She was positive now that she had simply left the back door
unlocked. One of Trouble's favorite tricks was to insert a paw in
the space underneath a door and pry until the door opened.
Obviously, the cat had let herself in.

With a rueful smile, Vali remembered other times the kitten
had maneuvered herself into a closet or a room using the same
trick.

But could she have shut the closet door behind her?

Vali glanced back toward the bedroom. It was possible, she reassured herself. Trouble was always doing things other cats never seemed to think of.

But shutting a closet door?

Determined to shake off the unease still plaguing her, Vali went back to the couch and sat down. She was no longer in the mood to read, so she reached for the television's remote control.

Unexpectedly, the telephone beside the couch rang. Vali jumped, stared at the phone for a moment, then lifted the receiver.

"You should be more careful about locking your doors, Vali."

The voice was a harsh, unpleasant whisper. Startled, Vali jerked the receiver away from her ear, staring at it as though it were a snake about to strike.

She waited, drawing in a long breath before lifting the receiver to her ear again.

"Don't worry about it, Vali. I'm going to be looking after you tonight . . . *all* night. I'll be right there with you."

Vali's throat seemed paralyzed. She tried to speak but could only choke out a strangled sob.

"Be sure to keep your doors locked until I get there, Vali. But don't worry about waiting up for me. I'll let myself in . . . just as I did earlier. By the way, did you ever find that troublesome cat of yours?"

Vali slammed down the receiver, her entire body shaking violently.

The phone rang almost immediately.

She covered her ears with her hands, staring at the telephone in horror.

The phone went on ringing for a full two minutes before it stopped, leaving an ominous silence in the cottage.

Vali looked around the room, then went to the large picture window. She edged the drapes back enough to peer out, but saw nothing. Suddenly she remembered the broken air conditioner— and the open bedroom window.

As she was on her way to the bedroom, the telephone started ringing again.

Frantic, she ran into the bedroom, cranked the casement window shut, and locked it.

The phone was still ringing.

Her back to the wall, Vali stood staring numbly through the open doorway, across the hall into the living room.

Make it stop, Lord . . . please make it stop. . . .

Finally there was silence. Vali pushed away from the wall and went to check the kitchen window, then the door, even though she had locked it only minutes earlier.

She had to think. She stood in the middle of the kitchen, then remembered the small jalousie window in the bathroom and hurried back across the hall to check it.

The kitten trailed behind her, curious and wanting to play. She pounced at Vali's feet and ran between her legs, tripping her. "Stop it, Trouble!" Vali screamed, and the cat fled back to the living room.

The front door . . . had she locked it?

She went to check and found both the lock and the dead bolt secure.

No one could get in. She was safe.

Unless they wanted in badly enough to break a window.

Should she turn out the lights?

No. He might think she'd gone to bed. She wanted him to know she was awake and watching. Besides, she couldn't spend the rest of the night in the dark. She would go crazy.

She had to call the police. Now.

The jangle of the telephone made every muscle in her body go into spasms again.

She yanked the receiver off the hook. *"Stop it!"* she screamed.

"I hope you've found your naughty kitten by now, Vali. I put her in the closet for you so she couldn't run away again. You have such pretty things in your closet, Vali. I especially like the pink silk dress. It's real silk, isn't it? It must feel cool and soft against your skin."

Sobbing, Vali threw the receiver against the table.

Then the lights went out.

Vali panicked, cried out, then dropped to the floor, crouching in a terrified huddle against the back of the couch. Her pulse was out of control, her breathing labored in the inky darkness.

Trouble came padding noiselessly over to her, nuzzling Vali's clenched hands and purring softly as she pressed her small head into her owner's lap.

Call someone while you still can . . . call the police.

She wouldn't be able to see the number in the dark. . . .

Try to find it . . . call the Kaines . . . call Leda.

Yes! She knew Leda's number by heart. She would call her, and Leda would send the police.

She began to crawl around the couch, fumbling for the receiver. It was dangling over the side of the table. She got to her feet, grasping the receiver with a shaking hand.

The phone was dead.

Now she was completely cut off from any hope of help. She was alone. Alone in the dark.

She picked up the telephone, yanked it out of the wall connection, and hurled it across the room.

Something moved outside, close to the wall of the cottage. Then something snapped, as if someone had stepped on a branch.

Vali whipped around.

The knife . . . what had she done with the knife?

Something began to scrape softly at the screened window, slowly, then faster, rougher, louder. The scraping gave way to a brutal pounding against the outside wall. The banging grew louder and more frenzied, until the very walls seemed to shake.

Vali backed away, her gaze riveted on the wall. Slowly she slid down the wall, her hands covering her ears, as she sobbed in mute appeal.

The pounding went on and on. Even with her ears tightly covered, Vali could still hear it, could feel the vibrations, her body shaking with every *thud*.

She screamed once more in desperation, then sat huddled weakly against the wall, waiting.

Help me . . . oh, please, please, help me. . . .

ELEVEN

JENNIFER set a cup of hot tea on the table in front of Vali. "Drink this, Vali," she urged softly. "Is there anything else I can get for you?"

Vali shook her head and squinted against the morning sunshine. She lifted the cup with a trembling hand, spilling some of the tea before it reached her lips.

Sunny stirred restlessly as Dan drummed his fingers on the table—the only sound in the kitchen. Jennifer had a fleeting, unpleasant sensation of the stillness of a house after a death. It was as if, given the extraordinary circumstances of the night before, an ordinary level of noise would have been intolerable.

Graham Alexander stood directly behind Vali, his hands resting protectively on her shoulders. His mother sat beside Vali, studying the younger woman's face with maternal concern, absently patting her hand from time to time in a reassuring gesture.

Leda Alexander had been a surprise to Jennifer. The Greek-born novelist looked to be in her early fifties. She was short and attractive, with dark hair and olive-toned skin. Instead of the cosmopolitan sophisticate Jennifer had expected, the internationally acclaimed novelist was slightly overweight and plainly dressed, and gave off an unaffected air of common sense and comfort. Her warm smile and direct manner had immediately put Jennifer at ease. Without question, she found Graham's mother far easier to like than her son.

Jennifer had to admit, however, that Graham's concern seemed genuine enough. "We're deeply indebted to you and your wife, Mr. Kaine," he was saying. "If you hadn't been worried enough to come over here last night and check on Vali, there's no telling what might have happened."

Dan quickly dismissed the man's gratitude with a slight shake of his head. "I'm just sorry we had to break down Vali's door. But as we explained to her last night, when she didn't answer the phone, we had the operator check her line; we were almost certain she was here. When the operator said the line was out of order, we thought we should make sure she was all right."

Jennifer drew up a chair beside Dan, continuing where he left off. "We were just so worried about you, Vali. And when you didn't come to the door, I really got scared. We were afraid you might be hurt and need help. That's when Daniel decided to break in."

Vali finally spoke, her voice halting and uncertain. "Please, Daniel . . . don't apologize again for the door. I don't know what I would have done if . . . you hadn't come when you did. I'm so grateful to you . . . and to Jennifer . . . for taking me back to your cottage."

"Yes, that was awfully kind of you," Leda Alexander put in. "And I can't thank you enough for calling us first thing this morning."

"But Vali . . . dear . . ." Jennifer looked up to find Graham Alexander frowning down at Vali. "What I don't understand is why you didn't simply answer the door when the Kaines arrived."

Jennifer saw Vali tense even more.

"I told you, Graham, I—I suppose I must have panicked. I was terrified by then!"

Graham nodded his head knowingly, darting an "I told you so" glance at his mother.

Leda, however, seemed unaware of her son's pointed look. "Of course you were, darling. Anyone would have been."

Graham sounded less convinced. "But surely you recognized Mr. Kaine's—*Daniel's*—voice, dear."

Vali darted an embarrassed glance at Dan and Jennifer. "I should have . . . I know . . . but I was so frightened. . . ."

Graham nodded with no apparent conviction, patting her gently on top of her head as though she were an unreliable child. "It's all right, dear. We understand."

Jennifer was surprised to see anger spark in Vali's eyes as she turned to look at him. "No, I don't think you do, Graham! You weren't here—you couldn't possibly know what it was like for me!"

The scientist lifted a disapproving eyebrow but said nothing.

"I didn't *imagine* it, Graham!"

"Vali," Graham's mother quickly interrupted, "Graham knows that. He's just concerned for you, darling. We both are. Now—" she squeezed Vali's hand and smiled at her— "I want you to throw some things in your overnighter. You can spend a few days with me until the police get this awful thing straightened out."

Vali looked at Leda uncertainly. "I don't know, Leda . . . I don't think—"

"Mother's right, Vali," Graham said firmly. "You can't possibly stay here until we get the door repaired and police take care of—this other business."

"But Graham, I don't want—"

"Vali? You in here?"

Without waiting for a reply, David Nathan Keye walked in, stopping in the doorway of the kitchen. In one hand he held a bouquet of rosebuds wrapped in green floral paper.

His dark gray eyes took in each person in the room for an instant before finally coming to rest on Vali.

"Well," David said, "I was about to wish you a happy birthday, but it looks as if the party's already begun. What happened to the front door?"

Jennifer turned to Vali. "Today is your birthday? And you haven't said a word!"

David crossed the room and, with a low bow and a wide, sweeping motion, presented the bouquet to Vali. "Happy birthday, Princess."

Jennifer looked at Graham Alexander, whose features had tightened to a hard, unpleasant mask.

David, too, flicked an indifferent glance at the scientist, then greeted Leda with what appeared to be genuine warmth. Finally he returned his attention to Vali.

"Thank you, David," she said softly, pushing her chair away from the table and starting to rise. "I'll put these in water."

But Leda Alexander stopped her with a restraining hand. "I'll do it, darling. You rest." Getting to her feet, she stopped for a moment to give David a peculiar look. "Vali had some trouble here last night. She's terribly upset."

The composer dropped to one knee beside Vali. "What kind of trouble? What happened?"

Graham answered for Vali. "I don't think Vali needs to go into the details again," he said coldly. "It will only make it more difficult for her."

David ignored him. "Vali?" he prompted, covering her hand with his own.

Vali glanced up at Graham, then turned back to David. "Someone . . . someone was in the cottage last night."

"What?" The composer's mouth went hard.

Vali described to him then, in her soft, hesitant voice, the events of the night before. When she was done, David gently released her hand and stood.

"You've called the police?" David asked, looking at Graham.

The scientist bristled. "Of course we called the police," he answered caustically. "They've already been here. When you arrived, we were about to help Vali get some of her things packed so she can spend a few days with my mother."

David looked from Graham to Vali. "Is that what you want to do, Princess?"

"I . . . I suppose," Vali said, not meeting David's gaze but instead staring woodenly down at her lap. As she spoke, she hugged her arms tightly against her body. "I can't stay here until the door is fixed."

David nodded and once again dropped down beside her. "Is there anything I can do, Vali? Any way I can help?"

Jennifer's throat tightened at the way the composer's gaze went over Vali's face. *He adores her,* she realized. *He truly does love her.*

The thought gave her no satisfaction. She still felt a sense of apprehension about Keye, in spite of his undeniable charm and apparent devotion to Vali. It puzzled her, how she could like him— and she did—yet at the same time not completely trust him.

It occurred to her that Vali might be better off without *either* of the two men who seemed so intent on claiming her affection. David Nathan Keye made Jennifer uncomfortable; she couldn't quite shake the feeling he was hiding something. As for Graham Alexander—well, she simply didn't like the man. Not a very Christian sentiment, but there it was. She thought him cold, arrogant, and decidedly overbearing.

The scientist's frosty, precise voice abruptly pierced her thoughts. "Vali said you were out of town, David. When, exactly, did you return?"

The composer glanced up at Alexander, studying him for a long moment. "I was in Nashville, Graham. And I returned just this morning." He got to his feet, his eyes glinting with challenge. "Why do you ask?"

Graham Alexander scrutinized the musician with a raking stare.

"The man who called Vali last night spoke in what she described as a . . . hoarse whisper."

The underlying accusation hung tensely between them. No one spoke as the two men glared at each other. David's face was ashen, but he continued to meet the other's look with a steady gaze of his own. "A common enough method of disguising your voice, I believe," he said. "One that's used rather frequently, I imagine."

Something flared in Graham Alexander's eyes, then subsided. He shrugged, and the tension was broken.

"Vali," Graham said solicitously, moving from behind her chair to interpose himself between her and David, "let Mother help you pack now. We need to get you settled so you can rest. I'll see to it that your door is repaired as soon as possible."

"And the phone, too," Vali reminded him.

"The phone?" David looked questioningly from Vali to Graham.

"The line was cut," Graham answered curtly.

David blanched, but he remained silent.

"Vali, darling," Leda began, "this was supposed to be a surprise, but I'm going to tell you now because there's no way I can keep it a secret all afternoon if you go home with me. Besides, I think you'll want your new friends to know."

She smiled at Dan and Jennifer, then explained, "I had planned a small party for this evening—to celebrate Vali's birthday."

"Oh, Leda—I don't want—"

"I knew you wouldn't *want*." Leda waved away Vali's objection. "That's why it was going to be a surprise. Just us, and Graham and David, of course. And Jeff Daly."

Graham gave her a clearly disapproving look. "You're still seeing him?"

His mother flushed, then countered, "As often as possible, Graham."

He pursed his lips but said nothing.

"Anyway," Leda continued, "now that you know, Vali, I thought you might like Daniel and Jennifer to come, too." She smiled at Jennifer and added, "If you can, that is."

Jennifer glanced at Dan, who seemed to sense her question. "It's up to you, love," he said.

"We wouldn't want to intrude on a family evening," Jennifer said hesitantly.

"Oh, but you wouldn't be," Leda insisted. "We'd love to have you."

"Please, Jennifer," Vali added. "I'd really like for you and Daniel to come."

"Mother, the Kaines are on their honeymoon, I believe," Graham Alexander put in. "We're making it difficult for them to refuse, but I hardly think they'd be interested in a family dinner."

Jennifer was surprised when Daniel settled the issue. "We'll be there." Rising from his chair, he added, "But I think we'd better be going now."

Jennifer got up and, after studying Vali's forlorn expression for a moment, walked over and impulsively gave her a hug. "We'll see you tonight, Vali. Try to get some rest."

She could have wept at the look of gratitude that washed over the singer's face. She wished she could just bundle Vali up and take her home with her and Daniel. She guessed Vali Tremayne to be within a year or two of her own age, and yet at times the sad young woman evoked a protective instinct in Jennifer nearly as strong as her maternal affection for little Jason.

David walked out with Dan and Jennifer, with Sunny in the lead. "I'm glad you're coming tonight," he said. "Vali's really very fond of both of you."

"She's so special," Jennifer said quickly. "I just wish last night had never happened. It must have been a nightmare for her."

"How . . . was she?" David asked hesitantly. "When you finally found her?"

Jennifer evaded his question, uncertain as to how much she ought to tell him.

But Daniel surprised her with his candor. "She was hysterical," he said quietly but with conviction. "It took at least ten minutes just to get her calmed down enough to find out what happened."

Jennifer watched Keye carefully but couldn't gauge his response to Daniel's words.

"But . . . you do believe her?" asked the composer.

"Believe her?" Daniel repeated.

"That it actually happened."

"Oh, it happened all right," Daniel replied. "She was terrified." He paused, then said even more emphatically, "Vali didn't imagine it. Someone scared her almost witless."

"And the phone lines *had* been cut, David," Jennifer reminded him.

The musician raked an unsteady hand through his already tousled hair. Jennifer suddenly noticed how weary he looked.

"David, do you have any idea who could be behind this?" asked Dan. "Has Vali been having any particular problems with someone lately? Someone who might be trying to terrorize her?"

"Vali?" David gave a short, voiceless laugh. "No, certainly not. For one thing, she's almost a recluse. She sees no one but me, Graham, and Leda, except when she goes to church—and even there, she avoids any real contact. Besides, Vali would walk a mile out of her way to avoid causing offense. No," he repeated tersely, "I can assure you that whatever is going on, it's none of Vali's doing."

Dan said nothing for a moment. When he finally spoke, his tone was faintly puzzled. "It seems to me that whoever was responsible for last night had no intention of hurting Vali. It was more a deliberate attempt to frighten her." Another thought seemed to strike him, and he added, "You know, I wouldn't be surprised if our runaway carousel wasn't the same kind of incident."

"Daniel, do you really think someone would go to that much trouble just to scare Vali?" Jennifer asked in surprise.

"I think it's possible," Daniel replied. Jennifer glanced at David Nathan Keye, disturbed by the intense gaze he had fastened on Daniel. As if the composer suddenly realized she was watching him, he looked away, whispered an abrupt good-bye, then started down the beach toward his house.

TWELVE

L EDA Alexander lived in a Gothic house right off the pages of a Victorian novel. It loomed in shrouded, mysterious dignity on a corner lot in one of Sandusky's oldest and most graciously restored neighborhoods. Jennifer took one long look at its gables and towers above the wraparound veranda and sighed longingly.

"Is that a sigh of appreciation or envy?" Dan asked as they started up the long, narrow walkway to the front door.

"Both. It's *wonderful,* Daniel! It looks like a giant dollhouse."

Before Jennifer could press the bell, the massive oak door with its stained glass panels was thrown open. Vali stood just inside, smiling warmly at the two of them.

She goes with the house, Jennifer thought.

In a flowered dress with long sleeves and a high neckline, Vali looked exquisitely feminine—and extremely young. The two men in her life had already arrived and were standing behind her, much like sentries at the castle gate.

Graham, impressively well groomed and proper as always, had exchanged his customary suit for a navy pullover and tan slacks. His polite-but-distant smile was firmly in place as Jennifer and Dan entered.

David, in a pair of white jeans and his usual striped shirt, looked comfortable but still tired, Jennifer noticed. He grinned at her, then pulled a stick of gum from his shirt pocket.

Jennifer was describing the spacious, ornate entry hall to Daniel when Leda Alexander appeared. Brushing away a smudge of flour from her nose, she dried her hands on a kitchen towel. "Where's your dog, Daniel?" she asked in her blunt, strident voice.

"We left her at the cottage. I wasn't sure whether we ought to bring her along."

"Oh, she wouldn't be a problem at all!" Leda insisted. "I should have thought to include her in the invitation. I like dogs."

"That's all right. We really can't stay too long."

"I don't think we want to hear that," the novelist said, firmly grasping his arm. "Let's go into the library. I put the snacks and punch in there." She flashed a quick smile at Jennifer before turning to guide Dan through the large double doors off the hall.

"What a wonderful room!" Jennifer exclaimed as they entered the library. A tasteful blend of fine hardwood, massive furniture, velvet drapes, and intricate cornices, the room was sumptuous with rich, deep colors of rose and gold. It apparently served as a combination study and music room. Floor-to-ceiling bookcases were filled to capacity. A concert-size ebony grand piano dominated a large space at the far end of the room, dwarfing a nearby electronic keyboard and a music cabinet.

Leda stopped at a giant sideboard heaped with a variety of snacks and two towering punch bowls. "Here, Daniel—we've arrived at the food. I'll run down the list, and you can tell me what you'd like."

Appreciating the novelist's direct, comfortable attitude toward Daniel's blindness, Jennifer offered, "I can do that, Leda. I already know without asking what he'll want."

With an interested smile, Dan inclined his head toward his wife. "Tell *me*, why don't you?"

"Well, for starters, Daniel, there's an enormous bowl of shrimp." His eyes widened, and so did his smile.

"Oh, Vali—I almost forgot." Jennifer reached in her purse

and pulled out a small gift-wrapped package. "For your birthday," she said.

With a shy word of thanks, Vali took the gift and placed it on a long library table with some others. Then, at Leda's instructions, she went to get ice for the punch, taking Graham with her to fetch the coffee urn from the kitchen.

"Leda, Leda, you made *baklava!*" David stared down at a large tray of pastry, his eyes glinting with anticipation.

"Baklava?" Daniel repeated.

"It's a Greek pastry," Leda explained. "Have one."

Daniel bit into one of the delicate sweets, and his face lit up with pleased surprise. "Mmm. I've never tasted anything like this. Did you make it yourself, Leda?"

"Yes. It takes forever. I used to make it more often. It was one of Paul's favorites. . . ." She stopped, glanced away for an instant, then brightened. "I'm glad you like it, Daniel. You and Jennifer can take some home with you tonight."

"I thought Jeff was coming," David said, reaching for a second pastry.

Leda glanced at the doorway Graham had just exited. "He had planned to be here, but he called about an hour ago to say he isn't going to make it. A former client is in Port Clinton, and they're having dinner tonight." She turned to Dan and Jennifer. "Jeff is my next-door neighbor," she explained. "He's an attorney."

David gave Jennifer a conspiratorial wink. "Just moved in this summer, and already he's fallen for the girl next door."

Leda colored and darted a warning look at David.

He grinned at her. "Hey—I'm cheering you on. A good man is hard to find, Leda. Go for it."

The author shook her head in hopeless resignation, but Jennifer noticed that the smile she gave David was affectionate. "Well, it will save Graham from glaring at the poor man all evening, anyway," she said wryly.

"Graham just hasn't accepted the fact," David said archly, "that his mother is still a young and attractive woman."

"That will get you all the *baklava* you want, young man," Leda said with a droll smile. She turned to Jennifer. "I think what Graham can't accept is my being interested in anyone other than his father. My husband died several years ago. Farrell was a wonderful man, but it *has* been a long time. . . ." She shook her head. "I can never predict Graham. Paul was always easier," she said with a sigh. "Graham has always been so . . . complicated. But, then, they say he's a genius. I don't suppose there's any such thing as an uncomplicated genius."

A few minutes later, Jennifer tugged at Dan's arm and led him down to the other end of the room. "This piano is magnificent, Daniel." The lid was closed, but she couldn't resist touching the top of it gently. It was obviously an instrument crafted by experts.

Leda came to stand beside them. "This was Paul's piano," she said softly. "After the accident . . . I had it brought here." She paused. "Vali says you're both familiar with Paul's music."

Daniel nodded with a sad smile. "Familiar with it—and in awe of it. If your one son is a scientific genius, your other son was a musical genius, Mrs. Alexander."

"Please—call me Leda. Yes, I think you're right about Paul—he was definitely gifted," she said with quiet pride. "He was also a good son. A fine man."

Seeing the older woman's eyes mist, Jennifer reached out to touch her arm. "It was a terrible loss for you."

Leda gave a small shake of her head. "Yes. And for many." She turned toward the opposite end of the room, where Vali stood talking with Graham.

After a moment, Leda began to herd everyone into the dining room for cake and ice cream. Two enormous sheet cakes rested in the middle of a long walnut table. One was lavishly decorated and heaped high with fresh strawberries. The other was plain, with white frosting and candy flowers.

Vali exclaimed with pleasure as she bent over the strawberry-topped cake. "Oh, Leda! It's absolutely beautiful!"

Leda laughed at her enthusiasm. "This child is positively wild about strawberries," she explained to Jennifer and Dan. "But I had to make another cake for Graham—he's allergic to them."

At Leda's request, David asked the blessing. For some reason, Jennifer wasn't surprised to catch a glimpse of Graham Alexander's look of mild scorn just before the composer began to pray.

Leda cut the strawberry cake, first handing a generous piece to Vali.

"No candles, Mother?" Graham asked.

"Oh dear, I forgot!" Leda looked flustered.

Vali laughed and reached to squeeze the older woman's shoulder. "I don't need candles! Just give me the strawberries!"

Leda cut another piece, put it on a plate, and offered it to David, who hesitated, then shook his head. "I'm afraid I'll have to share Graham's cake. I don't tolerate strawberries very well, either."

Leda raised her eyes to his face. "Well, David—so you and Graham *do* have something in common after all, even if it is only an allergy." A look of dry amusement crossed her face.

David stared at her for a moment. A hint of mischief gleamed in his eyes, and he said, "I think Graham and I have more in common than you might realize, Leda."

The novelist lifted her dark brows. "Mm. Yes, that's likely so," she agreed, glancing at her son, who stood behind Vali, looking as if his face had been chiseled from stone.

After they had eaten, Vali opened her presents. Conspicuous by its absence was a gift from Graham. Jennifer wondered about this until she saw him draw Vali to one side. "My gift for you is private, dear," he said quietly. "I'll give it to you tomorrow night at dinner, when we're alone." Vali paled at his words, appearing to be more disturbed than pleased.

It was David's gift, wrapped in a thin package resembling a stationery box, that seemed to give Vali the most pleasure.

With a puzzled smile, Vali unwrapped it and lifted a few sheets of paper from within, staring at them for a long time before finally lifting her eyes to look at David, perched on a hassock. "You wrote this for me?"

He studied her expression anxiously, then smiled at her. "With a title like *Vali's Song,* it must be for you."

They continued to stare at each other. Jennifer couldn't resist a covert glance at Graham Alexander. His face was crimson, his mouth a tight line, his eyes glazed with what could only be anger.

Leda broke the silence. "What a nice thing to do, David! But this is a gift that's meant to be shared, Vali. Won't you sing it for us, darling?"

Vali cast a startled glance at the older woman. "Oh—I don't think so. . . ."

David rose and, still smiling, closed the distance between them. He took Vali's hand, coaxing her out of her chair. "Leda's right, Princess. That magnificent voice of yours is meant to be shared." His eyes never left her face. "Sing your song for us, Vali. Please."

Everyone but Graham added their own appeal to David's. Vali hesitated. Her gaze traveled to the piano at the other end of the room. Finally, she seemed to make her decision, squaring her shoulders and giving Leda a ghost of a smile. "I haven't sung for anyone other than David for so long—"

"What better time to begin than now, when you're surrounded by people who care for you—and with a song that was written just for you?" Leda asked softly.

Gently, David urged her toward the piano, the others following.

"Will you play it for me first?" Vali asked him as he propped the lid on the piano.

David smiled at her and eased himself onto the piano bench.

When Vali would have handed him the music, he shook his head, smiling as he began humming, then running through a sampling of chord progressions with no particular pattern. He stopped once, glancing up at Leda as if a thought had just struck him. "Are you sure it isn't going to bother you—my playing Paul's piano?"

Leda met his gaze. "No, Paul allowed all his friends to use the piano. Even their children." She gave him a small, sad smile. "He always said . . . that a musical instrument was worthless when it was silent."

Jennifer saw the composer study Leda's face with a look of tenderness and understanding. Then his hands began to caress the keys with the touch of a master, finally settling into a plaintive, haunting melody. "This is your song, Vali," he said at last, the music flowing effortlessly.

At first, Vali merely scanned the music as David played. But it wasn't long before she began to sway gently with the rhythm. Soon she began to hum, then sing the words, faintly at first, then with more strength and assurance. Finally, the unforgettable voice that had made her famous began to wrap its incredible power and richness around the melody.

Jennifer clung to Daniel's hand, holding her breath as she listened to the voice that had once thrilled her on recordings. She heard Dan sigh with admiration and knew he shared her feelings.

The song was achingly beautiful, an unforgettable tribute to the singer that stopped just short, Jennifer thought, of being a love song. When it was over, there was a long silence before everyone—everyone but Graham—exploded into applause and mingled outbursts of appreciation.

Jennifer glanced at David and caught her breath at the expression on his face. She knew she would never forget the depth of emotion she saw in that look—the inexplicable pain, but most of all, the love. At that moment, Jennifer knew that, whatever else David Nathan Keye might be, he was, above all else, a man consumed by love.

Everyone begged for more, and Vali complied, although with some hesitancy at first. The longer she sang, however, the more she seemed to respond to the music. Like a rose that had been buried in the snow over a long winter, the young singer opened herself one petal at a time, revealing what seemed to be a limitless supply of ability and incredible power. Jennifer stood in dazed awe, knowing she was watching the renewal of a talent only God could have created.

She was so absorbed in the event taking place before her eyes that she was startled when Vali, still singing, wedged herself between Jennifer and Daniel and tugged them closer to the piano. David, grinning his approval, kept playing but told Dan, "Have a piano, Daniel. I'll furnish the orchestra." He then slid smoothly from the bench, at the same time guiding Dan onto it before turning to the electronic keyboard nearby.

Dan moved effortlessly into the song David had been playing without missing more than a beat.

Vali linked her arm through Jennifer's. "This act needs a little harmony, Jennifer—and your husband says you're a great singer. Help me out."

Jennifer stared at Vali in astonishment. "I couldn't sing with *you!*"

"Hey—I'm not so bad," Vali teased. "Come on, let's try."

Their banter was lost in a thundering, driving cadence from the keyboard. Dan took his cue from David, jumping quickly into the upbeat, rousing tempo of a popular contemporary number. Dumbfounded at the position she now found herself in, Jennifer nevertheless launched into the song, surprised at how easy it was for her to fall into harmony with Vali.

Wait until our folks hear about this! she thought, almost overcome with excitement.

They sang for the next twenty minutes. Jennifer, though she had originally been trained in operatic music, was an avid devotee of Christian contemporary and knew every song Vali ran by her. She didn't miss Graham Alexander's glare of disapproval throughout the entire time, but she was having too much fun to care. They stopped only once, to enjoy a friendly duel between Dan and David at their respective keyboards.

Daniel was a highly trained musician with a wealth of natural ability, and Jennifer felt herself about to explode with the pride and pleasure of watching him hold his own with one of the foremost musicians in the industry. David challenged him playfully, throwing one variation after another at him, each of which Dan met easily with an improvisation of his own. Finally, they blended their instruments together and broke into a medley of well-known praise numbers, bringing Jennifer and Vali back into the music, and ending at last with Dan and even Leda singing along.

When they were done, Leda grabbed Vali and embraced her, weeping unashamedly. "It's been so long, darling, . . . so long!"

Only Graham stood back, watching with an expression of open displeasure.

Finally David turned off the keyboard and reached to shake Dan's hand. "Daniel, you belong in the business! You're *good,* man! Really good."

Dan's smile was modest but pleased. "Thanks, but I believe I'm right where I belong. I have everything any man could ever hope for—and more." He turned his head in Jennifer's direction. "Much more."

David glanced from one to the other. "Well, I hope you'll at least keep up with your writing. Give us another *Daybreak.*"

"I didn't actually write *Daybreak* because I wanted to, David," Dan said, rising from the piano bench. "I wrote it because I *had* to. The truth is, I had never even thought of writing music. The station has been my ministry for years."

"The station and your counseling," Jennifer reminded him.

David studied Dan curiously. "What kind of counseling?"

"I just finished up a degree in Christian counseling a few weeks ago," Dan explained. "Mostly I work with the blind."

"What a full life you have, Daniel," Vali said softly. "I don't know how you manage everything."

"I don't." Dan grinned and motioned to Jennifer at his side. "She does the managing." His expression turned serious. "One thing's for sure, Vali," he said. "There can't be any doubt about *your* ministry. What an absolutely incredible gift God has given you."

At that point, Graham stepped in, wrapping his arm possessively around Vali's shoulders. "We're all aware of that, Daniel," he said stiffly. "However, the frenzied pace of her career hasn't always been . . . healthy for Vali. That's why it's so important that she take her time and not rush into anything."

Jennifer saw an expression flicker across Dan's face, but his voice revealed nothing. "I can understand that."

David, watching the exchange, flashed an impish smile at Graham. "Ah, Graham . . . ever the careful, analytical scientist. We emotional musician types must really frustrate you."

"The world needs all kinds," Graham returned smoothly.

David lifted both eyebrows in mock surprise, obviously readying his comeback.

As if she sensed a confrontation brewing, Leda broke in. "Graham, would you and David help me for a moment, please? I need to move the sideboard back into the dining room."

As soon as Leda and the two men left the room, Vali spoke up.

"Daniel—" she paused, looked at Jennifer, then went on in a soft, hesitant tone— "I was wondering . . . about your counseling. . . ."

Dan nodded, giving her a questioning smile.

"I was wondering . . . would you . . . could I . . . talk with you
. . . sometime?"

Dan looked surprised. "Vali, most of my experience has been
with people who are disabled in some way—particularly the
blind."

Vali didn't reply immediately. When she finally spoke, her voice
was low and strained. "Daniel, I *am* disabled."

Jennifer touched her lightly on the arm. "Vali, I'll leave so you
can talk to Daniel."

"No," Vali protested. "Please don't." Once more she turned to
Daniel. "Daniel, I need help. There's something wrong . . . with
my mind, I think."

He frowned. "Why would you think that?"

"I'm afraid, Daniel. I'm afraid almost all the time! And I don't
even know what I'm afraid of. I've seen doctors, . . . and I've
prayed for healing. But I never seem to get any better."

Jennifer watched the frail young singer clench and then relax
her hands. The contrast between the dynamic, joyful performer of
a few moments before and the uncertain, faltering girl now staring up at Daniel was almost incomprehensible.

"Vali, it takes a long time before a counselor can really help,"
Dan said kindly. "We'll be going home in a few days."

"I know that," Vali said quickly. "But I thought perhaps you
could at least—" She stopped. "I'm sorry. I can't seem to remember that the two of you are supposed to be on your honeymoon. I
insist on barging into your life, don't I? I'm really sorry—please
forget I said anything."

"No, Vali—that's all right." Dan's expression was troubled.
"Listen, I'd be glad to talk with you. I just don't want to mislead
you, that's all."

Vali stared miserably down at the floor.

"Vali—," Dan pressed gently, "will you be coming back to your cottage soon, do you think?"

"Tomorrow, I hope. If everything is repaired by then."

"When you get back, why don't you give us a call—or just come over. We'll talk, OK?"

"Are you sure, Daniel? I hate asking you, but—"

"It's perfectly all right," Dan assured her. "You're a friend. Right, Jennifer?"

Jennifer caught Vali's hand. "Daniel's right. You're not imposing at all, Vali. We want to help if we can."

She stopped, startled by Graham Alexander's sudden reappearance.

"I couldn't help but overhear part of your conversation," he said, his voice hard as he came to stand next to Vali. "I must tell you that I think this could be a very risky idea, Vali."

"Graham—please . . ."

"If you feel the need for professional help," he went on in the same cold tone, "then we should consult a physician. A specialist." He glanced at Dan with obvious pique. "I don't want to be rude or denigrate your competence, Mr. Kaine, but as you pointed out to Vali, you'll be leaving soon."

He turned back to Vali then, and Jennifer had never seen him look quite as stern as he did at that moment. "I do wish you had discussed this with me, dear."

At that moment, David walked up. "Is there any particular reason why she should have?"

Alexander bristled noticeably. "This is none of your business, Keye!"

Seemingly unruffled, David clucked his tongue and gave the other a wicked grin. "Careful, Graham. You're going to show some emotion here, if you don't watch it."

"You insolent—"

"*Stop* it!" It was Leda who put an end to the developing skirmish. "That's enough from both of you," she said sharply. "This is Vali's birthday." She turned to the composer. "David, you're a guest in my home and always a welcome one, so long as you don't upset Vali. And Graham, you may be my son, but the same thing applies to you."

The determined thrust of her chin and her steady, censuring glare silenced both men.

"I'm sorry, Leda," David offered apologetically. "You're absolutely right. I was out of line."

Graham's eyes never left the musician's face as he muttered a grudging, "Sorry, Mother." He then turned to Vali. "But I meant what I said, Vali. Your emotions are too important to toy with. If you're serious about this, there are a couple of excellent men in the area who would accept you as a patient, I'm sure."

"For heaven's sake, Graham, I don't want to commit myself to an asylum! I just want to talk with someone—another Christian, preferably—who might be able to help me sort out my problems."

Graham flinched, but his tight mask of control never slipped. After a long, awkward silence, he said, "We can talk about this tomorrow. I have to leave now; I still have notes to dictate tonight. Will you see me out?"

"I—yes, of course," Vali stammered, moving quickly toward the door without looking at anyone.

As soon as Vali returned to the room, Jennifer and Dan said their good-byes and went to the car.

Jennifer was securing her seat belt when she saw David and Vali walk out onto the porch together. He reached for her hand, said something, then released her and started down the walk toward his Corvette parked at the curb. With a brief wave in Jennifer's direction, he unlocked the car and got in.

Just before she started the car and pulled away, Jennifer looked once more at Vali standing alone on the porch. Again she felt an involuntary tug of concern. She frowned and shook her head as if to banish her increasingly strong feelings of apprehension for Vali Tremayne.

As she turned the corner and headed for the highway, she glanced in the rearview mirror to see the headlights of David's car following close behind. Again, Jennifer wondered about the composer's role in Vali's life. Was he a part of the troubled young woman's problems? Or, although she considered it highly unlikely, could he possibly be a key to the solution?

THIRTEEN

A T ELEVEN o'clock that night, a man uttered a series of curt monosyllables into his telephone receiver. He shifted impatiently in his chair, waiting for a chance to make a statement.

Finally his opportunity came. "I think we need to do something about Kaine and his wife."

There was a long pause. "I thought you said they were harmless."

"That was my first impression. But apparently he's some kind of . . . counselor." The man pulled in a deep breath in irritation and tugged at the collar of his shirt. "Vali seems to think she wants to talk with him . . . privately."

"Why?"

The man glanced nervously around the room, focusing on a small photograph of Vali Tremayne. "Apparently she's feeling the need for help," he replied, his tone caustic.

"What did the blind man tell her?"

"He agreed. I think she's planning on trying to see him sometime tomorrow."

"I knew we should have acted on my original instincts," the voice at the other end of the line snapped.

"No! My way is best. Just keep an eye on the Kaines—I'll take care of the rest of it."

The other man said nothing for a moment. When he finally

spoke again, his voice was oiled with a smirk. "You want her, don't you? You've fallen for her."

"I've never pretended to be indifferent to her."

"That's quite true, you haven't. Up to now, however, you've shown an admirable restraint of your feelings."

"My feelings are my business."

"Only if they don't interfere with the work."

"They never have, have they?"

"Not until recently." He paused. "All right. Continue as you have been, at least for now. We'll take care of the Kaines."

"Be careful. The man is no fool."

"Don't worry, we'll be discreet. Just get on with your part." After a petulant sigh, he added, "All these complications annoy me. You used to be such an easy man to work with. Lately you've become troublesome. *Do* try to be somewhat less tiring, won't you?"

The man hung up, scowling at the photograph beside him. It was true that he wasn't entirely mindless of Vali's appeal. Still, he had no intention whatsoever of allowing her to complicate his life any more than she already had. Like anyone else who got in the way of the work, she was expendable.

FOURTEEN

THE ferry from Catawba to Middle Bass Island wasn't crowded. It was a weekday, and the tourist season was over. Still, several people were aboard, enough to provide a steady hum of conversation.

"I think we're going to have another beautiful day," Jennifer said to Daniel, shading her eyes with one hand as she glanced up into the bright, cloudless sky.

They were sitting on metal benches on the outer deck. Jennifer had tied a bandanna over her hair to protect it from the spray off the lake. Dan held a large picnic basket on his lap.

"What's for lunch?" he asked, tapping the cover of the basket.

"All kinds of good stuff from that deli up the road. Fried chicken, potato salad, ham and cheese, rolls—oh, and a pound cake."

"Mmm. We'll have to take a doggie bag back to Sunny."

"Poor thing, she hasn't had much fun on this trip," Jennifer said, linking her arm through Dan's. "I wish now we had brought her along. But it would have been awkward, with the ferry and going biking and all."

Dan pulled his mouth into a skeptical line. "We're really going to do this, huh? The tandem bike, I mean."

"That's the best way to see the island, Daniel."

"I can't *see* the island, Jennifer," he reminded her dryly. "And you've already seen it. So why can't we just walk around for a while and then eat?"

"Biking is good exercise, Daniel. You were grumbling just yesterday about needing exercise." She patted her abdomen. "And so do I. You're not worried about riding a bike, are you?"

He grinned. "You're probably the one who should be worried, darlin'. Having me along may cramp your style just a little."

"Not a chance. It'll be fun. And romantic. There's something very romantic about a bicycle built for two."

"Jennifer, take my word for it. There is nothing even remotely romantic about a grown man taking a tumble into the bushes. Even if the woman he loves is tumbling right behind him."

"Daniel, any man who isn't afraid to ride the *Magnum* can't possibly be intimidated by a bicycle."

"Wanna bet?"

She elbowed him and turned to survey their fellow passengers. Directly across from them sat two young Asian men with cameras strapped around their necks. On the same row of seats were an elderly man and woman. The woman had little round wire-rimmed glasses perched on an upturned nose and was smiling at Jennifer wisely, as if she could tell she was a newlywed.

Jennifer returned the woman's smile, then let her gaze move farther up the deck. A middle-aged man with a briefcase was reading a science fiction paperback. A few seats away, three college-age girls were deep in conversation.

Had her attention not been caught by the flaming red hair of one of the girls, she probably would never have noticed the man standing close to them. Her admiring glance went from the fiery curls of the coed to the glistening bald dome of the man towering above her. He looked familiar somehow, and when he moved, Jennifer caught a better glimpse of his profile.

She gasped, staring at him with astonishment. *He looked like the man she had seen at Cedar Point!* Unexpectedly, he moved toward the corner of the deck and disappeared. Jennifer got up, her gaze scanning the deck. But the man was nowhere in sight.

"Jennifer?" Dan called in a puzzled voice.

Jennifer went back and sat down, immediately searching the passengers again for some glimpse of the burly, bald-headed stranger.

"Honey? Is something wrong?"

Hearing the troubled note in Daniel's voice, Jennifer took his hand, hurrying to reassure him. "No, nothing," she said. "I thought I saw someone I knew, but I was wrong."

Still, she continued to study the other passengers, half hoping she wouldn't see the man again, yet at the same time disturbed that she had seen him at all—and that he had managed to disappear so quickly.

꧁꧂

"Well—did you or didn't you enjoy the bicycle ride?" Jennifer asked smugly as she pitched their napkins and paper plates into a nearby trash receptacle.

Dan stood up, gave a huge stretch, and yawned. "It was an experience, I have to admit."

"Is this the first time you've been on a bike since the accident?"

He nodded. "Gabe has tried to talk me into it a couple of times, but I didn't take to the idea."

"But you do so many other things," she pointed out. "You told me you go horseback riding with the kids at the farm. And you bowl. And swim, of course."

"Speaking of swimming—"

"You've already spoken of swimming," Jennifer interrupted. "Several times, as a matter of fact. I'm beginning to think my competition is going to be a pool."

"You'll never have any competition, darlin'. But you know what they say—if you can't beat 'em . . ."

"So you can laugh me out of the pool again, like you did at Gatlinburg last week? No thanks."

"I didn't laugh at you," Dan insisted, a suspicious hint of a smile playing at the corners of his mouth.

"I told you before we got married that I can't swim like a fish," Jennifer said self-righteously.

"But you *didn't* tell me," he countered with a smirk, "that you still used an inner tube." When Jennifer made no reply, he added, "Don't worry about it. As soon as we get back to Shepherd Valley, you're going to have yourself some private lessons. You'll be Olympic material in no time."

Jennifer rolled her eyes skeptically. "I'll settle for learning how to negotiate a decent front crawl."

Walking around to her side of the picnic table, Dan caught her hand and kissed her lightly on the cheek. "Find me a tree, love."

"A tree?" Jennifer stared at him blankly, then caught on. "You're about to take a nap, right?"

"Ten minutes?"

"I'm wise to your ten-minute snoozes, Daniel. It's like trying to wake a grizzly in December."

Protesting all the way, she guided him to an enormous old cottonwood tree, where both of them dropped to the ground. Dan leaned against the trunk and wrapped his arms around Jennifer. She rested against the broad expanse of his chest, glancing around their surroundings with lazy contentment. The picnic area was a quiet, secluded little glen with warm sunshine trickling through the trees overhead. The air was tangy with the faint, damp smell of the lake. It was a special time and a special place, and at least for now, it belonged only to them.

"Are you happy, Jennifer?" Dan asked quietly, tightening his arms around her.

"Oh, Daniel—if I were any happier, I'd . . . I'd explode!"

He rested his chin on top of her head. "Have I thanked you today for marrying me?"

"Mm. I think so. Once or twice, anyway." Jennifer tipped her head to look up at him. His smile was soft and thoughtful. "What about you, Daniel? Are you happy?"

He pressed his lips to her temple. "Ah, love, . . . 'happy' isn't a big enough word for it." He paused. "You know, before the Lord brought you into my life, I used to wake up every morning after the accident, and for the first few minutes I literally had to *force* myself to face reality, to . . . *condition* my mind all over again to the darkness. Even after five years, it was still hard for me to put on the truth each morning and start all over."

He brushed a gentle kiss into her hair. "But now . . . now I wake up, and I lie there listening to you breathing so soft and easy beside me. I feel your warmth, and I think about our love . . . and I don't mind the darkness anymore. Now I wake up to sunshine every morning."

Jennifer's eyes misted with tears, and she lifted her face for his kiss. Then she sighed and pressed her face against his shoulder. "Oh, Daniel, let's always love each other like this. Let's never, ever let our love get old or stale or—predictable."

He smiled at the depth of emotion in her voice, and there was a light chuckle in his tone when he answered. "Darlin'," he murmured into her hair, "somehow, I find it hard to believe that anything about life with you—or our love—will ever be predictable."

He kissed her again, and Jennifer snuggled close. After several minutes of silence, she turned in his arms to look up at him. "Daniel, what do you think about Vali? Do you think she's right about there being something wrong with her mind?"

He shook his head. "No, I don't think so. Oh, there's something wrong," he added quickly. "But if you're asking me if I think Vali has serious mental problems, no, I don't."

He shook his head. "Every time I'm with Vali," he said thoughtfully, "I get the impression of someone who's extremely insecure, someone with very little self-esteem. David has confirmed my observation, by the way." His tone was gloomy as he went on. "As serious as that can be in itself, I'm not so sure it's the primary problem."

His expression grew even more grim, and Jennifer felt her own concern deepen. "What are you thinking, Daniel?"

"I wish I could see Vali's eyes," he replied slowly. "There's something . . . not quite right about her speech, but I can't put my finger on it. Haven't you noticed that at times her voice has virtually no inflection at all? It's almost as if she's not entirely aware of her own words. There's a certain flatness there that isn't typical. And the way she stumbles over her words. Doesn't that strike you as a little peculiar for a singer?"

Jennifer stared at him. He was right. She would never have realized it on her own, but Dan had just pinpointed one of the things she had found vaguely disconcerting about Vali from the beginning.

"What do you think it means, Daniel?"

"I can't be sure, but one of two things, I think. If only I could see her eyes," he said again, "I could be more certain. That lack of expression and nuance in her voice could indicate a specific emotional problem—I'm thinking of depression. Or she could be on some kind of mood-altering prescription."

Jennifer frowned. "You don't think Vali is taking drugs, do you?"

He shook his head. "Not in the sense you mean. But she could be under a physician's care and taking a prescription drug."

"But you don't think so." Jennifer saw the doubt in his expression. "Do you?"

He hesitated. "I don't think it's likely that Vali would have asked me for help if she were already seeing a doctor for her problems. Besides, Graham made it fairly clear that she isn't."

"Well, whatever it is," Jennifer said with assurance as she settled back into his embrace, "I know you'll be able to help her."

He rubbed his chin across the top of her head. "Don't be so sure, Jennifer. It's not likely I'll have time to even find out what the problem is, much less help her solve it. I only agreed to talk with her because I thought I might be able to convince her to see a doctor who *can* help."

They remained silent for a long time. Jennifer found herself wondering if either of the two men in Vali's life played a part in her emotional struggles, and if so, which one. Or could *both* Graham Alexander and David Nathan Keye somehow be responsible for the troubled young singer's problems?

After a few more minutes, she heard Dan's breathing grow even and shallow. She turned to look up at him, smiling when she saw that he was sound asleep. She kissed him lightly on the cheek, then burrowed more comfortably into his arms for a short nap of her own.

Half an hour later, the man with the field glasses saw them get up, tie their windbreakers around their waists, and stow their picnic supplies in the bicycle basket. After a quick look around the area, they got on the tandem bike, the blind man on the seat in back of the woman.

The man lowered the field glasses and sprinted to the car parked a few feet away. He cranked the powerful engine to life and pulled out onto the narrow road.

As soon as he had the bike in view, he slowed the car, staying at least a quarter of a mile behind.

He followed at that distance for a few minutes, continuously checking the rearview mirror. There was no one else on the road. He glanced from one side to the other and, seeing no pedestrians, applied a little more pressure to the accelerator, keeping the couple on the bike clearly in sight. Staring straight ahead, he lowered the gas pedal even more, then floored it. The car belched a loud roar and lunged forward, directly toward the tandem bike just ahead.

Jennifer heard the sound of the engine and glanced back over her shoulder to see what was happening. She panicked at the sight of the car closing in on them and uttered a choked cry of alarm. The bike swerved sharply to the left.

"Jennifer? What is it?" Dan put a steadying hand on her shoulder.

Facing forward, Jennifer tried to pedal faster, then turned to look behind them once more. "There's a car—coming straight at us!"

A wave of terror swept through her. The sedan was barreling down on them like an angry black tornado.

For a split second, Jennifer froze and almost lost control of the bike. Her hands began to shake on the handlebars. Her throat constricted with a rising knot of panic.

"Dan—*he's going to hit us!*"

Staring back in shocked disbelief, Jennifer didn't see the deep chuckhole in the road until the bike hit it full force. Stunned, she heard Dan cry out, felt him grab for her, heard the squeal of tires and her own shriek of terror as the bike flew off the road and crashed into a ditch.

The speeding sedan roared past them without slowing. Jennifer caught only a fleeting glimpse of the driver when he snapped his head around to look at them, lying helplessly in the ditch.

It was the same man she had seen at Cedar Point—the same man she thought she had seen on the ferry. The bald man with the eerie, pale eyes.

FIFTEEN

WHEN the phone rang late the next morning, Jennifer was in the bathroom applying ointment to the scratches on her face and arms. She hadn't exaggerated when she told Daniel she looked as if she'd been dragged across a gravel road.

Daniel had somehow emerged from the bicycle crash without a scratch, although he had wrenched his shoulder and bruised a rib or two. He had done his best to absorb most of the fall, holding on to Jennifer and trying to keep her on top as they were thrown into the ditch. But the impact had thrown her away from him at the last minute.

Once the shock wore off, they walked to the bike rental and called the police. The officer who talked with them was polite and concerned, but offered little hope for finding the man who had tried to run them down. Without a license number or specific description of the car, he explained, it would be difficult, if not impossible, to trace the driver.

Only after they returned to the cottage did Jennifer tell Dan that she was positive the driver of the car had been the same man who had aroused her suspicions at Cedar Point. She also confided that she was now fairly certain he had been on the ferry that morning.

Dan had finally admitted that he, too, was beginning to believe there might be a link between the events at the amusement park, the intruder at Vali's cottage, and the incident with the black sedan.

103

He had gone on to explain that he suspected someone of trying to terrorize Vali—or, worse, actually harm her.

Jennifer was still staring at herself in the mirror, thinking about his troubling suspicion, when Dan walked into the bathroom. "Jennifer, are you sure you shouldn't see a doctor?"

"No, really, I'm all right." She replaced the tube of ointment in her travel kit and turned to him. "Who was on the phone?"

"Vali. She wanted to know if she could come over—or if we would mind stopping by. I told her what happened and explained that you're not feeling too great. She's going to walk over here in a few minutes. Is that all right?"

"Yes, of course. But—"

"What?"

Jennifer sighed. "I'm beginning to feel really guilty about all this."

Dan closed the distance between them, taking her hand. "What are you talking about?"

"Daniel, it's all my fault that we got caught up in this. If I hadn't been so curious our first day up here, we probably wouldn't have people trying to run us down."

"That's a little irrational, even for you, sweetheart."

"Daniel—"

He made a gesture to stop her protest. "I mean it, Jennifer. In the first place, we don't know that what happened to us yesterday has anything to do with what's been going on with Vali."

"You think it does," Jennifer said stubbornly.

He put his hands on her shoulders. "Even so, you didn't go looking for trouble."

"Well, whether I went looking for it or not, I've certainly managed to foul up our honeymoon," Jennifer said miserably.

For a moment Dan stood unmoving, as if he were considering her words. Then a trace of a smile touched his lips. "I don't know about you, darlin'," he said softly, framing Jennifer's face between his hands, "but *I* think our honeymoon has been nothing short of wonderful."

Jennifer studied him. "Really, Daniel?"

"Absolutely," he whispered. With infinite tenderness, he scanned her face with his fingertips, a mannerism Jennifer had grown to love. Gently, he brushed a wave of hair away from her cheek. Then, still smiling the sweet, soft little smile that never failed to make her heart spin, he pressed a kiss on her forehead. Jennifer closed her eyes, and he kissed them, too. Then she smiled, and he kissed her lips. Thoroughly.

At last he lifted his face from hers with a little sound of regret.

"Then you're not feeling neglected?" Jennifer murmured.

He touched one finger to her mouth and shook his head. "A little crowded, maybe. Husbands are like that, you know."

"I'm afraid I don't know very much about husbands yet," Jennifer confessed softly into the warmth of his shoulder.

"Ah, you're doing fine, sweetheart," he told her, pressing one more kiss to her cheek. "You're doing just fine."

Dan could hear the strain and uncertainty in Vali's voice almost from the moment she arrived at the cottage. Jennifer, pleading the need to soak her soreness away in a hot tub, left them alone. Even then, Vali avoided her reason for coming. After a few minutes of idle pleasantries, Dan finally took the lead.

"I thought we might hear from you yesterday," he said. "When did you come back to the cottage?"

"Early this morning. The phone was in service again by yesterday morning, but it took longer to get the door fixed."

"I don't imagine it was easy, coming back after that incident with the prowler," Dan said carefully.

"It was awful. I felt . . ." She hesitated.

"Violated?" Dan prompted quietly.

"Yes—that's it exactly! It was as if somebody had intruded not only on my privacy, but on my *self*—my person—as well."

Dan nodded with understanding. "I'm sure you could have stayed with Leda for a few days. She's obviously very fond of you."

"Oh, Leda is wonderful," Vali said quickly. "And I love her as much as if she were my own mother." She stopped, then went on. "At least, I think I do. I never knew my mother."

Over the next few minutes, she explained to Dan that her natural parents had abandoned her when she was still a toddler and that she had grown up in foster homes until, at the age of fourteen, she was adopted by a Nashville policeman and his wife.

Dan knew Vali was still being evasive, but he had been prepared for that.

"Do you still see your adoptive parents?" he asked.

"Uncle Bill—that's what I called him—died just before I graduated from college," Vali explained. "Aunt Mary still lives in Nashville. We talk by phone at least once a week."

Dan leaned back in his chair and smiled. "Vali, what did you mean the other night at Leda's? When you told me you were afraid, but you're not sure what you're afraid of?"

He heard her deep intake of breath, as if she hadn't expected his directness.

"After everything that's happened lately, I'm beginning to think I have even more reason to be frightened than I knew then."

"But that isn't what you meant the other night, is it?" Dan asked gently.

"No," Vali admitted after a long hesitation. "It's just that sometimes—often—I feel afraid. Anxious. Almost . . . terrified." She faltered, then went on. "It's as if I'm expecting something to happen, something awful, something that I can't control. But I don't know what."

Dan frowned. "You say this happens often. How often, Vali?"

"Oh, I don't know . . . maybe once every couple of days. Yes," she said after a moment, "at least that."

"And you have no idea why?"

"No," she replied, sounding forlorn. "I've tried to remember, but—"

Dan interrupted. "Why do you say 'remember'?"

Vali didn't answer right away. When she finally spoke, Dan heard a note of surprise in her voice. "I just realized that whatever it is I dread so terribly . . . it's something that happened a long time ago. Something bad."

Dan was quiet for a long time, lightly rapping his fingers on the tabletop. "Do you remember when you first started to have these anxiety attacks, Vali?"

After a long pause, Vali answered, her voice low. "Yes, I remember. It was. . . ." She stopped, then abruptly asked, "You know about Paul's death—the plane crash?"

Dan nodded.

"After Paul died, I had—they *said* I had—a breakdown. I was in a hospital for months. . . . I don't remember exactly how long."

Dan suddenly became aware of the gradual change in her voice. She was dropping back into the flat, expressionless tone he had heard before. The longer she talked, he noticed, the more pronounced the monotone became.

"After I was well enough to leave the hospital, I stayed with Leda for a few weeks. Then I bought my cottage here at the lake."

"But when did you start feeling so . . . afraid?" Dan prompted gently.

"Afraid?" There was a long silence. When Vali finally spoke, her voice had cleared and sounded stronger. "It was while I was still at Leda's, I think. Yes," she said with more assurance, "it started then. I remember, because I had to start taking the medicine again."

"Medicine?" Dan sat forward. "What medicine was that?"

"Let's see, what did Graham call it? I don't remember. Some kind of tranquilizer he got from Dr. Devries at the hospital."

"Your doctor prescribed it?"

"I suppose so. He gave Graham some samples the day I left the hospital. Once Graham found out what the medication was, he got a generic brand of the same thing from one of the doctors at the Center."

"The Center?"

"Graham's laboratory."

"They have medical doctors there, too?"

"Oh, yes. Graham says that more than half of the research people are medical doctors. They even have psychiatrists and psychologists."

"I see." Something flashed briefly in Dan's mind, then fled. "What exactly does Graham do, Vali? What kind of research is he in?"

"Oh, Daniel," she said, laughing a little at herself, "I'm afraid I don't understand it well enough to begin to explain. It's all very technical. Graham is primarily a chemist, I believe. He's the director of research at the Center. They do a number of different things, mostly with pharmaceutical research and development, I think."

Dan nodded slowly. "This medicine, Vali—Graham gets it for you?"

"That's right. I've tried to pay for it any number of times, but he won't let me. He says they get tons of samples at the Center and I might as well use some of it. I really don't like taking things from him—he and Leda have already done so much for me—but he refuses to let me pay."

"I understand." Dan *didn't* understand, not really, and his doubts about Graham Alexander were increasing by the minute. "Graham is very fond of you, isn't he?"

"Yes," Vali said, her voice even softer. "He wants to marry me. In fact . . ."

Her voice drifted off, and Dan prompted her again. "What, Vali?"

"He . . . bought me a ring. Last night he took me to dinner, and he had the ring with him."

Dan lifted his brows. "Are you wearing it now?"

"No," she said quietly. "Not . . . yet."

"Do you mind my asking why?" Dan said carefully.

"No . . . I don't mind. It's just that I'm . . . very confused about my feelings for Graham."

Dan waited, saying nothing.

"I still . . . can't seem to forget about Paul," she added, her voice strained.

"I don't think anyone would expect you to forget him," Dan said. "You loved Paul Alexander a great deal, didn't you, Vali?" he asked softly.

"He was my life," she said, her voice surprisingly strong.

Dan nodded, feeling a wave of compassion for her. "I'm sure Paul would want you to be happy, to love again, after all this time."

"I *want* to!" Her harsh outburst startled Dan. "I *want* to love Graham. He looks after me. He's wonderfully good to me. . . . I *owe* it to him to love him."

Dan measured his words with great care. "Vali, you can't use love to pay a debt."

He heard her voice falter. "I know . . . it's just that I want *so much* to love Graham. Sometimes I wish David had never come up here. I—"

"David?" Dan frowned and rubbed his hand over his chin. "So David is complicating things for you?"

For a moment he wondered if he had said too much. But she

finally answered, her tone halting and uncertain. "David . . . cares for me, too." She paused, then added, "At least, he says he does."

"And that disturbs you?"

"David is a . . . disturbing man." She paused. "Sometimes . . . sometimes he reminds me of Paul."

"Do you think that's why you're attracted to him?"

"I'm not!" She stopped, and Dan said nothing, waiting.

"That's not true. I *am*. But not because he reminds me of Paul. The very things I felt drawn to in Paul seem to . . . to intimidate me in David." She laughed weakly. "That doesn't make sense, does it?"

Dan shrugged. "Our feelings often don't make sense, I'm afraid."

"I'm not sure what I feel for David," Vali admitted. "I enjoy being with him—he makes me feel . . . good about myself. Paul could always do that, too."

Daniel heard the slight tremor in her voice as she went on. "But sometimes David almost . . . frightens me. It's as if there's something I ought to know about him, something important, but—" She broke off, then choked out a rush of words, her frustration unmistakable. "Oh, I don't know! I just don't *know!*"

Dan could hear the growing strain in her voice. The storm of emotions he had sensed in Vali over the last hour troubled him. The young woman sitting across from him was so complex, her emotional state so fragmented, that it was difficult to sort out what he had heard with any degree of objectivity.

As honestly—and as gently—as possible, he explained to her his own need to think about some of the things she had told him. "And there's something I want you to be thinking about, too, Vali," he said. "What you said, about Paul—and David—making you feel good about yourself, making you feel special . . . that's important, having people in your life who care about you and make you feel that you matter to them, that you're special. But it's absolutely vital that you realize you *are* special, no matter what anyone else may think."

"I'm sorry," she said, "I don't understand."

"Vali, you can't—and you don't have to—base your identity on what another person thinks about you." Dan leaned forward, intent on making her understand. "You *are* special, Vali—very special—because you're a child of God. Because God made you. Because he saved you. Because he loves you. It's your relationship with *God* that makes you what you are, who you are—and enables you to be everything you can be."

He tapped his fingers on the table, thinking. "Let me give you just a couple of things to consider and pray about, OK? If you have any question about what you are in the eyes of the Lord, read Psalm 139: 'For you created my inmost being; you knit me together in my mother's womb. I praise you because I am fearfully and wonderfully made; your works are wonderful, I know that full well.'

Dan went on, smiling. "One of my personal favorites is 1 John 3:1: 'How great is the love the Father has lavished on us, that we should be called children of God! And that is what we are!'"

He thought for a minute, then added, "Remember this, Vali. You count . . . you matter. If you weren't important to another soul in the world, you would still be someone very special. Not so much because you're *you*—but more because you're *his."*

Vali was silent for a long time. Finally she said, very simply, "Daniel . . . I'm not sure, but I think you may have just given me a very precious gift."

Dan sensed the unshed tears in her voice, but there was something else he was resolved to bring up before she left. "Vali, one more thing. I'm a little concerned about this medication you're taking. You don't really know what it is, and—"

Instantly defensive, she stopped him. "Graham wouldn't give me anything harmful, Daniel!"

Dan made a dismissing gesture with one hand. "I'm not suggesting he would. I'm sure Graham wants only to help. But apparently you've been taking it for quite some time without knowing what it is."

Dan took a deep breath and phrased his words carefully. "Vali, under normal circumstances I wouldn't suggest this, but it seems that there might be a connection between this medication and your anxiety attacks. If your personal physician had prescribed the medicine, I'd say you should talk to him about it. But—" He paused, groping for words. "I'd be interested in seeing what happens if you don't take the medication . . . if you wean yourself off of it gradually."

With a sigh, Dan shifted and listened for Vali's response. If he was right—and he was pretty sure he was—that unknown medication could account for a lot of Vali's problems.

"Vali?" he prompted after a moment. "What do you think?"

Vali's reply was slow in coming. "I suppose . . . if you don't think it would hurt me. But I only take one pill every other day, Daniel."

Dan thought that was a peculiar dosage. "When do you take it? What time of day?"

"Just before I go to bed."

"Did you have one last night?"

"No."

"So you'd be due to take a pill tonight?"

"That's right."

"How about skipping tonight's dosage? To see how you feel tomorrow?"

"Well . . . I suppose that would be all right."

Dan stood up. "If you start feeling bad, let me know right away. Or if you have any side effects at all, we'll get in touch with a doctor. But try to go through tonight and tomorrow without it, why don't you?"

"All right. But I doubt that I'll notice any difference, Daniel. Graham said it's very mild."

Dan heard her get up. "I really should be getting back to the cottage now. David will be coming by soon to rehearse."

"How's it going?" Dan said, matching her abrupt change in mood with a cheerful tone of voice. "Have you made any decision yet about your career?"

He could hear the uncertainty in her reply. "David's music makes it awfully tempting. To tell you the truth, this is the first time since . . . since Paul died that I've begun to feel a desire—a need—to sing again. But . . ."

When she didn't finish her thought, Dan completed it for her. "You don't know if you can handle it—emotionally?"

She sighed. "That's right." After a slight hesitation, she added, "And Graham doesn't want me to go back. He wants us to be married soon and live up here."

Dan walked her to the door, with Sunny following. "Well, speaking as a radio man, I'm going to be hoping for a new album from you soon. And speaking as a friend," he added, "I feel exactly the same way. I can't help but believe that a gift like yours is meant to be shared."

"Thanks, Daniel. And thank you for talking with me. Tell Jennifer good-bye for me."

After Vali had gone, Dan returned to the table and sat down. He was vaguely aware of Jennifer singing in the bathroom; then he heard her turn on the blow-dryer.

He raked a hand through his hair and sighed. Out of the entire conversation with Vali, two things bothered him most. One was her comment about sometimes feeling afraid of David, and the other was the discovery that she had been taking medication for years without a doctor's supervision. What especially troubled him about the latter was Graham Alexander's involvement. If the man cared as much for Vali as he pretended, wouldn't he be more conscientious about giving her lab samples for medication?

Dan admitted to himself that he was just as put off by the scientist as Jennifer seemed to be. It bothered him, however, that he and Jennifer were apparently at odds in their feelings about David Nathan Keye. Jennifer had had conflicting feelings toward David from the beginning, whereas Dan instinctively trusted the man. Still, he couldn't gauge Keye's facial expressions or body language as Jennifer could, so he tended to be cautious about trusting David too much. The truth was, however, that he had been silently cheering the composer on in the contest for Vali's affection.

This was one of the times he felt more keenly than usual the restrictive nature of his disability. Although he knew the Lord had given him a certain amount of discernment, he never felt wholly secure in his sightless perceptions of others.

Except, of course, for his perception of his wife, who suddenly interrupted his reverie by sliding onto his lap, the sweet sunshine fragrance of her hair falling across his face as she planted a kiss on his cheek.

His vision of Jennifer was altogether different. God had placed a picture of her in his heart—a picture painted with divine perfection and the unerring accuracy of love.

SIXTEEN

VALI awoke in a panic, bolting upright in bed, gasping for breath, her heart pounding wildly.

She had dreamed of Paul. But not Paul the way she remembered him. His face had been angry, thunderous; his mouth set in a thin, hard line; his eyes scalding with rage and dark with warning.

The digital clock beside the bed registered 3:00 A.M. With a sigh, she sank back onto the pillows and for a few minutes tossed restlessly, still unsettled. When she finally fell asleep again, it was only to have the dreams resume. Frame after frame of terrible images assaulted her—pictures of the plane crash in which Paul had been killed, pictures she remembered from the newspapers and those she had only imagined during the long, tortured nights at the hospital. Flashes of fire, the plane ablaze, everything burned. Paul inside the inferno.

No remains . . . everything burned . . . nothing but ashes . . . no remains . . .

This time when she woke up she was ill, her stomach pitching, her throat hot and swollen. Her hands trembled with fear as she clutched the sheet around her shoulders.

Four-thirty. Too troubled to sleep, Vali got up, went to the kitchen, and poured a glass of juice. She drank it fast. Too fast. Her stomach rebelled, and she ran for the bathroom.

Finally exhausted, her entire body covered with a film of

clammy perspiration, she went back to bed, pulled the sheet and the spread over her, and once again fell into an uneasy sleep.

This time she dreamed of the man at the Ferris wheel and the macabre carousel ride, then of Graham and Paul. Paul was staring at her with disappointment, as if she had failed him in some way. *"Betrayal . . . ,"* he said slowly, his eyes burning into hers. Over and over he repeated that one word. *"Betrayal . . ."*

At seven-thirty, she got up, feeling as if she had never been in bed. Her head throbbed, her eyes were grainy and irritated, and her stomach was in spasms. She tried to eat some dry toast but threw most of it away.

After making her bed and doing a load of laundry, she made a halfhearted attempt to do some breathing exercises and scale warm-ups. Within a few minutes, however, she gave up. She was tired—incredibly tired. With a sigh, she lay down on the bed and covered her eyes with her hand.

Her head was assaulted by a mind-squeezing pressure. A crashing wave of pain was followed by a brief, heavily veiled image of a bald-headed man walking toward her. His pale, icy stare loomed at her out of a mist. Someone was beside him . . . a tall man . . . a man with no face.

Vali lay there for an hour, trying to rest, but tormented by the images that would not go away. At last she got up and went to the kitchen. She needed busywork, something to occupy her hands, something that required little cooperation from her mind. Her eyes fell on a pathetic, pot-bound African violet, and she focused on transplanting it with all her energy.

The window above the sink was open, and she could hear the sound of whitecaps slapping rhythmically at the shore. The lake was choppy, the air close. She rinsed her hands, reached for a paper towel—and nearly slammed her head against the cabinet as another unexpected bolt of hot pain sent her groping for a chair.

Quickly, she put her head down, framing her face between her hands. A white blaze of light hurtled forward in her mind and froze like a halo around Paul's face. He was wearing the crewneck sweater and corduroy jeans he had been wearing the last time Vali had seen him. He had come to tell her about the unexpected trip, to say good-bye, to tell her . . .

She waited for her memory of Paul to end there, as it always did. He would walk into her living room in the townhouse in Nashville wearing the funny, crooked little smile he always wore when he looked at her. He would drop his hands gently to her shoulders, murmur, *"Angel"*—his private endearment for her— then disappear. Out of her vision, out of her life.

From that point on, she would remember nothing until the memorial service. She would see herself, sitting at the front of the church. . . . She would hear the organ sounding one of Paul's own praise anthems. . . . She would be aware of quiet weeping, subdued whispers, the chokingly sweet, heavy scent of flowers . . . Leda beside her, clutching her hand, looking strong and heartbroken at the same time . . . Graham on the other side of her, his taut features carved in restrained mourning.

Always, there was that gap in her memory, like a deep, silent chasm separating those last few moments with Paul from the memorial service. Until now. Now a misty vignette began to inch its way into her mind. Once more she saw Paul's smile, heard him whisper, "Angel."

But this time there was more. The vision was shattered, like pieces spilling out of a bottle. Paul gripped her forearms, his face lined with worry. *"If anything happens to me, don't trust anyone but my mother. Do you understand me, Angel? She's the only one you can trust."*

Startled, Vali sat upright. What did it mean? What had Paul been trying to tell her?

Chilled and still trembling, Vali got up from the chair and

began to pace the room. This was the first time since the plane crash that a new thread of memory had appeared. Why now?

A sudden thought struck her, and she stopped walking. *The medicine!*

She had skipped last night's pill, as Daniel Kaine had suggested. She thought it unlikely that the missing dosage could be responsible for the headaches, the baffling dreams, the bursts of memory. But over the next two hours, the flashes of memory repeated themselves. Each grew more intense, more troubling.

By noon, Vali was frightened to the point of panic and decided to call Daniel. She was surprised at how quickly he responded to her question about the medication.

"No, I definitely don't think it's coincidence, Vali," he told her. "I think we need to find out as much as we can about the pills you've been taking and whatever it is that's trying to fight its way out of your subconscious."

"But, Daniel—Graham wouldn't give me anything that would hurt me! And I have no idea what these . . . memory flashes are."

Dan was quiet for a moment. "Do you think Leda could be of any help?" he finally asked. "That statement of Paul's you mentioned—about not trusting anyone but his mother—maybe Leda would be able to shed some light on that."

"I can't imagine how . . ."

"Vali, I think we should talk with Leda," Dan said firmly.

"I suppose . . . if you really think it's important, I could call Leda and see if she'd mind our driving in later today. It would have to be after four, though. She writes from early morning until three-thirty or four every day."

"Fine. Listen, why don't Jennifer and I come over so you won't be alone?"

"Oh . . . no. I'm all right. But, Daniel—do you think Jennifer would drive, if we go to Leda's? I don't think I'd be very safe behind the wheel today."

"I'm sure she'll be glad to. We'll be there around four unless I hear from you, all right?"

When an insistent knock sounded at the door a few minutes later, Vali nearly jumped out of her skin. She opened the door to find David standing there.

"We were to rehearse at one-thirty, remember?"

"Oh, David—I forgot! I'm sorry, I should have called you. I can't possibly sing today."

He walked in without waiting to be asked. "What's wrong, Princess? Are you ill? You look awful."

Vali avoided his gaze, about to turn away from him, when he caught her arm. "Vali? What is it?"

"I'm . . . not feeling well," she said evasively. "I hope you don't mind if we cancel today."

"Can I do anything? Do you want me to call Leda?"

She shook her head. "No—I'll be all right. It's just . . . a bad headache."

Gently, he put a hand to her cheek. "You're sure that's all?"

Vali finally looked at him, her breath catching in her throat when she saw the tenderness in his eyes.

"Vali . . . Princess, what is it? What's wrong?"

Vali jumped when the phone rang, hesitating before crossing the room to answer.

Graham's warm, confident voice helped to steady her. "Are you all right, dear? You sound . . . peculiar."

"I'm fine . . . fine," Vali assured him. "I've had a headache most of the day, that's all."

"Probably your nerves," he said quickly. "Vali, I've been doing some thinking about this business of talking with Daniel Kaine. I really don't think it's wise. I spoke with a friend of mine earlier today. A psychologist, with an M.D. as well—very well respected in his field. If you really think you need counseling, he'll be glad to take you as a patient."

Vali drew in a long breath. "I . . . Graham . . . I've already talked with Daniel."

Instantly, his voice turned cold. "Wasn't that rather impetuous?"

"I—" She glanced at David, unnerved by the way he was studying her.

She heard Graham's deep sigh and knew he was groping for patience. *"And?"* he asked sharply.

Vali hesitated, reluctant to anger him. Still, he *was* responsible for giving her the medicine.

He was furious when she told him about the pills. "What an *incredibly* irresponsible suggestion for Kaine to make!" he exploded. "And you actually *listened* to him?"

"Graham, please . . . I have to do *something.* Don't you see that? I can't go on like this."

"What does that mean?"

"You know what it means." Vali felt an uncommon stab of irritation with him. *"You're* the one who's always reminding me of how fragile my emotions are."

There was a long silence. "I thought you trusted me," he finally said.

"I *do* trust you, Graham! But I can't go on living my life dependent upon you and your mother to make my decisions for me. Can't you understand?"

Graham's tone softened slightly. "Vali, I do understand. But you must be patient with yourself. And," he said pointedly, "you have to use good judgment. Now then—tell me exactly what Kaine suggested and how you've been feeling since."

He said little as Vali told him about her talk with Daniel. Occasionally he muttered a short sound of agreement or disagreement. But at least he no longer sounded angry.

"Vali, as mild as that medication is—and I can assure you that it *is* mild—you can't simply drop it all at once. Not without suffering at least some nominal side effects. And if Kaine were as qualified as he's led you to believe, he would have warned you of the possible consequences of missing even one of the pills."

"Graham, Daniel didn't try to mislead me. If anything, he was reluctant to even talk with me; he—"

"Yes, yes—I'm sure," he interrupted brusquely. "However, the point is that he had no business giving you advice at all." He paused. "So the headaches and these—*dreams* started last night."

"Yes."

"And you think they may be related to the pill you *didn't* take." He made no attempt to hide his sarcasm.

"I . . . I don't know what to think." Vali hesitated. "I thought perhaps if I talked with your mother—"

Graham didn't let her finish. "What in the world does *Mother* have to do with any of this?" he burst out.

Vali bit her lip, hesitating. "Daniel thought Leda might be able to help. Graham," she said carefully, "are you positive you can't remember anything at all about the last time you . . . were with Paul? You said the two of you talked. . . ."

"Vali," he said after a long silence, "I've already told you— several times—all there is to tell about that night. Paul came to the Center. We had coffee, talked for a few minutes, about you, mostly, and then he left."

Vali heaved a sigh of disappointment but said nothing. The weariness she had felt earlier now settled over her anew.

"I'll drive you in to Mother's later," Graham was saying, his tone now less annoyed. "I think I should be there, the way you've been feeling today."

He was so protective of her.

Too protective, something whispered at the back of her mind.

Vali shook off the thought. There really was something wrong with her if she could resent Graham's unflagging devotion to her, his thoughtfulness and consideration of her needs.

"I'd like you to be there, Graham. I was going to ask Jennifer to drive me, since I'm so shaky. But if you really want to . . ."

"I insist," he said firmly. "It will give me a chance to see you, after all." Sounding somewhat mollified, he told her good-bye and hung up.

Vali delayed turning back to David. When she did, she found him slouched against the piano, studying her with a searching stare.

"What kind of pills has Graham been giving you, Vali?" he asked harshly.

Vali had suddenly had enough. Her nerves were raw, her head was hammering, and she simply couldn't face another long explanation. "Since you obviously overheard our conversation, David, you shouldn't need any details," she snapped.

Something flared in his eyes—anger, she thought—but it quickly disappeared. Slowly he pushed himself away from the piano and walked over to her, his gaze never leaving her face. "I'm sorry. I suppose I shouldn't have listened. But you're right— I did hear the conversation. That's why I'm worried, Princess."

When Vali saw the soft warmth in his eyes, she regretted her sharpness. "David, I didn't mean to snap at you. It's this headache . . . and I didn't sleep. I must be more on edge than I realized."

"Vali." Gently, he put his hand on her shoulder. *"Do* you trust Graham? Do you really trust him?"

"Of course I trust Graham!"

David searched her gaze. "Are you in love with him?" he asked directly.

Surprised, Vali stammered, "I . . . you know I care for Graham. . . ."

"I asked if you're in love with him."

"You have no right, David. . . ."

"You still haven't answered me, Vali."

"I don't think that's any of your business."

Vali saw him swallow hard—once, then again. As she watched,

his expression gentled and his mouth softened to a sad, uncertain smile. "You're right. It's not."

Vali felt an unexpected sting of shame. "David . . ."

Slowly he lifted one hand, lightly grazed her cheek with his fingertips, then touched her hair. "I just want to see you happy, Princess," he whispered, his eyes caressing her face. "You're so special, Vali . . . so very, very special."

Vali felt tears scald her eyes, and she tried to turn away. But David caught her by the shoulders, turning her gently around to face him. Vali's heart stopped when she saw the look on his face. He was smiling at her, not a happy smile, but a wistful smile of regret that made her heart ache. For some inexplicable reason, she suddenly felt the need to comfort him.

"David . . ."

She stopped breathing as he bent his head to touch a featherlight kiss to her forehead. For one brief, tender moment, he circled her with his arms and gathered her carefully to him. Vali didn't know what to do, what to say. Awkwardly, she put her hands on his shoulders and stared up into his face.

"I'll go now, Princess," he whispered. "Try to get some rest, won't you? And forgive me if I upset you. Please?"

Vali nodded weakly as David slowly released her from his embrace and turned to go. She stood in silence, watching him leave, the tears fighting to spill over. She didn't understand the sweetness of emotion she had felt in his arms, nor the overwhelming sorrow she now felt in his absence.

But he had left something behind, something she knew she would cling to, just as she had savored the hope Daniel Kaine had given her yesterday. Dan had told her she was "special . . . not so much because you're *you*—but because you're *his* . . . because you're a child of God."

David, too, said she was "special . . . so very, very special." She wanted—she *needed*—to believe them both.

SEVENTEEN

THE man answered the telephone reluctantly, muttering a grudging hello.

"So—did she talk to the blind man?" the voice at the other end of the line asked without preamble.

He hesitated, but not for long. "She talked to Kaine, yes."

"And?"

Again he paused before replying. "He . . . suggested that she skip the medication for a couple of days. To see how she would feel."

"And did she?"

He sighed. "Yes."

"With what consequences?"

"If the block isn't reinforced every forty-eight hours, control begins to fragment. At that point, it's quite possible for partial memory to break through."

"Am I to assume that this . . . breakthrough . . . has begun?"

He cleared his throat and mumbled a short, "Yes."

"Is there any possibility of getting her back on the medication immediately?"

"Not likely," the man grated. "I think Kaine has made her suspicious of the pills. She'll probably resist taking any more, at least for now."

"I see. So, my friend . . . are you ready to put an end to this business yet?"

He had anticipated the question, indeed had already reviewed his choices. They were few and impractical. "Yes. Let's get it over with."

"Ah . . . finally, an objective attitude." The caller paused. "Do you know where she will be tonight?"

"She and the Kaines are going to Sandusky," the man replied thinly. "They're looking for additional clues."

The caller laughed shortly. "Fine. We'll provide them with a few they aren't expecting. Kaine and his wife are both going?"

"I think so."

"Good. This will be easier than we thought. We can take care of all of them at the same time. Now—it would be wise for you to absent yourself from them for the entire evening. Also, we'll need to be certain the singer drives her own car."

"She's not planning on driving at all. She was going to ask the Kaine woman . . ."

"That's no problem. We'll simply render the Kaines' automobile useless, at least for the evening."

"What are you planning to do?"

"You needn't concern yourself with that. Just rest assured that everything will be handled quietly and neatly. After tonight, there will be no more loose ends."

"But shouldn't I be there? To make sure everything goes according to plan?"

"Not unless you want to die with the rest of them, my friend."

EIGHTEEN

JENNIFER, are you sure you don't mind driving?" Vali asked from the backseat. "Graham intended to take us until he got that phone call from Ohio State," she explained, adjusting her seat belt. "It turned out that he and David were both busy tonight."

"I don't mind a bit." Jennifer glanced in the rearview mirror as she pulled out onto Cleveland Road. "Just so long as you don't care if Sunny rides in your car."

Vali reached over to pet the retriever, who was perched on the seat beside her, staring out the window. "Sunny can go anywhere with me," she said, smiling. "Did you call the garage about your tire?"

Jennifer nodded. "I don't know where we picked up that nail, but I sure didn't want to drive all the way to Sandusky on that little doughnut they call a spare."

"Did they say when you can pick up your car?"

"Later this evening. I asked the mechanic to go ahead and change the oil and do a couple of other things while he was at it."

"I told you I'd do that when we get home." Dan, seated beside her, shook his head. "You're just wasting money."

Jennifer rolled her eyes at Vali in the mirror. "I thought I'd save you the trouble this time, Daniel."

"I *can* change the oil, Jennifer," he said somewhat testily.

"I know that."

"I change the oil in the station's Cherokee all the time."

She glanced at Vali again, lifting her eyebrows and grinning. "That's right, you do."

"How much is he charging you?"

"How much?" She looked at him.

"You didn't even ask?" Dan's expression was incredulous.

"Well . . . no, not exactly. I forgot."

Dan sighed.

"Next time I'll remember," Jennifer added meekly.

"Are you sure this guy even knows *how* to fix a tire?"

"All he has to do is remove the nail and patch the hole. He may not be Mr. Goodwrench, but I think he can handle it."

"Mm."

"Daniel . . ."

"Hm?"

"Are we having our first argument?"

"We had our first argument not long after we met, Jennifer."

"Good. I wouldn't want to have our first one in front of Vali."

After a second, Dan grinned. "Was I making noises like a husband?"

"That's what it sounded like."

"I'm just practicing."

"Well, you can quit. You got it right the first time."

"Turn your windshield wipers on, Jennifer."

She looked at him again. "How did you know it was drizzling?"

He shrugged. "The way the tires sound on the highway."

Jennifer muttered to herself but turned on the wipers.

"This road gets a little slippery when it's wet, Jennifer," Vali warned from the backseat.

"Don't worry, I'll be careful."

They drove along in silence for several minutes. Jennifer glanced in the rearview mirror every now and then, both for traffic and to watch Vali. She could tell by the way the singer was acting that she was still having "memory flashes," as Dan had called them. And she was massaging her temples. The headache must still be there, too.

Jennifer had a mild headache of her own, but she knew hers was weather related. It had been warm and humid all day, and the air was now close enough to be uncomfortable. She fiddled with the air conditioning control, turning it up a notch.

"We're going to have a storm later," Dan said, breaking the silence.

"Daniel has radar," Jennifer explained to Vali soberly.

"It's going to storm," he repeated with confidence.

"It probably will," his wife agreed grudgingly.

There was little traffic. Jennifer reached over to turn on the radio, keeping the volume soft so it wouldn't aggravate Vali's—or her own—headache. She played with the dial, eventually finding a weather report.

"Remember that a severe thunderstorm watch means conditions are favorable for heavy thunderstorms. These storms may include dangerous lightning and strong winds."

"See," Daniel said smugly, "his radar picked up a storm, too."

Jennifer groaned and switched off the radio, focusing her attention on the road as the rain started to come down more heavily. The two-lane highway to Sandusky was fairly flat, unlike the roads back in West Virginia. But the rain was making the surface slippery. As they headed into a curve, she felt the wheels slide, and she gently tapped the brake.

"Take it easy, honey," Daniel cautioned.

"Sorry." Jennifer didn't dare hit the brakes any harder. She gripped the wheel, relieved to feel the car settling into the curve.

As she came out of the turn, she glanced into the rearview mirror. Vali was sitting with her eyes tightly closed.

"Are you all right, Vali?" she began, then gasped as she saw a dark sedan careening up behind them at too high a speed to be safe on slippery roads.

Jennifer pushed on the accelerator, and Vali's Sentra lunged forward.

"What's wrong, Jennifer?" Daniel asked. "Why are you driving so fast?"

"Some idiot behind me is tailgating," Jennifer grated out, her eyes darting to the rearview mirror.

"Well, let him pass."

Jennifer let up on the gas, but the black sedan didn't go around her. Instead, it drew even closer, bearing down on them at an alarming speed. Panicked, Jennifer scanned the road ahead. A long curve to the right was coming up, a place where the car couldn't possibly pass unless the driver wanted to take the risk of a head-on collision with a vehicle on the blind curve.

Again she glanced in the mirror. The sedan was almost on her bumper now, and through the rain-glazed rear window she couldn't see the driver's face—only his bald head, bent low over the steering wheel, one hand holding a cellular telephone to his ear.

Jennifer's heart leaped into her throat. Instinctively she hit the brakes, intending to slide off onto the right-hand berm. Nothing happened. The black car lurched forward, slamming into the rear bumper of Vali's car, then began to accelerate, pushing them ahead, faster. Again Jennifer tried to apply the brakes. Her foot went all the way to the floorboard, with no result.

"We've lost the brakes!" she shouted, gripping the wheel until her knuckles went white. As if from a great distance, she could hear Daniel's voice, barking instructions to her, trying to help. Still the sedan pushed them forward, ever faster.

Jennifer hung on, praying frantically as she guided the car around the curve. The black sedan was still behind them, pushing them forward. Suddenly, on the other side of the curve, a huge panel truck appeared out of nowhere, blocking the highway.

"Hold on!" she screamed. With a final prayer, she wrenched the steering wheel sharply to the left. On two wheels the Sentra crossed the oncoming traffic lane and landed with a bone-jarring *thud* on the access ramp on the other side. Jennifer fought for control, narrowly missing a small green pickup truck coming down the ramp onto the highway.

When the incline of the ramp finally brought them to a stop, Jennifer threw the emergency brake, leaned over the wheel, and began to shake. No one said a word. Sunny whimpered once, and Daniel turned to give her a reassuring pat. Through the rear window, Jennifer could see the black sedan still sitting in the middle of the highway, its rear end fishtailed into the panel truck. The bald driver was nowhere in sight.

With a shuddering sigh, her hands locked on the steering wheel, she fought back the tears clouding her vision. Her chest felt as if someone had strapped a boulder on it. Her stomach began to riot, and her head felt about to explode.

After a few seconds, Dan drew in a long, shaky breath. "Jennifer? Are you all right?" His voice was thick and unsteady.

Jennifer had to wait until her teeth stopped chattering to answer him. "Y-yes," she said, still clutching the steering wheel.

"Vali?" Dan asked.

"I—yes. I'm . . . all right."

Dan reached over to touch Jennifer's hands. Very gently he pried one finger at a time from the wheel. "You did real good, love," he said softly. "That was quite a landing."

Finally able to move, Jennifer looked over at him. "There were no brakes," she said in a dazed voice. "Nothing."

Nodding, he squeezed her hand. "I know. But we're all right now; we're fine."

"I . . . couldn't stop . . . I couldn't . . . pull over . . . I . . ."

Quickly, Daniel released his seat belt and drew her to him. "Easy . . . easy. It's all right," he murmured, lightly stroking her back.

"It was the same man," Jennifer said in a low, tight voice against his shoulder. "He tried to kill us."

"What?"

"Vali, . . . did you see?" asked Jennifer. "The black car?"

"Yes," Vali said in a low, tremulous voice. "I saw it."

Daniel started to say something, but Jennifer stopped him. "It was *him*, Daniel. It was the man I saw at Cedar Point—the same man who ran our bicycle off the road. He . . . he's trying to kill us, Daniel!" She stopped and caught her breath. "Who *is* he?" Her cry was muffled against his chest.

"I don't know, honey. But what we have to do now is get some help. We can't drive without brakes."

Holding her with one arm, he pulled a handkerchief out of his back pocket.

"Is this white?" He held out the handkerchief for her inspection.

Jennifer stared at it for a moment, then looked blankly at Dan. "White?"

"For a signal," he explained.

"Oh—yes. Yes, it's white."

"Tie it to the antenna and raise the hood," he told her as the rain pattered softly on the car. "We'll just have to wait here until someone stops to help."

Within half an hour, a deputy sheriff arrived. After a few questions, he radioed for a wrecker to pick up the car, then drove all of them back to Vali's cottage.

It was nearly nine o'clock that night before Dan could get any information from the garage in Huron where Vali's car had been taken. Jennifer and Vali sat waiting on the sofa as he hung up the phone and turned toward them.

"The brake lines were cut," he said tersely.

"Cut?" Vali repeated in a shaky voice. "You mean someone deliberately . . ."

"That's right. Someone deliberately took out the brakes."

The room was thick with tension for several minutes. Vali finally broke the silence. "There's something I probably should have told you before now. But at the time, I didn't think it was important."

She told them about seeing the bald-headed man at the Ferris wheel at Cedar Point—the same man who had been driving the black sedan today.

"So you saw him at the Ferris wheel, before it broke down," Dan said thoughtfully. "And Jennifer saw him again at the carousel before . . ." He let the rest of the sentence drift off, unfinished.

He remained quiet for a long time. When he finally spoke, his voice was grave, his face as sober as Jennifer had ever seen it. "I think we need to consider something. I don't believe it's just coincidence that our car was put out of commission and Vali's brakes were tampered with anymore than it's coincidence that this guy— whoever he is—keeps showing up every time something weird happens."

When neither of the women said anything, he lightly rapped his knuckles against the countertop where he was standing, then went on. "It seems to me that someone wanted to make sure we drove Vali's car tonight instead of Jennifer's. And I'm afraid we can all figure out why."

He moved to the cabinet, felt for a mug, then poured himself some coffee.

"I'm so sorry for what I've done to the two of you," Vali said suddenly, her voice strained. "For dragging you into this . . . nightmare. You could have been killed today—and apparently because of me!"

Dan turned back to her. "It's not your fault, Vali. Can you think

of someone—anyone—who would have a reason to hurt you?"
He paused. "You say you didn't recognize this man?"

Vali shook her head. "No. When I first saw him at Cedar Point,
I thought he looked vaguely familiar. But later—No, I'm sure I've
never met him before."

"What are we going to do, Daniel?" Jennifer asked.

Dan took a sip of coffee, then set the mug on the counter. "I
think the first thing we'd better do is talk to the police. Vali, who
else knew we were going to Sandusky tonight?"

"Who else?" Vali hesitated, then replied slowly, "Well . . . Graham, of course." She paused. "And David," she added softly.

"No one else?" Dan pressed.

"No."

"What about Leda? Did you call her?"

"I tried. But I got her answering machine—she uses it through
the day when she's working. I left a message for her to call me
back if there was any reason we shouldn't drive in tonight."

"What time did you call?"

"Late this afternoon—three-thirty, maybe."

"Then Jennifer's tire had already been vandalized by the time
Leda could have known we were coming," he said, mostly to himself. He raked a hand down one side of his beard. "So . . . that
leaves Graham—who's in Columbus—and David. They're the
only ones who knew where we were going." Another thought
struck him, and he asked, "Did both of them know *why* we were
going to Leda's?"

Vali looked at him. "What?"

"Did you tell both David and Graham that we wanted to talk
with Leda about your dream?"

Vali was silent for a long time. "No," she finally said, her voice
uncertain. "I don't think I told either one of them. I *did* tell Graham everything else, though—about the headaches, the memory
flashes . . . everything. And David was here when I was on the

phone with Graham. I'm sure he heard the whole conversation. But no," she said again, "I'm almost positive I didn't say anything about Leda, except that we thought she might be able to help."

As Jennifer watched, Vali's expression changed from bewilderment to what looked like anger. "Graham was in Columbus," she said slowly. "So only David . . ."

Daniel put up a restraining hand. "Vali . . . I don't think we ought to jump to any conclusions. I *do* think it would be a good idea to call the police, though."

Vali got up and walked across the room toward the window. "I suppose you're right," she finally said in a soft voice, her back to them. "But if you don't mind, I'd like a little time. For one thing, I should call Leda and explain what happened. She'll be worried that we didn't show up. And I need to . . . get myself together."

Dan nodded and started to move toward the door, with Sunny at his heels. "Jennifer and I will go back to our place, get cleaned up a little, then come back over here, if you want."

Jennifer walked over and put her hand on Vali's shoulder. "Maybe you could rest for a little while, too. You look awfully tired, Vali."

"I . . . yes, I am," Vali admitted, still facing the window.

"Vali," Dan cautioned, "I don't think you should let anyone in—or talk with anyone—while you're here alone. No one but Leda. Until we know for sure what's going on."

Vali nodded, her head down.

Troubled, Jennifer watched her, then went to Dan, putting her hand on his arm. "We'll come back soon, Vali."

Finally, Vali turned away from the window. "Yes. All right. Thank you, Jennifer."

It was raining steadily when Jennifer and Daniel walked outside. Neither of them had a raincoat or jacket, so they jogged most of the way to the cottage. "Daniel, do you think it's David?"

"I don't know. The only thing I'm fairly sure of right now is that someone wants Vali out of the way." He stopped. "And it's beginning to look as if they've got the same thing in mind for us, too."

Jennifer shivered but said nothing. She glanced nervously around at the dark, deserted beach, then tightened her grip on Daniel's arm as they went on running.

NINETEEN

OON after Daniel and Jennifer left, Vali called
Leda, telling her only that they had had car trouble
and wouldn't be coming in that evening after all.
A few minutes later, she threw on a windbreaker and left the
cottage. She suspected that the rain now falling steadily was
merely the prelude to a hard storm. The lake was rolling with a
gathering wind, and the night air seemed heavy and charged with
electricity.

Indifferent to the wind and rain, she half-ran the distance from
her cottage to David's house, guilt nagging at the back of her
mind all the way. For her own protection, Daniel and Jennifer had
asked her to talk with no one but Leda. If they had known she
was going to see David, they would surely have tried to stop her.

Vali didn't know what accounted for the urgency to confront
David alone, before the police—or anyone else—learned what
was going on. Perhaps she wanted to discover the truth about his
part in this nightmare before he could cover his tracks.

Or maybe she was secretly hoping he would produce an alibi,
some proof of his innocence.

At any rate, she intended to face him before he had time to put
up some sort of smoke screen. The possibility that David had
been lying to her all along was almost more than she could
believe. He had seemed so caring, so genuinely fond of her.

She had trusted him.

Tears spilled over and mixed with the rain pelting her face. She began to run even faster. There wasn't much time before Daniel and Jennifer returned to her cottage. She had to reach David first.

Vali deliberately ignored the fact that she might be placing herself in jeopardy by going to David's alone. Somehow, that didn't matter now. Besides, there was also a very real risk to Daniel and Jennifer. If David were the one responsible for all the treachery, confronting him alone might be the only way to protect her two new friends.

She raced up onto the porch to get out of the rain but stopped with her hand poised to knock when she heard music inside. It was David, of course. He was playing a Fauré nocturne, which surprised her; she had never thought of David playing anything but his own music. As she might have expected, he played it masterfully.

Vali had seen enough storms on the lake to sense that David's interpretation of the music was like the night itself—deceptively tranquil, but building to a brilliant storm of passionate, thundering force. Even as angry and hurt as she was, she found herself caught up in his artistry and command of the music. Only when silence fell did she finally manage to shake free of the compelling music and knock on the door.

The moment David appeared in the doorway Vali saw that he looked unusually tired and somewhat disheveled. His hair was tousled, his shirt not tucked in, and fine lines of fatigue bracketed his mouth.

Did she only imagine that his expression brightened when he saw her?

"What on earth are you doing out in this weather, Princess? Come inside and get out of the rain."

He reached as if to take her arm, but Vali brushed by him, avoiding both his touch and his gaze. She went to stand in the middle of the living room, near the piano.

"What's wrong, Vali?"

When he would have helped her out of her jacket, Vali threw it off, tossing it onto a nearby chair. Then she stood watching him, her hands clenched at her sides. "You look surprised to see me," she finally said.

He frowned, obviously puzzled by her behavior. "Surprised, but pleased. I have fresh coffee. Let me get you some."

"I don't want any coffee, David," Vali said tightly. "I want the truth."

He had turned to leave the room, but now stopped. "The truth?"

Vali swallowed down the knot of misery in her throat, suddenly aware that this was going to be even more difficult than she had thought. Physically and emotionally, she was stretched to the limit. Her head had begun to pound again, and she felt slightly ill.

David stepped a little closer. "Vali? Why don't you sit down, Princess? You look a little . . . shaky."

"I imagine I look considerably better than you expected, though, don't I, David?"

Again he frowned. "What are you talking about?"

"I think you know," Vali shot back, furious at his composure.

He shook his head. "Have I missed something?" He ventured a smile and reached for her hand. "Hey, Princess . . . I can see you're upset with me. But don't I at least get to know why?"

Vali recoiled from his touch, inching backward a few steps. "Why did you do it, David?"

"Do *what?*" He stared at her. "Look, I don't know what you're talking about, but I can't very well apologize unless you tell me what I've done."

Vali studied him in sick disbelief. "Oh, *stop* it, David!" she burst out. "Stop playing games with me."

His mouth tightened. *"What?"*

The thundering at the back of Vali's head intensified. For an instant she was afraid she was actually going to pass out. She pulled in a deep breath, trying to steady herself. "You should have thought your plan through a little more carefully, David. Oh, it probably would have worked if *I* had been driving. No doubt I would have panicked. But Jennifer's reflexes are much better than mine."

David closed the distance between them, grasping her by the shoulders. Anger sparked briefly in his eyes, then ebbed as he searched her face.

"You obviously think I know what you're talking about," he rasped. "But I swear to you, I don't. Vali—please, just tell me what's happened."

As limp as a rag doll under his hands, Vali was surprised to realize that she felt no fear. Only disillusionment. And a terrible sense of betrayal.

Betrayal. The thought acted like a trigger, exploding Paul's face onto the canvas of her mind. Paul's hands had also gripped her shoulders that night. His face, too, had been livid with anger. *Betrayal . . .*

Vali felt herself begin to sag. David caught her, led her across the room. She fought him, but he managed to ease her down onto the couch. His whisper-voice sounded distant, detached. She felt the blackness closing in, the pounding in her head racing faster and faster. She squeezed her temples between her hands with a soft moan.

"Vali . . . Princess . . . what is it? Are you ill?" When David coaxed her head onto his shoulder, Vali was too weak to protest.

She started to cry, silently berating herself for her weakness. Another wall of pain engulfed her, seizing her with such an excruciating agony that she gasped for relief.

"Vali, I'm going to get a doctor. Here, lean back. Lean back and close your eyes while I call a doctor."

"You tried to kill me . . . all of us . . . and now you're going to call a doctor?" Vali shot an incredulous look at him.

"*Kill* you—" David gaped at her, wide-eyed— "What in the name of heaven are you talking about?" He jumped to his feet, staring down at her.

For an instant, Vali wondered if she could have possibly been wrong. He looked so—stricken, so astonished at her accusation.

She pushed herself up off the couch, fighting the pain in her head, the crazy zigzags of color and shattered pictures racing before her eyes. "*Why*, David? What are you doing here? What do you want? What's so important to you that you'd try to kill three people?"

He shook his head slowly. "Vali—you've got to believe me. I haven't tried to kill anyone. I don't know what you're talking about, I tell you! I don't *understand!*"

Vali wished with all her heart she could believe him. Another thought struck her: She didn't *want* it to be David. He was too . . . important to her.

She looked away from him, trying to avoid his searching eyes. *Whether I want to believe it or not, he tried to kill me today. I mustn't forget that. I don't dare forget it.*

Without trying to touch her, David lifted both hands in a gesture of supplication. "Just . . . tell me," he whispered. "Tell me what it is I'm supposed to have done, Princess. Please."

Anger flooded Vali all over again. She took a step toward him, then stopped, struck by the thought that she was alone with this man, that he had tried unsuccessfully to kill her once, and that there was nothing to stop him from trying it again.

Why, then, didn't she feel threatened?

She heard her own voice as if coming out of a thick fog. "Did you know about the panel truck, David? Did you hire the driver? Or just the psychopath in the black sedan?"

She hurled words at him like stones, a furious, disjointed

account of the entire incident. She told him about the useless brakes, the slick highway, the black sedan and the driver. She told him everything she was sure he already knew. By the time she had finished her passionate recital she was drained, totally depleted of any strength she might have had.

"Vali . . . Princess . . ."

Suddenly she realized that David was holding her again, gripping her forearms, his gaze raking her face.

"Vali, did you say the brake lines were cut?"

Vali nodded, studying him with a dull, leaden stare. "You know they were," she said woodenly. "You know."

David winced, and she saw a small muscle by his left eye jerk spasmodically.

"You think I did that, Vali? Do you really think I'd do anything to hurt you?"

Vali tried to look away from him, but he wouldn't let her. He caught her chin with his hand and forced her to meet his gaze.

"Vali, listen to me. *Listen!*" he demanded when Vali tried to twist free. "It wasn't me, Vali. I would never do anything to hurt you. Don't you know that by now? I could never hurt you!"

How could he lie so convincingly, even now?

Vali felt tears splash down her face. She tried to free her hands, but David's grasp was unyielding. Before she realized what she was saying, the words tumbled from her lips. "Oh, David! Why— *why* did it have to be *you?*"

"Vali—" There was a new urgency in his whisper. "Please listen to me. Whose car was Jennifer driving—her own or yours?"

Vali gave him a blank look. "Whose car?" She hesitated. "Mine. She drove my car."

"Why? Why didn't she drive her own?"

Again Vali delayed her reply. "Her tire—someone put a nail in her tire."

His eyes narrowed. "Who else knew you were going to Sandusky tonight?"

Vali's throat was tight, her mouth dry. Her heart was racing as if it were about to explode out of her chest.

"It's important, Vali. Did anyone besides me—and Graham— know what you were planning to do tonight?"

She gave him an accusing look. "Just you," she choked out. "And Graham. No one else."

For a moment, David squeezed his eyes shut. Then he looked at her and said, "It wasn't me, Vali. I *swear* to you—it wasn't me."

Vali continued to watch him, wanting desperately to believe him. "Then . . . who?"

He pulled in a ragged, shallow breath. "Graham."

Vali tried to jerk free, but he held her. "No! Don't you *dare* blame him!"

David clutched her shoulders. "It was Graham." His steady, unwavering gaze held hers.

"Graham was in Columbus!" she spat out.

He shook his head. "No. He didn't go. Vali, you have to believe me. Graham is the one responsible."

Vali stared at him, her mind spinning.

David took her hand and again began to lead her toward the couch. His action broke Vali's paralysis. Seizing her chance, she yanked free of him and bolted for the door. But he outdistanced her, blocking her escape. "You can't, Vali! You're not safe anywhere but here now."

Vali choked off a sound of disgust and backed away from him.

"Vali . . . Princess . . ."

"Don't call me that!"

"I wouldn't hurt you."

"You tried to kill me. . . ."

"Never . . . I would never hurt you, Vali."

"You would have *killed* me. . . ."

"No! I love you, Angel. . . ."

Vali closed her eyes, then opened them. "What did you say?" she choked out.

"I love you," he said again, his whisper broken and hoarse. "I could never hurt you. You're my heart, my life."

Vali's mind spun out of control. "You're lying."

"Come here, Vali." He extended his hand.

Vali shook her head furiously.

He caught her hand, tugging her gently to him. Slowly, carefully, he drew her into the circle of his arms.

Vali felt the trembling of his body, heard him utter a deep, ragged sigh. "My love . . ." His lips brushed her brow with infinite tenderness. "It's true I'm not what you think."

Vali stiffened.

He tightened his embrace and pressed his lips against her temple. "Vali . . . Angel. . . . I'm not David Nathan Keye. I'm . . . Paul."

TWENTY

THE world stopped. Vali's legs buckled under her. She couldn't breathe, couldn't move, couldn't speak. She could only tremble in his arms, in the arms of this stranger, this madman who seemed intent on stealing her last shred of sanity.

His arms tightened around her, supporting her. "It's true, Vali."

He tipped up her chin, forcing her to look at him. Vali shook her head. "You're insane," she choked out.

"No."

Vali stared up at him in horror. "How dare you?" she whispered. *"How dare you!"*

He put her slightly away from him, clasping her shoulders only firmly enough to keep her from pulling free. His eyes burned into hers, trapping her in his gaze. "I can prove it, Vali. I know I don't look like myself. My face, my hair—everything is different. But not my heart. My heart is the same. It still belongs to you, Angel."

It was his use of the endearment again—*Paul's* endearment—that shattered what little control Vali had left. She cried out once, then again. He pulled her to him, holding her, soothing her, sheltering her in the hollow of his shoulder.

He urged her toward the couch. "Here, Angel, sit down," he whispered, touching his lips to her hair. "Sit here with me. I'm sorry. . . . I'm so sorry I did this to you. I know it's awful for you.

Here, sit close to me. . . . I'll tell you everything. . . . I'll tell you the truth, all of it."

Vali allowed him to pull her down beside him on the couch. He continued to hold her, gently but securely within his arms, stroking her hair. "I don't know where to start. There's so much . . . so much to tell you. . . ."

Tears streamed down Vali's face. Abruptly, she drew away from him as another thought struck her. "You're lying!" she said, her words spilling out in a breathless rush. "You can't be Paul. Your eyes—"

He held up an unsteady hand. "Wait," he said. He turned away for a moment. When he again faced her, he extended his hand, palm upward. He was holding two tinted contact lenses.

A stunned cry ripped from Vali's throat when she looked into his eyes—light gray, not dark. Pressing a fist against her mouth, she stared at him with a mixture of fear and disbelief.

He lifted a hand to gently smooth a wave of hair away from her temple. His touch was achingly tender when he brushed the tip of his index finger over her ear. "Little seashells," he whispered. "Remember? I always teased you that your ears looked like little seashells."

Vali shuddered on a choked, incredulous sob.

"Remember the day we spent at Radnor Lake?" His face softened to a smile that was both sad and reflective. "You took off your sandals so you could run free. But you sprained your ankle, and we ended up in the emergency room. Remember the nurse who admitted you? Her name was Sam. When she found out who we were, the only thing she was interested in was whether or not we knew Amy Grant." He threaded his fingers through her hair, then watched as if fascinated by the waves sifting through his fingers.

Tears began to spill from Vali's eyes again as she stared at him, remembering a man of incredible gentleness, a man whose love had always been sweet and steady and dependable. She squeezed her eyes shut, her shoulders heaving with the force of her silent weeping and tumultuous emotions.

He wrapped her more snugly in his arms. "Don't cry, Angel . . . don't cry anymore," he whispered against her lips. His kiss told her the truth as nothing else could have.

She dragged his name out of her heart as if it were the first time she had ever said it. *"Paul . . ."*

"Ah, what a feeling, hearing you say my name again, holding you again. . . ."

Vali reached up to touch his face, taking in every line, every plane of it as if seeking a familiar landmark. "Your eye," she choked out.

He closed his heavy left eye under her gentle touch. "The plane crash, Angel. My face was . . . destroyed. They had to give me a new one. A few weeks after the surgery, they noticed my eye was drooping a little. I told them to leave it. I wasn't about to start over."

She put her hand on his throat. "Your voice . . ."

"This is permanent, I'm afraid. My voice box was crushed."

"Your beautiful voice . . ."

Quickly he pressed his lips against the palm of her hand. "It doesn't matter. After everything else that's happened, it's not important. As long as I can still tell you I love you, that's enough."

Vali ran her hands over his shoulders. "You're so thin."

He shrugged and managed a wobbly grin. "Don't you remember? I don't eat when I don't work. And I wasn't able to work for months."

Choking on her tears, Vali examined his face with her hands much as Daniel Kaine had a few days before, slowly shaking her head in wonder. "But they said you were dead—the papers, the television—everyone told me you were dead!"

He grabbed her hands, framed them with his own, brushed his

lips over her knuckles. "You don't know how I hated that . . . but that's how it had to be." Suddenly he stopped. Looking up, he searched her eyes. "Angel, don't you remember anything about that last time we were together? The day I came to see you in Nashville, before I went to Washington? Anything at all?"

"Remember?" Vali shook her head. "No. Just . . . your coming to my apartment. You said you couldn't stay long, that you had to leave for Washington. You kissed me. . . ."

He nodded, a sad smile hovering about his mouth. "Nothing else?"

"No. I can't remember anything after that until . . ."

"The plane crash?"

"Yes," she whispered, then moved her hands to clutch his shoulders. "I wanted to die, too!" she cried.

"Oh, Angel, . . . I'm so sorry you had to go through that." His eyes misted as he studied her face.

Vali drew back from him, suddenly angry again. "How could you do that to me? How could you let me believe you were dead when you were alive? And for *three years!*"

A violent shaking racked her body. "Do you know what happened to me? I almost lost my mind! I was in a hospital for months; I was . . ." The words died in her throat.

He started to reach for her again, then let his hands drop away. "I know. . . . I *do* know, Vali. But there was nothing I could do. You see, while you were going through *your* nightmare, I was going through one of my own. Almost two years of plastic surgery, one operation after another—skin grafts, bone reconstruction, physical therapy. Then they started on the psychological conditioning. They turned me into a new person, gave me a whole new identity."

He reached for her hands, and Vali watched as he enfolded them in his. "What you have to understand, Angel, is that I *would* have been a dead man if I had come back into your life as Paul

Alexander. For months after the plane crash, I didn't know what they had told you. By the time I learned, everything had been set in motion, and there was no going back. They made it clear that my life—and quite probably yours—depended on my silence."

"They? Who are *they?*" Vali cried in frustration, yanking her hands away from him. "And carry *what* off? *Who* put you through the surgery? And where were you all that time . . . when I thought you were dead? I still don't understand how you could have let me believe I'd lost you, when you were alive the whole time!"

"It was the only way, Vali. You'll understand when I explain the whole story—"

"And when you finally *do* come back into my life, you don't look like yourself or talk like yourself or even *act* like yourself! You carry on this horrible . . . masquerade! You let me believe you're someone else, you lie to me—" Vali pressed the fingertips of both hands hard against her temples. *"Why?* Why didn't you just tell me the truth?"

He caught her shoulders and pulled her close, holding her gaze with his. "I couldn't. Telling you the truth would only have placed you in jeopardy along with me."

He continued to search her face as if he couldn't get enough of the sight of her. "Vali, after the plane crash, I was unconscious for days, then out of my head for weeks. I was totally irrational— delirious with pain. I was burned . . . horribly. Third degree burns over much of my body. You can't imagine the pain—"

He shook his head as if to banish the memory. "I, too, wanted to die. In fact, I *prayed* to die!"

Suddenly he seemed to realize the force of his grip and he released her. "All that time," he went on, "all that time they were rebuilding me, restoring me, pounding at me to make me realize that this was the only way I'd ever be able to come back into your life. If I were to . . . *live* again, it had to be as a new man. So I could come back to you and protect you from Graham. And, at the same time, help them get the evidence to stop him."

The impact of his words stunned Vali into silence. When she finally tried to speak, she felt as if her mouth had gone numb. *"Protect* me . . . from Graham? What do you mean?"

He studied her for a moment with a measuring gaze. "Vali, the plane crash that supposedly killed me was no accident. The engines were sabotaged. Graham . . . and the people he works for . . . were responsible."

Vali felt a cold shroud fall over her. She began to tremble. "Graham?" She shook her head in denial. "No. Graham wouldn't hurt anyone, especially not you! He loved you; he admired you; he wouldn't—"

"Graham is totally incapable of loving anyone or anything," Paul rasped, his eyes blazing. "Graham cares about nothing but his experiments, his work!" He got up and began pacing the floor.

Vali sat watching him, listening mutely as he told her about a conspiracy of terror too incredible, too fantastic, to be anything less than the truth. As he spoke, his words began to set into place the missing pieces of the puzzle that had held her memory at bay for years.

"The last day of my vacation that summer—the day before I was to come back to Nashville—I spent most of it with Mother, then went to see Graham." He paused. "This was while he was still at the Woodson laboratory, remember? Before he built the Center. It was late—eight, maybe nine o'clock—but it wasn't unusual for him to work that late. Since I planned to leave early the next morning, I decided to go over to the lab and tell him good-bye."

He stopped in front of her, reached in his shirt pocket for a stick of gum, and tucked it in his mouth.

"You never used to chew gum." The thought was totally

irrelevant. Vali didn't even realize she had spoken until Paul smiled at her.

"New habit for the new me," he said dryly.

"Anyway," he continued, "I started into the lab, but I heard voices, so I waited in the adjoining office. The door was ajar just enough for me to overhear the conversation taking place inside. What I heard froze my blood. I sat there and listened to my own brother commit treason."

"Treason?" Vali gaped at him.

Paul nodded. "Oh, I couldn't hear everything. But I heard enough to tell me that Graham had been concealing the results of some of his experiments from the Woodson people and selling— or trading—them to someone else. Someone," he said slowly and meaningfully, "not affiliated with our scientific community. The man who walked out of the lab with Graham that night had an accent that even *I* recognized as European."

"What kind of experiments?" Vali hugged her arms more tightly to her body, struggling to take in what Paul was telling her. "This sounds like something out of a science fiction novel."

Paul smiled grimly and dropped down beside her on the couch. "Doesn't it? That's what I thought, too, at the time."

He sighed and took one of her hands in his. "You may not know that Graham's specialty for years has been in the field of psychotropic drugs."

"Psychotropic drugs?" Vali repeated.

He nodded. "Drugs that affect the mental processes: marijuana, hashish, hallucinogens. But Graham has gone far beyond all those. He's developed some real state-of-the-art stuff—consciousness altering, memory blocking, redirection of thought patterns, and a lot more. He worked at top-secret level with Woodson for years to develop ideas for our own government, but Graham has always been too ambitious to remain just another research man."

He paused and for a moment sat studying Vali's hand, clasped in his. "What I heard that night at the lab made it obvious that Graham had a partner willing to finance his experiments in exchange for Graham's furnishing the partner's government copies of his research. For Graham, there would be a new laboratory, plenty of money—a scientist's dream." He looked at her. "The Alexander Center," he said, his tone bitter.

Vali looked at him, understanding now dawning quickly. "You said you were still there when Graham and the other man came out of the lab. . . ."

Paul nodded. "That was my first mistake."

"What do you mean?"

He uttered a short, voiceless laugh. "I've never been too good at keeping my mouth shut—I'm sure you remember—"

She glanced down at her lap, and for the first time since she had entered the house, she smiled, just a little. "Yes, I remember."

"I lit into Graham as soon as the other guy was out the door. I told him exactly what I thought of him and what I was going to do about it. Like a fool, I issued an ultimatum—told him to bring his entire obscene operation to a halt—or I would go to Uncle Kevin."

"Uncle Kevin?"

"Actually, he's one of my dad's best friends, but we've always called him 'Uncle Kevin.' He's been with the CIA for years. In the back of my mind, I suppose I thought I could either shame or scare Graham into cleaning up his act."

"Oh, Paul . . ."

He gave her a crooked grin. "I know—totally stupid. But I was *furious.* Not only because Graham was betraying his country but because of the kind of garbage he was fooling around with. I think all this mind-control stuff is immoral, Vali! And dangerous. Graham used to rant about the way scientists would eventually bring an end to all wars, that ultimately it would be the scientists who would establish universal peace—" He gave a small sound of disgust, running his hand through his hair.

"What did he say when you confronted him?"

"Oh, he was cool. Graham is *always* cool, you know. He looked at me with one of those cold-fish stares of his, then proceeded to explain how he had been doing some research for a private business in Europe. It was a slick comeback, but I knew him too well—well enough to know he was lying. Graham's an uncanny liar, but he's never been too successful at conning me."

He twisted his mouth with self-mockery. "Then I made my second mistake. I let him know I didn't believe anything he'd said and went charging out of the lab."

He stopped for a moment when a strong sweep of wind rattled the living-room windows, waiting until the noise from a sudden roll of thunder subsided before going on.

"I carried out my threat. I went to Nashville and called Kevin from a pay phone near your apartment. I told him what I knew, and he insisted I come to D.C. He even arranged for one of his people in Nashville to fly me to Washington on a private plane."

He leaned forward, propping his elbows on his knees and framing his face between his hands. "What I hadn't counted on was that one of Graham's pals followed me and found out about my trip to Washington. A few minutes from D.C., the plane's engine failed. The pilot managed to get a Mayday out on a scrambled frequency before we went down. An Agency helicopter picked up Kevin and arrived on the scene within minutes after the crash. The pilot was already dead. I was unconscious and badly burned."

He tapped the knee of his right leg. "My leg was caught under the seat, and they had trouble pulling me free. They got me out just in time. Kevin knew enough to suspect that the plane had been sabotaged. He and the helicopter pilot made an on-the-spot decision to report me as dead so Graham and his friends would think they had nothing to worry about. The plane was almost completely destroyed by fire." He shrugged, leaving the rest unsaid.

Vali's mind groped to make sense of what she had just learned. "They said there were . . . no remains. Nothing but ashes."

Paul grimaced. "It wasn't the first time the CIA falsified records."

"But how could they be so sure it was sabotage, that it wasn't an accident?"

Paul raised his head to look at her, and Vali saw the anger glinting in his eyes. "They weren't sure, not a hundred percent. Not until they got it on tape, thanks to a high-tech listening device that was installed in Graham's condo. Installed, incidentally," he told her with a thin smile, "by the same people who were buying Graham's experimental drugs and journals from him."

Vali frowned in surprise, and he nodded. "Right. His pals didn't trust him, either. They bugged his lab, his condominium—" He paused for an instant, then went on. "That turned out to work in our favor. One of Kevin's agents traced Graham's contact and found out where he's been staying. The agent spent over an hour in the guy's apartment the other night while this character and Graham were together at the Center. He copied some very interesting tapes—one of which includes a conversation about the airplane crash." He stopped, watching Vali carefully. "On one of the later tapes, there was a discussion about the most effective way to . . . take care of you."

Vali felt a sick knot of fear tighten in her stomach at the significance of his words.

"The main reason for *me* coming here," he continued, "was to keep an eye on you while the Agency did their job. They knew I wouldn't last a day if I came back as Paul Alexander. Not only could I incriminate Graham, but I could also identify his contact. Without an eyewitness, Graham probably wouldn't have been indicted. With my testimony, the charges are almost certain to stick."

"Oh, Paul," Vali exclaimed, "how can you testify against your own brother?"

"What choice do I have?" Paul shrugged, a frown creasing his brow. "What complicated things for me was finding out that you apparently remembered nothing about that day in Nashville, before I left for Washington."

At Vali's questioning frown, he tried to explain. "Vali, I told you everything that day. What I had learned about Graham—and what I was going to do about it. I told you where I was going— and why."

He rubbed his hands down over his face in a weary gesture, then looked up again. "When I first stopped by to see you, you were unhappy with me. I had already been gone for several days, and there I was about to leave again. I knew I shouldn't tell you what I'd learned, but you were so upset with me I went ahead and blurted out the whole story. Later, when I learned about your loss of memory, I was terrified to think about what might happen to you if you ever *did* remember. I'm sure Graham has considered you a threat all this time—just because there was always the chance you might know something, and he had no idea how *much* you knew."

Vali stared at him. "But why can't I remember . . ."

Suddenly she realized that she *had* been remembering. Pieces. Fragments. Scraps of memory had been floating in and out of her mind all day. She simply hadn't recognized them, hadn't been able to fit them together. Paul's face, his anger—that anger had been directed at Graham, she now realized, not at her.

Betrayal. He had spoken the word when he'd told her about Graham's deceit. And the bald-headed man—

"Did you describe Graham's . . . partner to me?" she asked abruptly. "Did you tell me what he looked like?"

Paul nodded, his gaze locking with hers. "Our man with the shiny dome," he said grimly.

"That's why he looked familiar. . . ." Vali said softly. "Oh, Paul—"

"Up until now," he broke in, "I thought the shock of the plane crash—and my 'death'—had somehow erased your memory. You know—a type of amnesia." His mouth thinned to a tight line. "But after overhearing your conversation with Graham today, I've got a hunch those little pills he's been giving you have something in them besides a tranquilizer."

Vali touched her fingers to her lips. "You think Graham deliberately—"

"Blocked your memory," he finished for her. "You bet I do."

Suddenly another thought sent Vali reeling. *"Leda!* She doesn't know? Leda doesn't know that you're . . . *alive?"*

He met her gaze. "No. And that's been tough. You know how sharp she is. I was really squirming the night of your birthday party."

At her questioning frown, he explained. "The strawberries, remember? She zeroed in on me with one of her eagle-eyed stares when I said I couldn't eat them. For a minute, I thought she suspected something." He gave Vali a rueful smile. "And when I sat down to play my piano again—" He shook his head. "I had been itching to get to it every time Mother had us over for an evening. Not being able to touch my own piano was almost as difficult as not being able to touch you." The expression of love and longing he turned on Vali brought tears to her eyes again.

"Oh, Paul! She's going to be so happy! Leda was devastated when she thought we'd lost you."

A look of regret crossed his face. "I'm a little worried about that. I'm afraid any joy she might feel at the sudden discovery that her . . . *dead* son is alive is going to be quenched by the realization that her *other* son is a traitor."

Vali leaned toward him. "Paul, that day in Nashville, did you say anything to me about Leda—something about not trusting anyone but her?"

He thought for a moment, then nodded. "Yes, I think I did. I was trying to protect you."

Vali felt almost dizzy with the realization that she hadn't simply imagined things, that the images that had been bombarding her throughout the day were, in fact, actual memories.

"Kevin told me I had placed myself in danger by shooting my mouth off to Graham," he went on. "He warned me to trust *no one*. I suppose I was trying to warn you of the same thing."

"It will be such an incredible shock to Leda," Vali said. "But your mother is so strong. She'll be all right."

Paul nodded, smiling a little.

"What are you going to do now?"

"Get us out of this mess just as quickly as possible," he said without hesitation. "I've already been pushing Kevin to wrap things up. He had hoped to wait until they could get some photos of Graham and his partner together. But after our trip to Cedar Point, I started getting really paranoid. I knew that incident with the carousel was no accident. And when Jennifer described the man she had seen . . ."

He expelled a long breath, rubbed the side of his right leg a moment, then went on. "The night your cottage was broken into—you thought I was in Nashville, remember? And I was. With Kevin. He met me there. I told him that, photos or no photos, I was going to tell you the truth by the weekend. He agreed and promised to take Graham and his cohort into custody by Saturday. Then I got back and found out what had happened at your cottage. . . ."

He shook his head. "When I heard you telling Graham today about the memory flashes, I knew I couldn't wait any longer. Kevin has warned me all along they would never let you remember—that they'd kill you first. I called him from a pay phone tonight, and he agreed not to delay any longer. My intention was to tell you the truth first thing tomorrow morning."

Determination lined his face. "But we're not waiting. I'm going to call Jeff and have him meet us at Mother's tonight. We'll be safe there until Kevin gets Graham and his pal on a plane."

Vali looked at him. "Jeff?"

Paul grinned at her. "Jeff Daly. The new man in Mother's life? He's an Agency man. You don't think the CIA would turn an amateur like me loose without backup, do you?"

"That's *terrible!* Leda is interested in Jeff—and she thinks he really cares for her!"

"And he does, Angel," Paul insisted, smiling. "He does. In fact, it seems that Jeff has developed such a fondness for Sandusky he's giving some serious thought to retiring there in the near future. Says it's time he was settling down."

Vali shook her head. It was too much to take in all at once. Life had suddenly become something wonderful and at the same time something terrible. She had never felt so overwhelmed, or so bewildered. For a moment she closed her eyes, as if by doing so she could somehow shut out all the ugliness, the pain, and the heartache of the last three years.

But then she remembered that her world *wasn't* ugly or painful any longer. Paul was alive. Paul was back.

She opened her eyes.

"Vali . . . can you forgive me?" Paul said, searching her gaze. He made no move to touch her, but instead pleaded with his eyes. "I honestly don't know what I would have done if I'd been conscious and capable of making decisions for myself. It was all taken out of my hands. You'll never know the guilt I felt when I finally learned what you must have gone through because of me. And you'll never know how desperately I've prayed that God would somehow carry you through the nightmare until we could be together again."

Vali lifted a hand and gently touched his face. He no longer looked like David Nathan Keye. This was Paul . . . her Paul.

"Vali, do you think you could still love me . . . as I am now? Could we start over again?"

Vali studied his face, love welling up in her. "Oh, Paul, we don't have to start over," she said softly. "I was already falling in love with *David,* but I was afraid to let myself care too much. Somehow I knew I felt as I did about David because he reminded me so much of *you*. Oh, Paul . . . I've never stopped loving you! Never!"

His face broke into the tender, adoring smile Vali remembered so well, and he reached for her. She went into his arms as if she had never been away.

She searched his eyes for the one familiar sign she had been looking for ever since he had first begun to tell her his incredible story. There it was, shining out just as brightly as she remembered. The look of love, so long restrained, had finally been set free.

"Welcome home, Paul," she whispered from her heart, just before he reclaimed her love with a long, cherishing kiss.

They shared one blissful moment of sweet reunion before a loud pounding on the door shattered the silence and startled them apart.

TWENTY-ONE

AN HOUR later, Jennifer and Daniel sat in the kitchen with Vali and Paul Alexander.

Jennifer could not stop staring at David. *Not David,* she reminded herself giddily. *Paul. Paul Alexander. In the flesh.*

She had been almost speechless with amazement from the moment the musician had opened his door and motioned them inside. After getting no answer at Vali's cottage, she and Daniel had arrived here, ready for battle. But their offense had been squelched by the sight of Vali, looking slightly dazed as she clung almost possessively to David's—*Paul's*—arm.

Vali had hurried to assure them that she was perfectly all right, then indicated that she—and *Paul*—had something to tell them.

Jennifer was still wide-eyed, her mind scrambling to take in the incredible story.

From across the table, Paul Alexander was smiling at her as if he knew what she was thinking. "Jennifer, why do I have the feeling you're sitting there trying to decide a fitting punishment for me?"

"Punishment?" Jennifer stared at him blankly.

"For misleading you," he explained.

After a moment's hesitation, Jennifer managed a rueful smile. "At least now I know why I never felt totally comfortable with you. It was so frustrating," she said bluntly, "liking you in spite of the fact that I didn't trust you."

"It clears up a couple of things for me, too," Dan added. "That first day we met, when I looked at you with my hands, I got a real surprise."

Paul nodded knowingly. "I got very nervous about that encounter. I had a hunch you might realize something wasn't quite right about my face."

"That's right, Daniel!" Jennifer blurted out. "I remember—you were surprised when I told you he was probably in his thirties. You thought he was younger."

"Thirty-two, as a matter of fact," Paul inserted with a grin.

"There's scar tissue around your hairline, isn't there?" Daniel asked. "From the surgeries?"

Paul's smile was a little forced. "Yes. I have a whole new face, Daniel. Not perfect—but new." He paused. "You said a couple of things bothered you. What else?"

"Your music," Dan replied.

Paul looked at him with a puzzled frown. "What? I worked for months, changing my style, even my notation."

"It was just a small thing," Dan explained. "You used to have a special little flourish when you modulated between keys that I'd never heard anyone but Paul Alexander use. I don't imagine that's easy to change."

"Apparently not, since I wasn't even aware I was doing it," Paul replied with a light laugh.

"What *I* want to know," Jennifer said, "is how you managed to . . . come back to life . . . and back into *Vali's* life as a musician."

Paul shrugged. "It wasn't that difficult, really. I was settled in a California condo for a few months, wrote some songs, waited for the Agency to use their contacts—and soon I was recording again. It didn't take long to establish a reputation on the Coast as a composer and an accompanist. From there, it was just a matter of getting a meeting with Vali's agent and a couple of producers."

"Where were you," Dan asked suddenly, "during your recovery and while they were getting you ready for your . . . reentry?"

"Different places," Paul said. "I was in a private—*very* private—clinic in Canada for the first year. Some of the later operations were done in Oregon. Later I was moved from one safe house to another until they settled me on the Coast."

Dan was quiet for only a moment before something else occurred to him. "The day you went to Nashville—," he said, leaning forward on his chair— "the day Vali's cottage was broken into . . . do you remember the talk we had that morning?"

"Most of it, I suppose. Why?"

"You went to a lot of trouble to fill me in on Vali's background and your own concern about her and Graham. At the time, I didn't understand why you were confiding so much personal information to someone you barely knew." He paused. "You were trying to put me on alert, weren't you? About Vali?"

Paul smiled at Dan's perception. "Exactly. I judged you to be a man who wouldn't be easily deceived, Daniel. And I sensed you were also a man willing to involve yourself in another's trouble. It was my own way of trying to provide a little extra protection for Vali."

When the whole story had been told, the four of them sat in silence for a long time. Once, Daniel shook his head as if still trying to assimilate the incredible tale of intrigue. Jennifer darted an occasional covert glance at Paul, only to find him looking at her with a knowing, slightly apologetic smile. Vali simply gazed at him as if she couldn't get enough of what Paul referred to as his "new face."

Daniel finally brought an end to the silence by pushing back his chair and getting to his feet. The retriever sleeping beside him also stirred and sat up. "I think I'd better take Sunny outside for a bit. It sounds as though the rain's let up for now," he said. "Want to come with me, Paul?"

The composer gave Vali's shoulder a light squeeze as he rose from his chair. "When we come back, I'll call Jeff. If he can meet us right away, we'll drive in to Mother's," he told her. Turning to Dan and Jennifer, he added, "I think both of you should come with us to Sandusky. I'm afraid you won't be safe until this is finished."

Jennifer waited, watching Dan's face. When he nodded his agreement, she sighed with relief.

"We probably shouldn't stay out here too long," Dan said as he and Paul walked along the shore. Freed of her harness, Sunny trotted ahead of them, occasionally turning and running back to check on her owner. "I think we're right in the center of the so-called calm before the storm."

"How can you tell?"

"Sunny," Dan explained. "She gets extremely hyper when there's an electrical storm on the way." He lifted his face, enjoying the spray off the lake, but still he felt edgy. "And so do I," he added.

"You're probably right," Paul said. "There are some pretty wicked-looking lightning flashes out there, and they seem to be getting closer."

They walked along in companionable silence for a while. At last Dan slowed his pace, saying, "All this must have been extremely difficult for you. Trying to hide your true identity from everyone—even your own mother. Your fear for Vali, trying to conceal your feelings for her. Frankly, I don't know how you carried it off so well."

"It was Vali who kept me going," Paul told him. "At first I was afraid Graham would try to get rid of her to insure her silence. I should have realized that manipulation is more his style. I think he was probably pressured into the idea of killing her. Not that he ever really cared about her," he added bitterly.

"Well, she should be all right now," Daniel said reassuringly.

"I hope so. But I'm worried about the drug he's been giving her, what sort of long-range effect it might have."

"I think she ought to see a specialist right away," Dan agreed.

"I wish you could have known Vali before this, Daniel," Paul said. "She was just beginning to bloom, just starting to develop a real sense of self-esteem. Up until then, she had always depended on other people—on *me,* at that time—for her identity. I tried to encourage her to be herself, to be the person God had made her to be."

They stopped walking. From the abrupt silence, Dan sensed that Paul had temporarily drifted back to the past. They stood quietly, indifferent to the light, drizzling rain. It was several minutes before they went on.

"I wish there were a way you could continue counseling Vali," said Paul. "She admires you a great deal, you know."

"Paul, you can do everything I could do for Vali—and more," Dan assured him. "You possess an unbeatable combination to help her: your love for the Lord and your love for her. It'll take a lot of prayer and a lot of patience, but my instincts tell me that any man who could survive what you have during the past three years has an abundant supply of both."

"Thank you, Daniel." Paul gripped his hand and shook it firmly. "Thank you for everything. Especially for caring enough to get involved—and on your honeymoon, yet."

Dan grinned. "I anticipate a lifelong honeymoon. We can spare a little time this week for friends." He turned and called Sunny back to him. "But for now, we'd better get back to the cottage. I don't think it's a good idea to leave Vali and Jennifer alone very long."

TWENTY-TWO

T HAT lightning is getting fierce," Jennifer said, glancing nervously out a window. "Do you think we should try to find an oil lamp or some candles—just in case?"

"I think there's a lamp out in the sunroom," Vali told her. "David says he likes to sit out there at night and—" She broke off with a shy smile. "I wonder how long it will take before I remember to call him Paul again."

Jennifer reached over and squeezed her hand. "Probably not long at all. But somehow I don't think he's going to mind very much *what* you call him—just as long as you continue to look at him with those stars in your eyes."

"None of this seems real to me yet," Vali said softly. Her expression sobered. "I don't suppose anything could spoil my happiness in having Paul back again, but I can't stop thinking about Graham. What he's done, what he *tried* to do."

"Vali . . ." Still clasping her hand, Jennifer searched for the right words. "Try not to think about Graham right now. You've been through so much today. There are a lot of things you'll have to face later. But for tonight, why don't you just . . . be grateful?"

Vali looked at her for a long moment, then said, "You're right. Paul will help me through the rest of it, when it's time."

"I think I'd better try to find that lamp now," Jennifer said, turning to leave the kitchen.

The sunroom was dark except for the erratic glare of lightning streaking through the glass-enclosed walls. Startled by the sight of the jalousie door standing open, she fumbled for the light switch on the wall as she entered the room.

She heard the step behind her a second too late. She felt a painful wrench in her shoulder as someone grabbed her arm and pinned it hard behind her back. At the same time, a rough hand covered her mouth, cutting off her scream.

Suddenly, only inches in front of her, a second man stepped out from the shadows.

Graham Alexander! A sudden bolt of lightning illuminated him in an eerie, spectral glow. He stood unmoving, his cold gray eyes appraising Jennifer with an impassive, almost clinical stare. He wore his usual tailored suit, so incongruous with his surroundings.

Cold fear snaked through Jennifer. There was something terrifying about the sight of Graham standing there like an ordinary businessman, watching her squirm under his gaze.

In her struggle to break away, she twisted sideways and caught a glimpse of the burly man holding her. The sight of his smooth-domed head and sinister features made her legs threaten to buckle.

"You won't need the light, Mrs. Kaine." Graham Alexander's quiet, frigid voice broke the silence.

Panic surged through Jennifer, propelling her to act. She kicked backward and, twisting, caught the man behind her off guard just long enough for her to break free.

But there was nowhere to run. Graham Alexander stood motionless directly in front of her. The other man was poised, ready to jump at her again. Jennifer felt like a trapped animal.

Graham lifted a restraining hand. "You've made all this much more difficult than it should have been, I'm afraid. If you and your meddling husband had minded your own business from the beginning, there would have been no need for anyone to get hurt."

Lightning flashed, illuminating him in incandescence. Jennifer's heart hammered once, then seemed to stop when her gaze met the cold, calculating stare of the scientist.

This man doesn't hate me, she thought suddenly, stunned by the unexpected insight. *He doesn't feel anything. He's empty. . . . He has an empty soul. . . .*

At that moment, she knew with a sickening flash of certainty that Graham Alexander was far more dangerous than any of them had suspected. The word *sociopath* darted through her mind, and she cringed inwardly at the terrifying suggestion that this was a man without feeling, without conscience.

"What are you going to do?" she choked out, trembling.

Graham shrugged, not answering. He blinked once, started to speak, then glanced beyond Jennifer's shoulder when he heard Vali's voice coming from the direction of the kitchen.

In desperation, Jennifer screamed out a warning. "Vali—get out! Get out of the house!"

"Shut up, you little fool!" Graham snarled and lunged toward Jennifer, his hand raised. At the same time, the other man pulled a handgun from his pocket and yanked her tightly against him with one beefy arm.

When Vali appeared in the doorway, Jennifer cried out to her again, but Graham had already moved to the door. He grabbed Vali, dragging her roughly into the sunroom and pushing her toward Jennifer, then stood scowling at both of them.

The bald man released Jennifer from his grasp, but remained so close she could smell the sweet, cloying scent of his aftershave.

"You—" He waved the gun at Jennifer. "Get over there by the wall. You, too," he ordered Vali, turning the gun on her.

They're going to kill us. . . . They're going to shoot us, and then they'll wait in here for Daniel and Paul . . . and they'll kill them, too. . . . They'll never have a chance. Jennifer began to pray silently, knowing with sick assurance that she was only moments away from death.

The man with the gun grunted a menacing obscenity when she hesitated, then shoved her so hard she fell against the wall with a thud. Dazed, Jennifer turned to check on Vali.

The singer was facing Graham. Her usually gentle, uncertain gaze was turned on him in incredulous anger.

"How can you do this?" Vali's voice shook violently. "What kind of a monster are you? First you try to kill your own brother, then—"

Graham's cold eyes suddenly narrowed. "What exactly are you talking about, Vali?"

She was trembling visibly. "*Stop* it! Don't you dare stand there and lie to me!"

Graham closed the distance between himself and Vali in two steps. For the first time, Jennifer saw a glint of feeling in his expression. It was rage.

"Spare me your simpering!" he snapped. "I asked you a question. What about Paul?"

Vali lifted her face and glared defiantly into his eyes. "The airplane crash, Graham—that's what I'm talking about," she spat out.

His anger seemed to flare once more, then ebb. In its place was an icy mask of contempt. "Poor Vali," he finally said in a tone that was chilling in its malice. "You really should have continued your medication, dear. In your case, memory is a definite liability." He sighed, then raised a hand to lightly trace the contour of the singer's lovely, stricken face. Jennifer saw Vali's eyes spark with a mixture of terror and revulsion.

"Such a waste, really," Graham continued. "I'd grown rather fond of you, you know. I even argued quite a strong case for your survival." He paused, staring at her for a moment. Then something seemed to snap shut in his eyes, and he smiled thinly. "Ah, well—you've been an enlightening experiment, at least. It hasn't been a total loss."

"That's all I've ever been to you, Graham? An experiment?" Vali's voice held a tremor that hadn't been there before.

"Not entirely," Graham replied. "There was the matter of making sure you didn't know too much."

"About what you did to Paul."

He nodded. "Just out of curiosity, dear, what *do* you remember? Or perhaps I should ask you how much you knew to begin with? What exactly did my dear departed brother tell you?"

"Paul told me everything."

"Ah. I was afraid of that. That's why I had to start you on the medication right away. I saved your life, you know," he said with a deceptively guileless expression. "My partners were all for terminating you immediately, but I convinced them that your death coming so soon after Paul's might be a bit too . . . coincidental for some people. It seemed far more expedient at that point simply to keep you under observation."

"And now?" Vali's question was little more than a tremulous whisper.

"Now?" Graham fingered the collar of his white shirt as he stared at her. "I'm afraid you're no longer useful, dear. In fact, you've become a definite nuisance."

"So you're going to kill me." Vali uttered the words flatly, with no real evidence of fear. "Let Jennifer go, Graham. You can't possibly have any reason to hurt her or Daniel."

"You've only yourself to blame for what happens to the Kaines, Vali," he said reprovingly. "Had you not gone running to the blind man with your foolishness, they could simply have returned home in blissful ignorance. But now . . ." He let his voice drop off meaningfully.

"Graham, don't! Please."

He ignored her, turning instead toward his partner. "Get this over with. I'll go to the front and watch for the other two. Be ready to finish them when they come in the front door. We need to get out of here."

"No!" Vali lunged at him. "You nearly killed him once! You won't hurt him again!" Like a wild animal gone berserk, she hurled herself at the scientist, pounding at him and clawing at his face, sobbing as she struck out at him.

Graham's associate turned his gun on Vali, but Graham stopped him. "Wait!" he shouted. Grabbing both of Vali's hands, he held her captive. "What are you talking about? What's this about my 'almost killing' Paul?"

Suddenly Jennifer knew, with sickening certainty, what Vali was going to say. She tried to stop her, but it was too late. Vali flung the words out in a frenzy. *"He's alive, Graham!"* Vali watched his stunned look of bewilderment with apparent satisfaction. "You *failed!* Paul is alive!"

"You really *are* insane, you little fool!" Graham seized her by the shoulders and began to shake her.

"He's been right under your nose all along—"

Suddenly Vali gasped, pressed a fist to her mouth, and stared at him. Too late, she realized that she had placed Paul directly in the line of fire. She continued to stare at Graham Alexander, her face taut with fear.

He tightened his grasp on her shoulders, studying her in ominous silence. "Under my nose?"

Jennifer could almost see his mind working. His eyes glinted with suspicion, his face twisted to a menacing scowl. Suddenly his expression changed. "Keye," he said quietly.

Vali shook her head furiously. "No! No, I didn't mean it, I—"

Jennifer saw Graham's hand circle Vali's throat. "How long have you known?"

Vali's eyes went wild with terror, and she shook her head from side to side. "No, you're wrong. . . ."

Graham's face turned even uglier as he brought his other hand to her throat and began to squeeze.

Jennifer screamed—once in horrified denial, then again as a deafening peal of thunder rent the night and lightning struck a huge old cottonwood tree only a few feet from the sunroom.

Vali cried out, and both men turned just as the massive tree pulled free of its roots. Like a slow-motion sequence from a movie, it toppled directly toward them, its branches dragging a mass of power lines down with it.

Jennifer watched in horror as the entangled wires and tree branches struck the propane gas tanks directly outside the sun-room. Live electric wires sparked across the tank. There was a loud *whoosh,* followed by a blast. Flames shot up, and the glass wall at the end of the room exploded.

The bald man with the gun was closest to the explosion. Rocked by the blast and shards of flying glass, he collapsed at once. Graham Alexander lurched backward with the force of the blast, knocking Vali to the floor and pinning her under him as he fell.

Jennifer felt the sting of flying glass against her arms and fore-head, and immediately dropped to the floor and covered her head. When the noise finally subsided, she lifted her head and looked around. Glass was everywhere. The entire far wall of the sunroom was in ruins, and fire was beginning to snake up the remains of the broken window frames. She could see the bald man, lying facedown in the rubble. Graham lay motionless on top of Vali's crumpled form.

With a cry of alarm, Jennifer scrambled across shards of broken glass to get to Vali. Still caught under Graham Alexander's uncon-scious body, the singer lay deathly still, a trickle of blood across her forehead.

"Vali! Vali!"

Vali's eyes fluttered open. "What happened?" she moaned.

"You're hurt—we've got to get out of here!"

With a valiant effort, Jennifer rolled Graham to one side and tried to pull Vali to her feet. Behind her, fingers of flame were already lapping at the garden chairs and tables at the other side of the room.

"Vali, come on! Can you walk?"

Vali's knees buckled, and she sank to the floor. "My ankle," she gasped. "It's—it's broken, I think."

Jennifer grabbed Vali under the arms and began to drag her across the floor. The room was filling up with thick, heavy smoke. Her eyes watered, and her throat burned. "We don't have much time," she coughed.

Vali shook her head. "Graham's still alive. We can't leave him here!"

Against Vali's protests, Jennifer staggered toward the kitchen, dragging Vali along with her. "The smoke won't be as bad in the kitchen," she shouted.

"Don't leave him, Jennifer! Please!"

By the time they reached the doorway, the kitchen had also begun to fill with smoke. "I can't breathe," Vali choked out, wheezing. "Leave me . . . get Graham."

Exhausted, Jennifer laid Vali down on the kitchen floor. "He tried to kill you!" she protested.

"He meant . . . something to me. And he's Paul's brother." Vali tried to take a breath but was gripped by a wracking cough.

Jennifer shook her head. "I don't have the strength to carry him out."

"Get help." Vali gripped Jennifer's arm with surprising power. *"Please!"* Then her head sagged to one side, and her eyes closed.

Jennifer looked through the doorway into what was left of the sunroom. Flames were beginning to lick up the walls, and smoke was pouring out. Vali was pale and clammy, her breathing shallow—probably in shock. She had no choice. If she stayed here with Vali, they would both die.

Frantic, she scrambled to her feet and tried to stand. Her legs would barely hold her. Gripping the kitchen counter for support, she made her way through the living room to the door, flung it open, and staggered out onto the porch.

Dan and Paul heard the explosion when it hit. With his hand in a death grip on Sunny's harness, Dan began to run as fast as he could toward the house. He could hear Paul's labored breathing behind him.

He pivoted toward the sound. "Are you all right?" he yelled.

"My leg—I can't keep up," Paul rasped. "Can you make it without me?"

"I've got to get to the house—"

"Go on! I'll be right behind you!"

Dan kept going, with Sunny beside him. Once he tripped in a hole and nearly fell, but he scrambled to his feet, fumbled for Sunny's harness, and kept going. His senses filled with the sound of the storm and the scent of smoke.

"Daniel!" Jennifer's frantic voice reached him above the wind and thunder. *"Daniel!"*

"I'm here, Jennifer!" With relief, he felt her hand on his arm.

"Daniel, where's Paul? Vali needs help!"

"He's right behind me—or should be. What about Vali?"

"She's inside. Daniel, the fire . . . Graham . . . we've got to get them out!"

Dan gripped her arm firmly. "Slow down. What about Vali and Graham? Where are they?"

"Vali's in the kitchen. She broke her ankle, I think. And she's swallowed a lot of smoke. She passed out—I'm pretty sure she's in shock. Graham's in the sunroom, but—"

Paul limped up behind them, panting heavily. Daniel turned toward the sound of his gasping breath. "Vali's inside. Let's go!"

When they got to the front door, Daniel turned to Jennifer. "Take Sunny. Go to a neighbor's and call the fire department—and an ambulance. Paul and I will go in."

"Daniel, I'm not leaving you here."

"We'll be OK. Paul will be my eyes. Now, go!"

Dan listened to Jennifer hurry off with Sunny in tow, then turned to Paul. "Can you do this?"

"I'll be all right," Paul rasped.

But Daniel heard the slight hesitation in Paul's reply. *Of course,* he remembered. *The plane crash . . . the fire . . .*

Daniel reached for him. "I know this is tough, after all you've been through. But we'll make it. We *have* to." He groped for the doorknob and flung open the door. He could feel the heat, smell the smoke. "You go first—on all fours. I'll grab your ankle and follow you. Don't go too fast—and don't stand up."

He heard Paul drop to his knees. "Ready, Daniel?"

"Ready."

They started to crawl slowly through the living room. The smoke was thick and heavy. "It's so hard to see," Paul muttered.

"Can you see the flames?"

"Not yet," Paul rasped. "But the smoke is—" The rest of his sentence dissolved in a fit of coughing.

"How much further?"

"We're almost . . . to the . . . kitchen."

Dan could feel the effects of the smoke in his lungs. His chest felt as if it could explode, and his eyes burned and watered.

"I see her!" Paul's raspy whisper reached his ears.

"How much further?"

"Only a foot or two. Vali!"

They reached her, and Dan groped to feel her pulse. She was

unconscious, but her pulse was fairly strong. "We have to get her out of here!"

Paul didn't answer.

"Paul?" Dan repeated. "Are you all right?"

"I'm here." The raspy voice began to cough. "The fire's moving this way. Part of the wall is gone."

"Then let's go!"

"I *can't.*"

Dan's lungs felt as if they would burst. He tried to get a breath and began to wheeze against the smoke. "We don't have much time!"

"I've got to go after Graham," Paul's whispery voice said. "Can you take care of Vali?"

"I think so, but—"

Paul squeezed Dan's shoulder. "I have to do this. I . . . I know what it's like to burn—to nearly die in a fire. Nobody deserves that—not even Graham."

Dan was acutely aware that their time was limited. In spite of the rain, the blaze was sweeping through the house and might be upon them at any minute. But he heard the plea in Paul's desperate whisper, and he couldn't bring himself to argue. "He's in the sunroom, Jennifer said. Can you get that far?"

"I'm going to try. Just get Vali out. *Please.*"

Then he was gone, and Dan was alone. A sense of hopelessness swept over him, but he fought against it. For once, his sightlessness was more of an advantage than a burden. He didn't need to see in order to crawl, and he didn't have to see to pull Vali's limp body through the room. All he had to do was go out the way they had come in. And keep praying as he went.

When you pass through the waters, I will be with you; and through the rivers, they will not overflow you. When you walk through the fire, you will not be scorched, nor will the flame burn you. . . .

The enormous lung capacity Dan had developed during his

years of training as an Olympic swimmer served him well. He could hold his breath for an incredibly long time, even under physical exertion, and he now used that ability to keep from being overcome with smoke.

He shall cover you with his feathers, and under his wings shall you trust. . . .

He felt a little more secure when he reached the edge of the living room carpet. But then he felt Vali begin to move, to thrash against him as he dragged her forward.

"Vali? It's me, Daniel. Don't struggle. Just stay with me, OK? We're almost out."

Dan heard her gasp, then begin to choke. When her coughing had subsided, he began to inch forward again, dragging her with him.

"Dear Lord," Daniel muttered, staggering forward. "Help us!"

The Lord will guard your going out and your coming in from this time forth and forever. . . .

At that moment he felt a touch of damp night air from the open front door.

"Oh, Daniel—"

"Jennifer?"

"I'm right here, Daniel! I'll take Vali now."

He felt her brush past him. "She's alive, Daniel. She's all right."

Exerting the last ounce of his energy, Dan stumbled out onto the porch. From a distance so far away that it seemed to be coming from another world, another time, he heard the urgent wail of approaching fire engines. Then voices. Someone helped him off the porch and set him down in the wet grass on the far side of the yard. He felt a hard shove from a furry body and smelled the musky scent of wet dog as Sunny nuzzled against him and licked his face.

The fire had not harmed their bodies, nor was a hair of their heads singed. . . .

TWENTY-THREE

P AUL Alexander knelt on the grass behind the house. All around him, he could hear sirens wailing and voices shouting, but none of it mattered to him. He was aware only of the burned and dying form of the man who lay in front of him.

Graham. His twin brother. His brother who had betrayed him, had tried to kill him.

But still . . . his brother.

Now they were truly twins. Graham had been burned, severely burned, just as he himself had been in the plane crash. Graham had felt the same pain, the mind-destroying, crushing pain of fire. He was alive, but just barely.

"Graham," Paul whispered. "The medics are on the way."

The eyes flickered open, wild and stark against the blackened face. "Too late . . ." he rasped.

Paul knew he was right, yet his heart wrenched at the reality of his brother's impending death. Graham shuddered, and Paul felt his pain.

He remembered. He remembered the agony, the terror, the devastating sense of helplessness. He knew what his brother was going through, and in a way, he was going through it with him.

As he stared down at the disfigured, ravaged body, Paul felt no anger. Only pity. Pity and an overwhelming sense of despair and loss. It shouldn't have been this way. They were brothers. How had it come to this?

Graham's breath rattled in his throat. He gasped for air. His head lolled to one side, and the life left his body.

"God, be merciful to him," Paul whispered. "God, be merciful to us all."

Then with infinite tenderness he reached to close his brother's eyes.

Sprawled outside on the lawn, as weak as he had ever been in his life, Daniel lay resting, enjoying the feel of Jennifer's arms around him, her murmurs of wifely concern.

"Are you sure you're all right, Daniel?"

"I'm fine. But Vali—"

"Vali is already on the way to the hospital. The medics said her ankle was broken, and she took in an awful lot of smoke. But she'll be all right."

"Paul—"

"Paul followed the ambulance to the hospital. He'll stay with Vali."

She said nothing for a moment, then started in on him again. "Daniel, are you absolutely positive that you're all right?"

He smiled. "Don't I look all right?"

"You look beautiful," Jennifer assured him between sobs. "Your face is black and your eyes are all red and your clothes are ruined. But you look beautiful, Daniel!" She hugged him to her as if to confirm her own words, smothering his face with kisses.

"We're quite a team, aren't we?" said Daniel.

"We're a *great* team!" Jennifer agreed.

Dan thought for a moment. "One thing, though," he said.

"Yes, Daniel?" She was still sobbing.

"Now that I've seen your idea of a honeymoon—" He paused as she kissed him again. "Would you mind very much if I handle our vacation plans in the future?"

"I still can't believe we're here, Daniel. This has to be one of the most exciting things that's ever happened to me!"

"Thanks," Daniel said dryly. "Where are our seats?"

"Orchestra section," Jennifer said distractedly, her head swiveling back and forth to watch the crowd pouring into The Performing Arts Center.

"Mm. First class. Do you see Leda anywhere?"

"No. I can't see much of anything from here."

A red-haired man wearing a sport coat and sweater vest approached them, smiling. "Mr. and Mrs. Kaine? I'm Grandy Hayden—Paul's manager. He asked me to meet you." He shook hands with Dan and Jennifer, glancing with interest at Sunny, who stood patiently at Dan's side.

"Your seats are down front. Paul's mother is already there. I'll take you to her, if you like."

He stepped in front of them and started walking. "Have you been at TPAC before?"

"No, we haven't," Jennifer replied. "We've been in Nashville, but this is our first time at the Center."

"Looks like most of Nashville is here tonight," Hayden said, glancing around. "I think we're going to have people hanging from the ceiling before long." He stopped to let someone pass, then went on. "Paul says the two of you are providing the music for the wedding tomorrow."

Jennifer nodded energetically, trying to ignore the butterflies in her stomach.

The concert hall was enormous, and already every inch of available space, both downstairs and in the tiered balcony, was packed.

As they neared the front, Jennifer spotted Leda, who stood when she saw them and waved. She embraced them warmly when they reached their seats, and Jeff Daly, at her side, stood and shook hands. Leda then introduced Vali's Aunt Mary, who was sitting on the other side of Jeff. Grandy Hayden waited until they were settled in their seats, then left to go backstage.

Leda continued to squeeze Jennifer's hand. "I think I'm more excited than the kids tonight!" she said. "Isn't this an event, though? The two of them together on a stage again for the first time in over three years?" She glanced toward the stage, then back at Jennifer. "So—are you ready for this big weekend? I'm already exhausted! And Vali—" She rolled her eyes heavenward. "I don't think that child has slept for a week. I told her she's going to collapse before the wedding tomorrow if she doesn't get some rest, but she doesn't hear me—she's too busy!"

Dan grinned at her. "How's Paul doing? Is he nervous?"

Leda arched one dark brow in amusement. "About the concert? No. He doesn't get too tense about performing. But the wedding?" She shook her head and threw up both hands. "He's hopeless."

As if by mutual consent, no one mentioned Graham. Jennifer knew it had to have been a shattering experience for Leda to have one son returned to her while losing the other to a horrible death.

According to recent newspaper accounts, Graham Alexander's research company was under investigation. The CIA had discovered ample documentation of treason. Graham's cohorts would be behind bars for years.

With a meaningful glance at Jeff Daly, Jennifer lowered her

voice to a conspiratorial whisper. "Is it possible there's going to
be another wedding in the near future, Leda?"

"It's under discussion," she answered slyly. "But I think we'll
elope. I'd never muster the energy to survive two big—"

The sudden dimming of the lights, followed by a crashing,
reverberating cadence of synthesized chords, made her stop and
turn toward the stage.

Jennifer clutched Dan's hand in anticipation as the music continued to echo from a darkened stage. The waiting crowd began
to cheer, already recognizing the unique sound of Paul Alexander's music.

A spotlight isolated Grandy Hayden as he hurried onstage, and
the music ebbed to a soft backdrop when he started to speak. He
grinned and waited to make himself heard.

"I won't draw this out—" The crowd applauded. "You've
waited long enough. Besides, there's probably nothing I could tell
you that you don't already know. By now you've heard their story.
You know where they've been and what they've gone through."
His expression sobered and he paused a beat before going on.
"Three years ago, you thought you had told them good-bye." His
smile returned. "Now, say hello . . . to Vali Tremayne and Paul
Alexander! By the grace of God—together again!"

He made a sweeping gesture with one hand, backing off the
stage as the lights went up and the music thundered. The crowd
rose to their feet in unison, exploding into a deafening roar of
cheering applause.

"Tell me *everything*," Daniel said in a voice loud enough to be
heard above the crowd and the music.

"There's Paul! Oh—Daniel—there he is!" Jennifer cried,
clutching eagerly at Dan's arm. "He's at his keyboard! Oh, my
goodness, he looks so different! He's gained weight. And his hair
is darker again . . . it still has lots of silver, though . . . and he still

has a beard. He looks *wonderful!* He looks *happy!* And he's still chewing gum, bless his heart!"

The din in the hall increased to a roar as Paul and his group moved into the familiar hit song associated with Vali throughout her meteoric career. Even lovelier than Jennifer remembered, she ran onto the stage wearing white silk, her magnificent hair blazing about her head. She faced the people once, opening her arms wide in welcome, then crossed to Paul and took him by the hand.

The two of them came center-front, their faces beaming with love for the crowd and for each other. Twice Vali had to wipe the tears from her eyes. Once she was overcome and pressed her head against Paul's shoulder for a moment until she regained her composure.

Leda was crying openly. It seemed to Jennifer that everyone in the hall was crying, and she was no exception. Even Daniel was dabbing at his eyes with his handkerchief.

It took almost ten minutes before the crowd settled down, and even then Paul had to call for order. Taking a microphone, his eyes twinkled with mirth as he looked out into the audience. "For those of you who were expecting David Nathan Keye, I apologize for the last-minute switch."

After their laughter subsided, he grinned at them and asked, "Well—you want to stand here and cry all night, or do you want some music?"

The uproar made it clear they wanted music. And they got music—a wide variety. The well-loved and familiar numbers Vali and Paul had made popular years before—the golden oldies, as Paul referred to them—plus a wealth of new numbers Paul had turned out since moving back to Nashville. There were hand-clapping, joyful praise songs, melodic ballads like *Vali's Song,* gospel songs and hymns and Scripture songs. Years of treasured Christian music were poured out as a love offering to the Lord in the presence of his people.

"Vali seems so much more confident," Jennifer remarked to Dan once, noting the pleased smile her words brought to his face. "She's just dynamite up there!"

"We're in the presence of greatness, darlin'," said Daniel.

"They're so *good* together!"

"Like us," he said with a sage nod.

"Like us," Jennifer repeated, checking his expression for any hint of levity but finding none.

Returning her attention to the stage, she saw Paul grab a microphone and drape his other arm around Vali. He looked exhausted but happy as he began to address the crowd.

"We really have to quit sometime tonight, people," he said, meeting the chorus of protests from the audience with an upraised hand and a grin. "Wait . . . wait a minute . . . just in case there's anyone out there who doesn't know this by now, I have something to tell you."

He brought the mike a little closer to his mouth and leaned forward to the audience, his eyes sparkling with mischief. His teasing grin broke into a broad smile of unrestrained joy with his dramatic announcement. "We're . . . getting . . . married . . . tomorrow!"

He turned to a blushing Vali and kissed her soundly, with loud and energetic approval from the audience.

Paul waited until the din subsided, then spoke again into the microphone, slowly and distinctly so his whisper-voice could be understood.

"Tonight is a special time of reunion for Vali and me. Our being together again is a miracle for which we'll never cease to thank God. We're grateful beyond words to be able to stand up here together and look out and see the people we love. Among those people are two very special friends the Lord brought into our lives at a time when we needed them most."

Paul smiled out at them and continued. "Most of you have

probably heard of one member of this marvelous duo. A few months ago, a musical by the title of *Daybreak* swept the Christian community. Not only has the musical itself changed numerous lives, but the title song has become an anthem of hope for Christians throughout the country. It will be a part of our wedding service tomorrow, but we wanted to share it with you tonight. *Daybreak* was written by a great man named Daniel Kaine. We'd like for you to meet him and his beautiful wife, Jennifer, . . . right now."

The next thing Jennifer knew, Paul had bolted from the stage, slowed very little by his stiff leg, and was headed toward her and Daniel. The crowd broke into pleased applause as they embraced, then linked arms. Paul coaxed them up to the stage, where they were welcomed by a misty-eyed Vali. She gave each of them—including Sunny—a fervent hug.

After leading Dan to the grand piano, Paul returned to his keyboard. A hush fell over the entire auditorium. Dan hesitated only a moment before sounding the opening chords of *Daybreak*. Paul waited a few measures, then added the electronic equivalent of a full orchestra, and the two of them began to offer a sacrifice of praise that Jennifer felt sure had the angels in heaven singing with them. Finally she and Vali, coming to stand behind Dan at the piano, added their voices to the music.

There was not a dry eye in the auditorium or a single person remaining in his seat as the four on stage repeated the *Daybreak* finale. They built in volume as they built the emotion, giving their voices, their hearts, and their spirits over to the music that God had used time after time, first for Daniel . . . and now for others.

Standing behind her husband, Jennifer watched the mastery and the consummate skill of his hands at the piano. As he played, she felt the power in his massive shoulders and the power in his spirit. Then a sudden flash of insight shook her to the very core of her being.

She looked up from Daniel and out into the mass of people whose voices were raised in one thundering hymn of communal praise and saw, not a sea of strangers, but a family of loved ones. In that moment, she caught a glimpse of what the Lord had desired for his children from the beginning of creation . . . a oneness, a unity of heart and spirit and purpose with the power to transcend individual needs, bridge nations, unite governments, and join worlds as a body fitted together and secured in place by the love of Jesus Christ.

After the last chord had sounded, Daniel stood, and Paul came to join them. The four linked hands and walked to the front of the stage, basking in the unity and the love that filled the hall.

As the cheering continued across the immense, overflowing auditorium, Jennifer glanced from Vali to Paul, then to the audience, and finally to her husband.

"What are you thinking, Daniel?" she asked, close to his ear in order to be heard.

He hugged her tightly and gave her a smile that went straight to her heart. "I was thinking," he said quietly, "how much the Father must enjoy these family reunions."

What readers are saying about the Daybreak Mysteries:

"*Storm at Daybreak* helped me through a broken romance. . . . I've read the book at least four times and had my faith re-anchored each time."

"I've discovered gold when I came upon your books—indeed a rare treasure!"

"Today I finished your book *Vow of Silence.* I picked it up two days ago and haven't been able to put it down."

"I have read hundreds of Christian novels. . . . I want to tell you that yours surpasses them all."

"As a church librarian, I want to tell you how well received your books are to our people . . . and at many other church libraries."

"We all agree you are tops in fiction, and we anxiously await any new books coming on the market."

What the media is saying about the Daybreak Mysteries:

"Dramatic Christian fiction at its best . . . "
  Christian Retailing

" . . . a fast-moving, spine-chilling story that weaves the Christian message throughout its pages."
  Librarian's World

"Christianity right at the grass roots, in your lives, where you live . . . "
  WCRH FM, Williamsport, Md.

"Hoff is an excellent storyteller who spins a tale that can be enjoyed by men, women, and younger readers alike."
  The Bookshelf

The Tangled Web

B. J. HOFF

Tyndale House Publishers, Inc.
WHEATON, ILLINOIS

Library of Congress Cataloging-in-Publication Data

Hoff, B. J.
   The tangled web / B. J. Hoff.
      p.   cm. — (Daybreak mysteries ; 3)
   ISBN 0-8423-7194-X (softcover)
   I. Title. II. Series: Hoff, B. J. Daybreak mysteries ; 3.
PS3558.034395T3   1997
813'.54—dc20   96-27246

Printed in the United States of America

01   00   99   98   97
7   6   5   4   3   2   1

FOR JIM

Husbands are the real heroes. . . .

Like a father who untangles
What small, clumsy hands ensnare,
God unsnarls and smooths our problems
Once we trust them to his care.

B. J. Hoff
From *The Weaver*

PROLOGUE
Pittsburgh, Pennsylvania
Saturday

Teddy Giordano felt his stomach wrench when he saw Nick's body slumped over the massive mahogany desk in the library. He closed his eyes and fought back a rush of tears.

Nick . . . oh, no, Nick . . .

He shuddered, forcing down the rancid taste of his own fear. He touched Nick's lifeless shoulder, then felt for a pulse at the side of his neck. Nick had been shot execution style, obviously by one of the *Family.*

Teddy yanked his hand away. *Had he suffered? Or had it been quick and painless, with death coming before he had even known what was happening?*

He dragged his eyes away from Nick's body and scanned the room. The heavy, rust-colored drapes were closed against the late afternoon light. The library was dim, illuminated only by a hand-painted desk lamp.

Only then did he realize that the telephone receiver was off the hook, its high-pitched wail insistent. He moved to pick it up, then stopped. Did he really want his fingerprints on anything in here?

He glanced down and saw the drawer of the desk standing open. Someone had had to force it—Nick always locked that drawer. Always. That was where he kept his gun . . . and, until recently, the small, black notebook.

The drawer was empty. No gun. No notebook.

Teddy hadn't expected the notebook to be there. It had already been hidden. *But what about the gun?*

He wiped his hands on his jeans, then raked his fingers through his hair. For an instant, his shock at finding Nick dead was replaced by an unexpectedly powerful wave of grief. The man slumped over the desk had been his boss—no, more than a boss. He had been almost like a big brother to Teddy. Nick had been good to him, had cared about him.

"Stay out of the business, Teddy," Nick had often warned him. "It's not for you. You're a good kid. You shouldn't sell yourself out. Just work for me, personally. Not the Family."

Nick Angelini was the only man Teddy had ever trusted. Nick had become his family, he and the kids.

The kids!

Teddy's head snapped up sharply. *Where were the kids?*

ONE

T EDDY'S boots whacked the glistening wood floor as he bolted from the library. He stopped in the hall, squinting up the dark stairway.

"Nicky?" His voice echoed in the high-ceilinged entrance hall. "Stacey? You up there?"

As he stood there, listening, his mind replayed his earlier conversation with Nick. At the time, he hadn't realized it would be their *last* conversation. . . .

"They're going to hit me, Teddy. At least, they're going to try. I violated the *omerta,* the code of honor. They know about the notebook, that I'm going to turn it in and testify against Sabas." His dark eyes raked Teddy's face, studying him closely. "I hate to do this to you, *compagno.* But I've got no one else. You have to take the notebook and the kids, Teddy."

Teddy backed away from Nick, shaking his head. "Uh-uh. No way. I'm a driver, a gofer, not a hero."

"You're more than that, and you know it," Nick said with soft rebuke. "You are *fratello mio*—my brother. You love my kids. And they love you. If they lose me, they have nobody. A dead mother they don't even remember, a dead father—"

"What about your sister?"

"My sister is a stranger to them. You're family."

"No one's going to hit you, Nick," Teddy protested. "Get out. Take the kids and leave."

1

"Teddy, Teddy," the older man said, shaking his head sadly, "you know better. I've betrayed the Family. There's nowhere to run. Nowhere."

"I can't do it," Teddy insisted. "I'm not like you, Nick. I drive cars, that's all. I can't take care of your kids. I have nothing to offer them. Besides, how could anyone know about the notebook, about what you're planning to do?"

Unexpectedly, the older man grabbed the front of Teddy's jacket. "Sabas is going to have me killed," he grated roughly. "The word is out. I'm a dead man. And you know as well as I do what will happen to my kids. They'll be raised by one of the other *caporegimes*. I don't want that for my kids, Teddy! I want them to grow up clean and decent, not caught up in the business."

He dropped his hand away then, slapping Teddy lightly, affectionately, on the cheek. "Sorry, kid. I'm nervous today, that's all."

"What do you want me to do?" Teddy didn't even try to mask his resentment. He owed Nick. *But this much?*

"I want you to take the kids and the notebook and get out of here," Nick said. "Before tonight. I have money for you—a lot. Enough to take care of the three of you for a long time, if necessary. But you've got to go *now*—as soon as possible!"

"But *where,* Nick?"

"To Virginia. There's a man there who works for the Federal Witness Protection Program," Nick explained hurriedly. "He's been straight with me. Once you get the notebook to him, they can move on Sabas and put him out of business. For good. Everything they need is in that notebook, Teddy. Even without my testimony, they can finish him."

A shadow of hopeless resignation clouded Nick's eyes. "I'll never testify, Teddy. But you can save the evidence. And you can save my kids, if you do what I ask."

They studied each other in silence. Then Teddy nodded shortly. "I'll need a car."

"Take the limo."

"It's low on fuel. I was planning on going into town later this evening and filling it up."

"Do it now. I'll have Nora pack for the kids while you're gone."

"Nora's off today, remember?" Teddy felt a pang of sympathy for the kindhearted, elderly housekeeper. She adored both Angelini children. She would be inconsolable when she realized they were gone.

"Then Nicky can pack for both of them."

"You're coming with us, or I'm not going."

"No! the only chance you and the kids have is to go without me. If I go, they'll kill us all." He paused. "I can buy you a little more time by staying here."

Nick took Teddy into the library and gave him a bundle of money from the safe, more money than Teddy had ever seen. "Now get moving," Nick ordered. "I'll talk to the kids while you're gone. They'll be ready when you come back."

Still Teddy hesitated. "Nick . . ."

The older man swallowed hard, then reached out to grip Teddy's shoulder. "Thank you, *compagno.* You've been a good friend."

Some friend, Teddy thought with self-disgust as he called the kids' names once again. *I've let Nick be murdered and lost his kids, all inside of two hours.*

He bounded up the stairs, taking them two at a time, then raced down the carpeted hallway to Stacey's room. He threw open the door, only to find the pink bedroom empty.

Next he went to Nicky's room, but there was no sign of the boy.

He went on down the hall, flinging open one door after

another. After checking the entire second floor and finding nothing, he ran back downstairs, charging through the enormous, drafty rooms with mounting anxiety.

Had they taken the kids?

In desperation, he hurtled down the basement steps.

"Nicky? Stacey? Are you down here?"

A soft thump sounded overhead, a few feet away. Cautiously, Teddy followed the sound.

"Stacey? Nicky? Can you hear me? It's Teddy."

A faint whimper answered him. He looked up, then raised both hands to unlatch the hook on the laundry chute.

Stacey tumbled out first, practically falling into Teddy's arms. She was crying. Teddy tucked the little girl securely against his chest with one hand, then reached up to help her brother.

Nicky landed lightly on his feet and stood staring at Teddy, his dark eyes burning with a combination of fear and anger behind the thick-lensed, silver-framed glasses.

"What were you guys doing in the *laundry chute?*" Teddy snapped incredulously.

The chunky little girl in his arms began to cry harder, and he quickly gentled his tone, patting her helplessly on the back. "Don't cry, baby. It's all right." He gave one stubby dark pigtail a gentle tug. "Look at Mrs. Whispers," he said, pointing to the frayed rag doll Stacey was clutching tightly against her. "She isn't crying."

Teddy turned to the boy. "Are you kids OK?"

With the back of his hand, Nicky brushed a tangle of dark, ragged hair away from his forehead. "He's dead, isn't he? Papa's dead."

Teddy stared at him without answering, still cradling the sobbing little girl against his shoulder. He glanced at Stacey, then nodded curtly to the boy.

"Where were you? Did you see anything?"

Nicky swallowed, his thin neck making the reflex motion

appear strangely pathetic to Teddy. "No. Papa sent us upstairs. He told us to hide if we heard anyone in the house."

The boy removed his glasses and, in a decidedly adult gesture, wiped a hand over his eyes. "Someone kept banging on the door." His voice wavered for an instant. "It was quiet for a few minutes. Then we heard a shot."

Teddy moistened his lips and glanced from Nicky to the weeping little girl in his arms. He wished he could think of something to say. He wished he could *think*.

"Papa said you were going to take us somewhere," the boy went on in an odd, flat tone of voice. "He told me to pack a suitcase for both of us. Are we still going to leave?"

Teddy nodded. "Yeah. Right now. You got your stuff together?"

"In the kitchen."

"Let's go." Still holding Stacey in his arms, Teddy turned and started up the basement stairs.

When they reached the hallway, he glanced toward the open library door.

The boy started toward the room.

"Don't go in there, Nicky!" Teddy cautioned sharply. "Get your coats, both of you. We have to get out of here."

Nicky looked at him, then at the open door, hesitating.

"Don't, Nicky," Teddy repeated tersely.

The boy continued to stare toward the library for another moment, then crossed the hall and opened the closet door.

Teddy set Stacey on her feet and took her hand. "Come on, baby. Let's get you into your coat."

Quickly, he zipped up his own jacket, then helped Stacey into her red parka. "That's my good girl," he said softly, managing a smile as he straightened.

She was no longer crying, but her dark brown eyes were large and solemn. "Nicky said we can't see Papa anymore, that he isn't going with us." Her small voice sounded frightened and much younger than her six years. "Mrs. Whispers is going with us, isn't she?"

"Anywhere you go, Mrs. Whispers goes, sweetheart," Teddy assured her with a hug.

In the kitchen, Teddy looked out the window, then cracked the door connecting to the garage, peering into the dimness.

A thought struck him, and he twisted his mouth to one side impatiently. "You kids wait here a minute. I have to make a quick call before we go."

Teddy returned to the library, resolutely averting his eyes from Nick's body. His hand shook as he dug a handkerchief out of his back pocket and used it to pick up the receiver. He pressed the button to clear the line and get a dial tone, then called Frank Vincent, Nick's lawyer.

Disguising his voice, Teddy hurriedly advised Vincent of Nick's murder. Then he fled the room, not looking back.

In the kitchen, he picked up Stacey's suitcase, started to open the door to the garage, then turned to Nicky. If Nick's death was not to be a total waste, Teddy had to be sure about the notebook. "There's a book," he said. "One of those little pocket jobs. It was important to your papa—"

Before he could finish, Nicky nodded. "I know all about it. Don't worry—it's safe."

Teddy heaved a sigh of relief. "Get your stuff and come on," he said, gesturing toward Nicky's suitcase. He wished he'd had time to pack a few things for himself.

Teddy hurried them into the garage, fumbling for his keys as he went. If only they could get out of here without being seen, maybe they had a chance.

Nicky lifted his suitcase into the silver limousine's large trunk. "Where are we going?"

Without answering, Teddy hustled both children into the front seat, then ran around the car and got in on the driver's side. He pressed the power door-locks and gunned the engine to life. As soon as the garage door went up, he backed out of the garage, tires squealing.

"Where are we going, Teddy?" the boy asked again.

Teddy righted the limo, glancing in the rearview mirror as the car surged forward. "On a long trip," he finally said. "I'm taking you to a place your papa told me about."

Without looking at him, Nicky replied knowingly, "Where we'll be safe."

Teddy glanced over at him. "Where you'll be safe," he repeated. "That's my job now," he said softly. "Keeping you and Stacey safe."

"We can't get away from them, you know," Nicky said woodenly. "There isn't anywhere we can go that they won't find us."

Teddy knew that Nicky Angelini was one smart kid. A genius, the headmaster at that fancy private school had told Nick. An honest-to-goodness nine-year-old prodigy. At the moment, however, Teddy fervently hoped even a genius could occasionally be wrong.

TWO

East-Central West Virginia
Palm Sunday

JENNIFER Kaine came awake in an instant, bolting upright in bed. She pulled the blanket up to
her neck and tried to focus her eyes in the dark
bedroom.

The room was thickly shadowed, unfamiliar. It was also cold.
Jennifer looked down toward the iron bedstead at her feet, then
across the room at the sliding glass doors.

Outside, huge pine trees and grasping maples fought each
other for control of the night sky. The blackness was relieved only
by a faint spray of light from the security lamp that stood a few
feet away from the cabin.

The cabin.

Finally, her head cleared. They were at the Farm, not at home.
She glanced over at Daniel. He was still asleep, his breathing deep
and regular. Sunny, Daniel's golden retriever guide dog, also
stirred restlessly from her rug beside the bed.

The digital clock on the bedside table showed almost midnight.
Jennifer had been asleep for nearly an hour, exhausted from the ride
to the Farm and the work they had done upon their arrival: carrying
in supplies, stacking wood for the fireplace, and loading the pantry
shelves. It had been eleven o'clock before she had collapsed onto the
plump feather bed, every muscle in her body rioting in rebellion.

Now, fully alert, she tried to figure out what had roused her from her deep sleep. There had been a noise—a noise out of place for her surroundings. With the covers still wrapped snugly around her shoulders, she lay listening.

Suddenly, a soft thumping sound, like the muffled thud of running feet, broke the quiet. At the same time, Sunny leaped to her feet, uttering a low, warning growl.

Someone was on the deck.

A wraparound wooden deck circled the cabin, with steps descending to the yard on both sides. It sounded to Jennifer as if someone was at the far end of the cabin, near the kitchen.

Then, abruptly, there was nothing but silence—a silence so total that Jennifer could hear her own heart pounding. She stared with growing dread at the glass doors at the end of the room, half expecting to see someone stop in front of them and gape back at her.

With another perfunctory growl, Sunny went to stand in front of the doors and look out. Chilled, Jennifer reached to shake Daniel awake.

"Daniel! Daniel, wake up!" Fear made her whisper scrape like sandpaper in the hushed bedroom.

Sunny now crossed to Jennifer's side of the bed.

Daniel was slow to stir.

"Daniel!" Jennifer shook him again, harder this time. "There's someone outside!"

Finally, he pushed himself up. "What's wrong?" he said, brushing the hair out of his eyes.

"I heard something outside," Jennifer whispered. "Like . . . someone running across the deck."

The instant Sunny saw that her master was awake, she went back to his side of the bed. The retriever stood watching Daniel shake his head and yawn.

"Someone running?" he muttered. "What time is it, anyway?"

Jennifer flipped back the blankets and swung her feet over the side of the bed. "I'm going to see what's going on," she said, grabbing her robe from a nearby rocking chair.

"Jennifer, wait a minute—"

But Jennifer wasn't about to wait. She wanted to make sure the glass doors were locked. She crept stealthily across the plank floor, flinching at the cold wood beneath her bare feet. There were no drapes at the doors, a condition Jennifer intended to remedy before sleeping another night in this room. She would use sheets or blankets if she had to.

She edged up to the glass, holding her breath as she peered outside. Nothing. The lock was secure.

After a moment, she went to the window at the other side of the room and opened a shutter. Daniel, blind for nearly six years now, shrugged into his robe and came to stand behind her. Sunny followed, wedging herself between the two of them.

"Can you see anything?" Daniel murmured, putting a hand on Jennifer's shoulder.

"Nothing." Jennifer strained for a better look, but her view was obscured by the dense grove of trees that rimmed the cabin. "It's too dark."

"How long have you been awake?"

"Just a few minutes. The noise startled me."

"You don't suppose Jason is up wandering around, do you?"

Jennifer tensed. Nine-year-old Jason, whom she and Daniel had adopted a few months ago, was mildly retarded; she continually had to fight her tendency to overprotect him. At the moment, Jason was supposed to be asleep in the loft bedroom, but Daniel's question prompted a stab of concern.

"I'd better go see. If he's up at this time of night, he must be sick."

"Wait. I'll go with you."

With Sunny following right behind them, Jennifer guided Daniel from the room with her hand in his. "I wonder if Gabe or Lyss heard anything," she whispered as they made their way through the darkened great room toward the stairway.

"I hope not. If Gabe wakes up, we're all up for the night," Daniel muttered. "It only takes a couple hours of sleep to charge him for the next day. He'll yak till dawn if he gets up now."

Gabe Denton and Daniel were as close as brothers. Not only had they been best friends for years, but Gabe also managed the radio station Daniel owned—and had recently married Daniel's sister, Lyss. The newlyweds had come along this week to help get the Farm ready for its first visitors of the year, weekend campers who would begin to arrive the week after Easter.

For the last four years, Daniel and Gabe, as well as others from the church, had worked to convert what had once been a family-owned farm into a Christian summer camp for disabled children. This year, the two couples had offered to fill in for the over-worked, year-round supervisor and his wife while the couple took a brief vacation before the summer camping season.

Jennifer's mind raced through all the possibilities as she hurried upstairs, leaving Daniel and Sunny below. She found Jason sleeping soundly in the enormous old four-poster that had once belonged to Daniel's grandparents. She stood watching him for a moment, then tucked the bedcovers more snugly around him and went back downstairs.

"Well, it wasn't Jason I heard," she told Daniel. "I don't think he's moved since we tucked him in." She paused. "Daniel, maybe we ought to wake Gabe and have him look around outside."

"It was probably just a wild dog, Jennifer. Let's go back to bed." He turned and would have started out of the room if Jennifer hadn't stopped him.

"A *wild dog?*" she repeated, clutching his arm.

He nodded. "We get them all the time out here. People dump them out on the highway, and they come around looking for food."

Jennifer's stomach knotted at the thought of stray dogs circling the cabin in the middle of the night. Still, she couldn't buy Daniel's explanation.

"That was no dog," she said stubbornly. "Not unless he was wearing shoes."

Daniel sighed. "Whatever you heard, darlin'," he said reasonably, "is gone now. Come on—let's get some sleep." He covered her hand on his arm and started toward the bedroom.

But he moved a little too fast for Jennifer, and she crashed into the corner of a large pine table.

"Ohhh, Daniel! My *toe!*"

Daniel caught her around the waist.

"What happened?"

"My toe!" Jennifer wailed. "I think I broke my toe!"

"How?"

"How?" Jennifer stared at him. "I ran into a table, that's how! It's pitch black in here."

Daniel pulled her to him and began to pat her back, much as he might have tried to comfort Jason. "But why?"

"Why *what?*" Jennifer's eyes smarted with tears of pain and exasperation.

"Why is it dark in here? Why didn't you turn on the lights? Just because I have to navigate in the dark doesn't mean *you* do."

At that moment the lights went on. Jennifer jerked in surprise, but it was only Gabe. Gabe, in a Chinese red monk's robe trimmed in gold satin. Directly behind him, peering over his shoulder with eyes that were little more than slits, stood Lyss. She looked lost and somehow forlorn in an oversized bathrobe that bore a strong resemblance to a horse blanket.

Gabe studied them, his hand still poised on the light switch. "What's going on?" he grumbled, flipping a shock of sun-streaked blond hair out of his eyes. "What are you guys doing out here in the dark?"

"We were looking for a wild dog wearing shoes," Daniel said

mildly. "But Jennifer—who apparently *isn't* wearing shoes—stubbed her toe. Will one of you take a look at it?"

Gabe studied Daniel for only a moment before giving a shrug and crossing the room. He helped Jennifer to the well-worn chintz chair by the fireplace, steadying her as she sat down.

Lyss watched them with a vacant stare and an enormous yawn. After another moment, she moved to help. "I don't think it's broken, Jennifer," she said as she examined the throbbing toe.

"Well, it *feels* broken," Jennifer muttered.

Behind Lyss, Gabe rolled his eyes and shrugged again. "So what were you doing, anyway? It's after midnight."

Daniel explained while Lyss went to make an ice pack for the toe.

"Probably a 'coon," Gabe said mildly. "Or maybe a stray dog."

Jennifer gritted her teeth. "If you don't mind," she grated, "I don't want to hear anything else tonight about stray dogs."

She saw Daniel barely suppress a grin, but his expression appeared convincingly sober when he spoke. "Why don't we help you back to bed, darlin'?" he said. "You can take the ice pack with you."

At that point Gabe offered to make coffee for everyone—"as long as we're all awake anyway."

Daniel grimaced, but it was Lyss who answered. "Some of us," she told her husband with a bleary-eyed glare, "are *not* awake. Nor do we want to be. At least not for another eight hours."

Soon the cabin was again dark and quiet. Daniel had already turned over to go back to sleep, but Jennifer wasn't ready to let it go—not yet. "I *did* hear something, Daniel," she insisted, her voice hushed. "And it wasn't a dog."

She waited, but there was no reply except from Sunny, who whimpered sympathetically from her side of the bed.

THREE

AS the limousine slowed, then came to a stop, Chuck Arno roused from sleep and sat up in the backseat, grumbling. Boone, the stoop-shouldered driver hunched behind the wheel, glanced nervously in the rearview mirror, then at the passenger beside him. He started to speak, stopped, cleared his throat, and tried again.

"How much longer are we gonna keep lookin', Wolf?" Boone's voice was reedy, almost whining.

In the passenger's seat, Wolf looked at Boone. Arno could see his frigid blue eyes in the mirror as Wolf studied Boone for a moment. Finally, without answering the question, he turned his gaze back to the road. Pressing his index finger to one side of his nose, he sniffed, once, then again—a habit that never failed to irritate Arno.

"Where are we?" he muttered, leaning over the front seat. "Why'd you stop, Boone?" He wiped a hand across his eyes, forcing himself awake, then stretched to look at himself in the rearview mirror. Arno grimaced at his own reflection—an overweight middle-aged man with swarthy skin and dark eyes, now red-rimmed and bloodshot. Automatically, his mind snapped shut, denying what he saw. He looked away.

"Got to get some gas," the driver snapped. "Hard to tell where we'll find another station this time of night, out here in the sticks."

Wolf, a small, wiry man with the coldest eyes Arno had ever seen, finally spoke. "We should give the Boss a quick call. He'll be wondering what's going on."

"You call, Wolf," the driver wheedled. "You know he's gonna be mad."

Wolf picked up the cellular phone from the seat beside him and flipped it open. He listened for a second, then closed the phone again. "We're too far out of range. Use the pay phone at the gas station." He eyed Boone suspiciously. "Why would P. J. be mad, Boone?"

Boone killed the engine but continued to stare straight ahead. His large, gnarled hands were none too steady on the steering wheel.

From the back seat, Arno watched the driver squirm, mildly amused at his discomfort. It was a common joke that Boone Scavarelli spent half of his life being scared to death of the Boss— P. J. Sabas—and the other half being terrified of Wolf.

When Boone glanced back at him, as if looking for support, Arno felt a familiar sting of impatience. The man's wandering eye was an imperfection that grated on him. He could never quite tell where Boone was looking. Worse, Arno thought with distaste, the man was a bumbler—none too bright. For the life of him, he couldn't figure why Wolf insisted on taking old Boone along wherever they went.

The aging driver was still pleading with Wolf. "He'll likely think we should have caught up with them by now."

"P. J.'s a patient man," Wolf answered with another sniff. "Just tell him we're closing in."

"Closing in?" Boone looked at him incredulously.

Wolf smiled at him. In the backseat, Arno moistened his lips, fidgeting as he watched the two.

Jay Wolf was neither ugly nor good-looking. At first glance, he might have been labeled ordinary, with his acne-scarred complexion, his small, narrow-shouldered frame, and his limp, light-brown hair. But when he smiled, his appearance underwent a startling transformation. His lips opened on a wide mouth that was overcrowded with surprisingly large teeth, some of which tapered to fanglike points. At the same time, his pale eyes narrowed menacingly, making his surname, "Wolf," eerily appropriate.

Still smiling broadly, he nodded. "That's what I said, Boone. Closing in."

"But, Wolf, we ain't got a thought where they—"

The smile disappeared. "Here's how I see it, Boone," said Wolf, casually resting one arm against the car door. "We've temporarily lost Giordano and the kids, true. But if we cover every county road, every country lane, and every cow path, we'll eventually find them. Right?"

He paused, again smiling, as if he had generously forgiven the older man his temporary lapse of confidence. "Now, Boone, you know they can't hide a flashy silver limousine like Angelini's out here in the woods too long. It seems pretty simple to me. We find the car, we find Giordano and the kids. Even if they try to hole up somewhere, they can't ditch that limo without us finding it eventually. Isn't that right, Chuck?" He turned to look at Arno.

Caught off guard, Arno hesitated, then gushed, "Right, Wolf. That's how it looks to me."

Wolf nodded and turned around. "You see, Boone? Just tell the Boss we're closing in and things are looking good. Real good."

Without meeting his gaze, Boone pulled up the zipper of his hooded jacket and hauled himself awkwardly out of the car. He pumped his own gas, paid the attendant at the register inside, then lumbered over to the pay phone at the side of the stucco building.

"Boone's nervous," Wolf said conversationally, his eyes on the older man using the phone. "You nervous, too, Chuck?"

"Me?" Arno laughed, a little too loudly. "No way, Wolf. Noth-

17

ing to be nervous about, right? It's like you said. How hard can it be to spot that limo of Nick's?"

A cold finger seemed to touch the back of his neck when Wolf half turned and smiled at him. "Boone's getting old, I'm afraid. We'll have to watch him, Chuck."

Arno quickly agreed. "Yeah. Yeah, maybe we'd better."

Wolf was still smiling when Boone returned to the car.

"So, did you talk to the Boss?"

Boone nodded, giving Wolf an anxious look. "He's burnin'. Just like I said."

Wolf shrugged. "He'll be OK. Relax, Boone. You worry too much." He touched his nose and sniffed. "Let's move."

Boone started the car and eased away from the pump. "The Boss is really upset, Wolf," he said with an uneasy glance. "You know what he told me?"

"No, Boone. What did he tell you?" Wolf smoothed the velvet lapel of his gray chesterfield.

"He said to tell you to bring Giordano and the kids back by the end of the week or not to come back at all. He said that, Wolf."

Wolf looked at him for a moment, then turned away, saying nothing.

In the back, Arno folded his arms across his chest and slouched down in the seat. Sometimes he wished he was still collecting markers. At least then he wouldn't have to spend so much time with Wolf. The guy gave him the creeps, and that was the truth. There was something weird about him, something . . . scary.

He had never met anyone like Wolf. Even the Boss—who could turn mean as a snake sometimes—wasn't strange like Wolf. At least with P. J. you always knew where you stood; you could tell when you were in trouble with him.

But not with Wolf. The guy was totally unpredictable. Icy cold most of the time, except when he had one of those fits of his.

Then he turned into a crazy man, a real mental case. And you never knew when it was going to happen. He would be smiling that blood-freezing smile of his one minute, and the next thing you knew, he'd be roaring and crashing around like a rabid . . . wolf.

Arno shuddered inside his black leather jacket. When this was over, he told himself for the hundredth time, he was going to talk to the Boss about some new action. Something out of Wolf's territory.

B Y dinnertime the next evening, Jennifer had
decided that her sore toe might be a blessing in
disguise. Her work detail for the day had been the
lightest of all, and now, listening to the others rehash their efforts,
she could enjoy the conversation guilt free.

Her chief duties had been to help Gabe inventory the storage
pantry and give him a hand with lunch and dinner.

By mutual consent, Gabe had been appointed chef for the
group. His hobby was cooking, and he approached it as he did
everything else, with dizzying energy and unbounded creativity.

His menu for the evening meal was no exception, Jennifer
thought as she dished up a generous second helping of Creole
gumbo.

She glanced at Lyss, who sat studying the last bite of food on
her plate with obvious regret. "I guess I'll forgive you for not
helping us clean the cabins," Lyss told Gabe. "This is scrumptious
stuff, love." She lifted the final taste of gumbo to her mouth and
took her time finishing it off.

"Save room for dessert," Gabe warned as he started scraping
dishes in the sink.

Daniel pushed himself back from the harvest table with a contented sigh. "Dessert, too? What are we having?"

"Lemon mousse," Jennifer put in. "And almond cookies."

Daniel, who loved anything citrus, made a small sound of satisfaction and gave a deep stretch. "When's snack time?"

Jennifer watched out of the corner of her eye as Jason soaked up the last bite of gumbo on his plate with a piece of roll and started to put it in his mouth, then stopped. He looked at the retriever sitting next to him and then, after a furtive glance at the adults, quickly palmed the bread.

"Don't even think about it, Jason," Jennifer said warningly, eyeing the boy and the dog.

Jason studied her face. When he saw one corner of her mouth twitch, he grinned at her, as if he knew he was still on safe ground. Blinking once, he said gravely, "But Sunny hasn't had any dinner."

"Well, she's not going to have her dinner at the table," Jennifer said firmly. "You can feed her after we're done. Outside."

"But you'd better not give her any of that gumbo, Jason," Daniel told him. "It's too spicy."

"So spicy you had three helpings," Gabe countered dryly from the sink.

"I'm immune," Daniel said pleasantly. "I'm used to Jennifer's cooking."

Jennifer elbowed him. "Daniel will have gummy oatmeal for breakfast, Gabe. Nice and cold."

Gabe wiped his hands on a dish towel, then returned to the table. "My count in the storage pantry didn't tally, Dan," he said, scooting onto the bench across from Daniel. "Either Mac's first count was wrong, or there's some stuff missing."

"What kind of stuff?" Daniel crossed his arms over his chest and leaned back against the wall.

"Blankets and pillows. I was three short on each. Jennifer checked my count, just to make sure."

"Don't forget the food shelves," Jennifer reminded him.

"According to the list Mac gave us, there should be two large jars of peanut butter in addition to what we counted. Plus three bags of marshmallows and two boxes of crackers."

Daniel leaned forward, drained the milk from his glass, then dabbed his mustache with his napkin. "Mac is as accurate as a CPA with that storage pantry," he said, getting up to take his dishes over to the sink. "Maybe some things just got misplaced."

Gabe shook his head. "Nope. We checked every likely place. His gaze swept the room. "Who's up for the dishes tonight?"

When a long silence greeted his question, he shrugged. "OK. Who wants to get up at six tomorrow morning and cook breakfast?"

"Jennifer and I will take care of the dishes," Daniel quickly offered, pushing up his sleeves. "You just sit down and enjoy your coffee."

Gabe smiled at Lyss and Jennifer. "Cooperation. That's what makes this team *work.*"

Later, Jennifer sat on the overstuffed sofa in the great room, looking around. She loved this room—mostly because it was so *friendly.* The huge stone fireplace was the focal point of the entire room. A fire burned there anytime the mercury dipped low enough. The furniture was big, worn, and comfortable. Jennifer had come to think of the cabin as a second home, and this particular room as the heart of that home. It was a happy room, she often thought, a good-natured, smiling kind of room where people could be themselves and enjoy each other.

She looked across the room to see Daniel retrieving his old Martin flattop guitar from the corner. Lyss went hunting for her banjo, and soon they were singing camp choruses.

After a time of prayer together, Daniel got up and put his guitar away. "I'm ready for dessert."

"We'll get it," Gabe said, pulling Lyss up from the couch with him. "It's in hiding. You don't leave dessert within reach of Dan the Dumpster."

When they came back, Gabe was empty-handed and scowling. "OK, so you found the cookies, Kaine. Are there any left?"

Daniel, standing with his face toward the fire, turned with a puzzled frown. "What?"

"The cookies, Daniel," Gabe repeated with forced patience. "Where are the cookies?"

Lyss followed her husband into the room, laughing at his aggravation. "Better 'fess up, Dan. He's just stubborn enough to lock up the mousse if you don't share the cookies."

"What are you two talking about? I don't know anything about the cookies."

Jennifer thought Daniel's expression looked entirely genuine, but she could never be sure. "Gabe, you said you made two dozen. Even Daniel can't eat that many cookies in an afternoon."

They went on arguing for another few minutes, Gabe insisting that his brother-in-law was the only conceivable suspect, while Daniel's injured look of denial became more and more convincing.

"I've got it!" Jennifer exclaimed finally, her smile saccharine. "I'll bet it was that wild dog you fellows told me about last night."

Gabe shot her a disgusted look.

"I bet I know who took the cookies."

All four adults stopped talking and turned to look at Jason.

From his place on the hearth rug beside Sunny, the boy pushed a strand of straight blond hair away from his eyes. "Probably it was the children in the woods."

No one said anything for a moment. "What are you talking about, Jason?" Jennifer finally asked.

He looked up at her and smiled. "I saw them today, when I

took Sunny outside. While Daddy and Aunt Lyss were cleaning the cabin. A boy and a girl. I think they want to be my friends."

"Jason," Daniel said patiently, "didn't we just have a talk a few days ago about make-believe friends? I thought you were going to stop pretending."

The boy shook his head. "But these aren't pretend friends, Daddy. They're real."

Daniel frowned. "Jason—"

As if wounded by the unfamiliar note of irritation in his father's voice, Jason suddenly stopped smiling and fastened his wide brown eyes on Daniel. "They *are* real."

"Jason, *you* didn't take the cookies, did you?" Daniel asked, his tone sharp.

"No, sir." The boy's crestfallen expression reflected dismay that Daniel would even ask.

During the somewhat awkward silence that followed, Gabe and Lyss discreetly left the room. After a moment, Jennifer said, "Jason, these . . . children . . . where exactly did you see them?"

"Jennifer!" Dan's expression darkened.

"Wait, Daniel—please. Let him tell us."

"They came from behind the tree." Jason watched Jennifer's face carefully.

"What tree, honey?" she pressed.

"The big one, at the end of the gate."

"What did they look like?"

He thought for a moment. "The boy has black hair, like Daddy's. And big glasses."

"You said there was a girl, too?" Jennifer prompted gently.

Jason nodded. "She has tails that stick out, like this." He raised both hands to his ears and made a pulling motion.

"Pigtails? Is that what you mean?"

Again, he nodded. "She's little," he said in a condescending tone. "And round."

"Round?" Jennifer repeated.

"Not like you. She's—" He made the shape of a ball with his hands. "Round."

"Jennifer, do you really think we should encourage this?" Daniel asked shortly.

Jennifer studied him, surprised at the annoyance etched on his face. Finally, she turned back to Jason. "Why don't you go up and get ready for bed, honey. We can talk more about this in the morning. All right?"

Jason gave her an unexpectedly wise look, as if he knew no one believed him. He rubbed Sunny's ears once more, then got up. "Can Sunny go with me? Just for a while?"

Jennifer nodded. "But she has to come back downstairs soon. Daddy might need her."

The instant Jason and Sunny were out of earshot, Daniel turned to Jennifer. "You know I've been talking with him about these imaginary playmates."

Jennifer bit her lip and nodded. "Yes, I know. But I'm not sure I understand why it bothers you so much."

"Because sometimes he carries it too far." He shoved his hands into his pockets and turned away, saying nothing more.

Puzzled, Jennifer stared at his broad back. "Daniel? Don't you think you might be making too much of this?"

He turned back to her, his strong, dark-bearded face set in a stubborn mask. "No, I don't. But I think *you* could take it a little more seriously."

"Daniel—"

"Jason's different, Jennifer," he said, ignoring her attempt to interrupt. "He doesn't always think the way you and I do. Sometimes it's hard for him to tell the difference between what's real and what isn't. I just don't want his fantasies to become too important—or too real—to him."

Exasperation rose in Jennifer, then ebbed as she realized that her husband had been uncharacteristically touchy the past few days. "Daniel, what's wrong?" she asked carefully.

He frowned. "Wrong?"

"It isn't like you to make an issue of something so small."

He said nothing, but his chin jutted out a fraction more.

A totally irrelevant thought flitted through Jennifer's mind. Daniel suddenly appeared extremely . . . large to her. It wasn't so much his considerable height, nor the expanse of his shoulders, molded by years of strenuous training as a former Olympic swimming champion. In fact, she was seldom mindful of his size. Daniel was so gentle, so kind and tenderhearted, that it was easy to forget that he towered over her and others. His sweet and unfailing devotion to her, his consideration of her feelings—even his quiet, casual Appalachian drawl—somehow tempered his formidable size and strength.

The only time she thought much about his size at all was during a rare bout of anger—or stubbornness. Like now.

She took a deep breath. "Daniel, let's go for a walk," she said quietly.

Again he frowned. "A walk?"

"Yes. Would you like to?"

After a moment, he shrugged. "It's cold out. You sure you want to?"

"I'll get our jackets." Jennifer started for the closet, then stopped. "Do you want to take Sunny?"

"No, if you don't mind helping me."

Frustration welled up in Jennifer, but she kept her tone perfectly even. "You know I don't mind."

After getting their coats from the closet, she ducked into the kitchen to tell Gabe and Lyss where they were going.

Outside, she took Daniel's arm, waiting until he covered her hand with his own before starting to walk.

They went around the front yard, then down the narrow lane

leading away from the side of the cabin. The night was cold, blanketed with damp silence. Wind bent the low-hanging branches of the maple trees and moaned through the pines scattered over the grounds.

Jennifer shivered, as much from a sudden, unbidden clutch of apprehension as from the cold. She huddled a little closer to Daniel, and he slowed his pace. "You cold?"

"I'll be OK after we walk a bit. It feels as if it's going to snow."

He nodded but said nothing.

"Daniel," Jennifer ventured, "is something bothering you? Something besides this thing with Jason?" She looked up at him, feeling a familiar tug at her heart as she studied the strength and kindness molded in his profile.

His voice was soft when he finally answered. "It isn't Jason. It's me."

He stopped, but Jennifer continued to cling to his arm. "What are you talking about?"

He sighed. "I don't know. Maybe I'm just overcompensating."

"I don't understand," Jennifer said.

"Neither do I." His smile was grim. "All I know is that lately I've been feeling . . . anxious. Maybe even a little insecure . . . about being a father." He hesitated. "A *blind* father. To a mentally challenged boy."

Jennifer caught her breath in dismay. "But you're a *wonderful* father to Jason! And he absolutely adores you!"

"Oh, I know he loves me—*us,*" Daniel quickly agreed. "But I still want to be sure that I'm doing what's best for him. However I can, I want to ensure a decent quality of life for Jason when he grows up." He squeezed her hand. "It's always going to be harder for him, Jennifer. I have to do everything in my power to give him as much strength and wisdom as he's going to need someday. So he can do more than just . . . survive, if the time comes when he's on his own."

Jennifer studied his face, unshed tears lodging in her throat. "Oh, Daniel . . . don't you realize that Jason can't be anything *but* strong with the kind of love and caring he's going to grow up with?"

She reached up and placed her hands on either side of her husband's face, searching his sightless blue eyes. "Daniel, you're a *marvelous* father—truly, you are. And Jason is going to grow up to be a fine, strong man, in spite of his disability." She paused. "But just as your own father didn't try to limit you—even after you were blinded—you mustn't try to limit Jason either."

He rested his hands lightly on her shoulders, saying nothing.

"Daniel," she continued, still framing his face with her hands, "you told me once that your father taught you about boundaries by giving you freedom and combining it with responsibility. You said he taught you about right and wrong by letting you make some wrong choices and take the consequences of your mistakes. Remember?"

He nodded.

"And you said that you believe God teaches us in the same way," she went on, "enabling us to stretch and grow by giving us the freedom to be wrong sometimes."

Again he gave a small nod.

Jennifer dropped her hands to his shoulders. "Well, Daniel, I think that's what you have to do with Jason, too. You have to give him some freedom. And—" She hesitated. "And I think you have to give him time to be a little boy. That's an important part of growing up, after all."

They continued to stand close, unmoving, each of them clasping the other's shoulders as Daniel seemed to consider her words. Finally, a hint of a smile softened his features. "And I suppose you think Jason's make-believe friends are a part of growing up as well?"

"Yes, I do." Jennifer paused. "I had a pretend friend when I was a little girl. His name was Bob."

"Bob?" One dark eyebrow lifted.

"He was a big-brother type," Jennifer explained matter-of-factly. "Protected me from all the bullies on the block, that kind of stuff."

Daniel put his arms around her. "Somehow, love, I can't imagine you having too much trouble with bullies."

"No?"

"No. It's a lot easier to imagine you chasing the bullies away." He kissed her gently on the forehead.

"I did that, too. But only when Bob was with me."

He shook his head, then turned at the sound of voices drifting toward them from the cabin. "Are Gabe and Lyss out here, too?"

Jennifer turned to glance at the cabin. "They're on the deck." She smiled as she watched Gabe hold Lyss in his arms. "Acting like newlyweds."

Daniel tightened his embrace, coaxing her closer. Leaning into his strength, Jennifer smiled at how warm it always seemed to be in his arms. She tilted her face to his.

"And do *you* still feel like a newlywed, Mrs. Kaine?" he asked softly, a smile in his voice.

"As a matter of fact, I do," Jennifer murmured, reaching up with one hand to touch his bearded cheek. "Do you, Daniel?"

He pressed his lips to her temple. "Not really."

Hurt, Jennifer tried to pull away from him, but he held her, smiling at her indignation. "I feel," he whispered against her hair, "like a man who is more in love with his wife than any newlywed could ever be." His lips met hers in a gentle kiss. "I love you, Jennifer Kaine. I love you more right now, at this moment, than I've ever loved you."

"You do?"

"Absolutely." Daniel kissed her again, a kiss that took Jennifer's breath away.

"Let's leave the newlyweds out in the cold and go back inside to the fire, what do you say?"

They began to walk. "By the way," he said, "what did this . . . *Bob* fellow look like?"

"He was gorgeous."

"Thought you were just a kid."

"I was." Jennifer chuckled. "But *Bob* wasn't."

He stopped. "Someday I'm going to have the last word in one of these conversations."

"Want to bet?"

Someone was crying.

At first Jennifer thought she'd been dreaming. Still only half-awake, she reached out to touch Daniel. Her hand latched onto his pillow. He was gone.

She sat up and looked around, trying to focus in the darkness. "Daniel?"

When he didn't answer, she reached over to turn on the bed-side lamp, then changed her mind.

Again came the faint, muffled cries that sounded like a child weeping, penetrating the night with a chord of anguish.

For a moment, Jennifer couldn't move. Chilled, she clutched the blanket, again whispering Daniel's name. Finally, she slipped out of bed, fumbling for her robe.

Something must be wrong with Jason.

Trembling now, she pulled on her robe, then turned toward the window. The sound was coming from outside. But that was impossible. Jason was upstairs.

Seeing nothing from the window, she turned and went to the sliding glass doors. She had hung a sheet to serve as a makeshift drape, and now she pulled it back to look outside. The deck and surrounding yard were dark. Nothing moved.

And the crying had stopped.

Rushing across the room and out into the hall, she nearly careened into Daniel, who was coming from the great room. Instead of his robe, he was wearing jeans and a ski sweater. Sunny was with him, on her harness.

"Daniel! What's wrong?"

He found her hand and tucked it under his free arm. "I thought I heard something. Did I wake you?"

"You heard it, too?" Jennifer gripped his hand. "It sounded like a child crying. Is Jason—"

"Jason's sound asleep. That was my first thought, so Sunny and I went up to check on him. He's fine."

Jennifer's throat tightened. "Then what was it?"

He shook his head. "Must have been an animal. Maybe something's hurt outside. I'd better go check."

Jennifer threw a coat on over her robe and went with him. They walked around in the cold darkness for nearly half an hour but found nothing. At last they gave up and went back inside. If an animal *had* been nearby, it was gone.

"At least this time you heard something, too," Jennifer said as she hung up her coat. "Do you really think it was an animal?"

"What else?" He unfastened Sunny's harness and stroked the retriever's head for a moment.

"Daniel . . ."

"Hm?"

"What if Jason *did* see someone today? What if those children weren't make-believe?"

He frowned. "Children in the woods?" He gave a small laugh. "Jennifer, it's *cold* out there. Even a runaway wouldn't be hanging around in this kind of weather."

What he said made sense. But *something* had been out there. And Jason had seemed so *certain* about those two children.

"I hope the whole week isn't going to be like this," Daniel said wearily.

"Like what?"

"I'd like to get some sleep."

"Oh." Jennifer looked at him, wishing he felt more like talking. "Daniel . . . *could* someone be out there? In the woods?"

He sighed. "Would *you* be slinking around a youth camp in thirty-degree weather at midnight, Jennifer?" He reached for her hand. "Honey, forget it. Let's get some rest."

Reluctantly, she followed him into the bedroom. In her mind, she could still hear the mournful, heart-wrenching sound of a sobbing child. Daniel was probably right. It was a ridiculous notion to even think that a child—or an adult, for that matter—would be out there in this weather.

But an hour later, Jennifer was still awake, listening. Listening for a sound that never came.

FIVE

T HE next afternoon, Jason started off for the big tree at the end of the lane. "Come on, Sunny—this way." Jason glanced back to make sure the retriever was following him, then took off running.

"Hurry!" Jason called over his shoulder. He had to find the children before someone came looking for him. He was sure the children wouldn't come out if they saw a grown-up. He didn't know exactly *how* he knew that, but he knew.

When Daddy had agreed to let him take Sunny outside to play, he warned Jason to stay "within shouting distance." He wasn't disobeying, he told himself as he and Sunny pounded down the dirt pathway at top speed. He could hear if anyone called him. The important thing was to find the children and tell them they had to return the cookies.

But what if they had eaten all the cookies by now?

He remembered the way everyone had looked at him the night before. Daddy had seemed disappointed in him, and that had hurt a lot. Mommy had looked at him the way she always did, with a little smile that crinkled up her chocolate eyes and made him feel loved. Uncle Gabe and Aunt Lyss had just acted like they felt sorry for him.

He had gone to bed angry, angry with those children in the woods. This morning he was still . . . *gritty.* That was Mommy's word for upset, and that's how he felt. Gritty.

The children shouldn't have taken the cookies. It was stealing. And not only had they done something wrong, but what they had done had made Daddy angry with *him*.

"Sunny, stop!" To slow himself down, Jason grabbed at a low-hanging branch of the big old tree. This was where he'd been playing the day before, when he spotted the two children.

"Hey!" He peered into the woods beyond the clearing. But the trees were thick, and they went a long, long way—out across the field and up the side of the hill that overlooked the Farm. "Hey, are you in there?"

Sunny looked at him, then turned to stare into the trees. "Good dog," Jason whispered to her. "You can help me look."

Jason called out again, but all he heard was the funny hacking sound made by a crow. A strong gust of wind whizzed through the trees.

Disappointed, he dug at the ground with the toe of his hiking boot. That's what Daddy did sometimes when he was trying to work out a problem in his mind. Maybe it would help.

He tried shouting into the trees again. No answer. But Jason waited some more. He didn't want to give up until he heard the sound of his daddy's voice, calling him back to the cabin.

Finally he turned to go. They should have come. They got him in trouble and then wouldn't come to help him. Maybe he didn't want to be friends with them after all.

That night, after Mommy had given him the last in a whole series of goodnight kisses and left his bedroom, Daddy stayed. He sat down on the bed and patted the blanket for Jason's hand. When he found it, he wrapped his big hand around it. Jason always felt good when Daddy held his hand. It made him feel safe, like nothing could ever hurt him.

"Jason, I owe you an apology," Daddy said. "About last night. I know you didn't take those cookies. I shouldn't have even felt the need to ask you if you did." He paused, then added, "If I hurt your feelings—and I'm afraid I did—I'm sorry, Son."

Jason looked up at Daddy. Even though his father couldn't see, he always seemed to be looking right at him when they talked. Like what they were discussing was really important.

"I just want you to know I'm sorry," Daddy went on, "and I believe you when you say you didn't take the cookies. Will you forgive me?"

Jason hadn't seen his daddy look sad very often. He almost always looked happy. Aunt Lyss said he usually looked like he was about to play a trick on someone.

But right now, he looked very sad, and Jason hated that. He sat up in bed and put his arms around his daddy's neck. "It's all right, Daddy. I forgive you."

"I guess we still have a mystery, though, don't we?"

Still hugging him, Jason nodded his head. "You mean, because we don't know who took the cookies?"

"Right. I know what you said, about the . . . children in the woods taking them. But—"

"You still don't believe they're real children, do you? You think I made them up."

"Jason, if they seem real to you—"

Jason pulled back. "Daddy, why don't you believe me?"

He saw his daddy take a deep breath, then run his hand over his chin. "Jason, I just don't understand how there could be two children out there in the woods. It's cold, and there's nowhere they could go to get warm. Who do you think these children are? And where did they come from?"

Jason felt a little better. At least Daddy was *trying* to believe him.

"Maybe they ran away from home."

"But they sound awfully little to be runaways, don't you think? And how would they get way out here?"

"I don't know," Jason said, watching his daddy's face. Daddy might be trying to believe, but Jason could tell he didn't. The apology made him feel better, but he wanted his daddy to *understand,* to believe him. The children were real. He hadn't made them up; he was getting too old for that kind of stuff. He guessed he would just have to figure out a way to prove he wasn't playing make-believe.

He hugged his daddy hard and kissed him on the side of his cheek, on that place where his black beard was thickest. He liked the way it tickled his nose. When he grew up, he was going to have a beard, too.

Long after Daddy had left the room, Jason was still awake. It was important for him not to fall asleep. He had to think, and he always found it easier to think when he was alone.

Tomorrow, when no one was around, he would talk to Uncle Gabe. If anyone could help him figure out a way to catch the children, Uncle Gabe could. He had once heard Daddy tell Mommy that Uncle Gabe was the smartest man he'd ever known, even if he did act like a clown most of the time.

If Uncle Gabe was that smart, he could help Jason prove he wasn't pretending. Or at least he would *try.* Uncle Gabe wasn't like most other grown-ups. He was never too busy to help. Never too busy to hear what a little kid like Jason had to say.

Next to Daddy, Uncle Gabe was Jason's favorite man in all the world.

SIX

I RRITATION welled up in Gabe as he stared at the empty container. Last night there had been enough baked ham not only for today's lunch but for topping two or three pizzas as well. Now it was gone. All of it.

"OK. This has gone far enough. It's no longer funny. I can survive on peanut-butter-and-jelly sandwiches the rest of the week if you can."

"What's wrong, Gabe?"

He scowled suspiciously at the group gathered around the table. Jennifer's puzzled frown looked sincere enough, but she had learned that deadpan expression of hers from a real pro. Nobody was more gifted in the art of the impassive stare than his old pal Dan.

Jennifer had been a quick study, all right. A few weeks ago, she had successfully convinced him that she'd had nothing to do with the fluorescent sign that had been placed in the middle of the town square. In shimmering neon colors, the sign had proclaimed the birthday of one *Gable Scott Denton,* his age, and his telephone number—along with an open invitation for everyone to call, "after eleven tonight to give Good Old Gabe your regards."

After days of relentless digging, he had finally confirmed his suspicions. His wife and Jennifer had painted the sign, and Jennifer had erected it well after midnight the eve of his birthday. When confronted, Jennifer had given an incredible performance, first pretending to be horrified, then wounded that Gabe would point a finger at her. Not once did the woman actually lie to him; she simply skirted the issue. Only later, when she could no longer stand being left out, did she gleefully admit to her part in the escapade, confessing with what appeared to be a touch of pride that the entire caper had been her idea.

Small wonder that he wasn't the least convinced by the guileless stare she now leveled at him.

He sighed. "The ham, in case there happens to be one among you who is ignorant of the fact, is gone. At least," he said testily, "it's *almost* gone." He held up one small scrap of meat and dangled it between his thumb and forefinger. "Unless we want to divide this up for sandwiches."

"You're kidding." Lyss, his wife of mere weeks, whom he loved to the point of derangement, ambled up beside him looking beautiful, curious, and convincingly vacant. He knew his lady well enough, however, not to be taken in by her charm. Love him she might, but she could be every bit as devious as her sister-in-law if she glimpsed the possibility of a good laugh at her husband's expense.

"How could it possibly be gone?" she asked innocently, peering down into the empty plastic container.

Dan was next. Gabe would have been disappointed, of course, if his friend's routine had not outclassed the combined efforts of all present. Dan lifted his Roman-gladiator chin and with casual disapproval remarked, "How could anyone lose a ham?" The inflection in his voice made it less a question than an accusation.

Jennifer folded her hands primly on the table in front of her and gazed at Gabe with a look of great wisdom. "Probably a 'coon. Or a wild dog. There are a lot of them around here, you know."

Jason was the only one who remained silent, and Gabe didn't have the heart to question the boy after all the fuss about the missing cookies the night before.

He sighed. Their fun and games were not going to continue throughout the week. Not without a price.

He gave them his iciest smile and spoke with a tone usually reserved for a couple of rambunctious clowns in his church youth group. "All right, people. Enjoy your amusement. Just chuckle your way through the bread-and-butter sandwiches you're going to have for lunch . . . and dinner."

Lyss groaned, but he ignored her. "Sit," he ordered with an imperious nod at the harvest table.

Obediently, she shuffled across the room to join the others. They waited, all eyes riveted on him.

"Now, then," he continued, shifting easily to the role of maligned but forgiving patron, "let's look at the facts. We have a variety of items missing from the storage pantry—linens and assorted groceries. In addition, two dozen cookies and approximately five pounds of baked ham have disappeared within a twenty-four-hour period."

When no one offered to comment, he went on. "Since all present have vowed their innocence of any wrongdoing—" He paused, appraising each face looking up at him from the table. "The only conceivable answer is that somewhere on the grounds lurks an extremely clever, quiet, and well-fed thief."

A heavy silence descended upon the room. "You think it's one of us playing a joke. Don't you?" Jennifer asked.

Gabe fixed a bland expression on his face. "Why in the world," he drawled, "would I think a thing like that?"

They continued to argue good-naturedly among themselves for a few more minutes but got nowhere. Finally, with sighs of resignation, they put together bologna-and-cheese sandwiches for lunch. They ate quickly, without conversation. Jennifer and Lyss exchanged occasional wry glances. Dan, however, appeared to be giving the whole situation serious thought. He was uncommonly silent—so much so that Gabe began to wonder if he might have misjudged him. Certainly he didn't look like a man who was secretly enjoying a practical joke.

41

No one lost any time returning to their jobs at the campers' cabins after lunch. Only Jason remained behind, offering to help clean up.

"Well, cub, what do you think about our mystery?" Gabe asked, giving the boy's shoulder a squeeze as they put away the last of the dishes.

Jason studied Gabe's eyes for a moment. "Do you think I made them up, too? The children in the woods?"

Gabe's smile faded. The small towheaded boy standing before him was obviously troubled. He wasn't sure how to respond, but Jason clearly expected something from him.

"*Did* you make them up?" he countered bluntly.

"No, sir, I *saw* them." Jason bit his lower lip.

Gabe studied him. "A boy and a girl, you say?"

Jason nodded solemnly.

"And you think they're responsible for our missing food?"

Again, the boy nodded, this time with a little more hope in his eyes.

Gabe began to stroke his mustache with his index finger. The kid was convinced. And while he didn't pretend to know much about little boys, he thought he *did* know Jason. And Jason didn't lie. One thing was certain: Jason really believed he had seen a boy and a girl in the woods. It was probably foolish even to consider the possibility, but Gabe had a hunch that it was important to Jason that *someone* believe him.

He narrowed one eye. "All right, cub. I think you and I might just try to catch ourselves a couple of poachers."

He dried his hands on the dish towel, then slung an arm around the boy, now bright-eyed with excitement. With a grin and a quick hug, Gabe propelled him into the great room.

"What we need," he announced gravely as they sat down on the slightly sagging couch, "is a plan."

They put their plan into effect shortly after midnight that night.

"I'm cold, Uncle Gabe," Jason complained, pushing closer to him.

Gabe tucked the boy's muffler more tightly around his neck. They were lying on their stomachs just below a rise at the foot of the field, not far from the huge old sycamore tree by the gate.

The night was cold, damp, and heavy with the threat of rain or snow. There was no wind, but the stillness felt like the proverbial calm before the storm. Gabe shifted uneasily.

Sneaking out of the cabin unnoticed had not been as difficult as he had feared it might be. Waiting until Lyss was deeply asleep, he had slipped quietly from bed, dressed hurriedly in the bathroom, then crept up the stairs to the loft. Instead of having to wake Jason, he had found the boy waiting for him, wide awake and impatient.

Now they huddled together in the brush. "You're sure this is where you saw them?" Gabe asked again. "This is where you talked to the little girl?"

Jason nodded, his eyes half-hidden beneath the blond, shaggy hair spilling out from his cap. "I tried to talk to the boy, too, but when he saw me, he grabbed the girl's hand and ran away."

Gabe studied Jason's face carefully. "What were they wearing, cub?"

Jason frowned and pressed his lips together. "The little girl had on a bright red coat," he said after a moment. "With a furry hood. The boy's coat was black, with shiny white pockets."

If Jason *was* creating all this from his imagination, Gabe thought, he certainly wasn't sparing any of the details. In spite of his earlier doubts, he was beginning to get caught up in his nephew's story.

"You said the boy looked to be about your age?"

Jason nodded eagerly. "But he's—" He searched for the word

43

he wanted. *"Thin.* He's thin, Uncle Gabe. And he has dark hair, almost black, not light like—"

Gabe stopped him in midsentence, touching a warning finger to his lips and motioning to the far corner of the field.

Only yards away from where they were lying, a shadow moved from behind the end cabin in the boys' section.

Jason stirred, and Gabe quickly shook his head and put a restraining hand on his shoulder. As they watched, the shadow changed and broadened, then suddenly grew still.

It was difficult to make out anything other than dark, shadowy forms. Only one security light was on at this end of the field, and it was at the girls' side of the cabins. Gabe raised his head another inch or so above the rise, and Jason cautiously imitated him. When there was no sign of movement, Gabe began to wonder if they had seen nothing more than a clump of shrubbery being ruffled by the wind.

Then something moved. Gabe's eyes widened with disbelief as two small figures slowly emerged from the shadows. Jason caught a sharp breath, and Gabe warned him with a quick hug to stay quiet.

Even in the darkness, he knew what he was seeing. *Kids. Two kids. So Jason hadn't made them up after all.*

He held his breath, watching them. They hovered close to the cabins for a moment, as if to make sure no one else was around. Suddenly, they took off, one pulling the other by the hand, in a frenzied run across the field. They were headed in the direction of the main cabin.

"That's *them,* Uncle Gabe!" Jason's whisper, harsh and excited, broke the silence.

Gabe gripped the boy's arm. "Shh! Stay down. Give them another minute, then we'll—"

"Look!"

Gabe swiveled around to look back at the cabins. Another shadow was emerging, this one much larger. The figure, crouching low but moving with agile grace, broke out of the shadows between the two cabins at the end and bolted across the field after the children. As he ran, he snapped his head back and forth, as if to make sure he wasn't being watched.

They were too far away to get a good look at his face, but Gabe could tell two things by the way he moved—he was a seasoned runner, and he was a grown man, not a kid.

A needle of fear pierced the back of his neck. Finding out that Jason's "friends" really existed had been a surprise, but not a frightening one. However, the realization that someone was with them—an adult—was far more unsettling.

Who were these kids, anyway? And who was the man with them? What possible reason could they have for hiding at an isolated youth camp in weather like this?

"We're going to follow them," he whispered. "But don't let them see you." He pulled himself to his knees, helping Jason to his feet as he stood. "Until I find out what they're up to, we're going to keep our distance. Understand, cub?"

Jason nodded but tugged on Gabe's hand. "Hurry, Uncle Gabe," he whispered insistently. "We have to catch them!"

Gabe wondered uneasily just what, exactly, he intended to do when they actually confronted the two kids and their unknown cohort. This entire scheme might not turn out to be one of his better ideas. Here he was, out in the woods with a nine-year-old boy, chasing after three strangers who could be up to just about anything. The only other adult male he could count on was most likely sound asleep—not to mention the fact that he was also blind.

For one of the few times in his life, Gabe faced a situation in which he could not find so much as a trace of humor. All he could think of was the fact that the three most important people in his life were sleeping innocently and helplessly inside the main cabin while some creep and his two little sidekicks prowled around outside. And as if that weren't enough, the eager boy at his

side—who had also become extremely important to him—
seemed to have no idea that they might be in danger.

Staying low and out of sight, they reached the main cabin only
a moment behind the others. A few feet away, a fruit cellar was
banked against a small rise. Gabe ran around to the side of it,
motioning for Jason to follow him.

A nearby security light cast enough of a glow on the end of
the cabin that Gabe could see the furtive trio now standing on
the deck, just outside the kitchen door.

He pressed against the side of the building to avoid being seen.
With growing anger, he watched as the man on the deck, after a
quick look around, took something from his pocket and inserted
it into the space between the door and its frame.

At that instant Gabe realized that he was watching a burglar open
the kitchen door with a plastic credit card. To his astonishment, the
man stayed on the deck while the two kids went inside.

Furious, Gabe studied the man who now skulked across the
deck, surveying one end of the cabin, then the other.

Now Gabe could see him clearly enough to tell he was
young—in his twenties, maybe—and appeared wiry and trim in a
dark jacket and jeans. He was bareheaded, and his hair looked
thick and curly.

An impatient tug on his hand reminded Gabe that Jason couldn't
see around him. He frowned at the boy, then shook his head to warn
him to stay put. Glancing from Jason to the cabin, his mind reeled
when he saw the man ease himself carefully through the door.

"Come on," Gabe whispered to Jason. "We're going around to
the window."

"What are we going to do, Uncle Gabe?" Jason whispered back.

Gabe shook his head, trying to ignore the knot of dread lodged
in his throat. He reminded himself that, if these three were indeed
their thieves, the worst they had done so far was to steal some

food and supplies. If that were the case, they surely weren't all that dangerous.

Besides, even if they did decide to make trouble, he thought he could handle two kids and a man who looked to be several inches shorter and twenty pounds lighter than himself.

They climbed the steps and tiptoed across the wooden deck as quietly as possible. Gabe moved Jason safely behind him, then edged closer to the window.

He tried to be quiet, but he found it almost impossible to move without making a racket. His feet felt like frozen clubs in the sturdy hiking boots, and his legs were stiff and unsteady from the cold air and tension. Carefully he plastered himself against the wall of the cabin and looked through the side of the window.

At first, he could see nothing. There was no light inside the room, and the faint glow shed by the outside security light was only enough to cast shadows.

Then one of the shadows moved, arcing a thin stream of light from corner to corner across the room.

Gabe stiffened. A flashlight! No doubt so they could see what they wanted to steal.

He pressed the side of his face even closer to the glass. The shadows revealed only one of the children—the boy—who was now moving toward the storage pantry.

Gabe inched closer, trying to see the far end of the kitchen. He stifled a small murmur of disappointment when he saw that the man was standing right beside the door.

His eyes scanned the room, and he moved in closer for a better look. There was the little girl, bathed in a soft wash of light from the open refrigerator door. Apparently, she was about to help herself to the contents.

Gabe pressed his lips together in a tight, angry line. At his side, he felt Jason squirm. He glanced down at him, again warning him with a finger over his lips to remain quiet.

A soft thud from inside made him turn back to the window. The refrigerator door was shut and the flashlight had been doused.

All movement inside the room had ceased. With a pounding heart, Gabe's eyes locked on the dark form now standing in the doorway between the kitchen and the great room. Even in the darkness, he immediately recognized the towering silhouette.

Dan! What did he think he was doing, walking right into the midst of those three, when he couldn't even see what was going on. . . .

Gabe stared through the glass. Dan might not even know anyone was *in* the kitchen. Had he heard something and come to check—or had he simply walked into the room and stumbled onto them unknowingly?

Either way, his being there meant there was no more time to waste.

Gabe looked desperately around the deck, hoping to find some kind of weapon. But there was nothing, only a few empty clay pots and a discarded milk can.

Jason huddled against him, shivering. *What should he do now?* The guy inside might have a gun . . . or a knife . . . and there was Dan, who couldn't even see the others in the room. The women were probably still asleep.

Whatever he did, it had to be quick.

His decision made, Gabe gave Jason a quick, urgent directive, then began moving toward the kitchen door.

SEVEN

DANIEL immediately identified the sound he had heard upon entering the kitchen. Someone had just closed the refrigerator door.

So Gabe wasn't sleeping either. Good. He was wide awake and hungry himself. Might as well have some company.

"Gabe?"

He waited, confused by the silence.

"Lyss?"

Not a chance. Lyss wouldn't waste her sleep time on anything, even food.

Then it dawned on him. "Jason. Don't try to sneak past me." He walked on into the room. "You'd just better hope there's plenty of that pudding left, sport." He stretched out a hand, waiting for Jason to take it.

Only after a moment of absolute silence did Daniel begin to sense something wrong. Jason would have come to him, would have at least said something. Nor was it Gabe or Lyss. The two of them were great pranksters, but they never took advantage of his blindness. And he had left Jennifer still in bed, sound asleep.

Still another few seconds passed before a warning buzz finally went off in his mind.

There was someone in the kitchen, all right . . . but who?

He seldom used Sunny on harness in the cabin; the surroundings were comfortably familiar, and he didn't need her guidance to get around. Now, however, he wished he had brought her into the kitchen with him.

Daniel's heart skidded to a stop, then raced. He stood unmoving, suddenly frightened.

Were the lights on? If so, he was an open target for whoever might be watching. He lifted his chin and forced his voice into an authority he didn't feel. "Who's there?"

He waited, his chest tightening. "I said who's there?"

Silence was his only reply. Yet he was absolutely certain he wasn't alone.

For the first time in months, a familiar attack of vertigo hit him—a dizzying assault that bordered on panic, the kind that had so often seized him during those first few months after the automobile accident. He felt himself watched by an unknown adversary. He was exposed. Vulnerable.

Perspiration bathed his face, and he reached out for something to steady himself. With relief, he felt the edge of the large, vintage cabinet, clung to it, and waited.

Teddy stood frozen in place only inches from the door. He squinted into the shadows, trying to get a good look at the dark giant now standing in the middle of the room.

Silhouetted in the glow from the outside light, the guy looked huge, with shoulders broad enough to block Teddy's view, and arms that, even in a bathrobe, spelled muscle.

He glanced at Stacey. In the dim light from outside, he could see that the poor little kid looked like someone had shot an electric current through her system. Her dark eyes were round and frightened, her mouth half-open in astonishment.

Nicky, ducking his head out of the storage pantry at the sound of a strange voice, reached his little sister's side in three broad steps and hunched himself protectively between her and the big guy in the bathrobe.

For the second time, the giant spoke. "I said who's there?"

Obviously, he couldn't see too well in the dark. Teddy fleetingly wondered why he hadn't turned on the lights. One thing was certain—they had only seconds if they were going to get out.

With one hand, he threw the door open; then he jumped aside, yelling, *"Run! Now!"*

The words were no more than out of his mouth when a blond guy in a blue ski jacket hurtled through the open door, blocking the kids' flight with his body.

Stacey, unable to avoid crashing into the man at the door, hit him hard enough to make her bounce and reel backward. She started to cry.

With a strangled exclamation of fury, Nicky charged the man and swung at him with both fists. But the man easily grabbed the boy with one hand and pushed him firmly against the wall.

Flipping the light switch with his other hand, he called out, "Dan—are you all right?"

Teddy took a step toward the door, and the guy in the ski jacket shot a warning. *"Freeze,* man! Don't even blink!"

Teddy looked at him. He didn't see a weapon, but something in that level, green-eyed stare stopped him.

"Gabe?" The big man in the white bathrobe looked relieved. Relieved and bewildered. "What's going on? Who's in here?"

Without taking his eyes off Teddy, the one called Gabe snapped, "Fagin and friends. But instead of picking pockets, they're looting the kitchen."

The dark-haired man looked even more puzzled. "What?" His frown deepened as he turned in Stacey's direction. "Who's crying?"

Teddy studied the bearded man with dawning understanding. *The guy was blind!*

They could have gotten away! If it hadn't been for that hard-eyed linebacker, they could have gotten away without anyone being the wiser. He made a choked sound of disgust, and the guy in the ski jacket shot him a withering look.

Suddenly the room exploded with noise as a big golden retriever came charging into their midst, snarling and barking like a wild thing.

Teddy's stomach lurched when he saw the dog zero in on him, roaring its intention to attack. Instinctively, he flung his arm across his throat.

Stacey, still crying hard, screamed in terror.

The blind man stopped the dog with a sharp command. The retriever dug in with all four paws, lowered its head, and silently continued to challenge Teddy with a menacing glare.

"Stacey," Teddy was dismayed at the weak sound of his own voice. "It's OK, baby. Be quiet now."

She looked at him, her dark eyes uncertain, her tear-tracked face pinched and frightened. Gradually, her sobs quieted, but she continued to watch Teddy with an uncertain gaze.

Just then a good-looking woman in a furry robe came racing through the door. She ran up to the blind man and grabbed his arm. "Daniel! What's wrong? I heard—"

She turned from him to scan the room, her mouth falling open in bewilderment as her gaze came to rest on Teddy, then the children.

Teddy's head swiveled when another woman came marching out of the room behind the kitchen. She was tall, with hair the same charcoal color as the blind man's. She was wearing a plaid bathrobe a couple of sizes too big for her, and she looked irritable and sleepy.

"Gabe, what is going on out here? Do you guys have any idea what time it—"

She stopped just past the doorway, staring blankly at the assembly in the kitchen, shaking her head as if to clear it.

The room was a din of confusion and noise. Everybody started talking at once. The dog began to bark again, and Stacey renewed her crying. Teddy's mind whirled.

The woman in the fuzzy green robe broke into the bedlam with a sharp voice. "Daniel, where is Jason?"

Teddy stared at her. *How many people were crammed into this place, anyway?*

The blond guy answered. "Outside. In the fruit cellar. I told him to stay there until I came after him."

"The *fruit cellar?*" the woman repeated, her dark eyes widening with disbelief. "Why in the world did you put Jason in the *fruit cellar?*"

"Later, Jennifer," the linebacker snapped. "Right now, let's find out what's going on with our . . . *guests* here. I'll fill you in on the details later. Don't worry. Jason's fine."

"Well, for goodness' sake, I'm not going to leave him out there in the cellar!" the woman said, her eyes flashing with anger. She started toward the door, but the blind man reached for her.

"Don't go out there, Jennifer—"

She shrugged out of his grasp and went on, stopping at the door to rake Teddy's face with a look of incredulous fury. "There can't be anything *outside* to worry about, Daniel. All the trouble seems to be in *here!*" She slammed the door hard on her way out.

It was quiet for a moment, as if most of the excitement in the room had followed her outside. The only sound was Stacey's choked weeping.

The blond man named Gabe glanced at the little girl, then turned to Nicky. "Are you her brother?" he asked sharply.

The boy leveled a hostile stare at him and nodded, saying nothing.

"Then take care of her," he ordered curtly.

With interest, Teddy noticed that the linebacker's eyes, hard with anger only a few minutes before, softened as he watched Nicky go to his sobbing little sister and try to comfort her.

Nicky put his arm around Stacey, then coaxed her to sit down on the long bench behind the table. Pulling a handkerchief from his pocket, he pushed it at her, saying, "Stop crying now, Stacey. And blow your nose."

As if surprised to hear his voice, she quieted. She looked up at Nicky, then down at the crumpled handkerchief in his hand. After a second, she twisted up her mouth and said, very distinctly and with obvious distaste, "It's not clean. I don't want it."

Nicky scowled. "It's the only one I have. Use it."

Hearing the gruffness in his voice, she puckered her mouth and began to cry all over again.

The blond man looked at her for a moment, then, keeping one eye on Teddy, moved to the large white cabinet beside the blind guy, opened the bottom door, and tore off a paper towel from its rack.

He walked over to Stacey, stooped down, and offered her the towel. "Here. This is clean."

The little girl raised her eyes to the linebacker. She studied him thoroughly for a few seconds, then reached out a small, mittened hand and took the towel, dabbing awkwardly at her nose. With her other hand, she pulled the hood of her coat down, away from her face, revealing her stubby pigtails.

She wiped her nose, staring at the man. "Please, I want Mrs. Whispers," she said in a shaky voice.

The man frowned. "Who?"

Stacey pointed across the room, where her rag doll lay on the floor in front of the refrigerator.

Awareness dawned in the blond man's expression, and he went over and picked up the doll. When she returned and handed it to her, Stacey immediately hugged the doll fiercely to her heart. "Thank you," she said with surprising dignity between sniffles.

The man studied her for a minute. "Why did you name her Mrs. Whispers?"

"It's a secret," she said gravely. "I can't tell you."

He stared at her, then nodded. "Right."

Teddy saw his expression sober as Gabe walked over and started talking in a hushed tone with the blind man—probably, Teddy thought, to brief him on the situation in the kitchen.

A stab of anger sliced through Teddy as he looked at the kids— anger at himself for being stupid enough to get caught like this. These people would call the police, of course. And that meant further delay in getting to Virginia. His jaw tightened as he realized how little protection the local police would be. There wasn't a community police force in the country that was any match for the Family's henchmen.

His gaze went to the door when it opened. The woman in the green robe walked in, holding the hand of a small boy in a heavy coat and a knitted cap. The thatch of blond hair Teddy could see escaping from the child's cap was almost white, but the boy had eyes as dark as his own. He looked to be about Nicky's age, but when he spoke, his speech sounded like that of a younger child. Of course, Nicky talked more like an adult than a nine-year-old, so Teddy couldn't be sure.

"That's them, Mommy! I told you! Didn't I tell you?!"

He pulled free of the woman and marched up to the other two children. "Why did you run away from me? And why did you break into the cabin? You were stealing from us!"

Nicky's eyes darkened with hostility. "We weren't *stealing!* We were just borrowing what we needed for a couple of days. We were going to pay you back."

"Jason—" The blind man reached out a hand. "Come here, Son."

The boy went to him, but he continued to look back over his shoulder at Nicky.

The blind man put his hand on the boy's shoulder. "Jason, are these the children you saw? The ones you tried to tell us about?"

"Yes, sir," the boy replied excitedly. He looked at Teddy. "I didn't see *him,* though. Just the children."

Teddy studied the blind man. The woman had called him Daniel. The name somehow fit the man, Teddy thought. Strong. Solid. Teddy sensed that, blind or not, the big man standing in the middle of the room was very much like his name.

Daniel suddenly turned in Teddy's direction, as if he knew exactly what Teddy was thinking. "Who are you?" he asked bluntly. "What are you doing here?"

Suddenly Teddy became uncomfortably aware that everyone in the room was staring at him. Even the blind man seemed to be looking right through him with his piercing blue eyes.

"I think you owe us an explanation," the blind man said quietly. "And I think you'd better make it quick."

Teddy pulled in a long, resigned breath. "My name is Teddy Giordano."

"And the children? Are they yours?"

When Teddy hesitated, the man called Gabe shot him a look through narrowed eyes. "They're not, are they? What are you doing with these kids?"

"They're not mine," Teddy admitted. "But I didn't take them against their will, if that's what you're thinking."

"You don't even want to know what I'm thinking." The blond man's face was hard and cold.

The two men stared at each other for a long moment, then Teddy looked away. His gaze went to Nicky and Stacey, who were watching him with frightened, but trusting expressions.

"We're in trouble," he finally replied. "Bad trouble."

56

"You sure are, buddy." Again it was the blond man who spoke. His voice was deadly calm, but Teddy could feel the heat of his anger as he turned and started toward the other room. "I'm going to call the sheriff, Dan."

"No!" Teddy instinctively jumped toward him, and the man whirled, his eyes glinting with an unmistakable challenge.

Teddy looked from him to the blind man. "Wait. Please don't call the police. It'll only make things worse for us."

"I just bet it will," the linebacker said, his tone dripping sarcasm.

"Look, I know we shouldn't be here. But it's not the way it looks—"

"Right," the other sneered. "You were just making a late-night delivery."

"Why don't you just *listen* to him, mister?" Nicky turned on the man called Gabe, his black eyes snapping with frustrated anger. "We're not thieves."

"My mistake, kid," Gabe said harshly. "Where I come from, people who steal are usually called thieves."

The boy's angular jaw tightened, and with one finger he pushed his glasses up a notch on the bridge of his nose. "We're just trying to stay alive, mister!"

Ignoring him, the linebacker turned back to Teddy. "What are you doing with these kids, anyway?" he asked. "Where are their parents?"

Without warning, the little girl jumped up from the bench and ran across the room to Teddy. He bent down and scooped her up in his arms.

"It's all right, baby," he murmured against one pigtail. "It's going to be fine. Don't cry anymore, OK?"

"Gabe asked you a question," the blind man said quietly. He hadn't moved, and the dog, settled by its master's side, continued to watch Teddy with a hostile stare. "Where are the parents of these children?"

Again, it was Nicky who hurled an answer.

"They're *dead!* All right? What else do you want to know?"

A small muscle just below the faint scar at the blind man's left eye twitched as he turned his face in the direction of Nicky's voice. "Both of your parents are dead, son?"

"Yes," the boy hissed at him. "Both of them."

Teddy could feel the barely controlled fury emanating from Nicky.

"Nicky," he cautioned, "stay cool." He glanced from one man to the other. "Look—I've got money. I'll pay you for what we've used. I admit we took some food. And blankets and pillows." He dug his wallet out of the back pocket of his jeans. "Here, take this," he said, peeling off a roll of bills without even counting them and shoving them at the blond man, who shook his head in refusal.

"You'll pay, all right, buddy. But not *your* way."

Teddy glared at him in frustration.

"Are you in trouble with the police?" the blind man—Daniel—asked abruptly.

Teddy turned to him and uttered a small, harsh laugh. "I *wish.*"

Daniel frowned. "Then who?"

After a long pause, Teddy said, "You don't want to know, mister. Believe me, it's better that you don't know."

"You said you're in bad trouble," Daniel stated quietly. "Isn't that what you told us?"

Teddy hesitated, then nodded, forgetting for an instant that the man couldn't see. "Yeah," he mumbled. "That's what I told you."

"Then you need help. You and the children."

Teddy looked at him. It suddenly hit him that the blind man reminded him of Nick. There was the same unexpected blend of kindness and strength in the man's face, the same gentleness and humor, that had marked Nick Angelini. Missing, however, was the gruffness, the tough mask that years of fast living and crime had baked into Nick's features. Nick had once told Teddy his whole life had been like a big spider web—a web he had woven and in which he had trapped himself with his own youthful foolishness and greed.

It was crazy. This man was a stranger, but suddenly Teddy knew he could trust him.

"We can't help you unless you tell us the truth," Daniel pressed.

The blond man and the two women were staring at Teddy with open suspicion. Teddy knew he had to give them an answer. He felt a sharp sting of guilt at the jeopardy in which he was about to place them. Ignorance was the only real defense against the Family.

But guilt took second place to desperation. He *had* to get the kids to safety. And if there was the slightest chance that these people could help him, he had to take it. Nick's kids were at stake. He had promised Nick. He would do whatever it took to keep that promise.

"All right," he said, turning back to the man named Daniel. "Let's talk."

EIGHT

I T was after three in the morning before they
finally called it a night.

Long before then, Jennifer and Lyss had found
sleeping bags in the storage pantry and settled all three children in
the loft bedroom.

Now the adults sat in the silence of the great room, drained
from hours of talking and occasional arguing. Once in a while,
someone would take a sip of lukewarm coffee or glance uneasily
at the others. Mostly, they looked at Teddy Giordano, studying
him, appraising him, wondering about him.

Not for the first time since Teddy had begun to tell his story,
Daniel shook his head in a bemused gesture. "You've been here
for nearly four days."

Teddy nodded. "We spent most of Saturday night in a motel
just outside Morgantown. When I spotted the limo on our tail
Sunday morning, I just picked a road and started flying until I
shook them. We ended up here late that same afternoon. I saw the
sign on the main highway," he explained, "and took a chance. I
knew I wouldn't lose them for long if I stayed on the main road."

"Where's your car?" Daniel asked.

"In the woods. I covered it up with some tree branches and
stuff. It's Nick's car, not mine—a big silver limo, hard to miss. But
I think I've got it out of sight."

Fatigue seemed to overwhelm him as he rubbed his hands down both sides of his face and uttered a weary sigh. Jennifer watched him, wondering how old Teddy Giordano was. Probably not as old as he looked, she thought. With several days' growth of beard and his dark eyes hollowed by shadows, he appeared unkempt, haggard, and exhausted. Looking at him, thinking about the incredible story he had just related, she found it difficult to stay angry with the man.

"I never intended to stay this long," he said, still resting his head in his hands. His words shot out in a fast, staccato barrage that strengthened Jennifer's original impression of a tense, anxious person beneath the somewhat arrogant facade.

He dropped his hands to his knees. "I thought we'd hole up for a day or so, just until I was sure it was safe to leave again. But before you got here Sunday night, I tried to call the number in Virginia—the number Nick gave me. I found out that the federal marshal I need to talk with is in Florida until the end of the week." He lifted his hands, palms up, and shrugged. "I didn't know what to do. I decided our best bet was to just dig in here and wait."

"Are you aware that the little girl is running a low-grade fever?" Lyss asked him shortly. "Has she been ill?"

Teddy frowned. "No. At least, she hasn't said anything. I found one of those small electric heaters in the pantry," he admitted. "I thought it would take care of that little cabin."

"You're resourceful, at least," Lyss said, her tone softening. "Stacey may just be tired. Some children run a fever when they're tired. But she ought to stay warm and get some rest."

Frustration lined Teddy's face even more deeply. He flushed, then turned back to Daniel. "Look, I *am* sorry . . . about everything. My intention was to leave plenty of money behind us to pay for whatever we used. I'm no thief."

Jennifer heard an edge in Daniel's voice when he answered,

even though his tone was pleasant enough. "You've been in the end cabin all this time? What if one of us had just walked in on you? We've been working our way down the row of cabins since Monday, cleaning and getting them ready for spring campers."

"I always knew where you were," Teddy said without hesitation. "I had your routine down. I figured you weren't going to get to us much before Friday. Besides, all we had to do was go out the back door and we'd be in the woods. That's one reason I picked the cabin on the end." He paused. "When the kids told me about your little boy seeing them the other morning, though, I held my breath the rest of the day, wondering if you'd come looking for us."

"Unfortunately," Daniel replied, a look of regret crossing his face, "no one believed his story. At least, not at first." He lifted his chin, frowning as if something had just occurred to him. "Two nights ago, late, Jennifer and I both heard a child crying. Was that—"

"Stacey," Teddy finished for him. "We, ah, we were leaving the fruit cellar, and she forgot her doll. She went back to get it, and when she ran to catch up with us, she fell." He glanced down at the floor. "She got scared, started crying. . . . She was pretty upset."

"No *wonder* the poor kid is sick!" Gabe snapped, his tone knife-sharp with disgust. "You've had her running around after midnight every night in thirty-degree temperatures! What do you expect?"

Slowly, Teddy raised his eyes to Gabe, answering his outburst in a tone that was unmistakably defensive. "We had to eat. And there was always someone around in the daytime. What was I supposed to do?"

Instead of answering, Gabe merely glared at him, then uttered a soft sound of contempt.

"I think we can understand your actions," Daniel put in, as if he sensed a brewing confrontation between the two men. "And I don't see much point in belaboring whether you were right or wrong. It's done now. But I've got to tell you that I think it would be a mistake to take those children out of here too soon."

Jennifer bit her bottom lip, anticipating an explosion when Gabe rose from his chair. His eyes glinted with surprise and angry disbelief. "Dan!" he muttered. "You can't mean it! This guy is Mafia! Who knows what kind of danger he's put us in just by coming here?" Jennifer saw Gabe's eyes dart toward Lyss, his expression fiercely protective. Gabe was easygoing, but when the people he loved were threatened, his temper could blaze without warning.

"I know you're concerned, Gabe," Daniel said quietly, obviously trying to calm his friend. "And so am I. But I'm also concerned about the safety of these children." "What's done is done. They're here now. And I don't think we have much choice but to help them."

Dan turned back to Teddy. "You don't know exactly when this federal marshal will be back," he said. "You don't even know but what these . . . people who were following you aren't still around somewhere." He frowned as he leaned forward on his chair. "How long do you think you can keep running with those children?"

Teddy raked a hand through his already tousled hair. "What else can I do?" he countered. "The kids are tired; they're scared. I need to get them settled somewhere. And I *have* to get to that marshal. Once I deliver the notebook, maybe Sabas will lose interest in the kids and me. They're only after us now because I have something they want."

Daniel shook his head. "I wouldn't be too sure of that. They know you can probably finger the mob for your boss's murder. They may even think the children know something."

The significance of his words hung between them. Teddy stared, his face pinched and pale. "All the more reason I have to get the kids to a safe place soon," he finally said, his voice less steady now.

Jennifer watched him clench his hands together and crack his knuckles, once, then again.

He looked at her. "Their mother died of cancer four years ago," he said tightly. "Now they've lost their father, too. They're hurting. They're afraid. I've got to get them settled somewhere. They need a home. They're just kids. . . ."

At that moment Jennifer decided she liked Teddy Giordano. True, he was probably self-indulgent and shallow. He was sporting a watch that must have cost hundreds of dollars and a diamond ring that flashed its four-digit price tag every time he lifted his hand. His boots were obviously Italian, his jeans designer, and his sweater imported cashmere.

She had already detected more than a hint of arrogance in his manner, and she suspected a touch of the con man as well—a clever one, most likely. In addition, he seemed defensive and high-strung. Still, she also sensed a quick mind, a bold but generous spirit, and a great deal of loyalty.

When he looked at those children—even when he talked about them—his defiant dark eyes softened to an expression that looked very much like love. Jennifer decided that anyone trying to harm the Angelini children would have to get past Teddy Giordano first.

Daniel's voice broke into her thoughts. "Why don't you get yourself a sleeping bag out of the storage pantry," he suggested to Teddy, "and sack out with the kids upstairs for a few hours? Tomorrow is Thursday. You can try your man in Virginia again first thing and maybe still get help before the weekend." He paused. "Frankly, I think what you need to do is wait right here until someone comes for you and the children. You might be placing all of your lives in danger by leaving here."

"And he'll undoubtedly be placing *ours* in danger if he stays."

Gabe got up and crossed the room. He stopped directly in front of Teddy Giordano, staring at him with open resentment. His eyes never left Teddy's face, but his words were directed at Daniel.

"Are you really buying this, Dan? The guy's admitted to being part of the *mob!* He could have *kidnapped* those kids, for all we know." His usually smiling face was taut with outrage. "Who knows what we'll bring down on our heads if we let them stay here?"

Daniel gently released Jennifer's hand. He got up and walked over to the fireplace, where a low flame was still flickering. He stood, his back to the fire. "You think we should force them to leave, then? What about the children? You heard Lyss—the little girl has a fever."

Jennifer watched Gabe carefully. The tension between him and Teddy Giordano had been obvious from the beginning. She doubted if either of the two men recognized the reason for the resentment between them. Most likely, she thought with a touch of irony, it was a case of one con man bumping heads with another.

Gabe's cynical, somewhat abrasive nature had been tempered years ago, when he became a Christian. But that didn't mean he wouldn't recognize a coat he himself had worn when he saw it on another's back. He just might be reacting, she mused, because Teddy Giordano reminded him too much of himself.

"Gabe?" Daniel prompted quietly.

Gabe looked at Lyss, then Jennifer. "We can't just kick the kids out into the cold," he muttered grudgingly. "And if they stay, I suppose *he* stays."

"If you think I'm wrong, Gabe, say so. You and Lyss have as much at stake here as we do," Daniel cautioned.

Unexpectedly, Teddy broke the exchange by hauling himself up off his chair. "I'll settle it for you. He's right. If we stay, we jeopardize all of you." He flicked an apologetic look at Gabe. "There's no reason you should stick your necks out for us. We'll go," he stated, looking wearier than ever. "As soon as the kids get a couple more hours of sleep, I'll—"

Gabe didn't let him finish. "Don't be stupid! You owe those kids whatever protection you can give them." His gaze swept Teddy Giordano with contempt. "Dan's right, unfortunately. You'll have to stay."

The two men stared at each other without blinking until Teddy finally inclined his head in a reluctant gesture of agreement. "All right." He paused, then added, "Thanks. I owe you."

Jennifer understood Gabe's reaction, even though she doubted that Teddy Giordano could. Dear Gabe—so much in love with Lyss, his new wife, so wholly dedicated and loyal to Daniel, his best friend and brother-in-law. Gabe would give up his life for anyone in this room—including Teddy Giordano.

But as caring as he was, Gabe could also be hard and unyielding when the people he loved were threatened. Teddy couldn't possibly comprehend Gabe's kind of love, a combination of toughness and tenderness, gentleness and strength.

When Gabe asked his next question, Jennifer half expected Teddy Giordano to tell him it was none of his business.

"Exactly how involved were you with these goons, anyway?" His expression was suspicious and openly hostile. "This guy you worked for—was he some kind of . . . godfather or what?"

Teddy looked as if he was about to smile, then seemed to think better of it. "It's not quite like the movies. No, Nick had a lot of power, but he was no *padrone*. He was what you've probably heard called a *capo*—a boss, a chief."

"And I suppose you were one of the Indians?" Gabe's tone was edged with sarcasm.

Teddy shrugged. "I was his driver. I drove the limo for him, raced a couple of his cars, worked on them, that kind of stuff. And I helped out with the kids—took them to school, to the doctor, to the dentist." With a level look, he added, "If you're asking was I into the action . . . no. Never. Nick made a point of never letting me near the business."

"How long had you worked for him before his death?" Daniel asked.

Teddy thought for a moment. "Nine, ten years, I guess. Since I was about sixteen. I worked part-time in a garage he owned when I was still in school. When I graduated, he took me off the street, gave me a job with him at his house."

Daniel nodded thoughtfully. "So you were close."

Teddy glanced away, and Jennifer saw a look of great pain cross his face before he hardened his expression. "Nick Angelini was good to me," he said flatly, his tone making it clear that he would say no more.

The room was silent for a long time. Finally, Daniel moved away from the fireplace and walked over to Jennifer, holding his hand out to her. "I think we're all in agreement about what has to be done. But before we turn in, let's pray about this."

Jennifer took his hand and rose from the couch. She saw Teddy Giordano dart a startled and embarrassed look in their direction.

After a moment's hesitation, Gabe took Jennifer's other hand, then Lyss's. Daniel offered his hand to the stranger in their midst, waiting until Teddy, with obvious reluctance, joined them in their circle.

Although Jennifer kept her eyes closed the entire time Daniel prayed for their "new friends," she was sure she could feel Teddy Giordano studying each of them. She wondered if the troubled young man with the haunted eyes had ever heard anyone pray before. She clasped Daniel's hand more tightly, grateful as always for her husband's strength and goodness, and for the blessing of the family into which she had married.

Daniel gave her hand a gentle squeeze, as if he knew exactly what she had been thinking . . . and praying.

NINE

T HE snow began shortly after dawn the next morning, falling from a sky that Jennifer described to Daniel as a sheet of lead-colored canvas. Moderate at first, by midmorning it had increased to the kind of treacherous, wind-driven snow familiar to natives of the mountains. It came down fast, heavy and threatening. And as it fell, the air grew bitter cold.

The children cheered, but the grown-ups knew the storm was no laughing matter. Jennifer paced the floor. Lyss clanged about in the kitchen, dropping silverware. Gabe seemed to talk a little faster each time he looked out the window.

Eventually, Daniel began to drum his fingers absently on everything he touched. He had seen plenty of these spring storms in the mountains of West Virginia, and they were nothing to be trifled with.

During breakfast, Jennifer coaxed Gabe and Lyss into helping her clean the last two cabins on the boys' row. Daniel and Teddy agreed to stay with the children, who were begging to go out and play.

By eleven o'clock, Teddy had tried his call to Virginia three times.

Daniel heard him sigh with frustration when he returned to the great room after his last attempt.

"Still no answer?"

"No. I must have let it ring twenty times." He paused. "I don't know what to do."

Daniel was on his knees in front of the fireplace, trying to fix the stretcher on an immense old rocking chair beside the hearth. It had been his grandfather's favorite chair, then his father's, until Lucas had finally surrendered to his wife's plea to "retire" it. When he did, Daniel had immediately claimed it for his own.

"Not much else to do but wait," he said, half turning toward Teddy's voice. "Give me a hand here, will you? Just hold this steady for a minute."

Teddy braced the chair as Daniel forced the stretcher back into its opening.

"I can't believe it's snowing like this," Teddy muttered. "Isn't it supposed to be spring?"

Daniel smiled and cocked his head upward, his hands still working. "I grew up in these mountains, and believe me, this time of year anything can happen. The natives are used to unpredictable weather, but to outsiders it usually comes as a big surprise." He stood up, wiping his hands on his jeans and smiling at the sounds of laughter coming from outside. "Sunny's still in the yard with the kids, isn't she?"

Daniel heard Teddy move to the window. "She sure is," he said. "She just pushed Stacey into the snow, and now she's shoving at her with her nose. Stacey's obviously having a great time." He paused. "I think they're playing hide-and-seek. And I'd say your dog is winning."

"You don't beat Sunny at hide-and-seek," Daniel replied with a grin. "That's her favorite game." He walked over to the large pine table beside the couch and picked up his coffee cup, grimacing when he found it empty. "Lyss said Stacey's temperature was normal this morning."

"Yeah, she's fine," Teddy said warmly. "Are you two related, by any chance?"

"Lyss and I?" Daniel nodded. "She's my kid sister."

"I thought I saw a resemblance," Teddy said. "Is she a nurse or something?"

Daniel shook his head. "No, she's a teacher. Phys Ed." He started toward the kitchen. "Let's get some coffee. I think Gabe made a fresh pot before they left."

Teddy followed Daniel to the kitchen, watching as the blind man made his way to the stove. He lifted the coffeepot, and Teddy moved to help, then stopped. Obviously, the man knew what he was doing.

"There should be some clean mugs on the right-hand side of the cabinet," Daniel said, filling his own cup, then setting the old-fashioned porcelain coffeepot back on the stove.

After pouring his own coffee, Teddy joined Daniel at the table. He glanced outside to check on the kids, then stirred cream into his cup, studying the big man across from him as he did. For an instant, he sensed something familiar about Kaine. The feeling passed as quickly as it had come, but his curiosity remained.

Daniel Kaine had an unusual face—interesting, but not easy to read. Teddy supposed women would find him good-looking. Certainly, he had a kind of compelling presence about him. His bronzed skin made him seem robust, as if he spent a lot of time outdoors. His deep blue eyes were strangely unnerving as they followed the slightest sound or movement in a room.

Strong, Teddy concluded. This was a strong man. Even beneath his heavy black beard, Kaine's jaw looked firm, his chin stubborn. His dark brows were generous but not severe, and his prominent nose stopped just short of being hawklike. Teddy wondered about the small, vertical scar at Kaine's left eyebrow.

When Daniel lifted his arms above his head and stretched, Teddy had a sudden, peculiar sense of tightly harnessed power, a dynamic but fully controlled energy. Then the memory hit him.

"Daniel Kaine!"

Kaine lifted his dark brows in a question.

"I *knew* there was something familiar about you!" Teddy said excitedly. "I saw you on TV when you won the gold medal in the Olympics. You're the 'Swimming Machine'—isn't that what they called you?"

Daniel lowered his arms, a half smile crossing his face. "You remember that? You couldn't have been very old when I was at the Olympics."

"Oh, man! Do I remember? You were *great!*" Teddy exclaimed. "I was in junior high, but I'll never forget it." His words tumbled out with boyish enthusiasm. "'Course, you didn't have your beard then, and you weren't . . ." He broke off, embarrassed.

Daniel, however, only smiled. "No, I grew the beard later. It's easier than shaving in the dark."

"Can you . . . I mean, do you still swim?" Teddy asked without thinking, then realized he might be out of line.

But Kaine didn't seem to mind. "You bet I do. Every day. I've got an indoor pool in my home," he explained easily. "That's why I'm feeling kind of stiff right now, going most of the week without any exercise."

"How long—" Teddy stopped. He didn't want to offend Daniel, but the question was burning in his mind.

"How long have I been blind?" Daniel finished for him mildly. "About six years now."

Teddy stared at him, feeling a sudden wave of sympathy wash over him. This man had been a national figure just a few years ago, an American hero. Now he was blind. Blind and doing odd jobs in a youth camp. Talk about lousy luck.

"So, you work here now, huh?"

Kaine started to take a sip of coffee, stopped, then smiled. "Well
. . . just this week, actually. The couple who manage the Farm
haven't had a vacation in a long time, so we came up to give
them a break. As a matter of fact, we've been trying to find
another full-time assistant for Mac—he's the manager of the
camp. But until we hire someone, we're going to be helping out
as much as we can."

"What is this place, anyway?"

Kaine briefly explained the idea behind Helping Hand.

"Then this is your place? I mean, you own it?"

"Not really," Daniel corrected him. "It's been in my family for
years, but now it's owned by several people. When my Uncle Jake
decided to retire, a group of people from my church agreed to
help finance a camp if Gabe and I would get it going."

"So it's strictly for disabled kids?"

Kaine nodded. "Some of them stay here several weeks out of
the summer; others just come for a week or two. It's been so successful that we've almost outgrown our facilities. We're trying to
buy more land so we can expand, and, as I told you, we're going
to add to the staff."

Teddy was intrigued with the idea. "But you don't actually live
here?"

"No, we live in Shepherd Valley—that's about sixty miles from
here. I run a Christian radio station there."

"A *Christian* radio station?" Teddy repeated, frowning.

"It's a radio station with a Christian programming format,"
Daniel explained. "The music we play—our talk shows—all of
our programming is Christ-centered."

"I see," Teddy mumbled. He didn't, but he wasn't interested in
learning more. That prayer circle last night had been enough for
him. These people were church people, and church people had
always made him uncomfortable. Daniel Kaine seemed to be
OK—he didn't act like some kind of fanatic. Still, he was obvi-

ously serious about his religion. *Too* serious, as far as Teddy could tell.

"Is there money in that kind of radio?" he asked abruptly.

Daniel laughed. "Not much, I'm afraid. But we make a living. I do some counseling part-time, too. We get by."

They both smiled when they heard Stacey squeal with excitement, followed by the boys' laughter.

"I was really fortunate, having the station to go back to after the accident," Daniel said, continuing their conversation. "At least I didn't have to train for a new job. A lot of blind people have to take on a whole new career, and believe me, that's rough." He paused, then went on. "Learning to live without your sight is enough of a challenge. If you have to learn a new job, too, you've got double trouble."

Teddy was quiet for a long time, thinking. "Yeah, I'm sure that's true. But I'll tell you, Daniel, there are times when the idea of a whole new beginning sounds pretty good to me."

Teddy glanced out the window. He could see Stacey down on her knees with her arms around Sunny's neck, giggling as the retriever nuzzled her chin. The two boys seemed to be hitting it off great, too.

He turned back to Daniel Kaine. "Sometimes I wish . . ." He stopped, surprised at what he was feeling. "Sometimes I wish I could just . . . be a different person. Start all over, from scratch. A brand new life." He laughed at his own foolishness. "Crazy, I know."

Daniel shook his head. "Not so crazy. There are a lot of people who probably feel the same way. Sometimes it's the only thing to do."

Teddy uttered a small, humorless laugh. "And sometimes," he said bitterly, "it's the only thing you *can't* do. Your past is your past, man. And it's always with you."

"Unless you're willing to give it up," Daniel replied.

Teddy looked at him but said nothing. They were silent for a long time, during which Teddy found himself thinking about his past, especially about his family.

Things hadn't been so bad before his dad died, he remembered. He and his older sister, Gina, had always had to work to help out at home, but their parents had been decent to them. But his dad had died when Teddy was only eleven, and a year later his mother remarried. Jack Falio had immediately judged his new stepson to be a "wise-mouthed kid," a "son with no respect." Teddy thought Falio was a hardnose, and an old-country jerk.

At the same time, Gina had married and left home. Feeling deserted by his sister and betrayed by his mother, Teddy had made no effort to get along with his stepfather. When a new little half sister came along, Teddy started drifting farther and farther away from his mother and the home that, by then, had come to seem like a prison.

For the next two or three years, he spent most of his time on the street with a small-time gang. Later he picked up pocket money by doing odd jobs at a garage owned by Nick Angelini. "Nicky Angel," the other *capos* called him.

Nick Angelini didn't spend much time around the garage, but he kept a close eye on his employees, even a part-time flunkie like Teddy. For some reason, the older man took a liking to the defiant teenager, eventually putting him to work full-time, even letting him race a couple of his cars professionally. Finally, he asked Teddy to move into his home and become his driver.

Teddy didn't have to be asked twice. In spite of the fact that Nick Angelini was a known boss for P. J. Sabas, Teddy was in awe of the big, good-natured Sicilian. If Nick had tried to bring him into the business, he wouldn't have hesitated.

Surprisingly, though, Nick had made it clear from the beginning that Teddy was to stay clean. He took him under his protection, much as he would have a son or a younger brother. The closest Teddy ever got to the action was overhearing an occasional phone conversation between Nick and one of the other *capos*.

Teddy knew what Nick's business was, and he knew it was dirty business. But he told himself it didn't matter. In his own way, Nick was a good guy. He was good to his kids, good to Teddy, good to his friends. So he was mixed up with the mob. So what?

Daniel's voice startled him out of his thoughts. "What would you do, Teddy, if you could start over again? What kind of life would you choose for yourself?"

Teddy looked at him. He was surprised at how easily he could answer Daniel's question. He had never really thought it all out. But over the years, he had daydreamed about the way he'd like to live . . . if things had been different.

"I'd get out of the city, for starters," he said. "I grew up on the streets, and I hated it. The noise, the stench, the traffic. One reason I liked it at Nick's so much was that we lived outside town. It wasn't like this, you understand, on a farm and all; but at least the air was cleaner, and it was quiet most of the time." He hesitated. "I even had a garden."

"A garden?" Kaine smiled a little.

"Yeah. A *good* one, too. The kids helped me. We had flowers on one end and vegetables on the other. It was a beauty."

"So you like being outside. What else? If you could start over again, I mean?"

Teddy smiled to himself. "It's pretty wild, I guess."

"Some of my daydreams are, too." Daniel Kaine leaned back, crossing his arms comfortably over his chest, waiting.

"Well . . . I know it's impossible—" Teddy stopped, then went on. "But if there were any way I could, I'd . . . adopt the kids. Nicky and Stacey." He waited, expecting Kaine to laugh. Or maybe even frown in disapproval.

Daniel Kaine did neither. Instead, he dropped his arms and leaned forward, resting his hands on the table in front of him.

"That doesn't really surprise me, Teddy. I hear your love for those children in your voice every time you talk to them. Or about them."

Teddy swallowed hard. "Yeah . . . well, we both know it's never going to happen. But you're right. I really do care about the kids. They're like my own, you know? And I think they care about *me*, too."

"Yes," Daniel answered softly. "I believe they do." After a moment, he said, "You know, Teddy—there *is* a way you can start over again. You might not have everything you want, just the way you want it. But if you really decide you want a fresh beginning, there is a way to do it."

Suddenly, Teddy knew what was coming, and he tried to head it off. "I suppose you're talking about religion?"

Daniel leaned back in his chair, a small frown creasing his forehead. Finally, he nodded. "Well—in a way. I'm talking about Christianity."

"I've already heard that stuff," Teddy countered quickly. "I know the whole story, man. By heart."

A look of surprise crossed Kaine's face. "You do?"

"Yeah. Nora—that's Nick's housekeeper—she was all the time preaching at me. And the kids. She took them to church every Sunday, and she did her best to get me there, too."

"But you weren't interested." Daniel was still smiling.

"Not me. Oh, I went to church when I was a kid. I know about Jesus and all that."

"But you don't believe it?"

Teddy looked at him. "No, I don't believe it. At least not all of it."

"What part of it don't you believe?"

Teddy dragged in a deep breath. He liked this man and, without knowing why, wanted Daniel Kaine to like *him*. "Look, Daniel, where I come from, men don't *die* for each other. They *kill* each other."

His words fell heavily across the silence between them with the dull thud of reality.

Finally, Daniel nodded. "I see your point."

Teddy hadn't expected that. "It's just not for me, that's all," he muttered.

"That's where you're wrong, Teddy," Daniel said quietly. "It *was* for you."

Teddy stared at him.

Daniel sighed. "I think I know where you're coming from, Teddy. If you felt that your life was everything it should be, you wouldn't feel the slightest need to change it. Right?"

Teddy nodded, then caught himself and mumbled, "I guess so."

"But because you know your life *isn't* what it should be, you don't think you can have any part in Jesus, or that he wants anything to do with you."

Again, Teddy grunted his assent.

"You just can't quite swallow the story that one man would climb up on a cross and die for another man." Kaine paused. "Especially for a man like yourself."

Teddy looked at him but said nothing.

"Keep in mind, Teddy, that Jesus wasn't just another man. He was God . . . God in the flesh. When he did what he did, he was showing us a different kind of love . . . *his* kind of love. And the kind he wants us to have for one another."

Something about Daniel Kaine's assurance got to Teddy. Suddenly, Kaine was making him angry. "Nobody—*nobody*—willingly puts their life on the line for someone else! If you believe that, man, you've been out of the real world too long! Maybe, just maybe . . . if Jesus *was* God, like you say, he would do it. But *if* he did it, it wasn't for people like me."

"'Very rarely will anyone die for a righteous man, though for a good man someone might possibly dare to die.'"

"That's what I'm saying. . . ."

"'But God demonstrates his own love for us in this: While we were still sinners, Christ died for us,'" Kaine finished softly.

Teddy blinked, saying nothing as he realized that Daniel Kaine had been quoting from the Bible.

"Those are God's words, Teddy . . . not mine."

Teddy started to interrupt, but Daniel stopped him with a quick gesture. "Wait. Bear with me. This is for you, Teddy. 'It is not the healthy who need a doctor, but the sick. I have not come to call the righteous, but sinners to repentance.' Wait—," Daniel said again, almost as if he could see Teddy's attempt to protest. "There's more. 'He died for all. . . .' *All* Teddy. No exceptions. Just one more verse, OK? 'Therefore, if anyone is in Christ, he is a new creation; the old has gone, the new has come!'"

Kaine grinned. "Now, isn't that exactly what you're talking about?" He didn't give Teddy the opportunity to answer but went on in the same casual, good-natured tone. "It surely sounds to me," he said, "as if God wrote the answer before you ever asked the question."

Abruptly, Kaine stood up. "I'm going to lend you Jennifer's Bible—mine's in Braille," he said with a smile. "Maybe you might pass a little time today by reading though the Gospel of John." He started to leave the table, then turned back. "If you're a fast reader and want to find out more about this subject of new beginnings, go on to Romans."

"The Bible's hard for me to understand," Teddy said grudgingly.

Daniel grinned at him. "You ought to try reading it in Braille sometime, friend," he said dryly. Counting off his steps, he walked out of the room.

TEN

B Y EARLY evening, the tension in the cabin had sharpened until it was almost palpable, especially between Gabe and Teddy Giordano.

Jennifer knew Daniel was also feeling the strain. Earlier he had confided to her that he was particularly bothered by the fact that the snow had begun just after dawn. Both his grandfather and his Uncle Jake were men who knew these West Virginia mountains as well as they knew the inside of their own homes, and they always insisted that the worst snowstorms were those that began shortly after the first light of day. Their observations weren't infallible, but Daniel had seen enough mountain winters in his own time to be wary of the storm now in progress.

Under ordinary circumstances, being snowed in with her husband and family wouldn't have bothered Jennifer in the least—it would have been fun. Present circumstances, however, were anything but ordinary. Even the normally imperturbable Lyss had a flinty edge in her voice. Only the children seemed reasonably untroubled by their situation, although she had caught Nicky staring apprehensively out the window a couple of times.

Hour by hour, the day had trudged by into evening, clouded by a peculiar overtone of unreality. They did their work, ate their meals, made the obligatory small talk, and avoided discussion of the snow that continued to fall in a steady white onslaught.

At seven forty-five, Teddy again tried to reach someone with the Federal Witness Protection Program. Jennifer was surprised but relieved when she heard him begin a conversation. When he returned to the others at the far end of the great room, however, his cheerfulness seemed halfhearted.

"At least I got an answer this time," he said with an uncertain smile.

"That's good," Daniel said. "What did you find out?"

"I still didn't talk with Nick's contact," Teddy replied. "But the man who answered *is* a federal marshal, and he seemed to think the marshal who arranged everything with Nick is back in town. He promised to have someone call me within the hour. He said if he can't connect with the other marshal, he'll make the arrangements himself to get us out of here."

"That should make you feel better," Jennifer said, trying to smile. She and the children were sitting at a small table in the corner, stalled in what seemed to be an endless game of Monopoly. Stacey was too young to comprehend the strategy, yet insisted on being a part of the game, and Jennifer was too restless to concentrate. Consequently, Nicky had easily captured the board.

The children were getting tired—tired and irritable. Jennifer could hear it in their voices. And Gabe wasn't much better. He was as restless as she had ever seen him. She sighed, then brightened a little when Daniel suddenly pushed himself up out of his rocking chair. "Let's make some music," he suggested. "It's too early to go to bed and too quiet in here to stay awake."

Ignoring the stony silence that greeted him, he pushed up his sweater sleeves and said firmly, "Come on now. We're not going to stop the snow by sitting around worrying about it. Lyss, have you finished that dulcimer for Jennifer yet?"

"Mm."

"If that was a yes, go get it. Gabe, where's your fiddle? Jason, will you find my guitar for me, please? And get your Aunt Lyss's banjo, too."

Jason suddenly came to life, hopping off his chair and running to the corner of the room where Daniel's guitar and Lyss's banjo were propped against the wall.

With the help of the three now wide-awake children, the adults also seemed to find a reserve of energy. While Gabe tuned his fiddle, Jennifer oohed and aahed over the new dulcimer her sister-in-law presented to her.

Gabe even managed a civil comment to Teddy Giordano. The younger man was openly admiring of the finely crafted, hourglass-shaped instrument. "You *made* that?" he asked Lyss. "What *is* it, some kind of guitar?"

"Same family, but older," Gabe said. "It's a dulcimer. Lyss custom makes them." His pride was evident.

Teddy looked from the dulcimer in Jennifer's lap to Lyss. "What's it sound like?"

"Show him, Jennifer. Jennifer plays a lot better than I do," Lyss explained. "I just like to make them."

Jennifer began to pluck the four-stringed, sweet-voiced instrument softly. "The dulcimer is thousands of years old," she said, continuing to play as she spoke. "It goes all the way back to ancient Persia. The immigrants who settled here in the mountains brought it with them from Europe."

"The thing about Lyss's dulcimers," Gabe said, "is that no two are alike. She gives every instrument she makes its own unique personality—its individual voice."

"Just like the Lord makes people." Daniel, tuning his guitar, turned slightly toward Teddy Giordano. "He made each one of us exactly the way he intended us to be." He stopped, his smile softening. "You know, it never fails to amaze me how God can take the discarded scraps of a life and shape them into something brand-new and beautiful."

Jennifer, by now accustomed to Daniel's analogies, glanced from her husband to Teddy Giordano, then back to Daniel. She sensed a definite current between the two men—nothing hostile, but a kind of *challenge,* perhaps.

Delighted with the dulcimer, she continued to pluck it lightly. "Lyss, it's beautiful! It's *exactly* what I wanted!"

"Sing, too, Mommy," Jason begged, plopping down on the hearth and motioning for Nicky and Stacey to join him. Teddy Giordano followed the children over to the fireplace, dropping down beside Stacey and settling her snugly against his side.

Jennifer began to play and sing "Wildwood Flower," a sad old folk ballad about lost love. After a moment, Daniel added his guitar and started to hum, then sing along with her.

They sang another mountain love song before Lyss and Gabe joined in with their instruments. When they switched to church-camp choruses, the children began to sing with them. Eventually, they played a little bluegrass, then turned to hymns before ending with a number of folk songs.

When they finally stopped, Stacey tugged at Teddy's sleeve. "Teddy, could I have a fiddle? Like that one?" She pointed to the fiddle in Gabe's hand.

Jennifer smiled at the sleepy-eyed little girl. Her stubby black pigtails were sticking straight out from either side of her head, and her round face was flushed with heat from the fireplace.

"Maybe when you're older, baby," Teddy said, giving her a hug.

Stacey's face fell, but brightened when Gabe made a beckoning motion with his hand. "Come here, kiddo. You can play my fiddle."

Jennifer looked at him, wide-eyed, then glanced at Daniel, whose dark brows had also shot up with surprise. Gabe's fiddle was no ordinary instrument. It had been handcrafted by a master in North Carolina for an absolutely ridiculous amount of money, and it was Gabe's pride and joy. No one other than Daniel or Lyss dared to touch it, and even they were scrutinized by its owner's eagle eye the entire time it was out of his possession.

Now he was inviting a six-year-old girl—a child he barely knew—to play it?

Stacey squealed and went sailing over to Gabe, beaming as he allowed her to rake the bow awkwardly over the strings of the fiddle. Jennifer was fairly certain that that high-pitched screech very nearly sliced Gabe's spinal cord in half, but she gave him credit for being a good sport.

She saw Daniel shake his head and grin. Lyss, too, was gaping at her husband as though she didn't believe what she was seeing.

"No, no—you don't *push* the bow, dumpling—"

Dumpling? Daniel choked, then coughed, and Jennifer almost strangled at the look of amazement on his face.

"You draw it gently over the strings," Gabe went on. "That's it. Good, that's great! Try it again. Gently, remember. *Good!* You're doing fine!"

Jennifer rolled her eyes at Lyss, who continued to stare at her husband in astonishment.

"Wait, wait, careful now. You don't want a *harsh* tone, dumpling. You want a nice, even, *sweet* tone. Like this."

By now, the feeling of contentment in the room, the warmth from the fire, the children's laughter, Daniel's occasional dry comments and Lyss's good-humored replies, had all worked together to lull Jennifer into a comfortable, drowsy tranquillity. Suddenly, the mood was shattered by a loud, angry bark from Sunny. Stacey cried out as the room plunged into darkness.

Still clutching the dulcimer, Jennifer leaped up from the couch. Daniel also got to his feet. "What's wrong?"

Jennifer reached for him. "The lights went out, Daniel!"

He squeezed her hand and drew her a little closer. "The snow must have put too much weight on the power lines."

The faint light from the fireplace enabled them to see just

enough to move around. Sunny stirred restlessly beside Daniel, and Stacey began to whimper.

His voice gentle, Gabe attempted to soothe her. "It's OK, dumpling. It's the snow, that's all. Don't be afraid." Pulling her onto his lap, he began to rock her.

Jennifer heard a thump, then a muffled exclamation as Jason pushed up between her and Daniel.

"I hit my knee!" he mumbled, taking hold of Jennifer's hand. "Are you all right, Mommy?"

Jennifer smiled at the protective note in the small voice and bent to plant a kiss on top of his head. "I'm just fine, honey. I'll take a look at your knee when we get some light. Don't be scared."

"I'm not scared," he replied. After a moment he looked up at Daniel. "This is kind of what it's like to be blind, isn't it, Daddy?"

"Yes, it is, Son. Although I imagine you can see at least a little with the light from the fire."

"I wouldn't like being blind, Daddy," Jason said gravely.

"Well, Jason, I don't like it very much either," Daniel admitted. "But I've learned to get around fairly well in the dark. So right now, I want you and Sunny to stay here with your mother for a few minutes. Aunt Lyss and I will get some oil lamps and candles from the storage pantry, OK?"

"The snow must be awfully heavy, to knock the power out," Lyss said as she moved with Daniel across the room.

"How deep do you think it is by now?" Daniel had neglected to count off his steps and stumbled against the side of the cabinet. He muttered in annoyance, then went on.

"Gabe said he thought we had at least eight inches, maybe more," Lyss told him. "But that was earlier."

"Is it still coming down?" Daniel stopped as they reached the door to the pantry.

He heard Lyss go to the window.

"Heavier than ever," she said, her voice strained as she came back to stand beside him.

"There should be a supply of candles in the pantry," Daniel said, trying to reassure her. "What about oil lamps? Do you know where they are?"

"There's one in each bedroom, I think. And some in the great room."

"We've got plenty of drinking water. And wood. Gabe and I brought in several loads yesterday."

"We're going to need it tonight." She paused. "Dan? I'm a little worried."

Daniel slipped an arm around her shoulder. "What's the matter, Pip?" He had given her the pet name when she was still a little girl but seldom used it these days. He had heard the edge of fear in her voice, however, and for a moment, she was no longer a grown woman, but his little sister again.

"Lyss? What is it?" he prompted when she didn't answer.

"I don't know." She suddenly sounded very young. "I have . . . a really bad feeling. Like something awful is going to happen."

Daniel's heart constricted. Lyss was probably the most unflappable person he knew. She was a rock. Lyss simply didn't have *nerves*.

"It's been a strange day," he offered weakly. "With our unexpected . . . visitors . . . and the storm. And now the power going off . . ."

He jumped when she clutched his arm. "Dan, I'm afraid!"

In the silence following her tense admission, a gust of wind rattled the windowpane. Daniel had the sudden sensation of an oppressive weight bearing down on him, and he shuddered against the feeling. For one terrible moment, Lyss's fear became his own. Her alarm swelled to a wave of dread that threatened to engulf him.

He clenched his jaw and shook his head, drawing in a shaky breath of relief when he felt the apprehension finally ebb, then disappear.

"You know what's wrong with you, Pip?" He tried to laugh, but his voice sounded painfully shaky, even to him.

"What?" Her grasp on his arm tightened.

"You've got Grandma Lou's heebie-jeebies," Daniel told her. "You know, the creepers."

Lyss's small laugh sounded forced. "You think that's all it is?"

Daniel nodded and squeezed her hand. "That's what it sounds like to me."

"You're probably right. I've let my imagination run away with me." Her voice sounded a little stronger now, and Daniel drew in a breath of relief. "Let's find some candles," she told him. "I don't do so well in the dark."

"Relax," he said dryly. "You're with a pro, remember?"

The combination of high wind and heavy snow had resulted in zero visibility. Boone squinted nervously into the darkness as the windshield wipers pushed the snow first to one side, then the other, grinding with the effort.

The limousine's headlights projected a nightmarish, distorted scene into the darkness.

"What're we gonna do, Wolf?" Boone's voice trembled badly, as did his hands on the steering wheel. "It's impossible to see anything out there!"

"Pull off the road," Wolf said grimly. "I want to look at the map."

Boone went another quarter of a mile before spying a small house with a driveway that looked recently plowed. He eased the limo to a crawl and slid sideways into the driveway, letting the engine idle while Wolf studied a road map.

After a moment, Wolf looked up, glanced out his window, then leaned forward to look out the driver's side.

"What do you suppose that is?" he muttered, staring at a sign only a few feet ahead of them on his side of the road: HELPING HAND FARM—10 Miles.

The sign was barely visible because of the blowing snow. Boone peered through the windshield, frowned, then shrugged without answering.

"Let's find out," Wolf said. "Get back on the road. I'll help you watch for signs."

Boone looked over at him. "Wolf, if it ain't right on the highway, we'd better not try to stop," he said, his tone petulant. "If we get off the main road tonight, we may never get back on."

Wolf returned his attention to the map for another minute. When he glanced up again, he shot Boone a look that clearly said, What are you waiting for?

Boone muttered something under his breath, then started to pull back onto the highway. The wheels spun, and he slanted an I-told-you-so glance at Wolf. Again he coaxed the car, and this time the powerful limo moved backward, lurching only once as it bumped onto the road.

"Relax, Boone," Wolf said, without looking at him. "And go slow—I don't want to miss this place. If the snow gets much worse, we may need somewhere to hole up for the night. Whatever this Farm is, let's not announce our arrival. We'll just drop in on them unexpectedly."

ELEVEN

WHILE Jennifer and Lyss placed lighted candles and oil lamps around the great room, Daniel stoked the fire, adding more logs and punching it up to a roaring blaze.

"We'd better call the power company before things get any worse," he said to Gabe as he replaced the fire screen. "Maybe they can send someone out by morning if we get our names on the list."

Gabe secured a candle in its holder and set it on the table by the couch. "I'll call," he told Daniel. Crossing to the other end of the great room, he began to leaf through the telephone directory.

Jennifer settled all three children in front of the fireplace. Taking one of the oil lamps, she started toward the kitchen, stopping when she saw the look on Gabe's face.

"What's wrong?"

He scowled at the handset. "The phone's dead."

Jennifer glanced from Gabe to the phone. "Try again."

It was no use. He tapped the receiver a few times, then shook his head glumly as he replaced the handset on the hook. "Nothing," he said, his voice gruff, his face clouded with uneasiness.

Daniel, too, looked grim as he came to join them. "I was afraid of that," he said, raking a hand down his face.

"Afraid of what?" Lyss asked from across the room.

Gabe hesitated before he answered. "The phone's out."

Jennifer's stomach tightened. The expression on Lyss's face told all, and if *Lyss* was worried, maybe their situation was graver than she had first thought.

"What are we going to do?" Lyss touched Gabe's arm, her eyes fixed on his face.

"We're all right, babe." He managed a tight smile. "Relax."

"Gabe's right," Daniel seconded. "We've got the fireplace, plenty of food and water—and we'll probably have power in a few hours."

"I don't think so, Dan."

Gabe's flat disagreement seemed to surprise Daniel. "Why not?"

"We're going to have well over a foot of snow by morning if it keeps up," Gabe explained tightly. "They can't get through to work on the lines in this storm."

"So we wait," Daniel said with a shrug.

Jennifer studied her husband's face, wondering if he really felt as calm as he sounded. She realized then that she was counting on Daniel to remain unruffled. Daniel and Lyss. The two were always so steady, so cool-headed, that when either showed the slightest sign of anxiety it seemed to affect everyone around them.

She looked at Gabe, but he was staring across the room at Teddy Giordano and the children. When his gaze finally met hers, his expression was troubled and thoughtful. He glanced at Daniel. "Dan, I'm going to take the Cherokee and go into town."

"What? Are you *crazy?* You said yourself the utilities people probably couldn't get through."

"The Cherokee will."

A look of protest crossed Daniel's face. "No," he said flatly. "You can't risk it."

"Gabe, Daniel's right," Jennifer put in. "You *can't* go out in this—"

She stopped when he turned to her. She had seen that expression in Gabe's eyes before. He was going.

Abruptly he turned, flicking his gaze to Teddy Giordano and the children, who were still sitting in front of the fireplace.

"Giordano," he said, giving a quick jerk of his head.

"The phone's out," Gabe told the other man as he approached. "That means you can't get your call."

Gabe's voice was as hard as his eyes as he went on. "I'm going to drive the Cherokee into town and let the utilities people know we're cut off out here. If you want, I'll call that federal marshal again and explain what's going on. Maybe he'll give me some idea when they're going to come for you and the kids." As an afterthought he added, "They'll need directions, too."

Teddy looked at him. "I'll go with you."

"No," Gabe replied quickly. "You stay here. In case Dan needs help."

As Jennifer watched, the two men locked gazes. Finally, Teddy Giordano relented.

"All right," he said, nodding.

"*I'm* going with you." Lyss's announcement was quiet but firm.

Gabe whirled around. His jaw tightly set, he frowned. "No, you're *not.*"

Lyss was nearly as tall as her husband, and she met his eyes with a level gaze. "I'm going with you, Gabe. And don't use that tone with me." She paused. "I couldn't count the times I've heard you say that nobody in their right mind would venture out alone in a heavy snowstorm."

"She's right, Gabe," Daniel said quietly. He turned toward Lyss. "But *I'll* be the one to go with him, not you."

Lyss faced her brother, her blue eyes so much like his now flashing with irritation. Even at five-ten, Lyss still had to look up to Daniel. But her tone was steely with resolve. "Daniel, Gabe's my husband. I'm going with him."

Daniel started to say something, then stopped, inclining his head in a gesture of understanding. "It's for you and Gabe to decide."

"You can be every bit as hardheaded as your brother, do you know that?" Gabe challenged, exasperation lining his features.

"You so often tell me, love," Lyss said easily, turning to walk away, "it's a family trait. I'm going to change into warmer clothes. You'd better do the same."

Gabe watched her all the way out of the room before turning back to the others. "Give me that phone number," he told Teddy Giordano.

Teddy pulled his wallet from the back pocket of his jeans. "Here," he said, handing a yellow slip of paper to Gabe. "If someone answers, repeat this number before you say anything else. The man you'll talk with is named Keith." He paused. "Tell him to try to get someone here as soon as possible."

Gabe gave him a faint, unpleasant smile. "Oh, don't worry. I have every intention of asking for express service."

Daniel touched Gabe on the shoulder. "Gabe? Are you sure you ought to do this?"

Gabe hesitated for only an instant. "The snow is only going to get worse, Dan. And the longer I wait, the harder it's going to be to get out of here."

"You don't think you'll have any trouble making it into town?"

"The Cherokee's a tank, you know that. The old girl will take us anywhere we want to go." Gabe attempted a laugh, but it fell flat. "Relax, man, you're makin' me nervous."

Daniel's smile was also forced. "All right. But be careful. And get back just as soon as you can."

"Right." Gabe darted a glance across the room at Stacey, who was half asleep in front of the fireplace, her head bobbing against her brother's shoulder. A ghost of a smile flickered, then died.

"Take care of those kids. They've had enough trouble," he said to Teddy Giordano as he turned to leave the room.

Jennifer shuddered and clasped Daniel's arm. "Daniel, can't you stop them? They shouldn't go out in this storm!" She felt physically ill at the thought of Gabe and Lyss leaving the safety of the cabin.

Daniel took her hand as Teddy walked away. "I don't like it any better than you do," he said, his voice rough with emotion. "But I'm afraid Gabe's right. Someone needs to go for help. We don't know how much longer this storm's going to last." His tone gentled. "It's probably not a good idea for us to be isolated out here. Not with these children to look after."

Jennifer tightened her grip on his arm. "Daniel . . . you don't think there's any way those people who are looking for Teddy and the children . . . could know where they are, do you?"

He pulled her to him and smiled. "Don't you have enough to occupy that busy mind of yours?" After a moment, his expression sobered. "Nobody's going to be out in this unless they absolutely have to be. I don't think you need to worry about Teddy's 'friends' showing up."

Jennifer leaned against him. He was probably right. But when another gust of wind rushed against the side of the cabin, she shivered and drew even closer against him. She wasn't certain which bothered her more—the idea of being trapped out here alone in the middle of a mountain storm or the fear that they might *not* be alone. Either way, they could be in serious trouble.

TWELVE

T HE world outside was a nightmare, an angry bawl-
ing gale of shrieking wind and icy snow that
burned their eyes and stung their skin. By the time
Gabe and Lyss made their way to the garage, they felt as if they
had been outdoors for hours.

The Cherokee was cold, too. Gabe turned the ignition key
once, twice. On the third try it caught. He waited impatiently for
the engine to warm up.

They sat in silence, both trying to ignore the wind lashing the
frame walls of the garage. Gabe switched on the heater, but when
Lyss shivered at the sudden blast of cold air, he quickly cut the fan.

"You sure you want to do this? It's not too late to change your
mind," he offered, glancing over at his wife.

"I'm going," she said quietly.

"Crazy lady," he murmured. "Come here." He reached out his
hand to her.

A smile rose slowly in her eyes as she moved into his arms. He
gathered her against him, saying nothing for a moment, simply
holding her.

"I was afraid you were angry with me," she whispered against
his cheek.

"No, babe," he said softly, moving to touch her lips with his in
the gentlest of kisses, his hands going to her face. "I love you,

Lyss," he whispered. "I love you so much it makes me crazy sometimes."

Gabe felt her catch her breath as he held her gaze, blinking hard against the tears in his eyes. He had loved Lyss forever. At times his love seemed almost too big, too overwhelming to contain. It would spill over from his heart and explode from his soul into tears of almost unbearable happiness, embarrassing him.

He kissed her again. He wished he could somehow put all his love for her into that kiss, but he knew no one gesture could ever begin to convey the depth of his feeling for her.

Finally he released her, touched her cheek just once with the palm of his gloved hand, then slid back behind the steering wheel. He looked at her with a shaky smile. "We'll want to try that again later and see if we can get it right, Alyssa," he teased.

Lyss smiled at him. "Unless you want to take us both out with carbon monoxide," she said dryly, "you'd better get this vehicle out of the garage. And buckle up," she added, fastening her seat belt.

Gabe backed out of the garage and slowly began to plow the Cherokee down the narrow lane.

"So this is where you disappeared to after dinner," Lyss observed, pointing to the partially cleared road.

"I put the blade on the tractor and took a couple of swipes at it. Thought it might be a good idea to open a road to the gate, anyway."

They reached the foot of the hill, went through the double gate, and started up the unpaved road toward the highway.

It was almost impossible to see. Without the security lights that usually illuminated the road, the snowy night was a thick black-and-white curtain, distorted and forbidding.

The Cherokee, however, plugged confidently through the snow, and Gabe finally felt himself begin to breathe a little easier.

He was secretly glad Lyss had insisted on coming along; he was grateful for her company. He wasn't all that worried about getting into town. He and Dan had taken the Cherokee through some pretty severe weather. But he had never shared Dan's love for winter. Gabe was at home in the mountains and had a native's respect for them. But if he were to be completely truthful, he found these spring storms downright scary.

"It's even worse than I'd expected," Lyss said quietly beside him, breaking the silence.

"It's rough, that's for sure," he agreed. "But we're doing OK."

She nodded and tried to smile.

"What a week, huh?" He glanced at her quickly, then turned his gaze back to the road. They were nearing the exit to the highway now, and he was feeling more confident. The state route might be snow-covered—there would not have been any extensive plowing done yet—but it should at least be passable in a four-by-four

"It's been different," Lyss said, not taking her eyes from the road. "What do you think of our unexpected visitors?"

Gabe uttered a small grunt of disgust. "I wish they had found another place to camp out."

"You haven't been very nice, Gable." The only time Lyss ever called him *Gable* was when she intended at least a mild reprimand.

"What, I'm supposed to cozy up to the *mafia?*"

"Teddy's not really mafia," she protested. "I think he's probably a pretty good guy. And the kids are sweet."

He shrugged. "The little girl is. Her brother's a little too wise-mouthed for my taste."

"All the more reason the two of you should hit it off," she said drolly. "You were every bit as precocious as Nicky when you were a boy."

"How would you know? You were still in diapers when I was a boy."

"Mm. But I was advanced for my age."

He grinned at her. The Cherokee swerved, and he turned back to the road. He righted the wheels and pulled onto the state highway, shaking his head in disappointment when he saw the condition of the road.

"Remember how I used to follow you and Dan around when you were in high school?" Lyss asked.

"Yeah. You were a real pest." Gabe knew she was trying to take his mind off the treacherous road conditions.

"I bet you never thought then that you'd end up marrying me."

"Hardly. I considered strangling you a few times but never marrying you."

She grinned at him. "Was I really that bad?"

"You were a brat." He smiled as he remembered the long-legged, skinny, rather plain teenager she had been.

For years, he had thought of Dan's sister as a kind of younger sister of his own, probably because he spent more time at the Kaine house than he did at his own home. To him, Lyss had been just another kid, a fantastic basketball player, and an incredible nuisance.

The first time he had seen her as a *person,* rather than an annoying extension of his best friend, had been one sultry summer night shortly after he and Dan graduated from college. The three of them—Lyss, Dan, and he—had gone to a circus on the outskirts of town. An hour or so into the performance, he and Dan had gone to get popcorn. When they returned, one of the male trapeze artists was standing on the sidelines, openly flirting with Lyss, who was seated in the front row.

Gabe's first reaction had been disgust. Lyss was just a kid, after all, and the guy looked to be at least ten years older than she. He wasn't sure whether he was more put out with the performer or with Lyss, reasoning that she should have known better than to carry on like that with a stranger.

As they approached, Dan had muttered something about his little sister growing up, and Gabe had looked at her more closely. Lyss was no more than sixteen at the time, and while she hadn't lost all her coltishness, Gabe saw with surprise that she was no longer a child—and no longer plain. He stopped walking but continued to watch the repartee between her and the trapeze artist. Lyss was coy and somewhat awkward; the guy was confident and smug.

Gabe had been totally unprepared for the stab of white-hot anger that suddenly jolted him into motion. He spilled half his popcorn as he charged forward and planted himself between Lyss and the trapeze artist. With a gruff comment about robbing the cradle, he issued a veiled but unmistakable threat. His action caught Lyss so off guard, she was speechless. Only after the circus performer let go with a stream of incomprehensible invective in a foreign language did Lyss regain her composure enough to berate Gabe for "treating her like an infant."

The Kaine eyes flashing, she had sat haughtily between him and her brother for the rest of the evening, leaving Gabe to fume silently to himself. To make matters worse, Dan had worn a knowing smirk all the way home.

That had been the beginning. Somehow, he had managed to wait two more years—miserable years of watching her date a football hero, a swim-team captain, and a computer guru—before facing the fact that, ridiculous and impossible as the situation might be, he was in love with Dan's kid sister.

Her parents had made them wait until Lyss graduated from high school before they began to date. Even though Gabe had been like another member of the family since grade school, he *was* six years older than their only daughter, and his interest in Lyss had come as something of a surprise to the Kaines.

Even more surprising—to Gabe, as well as to the family—the

relationship endured, surviving Lyss's four years at college and a year working in Colorado afterward.

Within six months of her return home, she was wearing an engagement ring—but only with the understanding that they would not be married until they had the down payment for their first home in the bank.

Gabe was to learn that Lyss was never in a hurry. He was fairly certain they had had the longest engagement of any couple in the history of the county—almost five years. But now, finally, she was his wife, and he loved her in ways he was sure he could never have loved another woman. Lyss had been so many things to him for so many years—a kid sister, a buddy, a sweetheart, a confidante, and now his wife. It seemed that they had always been together, had always been a part of each other's lives. And it was good. It was extremely good.

Impulsively, he reached for her hand and squeezed it. "You know what, babe? I think one of the reasons I love you so much is because you're such a good sport."

"That's heartwarming, darling, to think that you married me for my sportsmanship."

"Yeah. You're a great basketball player."

"And you're such a romantic." She grinned at him, then sobered. "Gabe . . . you *are* happy, aren't you?"

He looked at her. "Of course I'm happy. What brought that on?"

Her smile was gentle. "Good. I want that for you. It's what you deserve."

He quirked one eyebrow. "Because I'm such a great guy, right?"

Lyss studied him for a moment. Her tone was surprisingly fervent when she answered. "Yes. You *are* a great guy. You're a truly good man, Gabe Denton. It's too bad you don't let more people in on your secret."

Gabe frowned dramatically and pressed a finger to his lips. "Shh. You'll blow my cover, Alyssa. You know I don't—"

His words died in his throat as he came out of a particularly sharp curve on the narrow highway.

Coming toward them from the other direction was a large, dark car. Gabe squinted against the headlights, trying to get a better look. The other vehicle appeared to be a limousine.

On *this* road?

Abruptly, he skidded off the highway, bumping onto the snow-covered berm and jerking the Cherokee to a stop just before they would have slid into an enormous drift.

"Gabe, what are you doing?"

"I'm turning around." Gabe cut the wheel and backed up, rocking the Cherokee forward as he eased back onto the highway.

"What's wrong? Why are you going back?"

"How many limousines are you likely to meet on this road?" he bit out, keeping his eyes straight ahead. "Even in broad daylight in good weather?"

Lyss glanced at him, then turned to look out the front window. "You think it's them? The people looking for Teddy and the kids?"

His face was grim. "You bet I do."

"Gabe, be careful. Maybe we should go into town for help."

"In this storm it's going to take us another forty minutes just to *get* to town and maybe another hour to get back to the Farm. Anything could happen in that time."

Underneath the snow, the road was slick with ice and extremely treacherous. But the Cherokee was having less trouble than the limousine ahead of them. Within a few minutes the back end of the Lincoln had become visible, and they saw it fishtail twice, swerving dangerously left of center before darting back into its own lane.

Gabe tightened his jaw and gripped the wheel in a death lock, staying just close enough to the limo to be sure he didn't lose them.

Lyss leaned as far forward as her seat belt would allow. "I can't tell how many people are in it, can you?"

"At least two," he said hoarsely. "Maybe more. It's hard to tell."

"You don't think they're headed for the Farm, do you?" she looked at him. "They couldn't possibly know that Teddy and the kids are—"

She stopped when Gabe started into a narrow, wicked turn. Almost at once, he cut his speed. His stomach clenched as the Cherokee started to slide, but with relief he felt the tires grip and hug the road.

"We'll stay far enough behind them so they won't know they're being followed," he told Lyss as they came out of the turn. "But I want to keep them in view just to—"

He broke off as he saw the limousine ahead zigzag and swerve. An oncoming semi, terrifying in the darkness and in its own immensity, fishtailed, then roared toward the limo on the wrong side of the road.

Panic slammed against Gabe's chest. He gripped the wheel, his hands shaking as he watched the truck start to jackknife, allowing the limo enough room to veer into the opposite lane and skid off the road untouched.

He clung to the steering wheel in a death grip as the semi kept coming, bearing down on them in a blaze of headlights, distorted by the wind-driven snow. He tried to swerve left, but the tires spun out of control on the ice.

The wheel wrenched crazily in his hands. He heard Lyss scream in terror, followed by the blood-chilling sound of crunching metal.

Then everything went black.

THIRTEEN

I N THE driver's seat of the limo, Boone sat shaking. With a trembling hand he reached for the door. "I'll see if we can help," he said. "It looks bad."

Wolf looked at him. "You just keep right on going."

Boone swung around, staring at Wolf in disbelief. "We can't do that! Those people may be hurt bad! We've got to see if we can help!"

"I said we don't stop," Wolf replied with chilling indifference. "Now get out of here before another car comes along."

In the back, Arno fidgeted. He secretly agreed with Boone. They ought to stop. But he wasn't about to argue with Wolf.

"There might not be another car along for hours, Wolf," Boone again tried to protest. "Not in this storm."

"It's a state highway. That truck driver was on the road, wasn't he? There'll be other cars. Now *move!*"

Boone eyed him for another few seconds, his mouth quivering. Arno followed his gaze as he finally turned to stare out the window at the accident. The semi and the Cherokee were meshed together in a silent, terrible embrace. Finally, Boone pulled forward. The car slipped, then leveled off, and they went on.

A tomblike silence enveloped the interior of the limousine for a long time. At last Wolf turned, and as his eyes caught Boone's, he smiled. "Turn off up there, Boone—at that sign," he said mildly, again looking back to the road. "Let's find out what this *Helping Hand Farm* is."

Gabe struggled toward consciousness, fighting against the pain. It held him prisoner, the weight of it pressing down on his head, his shoulders, suffocating him. He wanted to close his eyes, to return to the warm sea of darkness. But there was something he had to do. . . .

Lyss! Where was Lyss? And why was it so dark? He squinted, shook his head, tried to push himself up. Something held him. He fumbled at his waist to release the seat belt, surprised by the weakness in his hands. Awkwardly, he ripped off his gloves and tossed them aside.

Lifting his head, he saw the immense dark hull of a truck crushed against the right side of the car. Then he remembered. *The semi!* He tore the seat belt from his body and scrambled toward Lyss. The pain that ripped through his head at the sudden movement made him reel backward and fall against the seat. He squeezed his eyes shut once, pulled in a deep breath, then moved again, more carefully this time, reaching for her as he moved.

"Lyss . . . honey . . ."

He touched her hand, felt a sticky wetness on his fingers.

Blood . . . Lyss's blood . . .

He pulled at her seat belt, ignoring the pain in his head. He had to free her, had to get her out of the car. He couldn't bring himself to look at her. He fixed his eyes on the seat belt, forcing himself not to look at Lyss.

"It's OK, babe. . . . I'll have you out of here in a minute. You'll be all right. You'll be fine, babe. . . ."

Glass . . . there was glass everywhere . . . on the floor, on the seat, on her lap, her hands, her arms. . . . So much glass. . . .

She made a terrible sound, a wheezing, choking sound as though she were fighting for breath. Finally, the belt was free. He forced himself to look up. There was so much glass . . . so much blood. . . .

Again Lyss choked, an awful strangling noise. Gabe felt dizzy, then sick. "Lyss . . ."

Out of the darkness, he heard an engine coming toward them. It slowed, then stopped. In the gleam of the headlights, Gabe saw her face . . . his beautiful Lyss . . . shattered like a broken mirror. . . .

In that instant he could almost hear the sound of his own heart breaking and shattering into pieces.

FOURTEEN

AFTER Gabe and Lyss left, Jennifer took the children upstairs to bed. When she checked an hour later, she found all three asleep. Jason and Nicky had gallantly given the bed to Stacey and her doll. Sunny lay on the floor beside the bed, her eyes following Jennifer as she tiptoed around the room.

After watching them for a moment more, Jennifer gave Sunny a pat on the head, extinguished the small oil lamp on the bedside table, and went back downstairs.

Daniel and Teddy Giordano were sitting in the kitchen where she had left them. A lamp flickered softly in the middle of the table. In its glow, the men's faces were lined with fatigue and worry.

"We should try to get some sleep," Jennifer suggested halfheartedly. Teddy looked at her and shrugged, while Daniel nodded distractedly, saying nothing.

Earlier she had closed the kitchen curtains. Now she walked to the window, pulled one panel to the side, and looked out.

Snow and ice glazed the window, but she could see that the snow was still falling, could hear the wind wailing. With a sigh, she dropped the curtain and went to sit on the bench beside Daniel.

He covered her hand with his. "Why don't you go lie down for a while?"

"It would be useless. I can't even *sit* still, much less lie down."

"They'll be all right, Jennifer."

"It's such an awful night. . . ."

"Gabe could drive that Cherokee in his sleep," he pointed out.

"But the roads must be almost impassable. . . ."

"Honey—"

"I'm sorry." She took in a deep breath. "How long do you think they'll be gone?"

He shook his head. "It takes half an hour to get to Elkins in good weather. In this . . ." He left his sentence unfinished. "Did you hear something?"

Jennifer looked at him.

"I thought I heard a car."

Jennifer stood, then went back to the window and looked out, staring into the darkness. "Maybe Gabe couldn't get through," she said.

Teddy Giordano came to join her at the window. "I don't see any lights."

"Must have been an airplane," said Daniel. "I don't hear anything now. Jennifer, is there any coffee left?"

"No, but I'll make some," Jennifer said, glad for something to do.

Daniel pushed back from the table. "I'd better go up and check on the kids again."

"I was just upstairs, Daniel," Jennifer reminded him.

"Let me go," Teddy offered. "I need to stretch my legs anyway."

As Teddy left the room, Daniel came up behind Jennifer at the stove. "I wish you'd go to bed," he said, slipping his arms around her waist.

Jennifer turned to face him. "I can't, Daniel. Not until Gabe and Lyss get back."

He nodded, lightly resting his chin on top of her head.

Jennifer wished she could shake the growing knot of apprehension that had plagued her throughout the evening. "Lyss was worried, Daniel. I could tell."

His arms tightened around her. He said nothing but pressed a light kiss into her hair. Jennifer buried her face in the warmth of his sweater for another moment, wondering if the night would ever end.

Both of them jumped, startled, when they heard the sound of stamping feet on the deck. Upstairs, Sunny barked once, then again, as someone began to pound loudly on the door.

"They *are* back," Jennifer said, slipping quickly from Daniel's arms.

"Jennifer, wait—"

But Jennifer was already opening the door. "What happened, couldn't you—"

She stopped, staring blankly at the three men on the other side of the door.

The one standing in front of the others was thin and pale, but neatly dressed in an obviously expensive topcoat. Behind him, a bearded middle-aged man, with a coat hanging loosely on his gaunt frame, stood watching her. The third man was moderately tall and broad-shouldered in a dark leather jacket; he had thinning hair and a dark mustache. Snow clung to them, and they looked extremely cold.

"Excuse us, ma'am." The man in the well-cut topcoat spoke first. "We were wondering if we could use your phone? I'm afraid we're hung up in a snowdrift." He rubbed his gloved hands together and craned his neck to look past Jennifer into the cabin.

Daniel had come to stand beside her. "What's the problem?" he asked, putting his hand on Jennifer's arm.

"We're really sorry to bother you," the apparent spokesman of the group said, smiling pleasantly. "We must have taken a wrong turn somewhere. We got about halfway down the road leading in here before we realized we were lost. Then we got stuck in a drift and had to walk the rest of the way." He stopped, extending his hand to Daniel. "Jay Wolf here," he said amiably.

Daniel merely inclined his head, saying nothing. The other's expression darkened, and he dropped his hand to his side.

Jennifer's uneasiness grew as she watched the man's peculiar pale eyes narrow to a cold stare. "I'm sorry," she said, wanting only to be rid of these strangers, "but our phone—"

Daniel stopped her, his grasp tightening on her arm. "Where exactly were you headed?"

"Actually, we're looking for some friends of ours who live in the area. It's just that we don't know this part of the country, and the storm has made it nearly impossible to find their . . . farm."

"If they live around here," Daniel answered shortly, "I'm sure we know them. What are their names?"

Irritation flared in the man's eyes. "Can't we just use your phone?"

Daniel hesitated only an instant. "I'm afraid we can't help you." As he spoke, he released Jennifer's arm and reached for the door.

It happened so fast, Jennifer was never sure who made the first move. Teddy came back into the room, and she heard him choke off an exclamation behind her. At the same time, the man in the topcoat pulled a handgun. His hard kick at the door sent it slamming against the wall as he and the other two men came charging into the kitchen, guns drawn.

"Jennifer—" Daniel reached for her, but the muscular man in the leather jacket stopped him.

"Move back, big guy—against the wall."

When Daniel didn't react, he rammed the pistol hard into his stomach. "I said *move back! Now!*"

"Stop it!" Jennifer screamed at him. "He can't see you! He's blind!"

All three men froze, their eyes locking on Daniel. But only for an instant. Almost immediately, their attention went to Teddy Giordano, who now stood in the middle of the room, his face a taut, angry mask.

"Well, well . . ." The man with the cold eyes took a step toward

Teddy, then stopped, his gun leveled at him. "Will you look who's become a country boy."

Jennifer shuddered at the wide, toothy smile, the feral expression that suggested an underlying viciousness.

"You've been bad, Teddy-boy. Very bad." Still smiling darkly, the man in the topcoat closed the distance between them.

Teddy stood rigid and unmoving. Jennifer saw his hands clench into tight fists at his sides as he met the other's gaze with a defiant stare.

For a moment, they stood staring at each other in silence. It was Teddy who spoke first. "What do you want, Wolf?"

The man called Wolf smirked, then laughed—a high, almost shrill hacking sound that struck Jennifer as strangely obscene.

Abruptly, the man's expression sobered. His pale eyes watered as he fixed a contemptuous glare on Teddy Giordano. "What do we *want?*" He pressed a finger to the side of his nose and sniffed. "You know what we want, Teddy-boy. We want Nick's notebook." He sniffed again, then added, "And we'd also like to have a little talk with the kids."

"I don't know anything about any notebook, Wolf. Or the kids."

Wolf's eyes never left Teddy's face. "None of that, Teddy-boy. Don't lie to me. I hate it when people lie to me. I'm going to have the notebook. And I'm going to talk with the kids. That's what we're here for." Without warning, his gaze went to Jennifer. "In the meantime, why don't you introduce us to your new friends?"

Teddy looked at Jennifer, and his eyes seemed to plead for forgiveness. Then he turned back to Wolf. "This is between us, Wolf. Leave them out of it."

Wolf let his watery gaze play slowly over Jennifer, then Daniel.

Finally, he turned back to Teddy. "You're in a lot of trouble, Teddy-boy," he said, again smirking. "Kidnapping is bad business. Very bad."

Teddy shot him a startled look. "Kidnapping! What are you talking about?"

Wolf shrugged, tipping his gun to Teddy's chin. "Nabbing two kids that don't belong to you—" He shook his head in a gesture of mock regret. "That's kidnapping, Teddy. The feds are looking for you, boy. You'd better let us help you."

Teddy blanched, but his expression never wavered. "I don't know what you're talking about."

Wolf's smile faded. "OK, punk. You want to play games? We'll play *my* games."

His eyes still locked on Teddy, he snapped out orders to the other two men. "Arno, take the woman in the other room and tie her up."

As the broad-shouldered man in the leather jacket took a step toward Jennifer, Daniel uttered an exclamation of anger and moved.

"Boone, keep that gun on the blind man!" snapped Wolf.

The hunched, older man moved in closer to Daniel, his gun wavering slightly.

Jennifer gasped as the man called Arno dug a gun into her side. "Let's go, lady."

"Leave her alone!" As accurately as if he could see the man's arm, Daniel struck out with one large hand and knocked the other man's gun free, sending it skating across the kitchen floor.

Furious, Arno hurled himself at Daniel, poised to slug him.

Jennifer screamed, and Boone moved in with his gun between Arno and Daniel. "Stop it, Chuck! Didn't you hear her? He's blind. He can't even see you!"

"That's enough!" Wolf shouted. "Get your gun, Chuck! And this time hold on to it."

He motioned Teddy against the wall with the others. "Get over there, Giordano." When Teddy hesitated, Wolf shoved the gun against his ribs and growled, *"Now!"*

Teddy went to stand next to Daniel, whose face looked as if it had been carved from granite.

Wolf stepped up to them. "You don't look blind, mister," he snarled, tapping the barrel of his gun against Daniel's chest. "And you move pretty good for someone who can't see."

When Daniel remained stonily silent, Wolf turned his attention to Jennifer. She went weak with revulsion as she saw his expression change to a predatory stare. Her breath lodged in her throat, and she cringed, digging her hands into her sides so hard that pain shot up her arms.

"You're the blind man's lady?" Again, the ugly, chilling smile.

Jennifer nodded, trying desperately to look at something—anything—other than the man's face. "I'm his wife," she choked out.

One pale hand snaked out to capture her chin, forcing Jennifer to look at him. "His wife?"

Again she nodded, squeezing her eyes shut against the cold touch of his skin against her face.

Unexpectedly, he dropped his hand. "Then I suggest," he said softly, "that you convince him to be a good boy and do exactly what he's told. And I suggest that you do the same."

Jennifer shuddered at the corruption she could feel emanating from the man. It was almost as if she could sense his evil seeping through her own skin.

He's insane, her mind clamored. *He's insane . . . and . . . deadly.*

Suddenly the man seemed to lose interest in her, transferring his attention back to Teddy. "Where are the kids?" he barked.

Teddy didn't look at him. "Pittsburgh, I suppose," he snapped.

Wolf sneered and struck the younger man, hard, across the face. "I *said* . . . where are the kids?"

Teddy glared at him with undisguised fury but remained grimly silent.

"You're making me very angry, Teddy-boy," Wolf said mildly. "I should think by now you'd know it's a mistake to make me angry." He glanced at Daniel, his mouth twisting into a derisive smile. "Now then, punk," he said, still watching Daniel's face, "you're going to tell me where the Angelini brats are, or I'm going to put a bullet between the blind man's eyes." With an ugly, teasing motion, he turned the gun on Daniel and mimed the act of shooting him.

Jennifer cried out, but Wolf ignored her, now training the gun on Teddy.

A ring of sweat banded Teddy's forehead. He looked from Wolf to Daniel, then back to the man with the gun. Finally, his voice ragged with defeat, he said, "They're upstairs." He moistened his lips. "Wolf, leave them alone! They don't know anything!"

Wolf ignored him. "Get upstairs," he said, glancing at the tall, bearded man. "Stay with the kids."

His gun still on Teddy, he turned to Arno. "I *said* take the woman out of here and tie her up. Do it now." He inclined his head toward the doorway into the great room, adding, "In there. And watch her close." He smiled his chilling smile. "She looks like trouble to me."

Jennifer felt the blood drain from her face. Her entire body began to shake when Arno jabbed her with the gun. "You heard him, lady. Move it."

"Jennifer—"

She saw Daniel lunge as if to charge toward her, then stop when Wolf pressed the tip of the gun barrel to the side of his head.

"Sit down, blind man! And shut up! Or I'm going to make your woman a widow!"

Jennifer stole one last look at Daniel, his face white and lined with fury, as the two men prodded her out of the kitchen.

FIFTEEN

T HE great room that had earlier seemed so cozy to Jennifer now appeared eerie and forbidding in the flickering glow of the oil lamps and the dying embers in the fireplace.

The man called Arno looked around the room, then turned to his partner. "Where's the upstairs in this—"

At that moment a door above them opened, and his words were lost in the sudden din from the stairway. Sunny came roaring down the steps, snarling and barking furiously. She headed straight for Arno.

Standing behind Jennifer, his gun shoved hard into her back, Arno jumped and yelled, instinctively turning the gun on the retriever.

"No!" Jennifer screamed, hurling herself in front of the dog. "Sunny—*no!*"

The retriever thundered to a dead stop, all four legs stiff and poised. Her eyes, dark with confusion and distrust, flicked from Jennifer to Arno, and she bared her teeth in a low, menacing growl.

"Sunny . . ." With great effort, Jennifer kept her voice even and firm. "It's all right, Sunny." She turned to Arno. "Please, she's my husband's guide dog. Don't—"

A muffled sound from the top of the stairs made her whirl around.

"Nicky!" she cried out. "Go back inside the bedroom!"

117

The boy was poised at the top of the steps, staring down at Jennifer and the two men. Behind him, just beyond the bedroom door, stood Jason. He was holding Stacey's hand.

"Boone?" Nicky adjusted his glasses and peered down into the firelit great room. His gaze flicked from Boone to Arno, locking on the gun in the burly mobster's hand. "What are you guys doing here?" In the light from the fireplace, Jennifer could see the boy's face, hard and unexpectedly mature.

"Hey—Nicky!" Grinning, Boone started toward the stairs but stopped when Sunny's growl increased to a warning snarl.

"Mommy?" Jason's voice sounded small and uncertain. He led Stacey along beside him as he stepped closer to Nicky. The little girl rubbed at her eyes, staring down into the great room with a look of surprise. Her eyes widened when she saw the gun in Arno's hand.

The mobster grabbed Jennifer's arm from behind, again pushing the gun against her back. "Lady, you get that dog out of my way, or I'll blow her to bits!"

Jennifer swallowed hard, looking wildly from the retriever to the children standing at the top of the steps.

I mustn't panic. . . . Oh, Lord, don't let me panic.

"Jason . . ." Her voice was tremulous. She stopped, then began again. "Jason, call Sunny. Then I want you children to go into the bedroom, shut the door, and stay there. With Sunny. Do you understand?"

The boy looked at her, then at Arno and Boone. "Where's Daddy?"

"He's in the kitchen with Teddy . . . and another man. He's all right, Jason. Now, please, honey—do as I say."

"Who are *they?*" Jason asked.

Helplessly, Jennifer looked at Nicky.

Nicky glared at Boone with disgust. "Wolf's in the kitchen,

right? With Teddy? You guys are here to finish what you started with Papa, I suppose."

Boone's face sagged with a wounded expression. "No, Nicky," he whined, shaking his head. "We just need to talk to you and Teddy. Teddy's got something that belongs to Mr. Sabas."

Nicky didn't take his eyes off the man as he said, "Jason, do what your mother said. Call Sunny."

Jason moved a few steps into the landing, then stopped. "Sunny—come on, girl!"

The retriever turned and looked up the stairs, then back to Jennifer, her eyes uncertain.

Again, Jason called her. This time, she hesitated only an instant before sprinting up the steps.

"Go back to the bedroom, Jason," Nicky told him. "Take Sunny and Stacey with you."

Responding to the tone of authority in Nicky's voice, Jason again glanced down the steps. When Jennifer gave him a small nod, he turned and led Stacey back to the bedroom. The retriever followed obediently.

"Get upstairs with those kids," Arno growled at Boone. "And *stay* up there with them, you understand?"

As Jennifer watched, Boone hesitated, glancing from Arno up to Nicky. He put his gun away before starting to shuffle up the steps.

"Better keep your gun handy if you're coming up here to *guard* us, Boone," Nicky sneered, folding his arms across his chest. "An unarmed man wouldn't have a chance against three dangerous kids like us."

"Hey, come on, Nicky," Boone said peevishly. "You know old Boone wouldn't lay a hand on you or your sister. We just want to talk to you, that's all."

Nicky pushed his glasses up with one finger, then leveled a scathing look of contempt at the man on the steps. "Talk about what, Boone? How you killed Papa? What you're going to do to Teddy . . . and to us?"

By the time he reached the landing, Boone was gasping for breath. "Now, you just hush that kind of talk, Nicky!" he muttered defensively, wheezing hard. "I told you, Teddy has something that belongs to Mr. Sabas. We just came to get it back. No one's gonna hurt you or your sister."

"Cut the gab and get those kids in the bedroom!" Arno shouted up the steps. "And *keep* them there, you hear?"

"Come on, Nicky. We'd better do like he says," Boone grumbled.

The boy glared at him with a mixture of anger and contempt. "Still letting Rambo rattle your chain, huh, Boone?"

"Nicky—" Boone glanced back at Arno.

Nicky ignored him. "Don't let him scare you, Mrs. Kaine," he said, glaring down the stairway at Arno. "He thinks he's a real tough guy, but he has the backbone of a slug."

Arno scowled up at the boy but said nothing. After Nicky and Boone finally disappeared into the bedroom, he jabbed his gun into Jennifer's ribs. "Get over to the couch," he told her, his voice rough. He motioned for her to sit down; then, keeping his gun trained on her, he reached inside his jacket and withdrew a twist of rope.

"You don't have to tie me up," Jennifer said, wincing at the tremor in her voice. "I'm not likely to make any trouble, not when someone has a gun trained on my husband and my son."

As if he hadn't heard her, he laid the gun on the table beside the couch. "Put your hands behind your back," he ordered her.

Jennifer hesitated, and he pushed at her with one hand. "Lady, just *do* it!"

Arno bound her hands, then trussed her ankles together as well. Straightening, he retrieved the gun and glanced around the room. "What kind of place is this, anyway?" he asked Jennifer. "You guys farmers or what?"

120

She shook her head. "It's a camp. For disabled children," she said tonelessly.

His lip curled with distaste. *"Handicapped* kids? A camp for cripples?"

Jennifer stared at him incredulously, for an instant too shocked to answer. "They're not . . . *cripples!"* she finally managed to choke out. "They're children. Disabled children."

He looked at her with open disgust. "What's with you, anyway? You're married to a blind man, working in a camp for crippled kids—you got something against *normal* people?" He paused, moving in closer to her. "I bet there's something wrong with *you,* too, huh? Maybe something you try to keep a secret. Something that doesn't show, right?"

Another madman, she thought wildly. She squeezed her eyes shut. He was so close she could hear the rasp of his breath, could smell some kind of sickeningly sweet hair-grooming product, could feel his small cold eyes on her.

Unexpectedly, he moved away and started walking around the room. "Who else is here besides you and the others? Anyone?"

Jennifer hesitated. She was relieved that Gabe and Lyss hadn't been trapped in this nightmare with them, yet she half wished they were here. Two more adults might have made a difference.

"I said, who else is here?" He scowled at her.

"No one." The words were lost in a rising wave of panic. Jennifer forced a note of calm into her voice. "No one else. The couple who manages the camp are on vacation. We're just filling in for them while they're away."

"You got a phone here, don't you?" His gaze scanned the room, locking on the wall phone.

"It's . . . out of order," Jennifer told him. "The storm . . ."

"Yeah, it's a real monster, ain't it?"

Jennifer had a sudden, irrational urge to laugh. Here she was, tied up and held captive by a gunman; Jason was locked upstairs with an aging thug; and Daniel—her throat closed with sick fear—Daniel was the prisoner of a lunatic. And all the while she was expected to make small talk with this . . . *gorilla?*

"How long have Giordano and the kids been here, anyway?" She looked at him. "I . . . I'm not sure."

Again, he moved closer to her, his posture aggressive as he rolled the gun around his hand almost casually. "You're not real smart, are you, sweetheart? What a pair, a blind man and a dummy," he said scornfully. "You're a looker, though," he added, sounding almost surprised.

The warmth from the fire suddenly seemed to disappear, and Jennifer shivered.

"What's a classy chick like you doin' hooked up with a blind man?"

When she neither answered nor met his gaze, he moved even closer. As if to deliberately intimidate her, he kept the gun trained on her while with the other hand he lifted a strand of her hair, then let it tumble slowly over his fingertips.

Jennifer flinched and twisted her head to one side.

He laughed. "Nervous, are you? Relax, sweetheart. It could be a very long night."

Jennifer felt a wave of nausea sweep through her as he looked at her for a moment, then put his gun down and shrugged out of his jacket. "It's getting warm in here," he said with a leer. "Might as well get comfortable—we're going to be here for a while."

Daniel's apprehension mounted as he listened to the two men at the kitchen table. Seated beside Teddy on the harvest bench for what seemed like hours, he could sense the tension in the younger man.

"Stall as long as you like, Teddy-boy," the man called Wolf said, his voice smooth. "I'm in no particular hurry to go back outside.

I'm going to get what I came for eventually, but we can play games for a little longer, if you want."

"I'm not playing games, Wolf," Teddy said, his voice low and tight. "I told you, I don't have any notebook. And those kids know *nothing* about Nick's business. You know he always kept his family out of it. He even shut *me* out."

"Oh, I'm not worried about what the kids know about Nick's business, Teddy-boy. I'm only interested in what they know about Nick's—*execution.*"

When Teddy made no reply, Wolf went on in the same casual, unhurried tone. "You see, some people might get the wrong idea about Nick's death. If they listened to just anyone, they might even suspect that his friends had something to do with it. Or even someone in the *Family.*"

Daniel heard the chair creak as the mobster got up and began to pace the room.

"Now, we wouldn't want anyone coming to the wrong conclusions about the Family, would we, Teddy-boy? So if Nick's kids have any information at all about who might have murdered their papa, we need to know. Understand?"

"I already *told* you—the kids don't know anything!"

Teddy's voice was strained as he pushed away from the table with a thud. "Don't you have any feelings at all?" he grated out. "They're just kids, Wolf!" He stopped, then added, "Kids without *parents.*"

"Sit down, punk. I'll tell you when you can get up." Wolf's tone went hard. "I think maybe you don't understand how serious this is. This is important, Teddy-boy. *Extremely* important." He paused, and when he went on, there was no mistaking the threat in his words. "I want the notebook, Teddy-boy. I want it now."

When Teddy tried to interrupt, Wolf slammed his hand down on the table.

"Otherwise," Wolf went on, his voice softer but even more

menacing, "maybe I can convince your blind friend here to per-
suade you."

"Wolf—"

"Shut up, Teddy-boy." Wolf's tone was still deceptively quiet.
"Better yet," he continued, "maybe I can convince his *wife* to
help us out."

Daniel's pent-up rage finally exploded. He tilted the harvest
table with both hands and let it slam back to the floor. "Don't
you *touch* her!" he roared, jumping to his feet.

"Sit *down,* blind man!" Wolf shouted. *"Now!* I don't think you
understand what's going on here. I'll do whatever I please. *I've* got
the control! Now sit down and shut up!"

Daniel heard the safety of the gun click only a second before
Teddy grabbed his arm.

"Dan, do what he says! He's just crazy enough to shoot you!"

For a moment every fiber of Daniel's body seemed coiled to its
limit, stretched beyond endurance. Finally, he sank back onto the
bench, a mixture of defeat and helplessness washing over him in
one enormous, crushing wave.

*Merciful Lord, don't let him touch Jennifer. . . . Don't let these ani-
mals hurt her.*

He started in surprise at Teddy's next words. "All right, Wolf.
I'll give you the notebook."

There was a long silence. "I thought you'd come around, Teddy-
boy," said Wolf, "once you understood how important it is to us."

"But it's not here," Teddy added. "I hid it."

"Where?" Daniel heard the suspicious snap in the mobster's
voice.

"It's in one of the barns. At the other end of the camp."

Wolf softly rapped the table with what sounded like the butt of
the gun. "If you're lying to me, Teddy-boy," he said softly, "you
won't get a second chance. I'll line you and everyone else in this

cabin up against the wall and start shooting. Do you understand me?"

"I'm not lying," Teddy answered woodenly.

"I hope not, kid." There was another moment of silence. "All right," Wolf said. "Both of you, stay put. I'm going to talk to Arno a minute, and then we'll go get the notebook."

He stopped, sniffed once, then again. "Incidentally, blind man, the gun will be pointed at your head—so behave yourself."

Both Daniel and Teddy remained stonily quiet while the other men carried on a hurried exchange between the two rooms.

". . . I'm taking the blind man with us." Wolf's speech was fast now, his tone sharp and authoritative. Daniel had the distinct feeling that the man's next words were emphasized for his and Teddy's benefit. "You go up and tell Boone what's going on, and make sure he understands. If I'm not back here within an hour, have him take care of those kids." He paused. "And you take care of the woman."

Then he turned his attention back to Teddy and Daniel. "All right, punk. Get a coat for yourself and the blind man."

Daniel heard Teddy leave and return a moment later. "I need my dog if I'm going outside," he said as he slipped into the bomber jacket Teddy handed him.

Wolf uttered a groan of disgust. "Teddy-boy can be your guide dog, blind man! Now, *move!*" Without warning, he cracked Daniel across the back of the neck with the handle of the gun.

Daniel's knees buckled as a fireball of pain shot through him. He staggered and lunged forward, almost falling.

Teddy grabbed for his arm, steadying him as he led him through the outside door.

"Let up on him, Wolf," he grated angrily. "He's *blind!*"

"He's going to be *dead* if the two of you don't get moving."

"Let's go, Dan. The sooner I give them what they want, the sooner they get out of your life."

"You know better than that," Daniel muttered.

"Listen, Dan—just do what he says," Teddy whispered, his tone urgent. "Whatever you do, don't provoke him."

Outside, the snow had tapered to little more than a fine mist. Daniel slipped once, stumbling over a rock. Teddy caught him. "Wolf, this is crazy. Let him stay inside."

Wolf's only reply was to jab the gun even harder into Daniel's lower back.

"Dan . . ." Teddy whispered as he clutched Daniel's arm, guiding him through the deep snow. "Dan . . . I know it doesn't help, but I'm sorry. . . . I'm so sorry for what I've done to you and your family."

His head still ringing from the blow in the kitchen, Daniel could only nod and go on.

SIXTEEN

J ASON couldn't quite make up his mind about the man called Boone. He didn't have the same . . . *bad* look in his eyes that the other two men did. Yet Nicky seemed to be really angry with him, apparently because of something to do with his "papa."

Jason had never heard anyone call his daddy "papa" before. Maybe that was the kind of word *geniuses* used. He had heard Teddy talking to Uncle Gabe and Daddy about Nicky, explaining how Nicky was a *genius*. Apparently, being a genius meant you were different from other kids, because Nicky attended a special kind of school, too. Jason didn't think he was a genius like Nicky, but he knew all about being different.

Right now, though, Nicky looked just like any other kid who was angry with someone. He was frowning at the tall thin man, and he looked really fierce.

Jason held on to Stacey's hand as he listened to Nicky and Boone.

"I didn't have nothing to do with hurting your papa, Nicky. I wouldn't have laid a hand on Nick. No way."

Nicky pushed his glasses up a notch, staring up into Boone's face. "I know that," he said impatiently. "It was Wolf. Wolf and Arno."

The man stiffened, taking a step back from the boy. "How'd you know that?"

Nicky didn't answer but simply continued to watch Boone.

"Whatever you do, boy, don't let on to them that you know anything," Boone warned him in a gruff voice. "Now listen, Nicky, you tell me the truth. *Were* you in the house? Did you hear what went on the day your papa . . . the day he died?"

"Why do you want to know, Boone?"

Jason watched, fascinated, as the man swallowed. Boone's neck was extremely long and skinny, with a lump at the bottom that rose and fell every time he swallowed or even took a deep breath.

"Nicky, honest now—I'm tellin' you the truth! The only reason we're here is to get that notebook that belongs to the Boss—Mr. Sabas—and to make sure you and Stacey get back home safe. That's all there is to it, and you're just gonna make trouble for you and your little sister if you don't do what Wolf tells you."

Nicky's only reply was a sneer.

Boone glanced over his shoulder at the closed door, then moved closer to Nicky. He stooped down and lowered his voice. "Listen to me, Nicky. If you—" His eyes went to Stacey for a minute. "If you or your sister heard anything that went on at the house the day . . . your papa died, don't admit it."

Jason saw with surprise that Nicky's eyes had suddenly filled with tears.

"You were there that day, weren't you, Boone?" Nicky asked quietly. "You and Arno . . . and Wolf."

The man shook his head. "I wasn't! I swear to you, Nicky, I *wasn't!*" He looked away, then back to Nicky. "I was in the car. I didn't know anything until it was over. Arno told me later. That's the truth, boy. That's the truth."

He straightened, coughed, and went on. "Your papa did something he shouldn't have done, Nicky. He tried to get the Boss—and the Family—in trouble." Again he shook his head. "He shouldn't have done that."

"So Wolf killed him," Nicky said flatly. "And now he's going to kill Teddy. And maybe Stacey and me, too."

"No!" Boone laughed, but Jason could tell it wasn't a happy laugh—it was strained, as if it hurt Boone's throat to get it out. "Why would he kill Teddy? Wolf likes Teddy, you know that. We *all* like Teddy!" He grinned at Nicky. "For a kid who's supposed to be so smart, you sure got a lot of crazy ideas, you know that?"

Nicky stared up at him for a long time. The room was quiet, except for Sunny's shallow breathing.

Finally Nicky spoke. *"You* guys are the crazy ones, if you really think Teddy has that notebook." An odd little smile broke across his face as he watched Boone's reaction to his words.

"What?" The man's voice was gruff. "What do you mean?"

Still smiling, Nicky said, "I heard Arno talking to you out in the hall a few minutes ago. About Teddy and Wolf going to find the notebook." He squinted at Boone. "But *I'm* the one who hid the notebook, not Teddy."

Boone had straightened up, but he stooped down again. It must have hurt, because Jason saw him make a face as if he was in pain. He took Nicky by the shoulders and shook him a little. "Don't you lie about this, boy!"

Sunny growled and rose to her feet. Jason, too, stepped forward. He wasn't sure what he could do, but he wanted to help Nicky. Boone straightened again, holding up both hands, palms outward, as if to show that he meant no harm to Nicky.

Jason told Sunny to stay, and the dog settled down beside him, still alert and watching quietly.

"What about the notebook, Nicky?" Boone asked, his eyes on Sunny.

"Do you think Papa would have trusted anyone but me with that notebook?" Nicky said softly. He had an expression in his eyes that Jason didn't understand—like he knew some kind of secret he wasn't telling.

Boone shook his head. "Then why did Teddy run off with you kids the way he did? And why did he tell Wolf he had the notebook?"

"To protect us," the boy said, emphasizing each word as if he were the adult and Boone the child. "Teddy knows Wolf too well. He was trying to get him away from us."

Boone's eyes narrowed. "Are you tellin' me the truth, Nicky?"

The boy nodded, his gaze steady.

"What do you think Wolf's gonna do when he finds out Teddy lied to him?" Boone rubbed his beard and frowned.

Nicky's voice sounded hard and cold when he answered. "Wolf's going to kill Teddy no matter what. We both know that." Jason saw that same secret kind of smile spread across Nicky's face. "Unless we stop him."

"Stop him?" Boone's chin trembled, but he looked interested.

Nicky nodded. "If I were to give *you* the notebook before Wolf finds out what Teddy's up to, do you think you could convince Wolf not to hurt Teddy—or us?"

Boone looked from Nicky to Stacey, licking his lips. Finally he said, "Yeah. Sure." He nodded. "Sure, I could. Wolf would be so happy I got the notebook for him, he'd listen to me. Where is it?"

Nicky blinked, then said evenly, "It's not in *here,* Boone. I'm smarter than that." He nodded, and Jason thought he looked pleased. "It's in a safe place. No one but me is ever going to find that notebook."

Boone scratched his head.

"Listen, Boone, I'll take you to it. We'll get that notebook before Wolf finds out that Teddy lied to him." He stopped, lowering his voice even more. "But you've got to promise me that you won't let Wolf or that creep, Arno, hurt us."

Boone put a hand on the boy's shoulder. "Hey, Nicky—you've got my word." He pressed his thin lips together in a worried expression. "But how are we gonna get the notebook? Chuck's right downstairs underneath us with the woman. And I'm supposed to stay with you kids 'til Wolf gets back."

Nicky pulled his mouth to one side and pushed his glasses up on his nose. He looked at Jason and Stacey, then back up at Boone. "I know what we can do," he finally said, his tone firm. "We'll just have to tell Arno the truth. Now, here's what we'll do, Boone. You go downstairs and explain to Arno about the notebook. Tell him where we're going, and that Jason and Stacey will have to stay with him. Then you and I will go after the notebook."

Boone cocked his head to one side and scratched his chin. "Yeah," he said slowly. "Arno won't stop us, once he knows where we're goin'."

He glanced at Sunny. "I don't know about that dog, though." He gave Nicky a nasty grin. "He'd shoot me for sure if he knew I told anyone, but Arno is scared to death of dogs," he whispered to Nicky.

Nicky laughed with him. "We'll take Sunny with us. Hey, she can even help us dig."

"No," Jason argued uneasily, beginning to feel angry with Nicky. "Sunny won't go with you unless I tell her to. And I'm not going to tell her to. She's supposed to stay here with us." He suddenly felt very frightened. There was nothing familiar or safe in this room except Sunny.

Boone frowned at him. Jason stepped back but continued to watch the man.

"Now listen here, kid, we don't have time to waste. We're gonna go get that—"

"Wait a minute, Boone," Nicky interrupted, tugging at his sleeve. "You go on down and explain things to Arno. Let me talk to Jason a minute, OK?"

Boone studied him. "Well . . . all right," he finally said. "But

the dog will have to go with us. You get your coat on and be
ready."

Nicky stood watching Boone shuffle stiffly out of the bedroom.
Then he hurried across the room to bolt the door.

Puzzled, Jason watched him. "What are you doing?"

The other boy turned around, his back to the locked door. He
put a finger to his lips, cautioning Jason and Stacey to be quiet.
His eyes looked like black coals aas he looked from Jason to his
sister.

"Why did you lock the door?" Jason asked.

Nicky smiled. "I'm eliminating some of their ammunition," he
said.

"Am–ammunition?" Jason repeated with a frown.

Nicky left the door and quickly crossed the room. "Wolf
would have used *us* to get what he wanted from Teddy—or from
your parents," he explained. "He wouldn't think twice about
shooting all three of us if it would help him."

"How do you know so much about these men?"

"They work . . . for the same people my papa worked for,"
Nicky said. "They used to be at our house a lot. I got to know
them pretty well."

Jason knew he might not like the answer, but he had to ask the
question. "They're not good men, are they?"

Nicky shook his head, taking Stacey's hand when she came to
stand beside him. "No, they're not," he said without hesitation.
"Boone's probably the best of the three, but that's not saying
much. Lucky for us, he's not too bright. The one downstairs—
Chuck Arno—he's not a whole lot smarter than Boone, but he
can get mean. He's kind of weird, you know? Thinks everything
has to be perfect or it's no good."

He stopped and glanced down at Stacey. She still looked scared,
but she smiled a little.

"Wolf is the dangerous one," Nicky went on. "Wolf is smart.

Maybe as smart as I am," he said matter-of-factly. "But my papa said that Wolf's brain is probably rotten by now, from all the drugs he's done."

He pulled Stacey more tightly to his side. "Being around Wolf always makes me feel kind of . . . creepy. I think he likes to hurt people. I mean, really *likes* it." He shook his head. "Wolf's the worst of them, that's for sure."

Jason's stomach felt funny. "What are we going to do now?"

Nicky didn't answer right away. His eyes went around the room as if he was looking for something. Finally he pointed at the tall, narrow window beside the bed. "What's outside that window?"

"Just a porch." Jason tried to remember what Mommy called it. "A . . . balcony."

Nicky's eyes brightened. "A balcony?" He dropped his hand from Stacey's shoulder and went quickly to the window. Without opening it, he peered outside for a minute.

When he turned back, he was smiling.

SEVENTEEN

J ASON looked up from the ground at the support pole that ran from the balcony to the lower deck. He could understand why Sunny didn't want to jump. She was a *dog*. But why was Stacey making such a big deal out of it? There was a post all the way down. All she had to do was hang on and slide.

Nicky had already done it by throwing a pillowcase full of stuff over, then sliding down ahead of her. And Jason had done it, even though he wasn't a . . . a genius like Nicky.

Jason watched Stacey now and tried not to laugh. All three of them had pulled on jeans and coats over their pajamas. Stacey looked like an inner tube. She could hardly move. Jason didn't want to hurt her feelings by laughing at her, but she did look pretty funny.

Stacey glared down at her brother and Jason. "Let Sunny go first," she whispered, a little too loudly.

"Shh!" Nicky warned her. "They'll hear us." He glanced around. "Jason, try to get Sunny to jump. Stacey won't stay up there by herself. If Sunny comes down, *she'll* come down."

But for the first time Jason could remember, Sunny refused to obey. Jason tried motioning with his hand, the way he had seen Daddy do. But Sunny just stared down at him without moving.

Jason planted his legs apart and spread his arms wide. He

135

slipped in the snow and grabbed at Nicky to keep from falling. Opening his arms once more, he ordered as loudly as he dared, *"Sunny—come!"*

The retriever only cocked her head.

"Sunny doesn't want to jump," Stacey said. "She wants to stay here with me."

Jason didn't know what to do. He looked at Nicky for help.

Nicky studied both the dog and his sister for a moment. "Stacey, throw Mrs. Whispers down to me."

Stacey's face crumpled. "I *won't!*" she whispered back. Glaring down at him, she clutched the rag doll tightly against her.

"I'll catch her, Stacey, I promise. Just toss her down to me. Come on. You'll see why in a minute."

Stacey gave her brother one more look—a scrunched-up pout Jason thought was probably her "mean look"—then carefully dropped her doll over the banister. Both she and Sunny watched Mrs. Whispers fall into Nicky's arms.

As Nicky caught the doll, he said, "Now, Jason—call Sunny!" He looked up at his sister. "Stacey, help Sunny over the rail. Hurry!"

Jason was pretty sure that Stacey didn't trust what Nicky said anymore, but finally she stepped behind the retriever. Jason opened his arms. "Jump, Sunny!" he commanded in a harsh whisper. "Come on, jump!" The dog glanced from Jason to the doll in Nicky's arms, then at Stacey. Finally, she raised herself as much as possible on her hind legs, thrust her head forward, and pawed at the balcony rail.

"Now, Stacey," Nicky rasped. *"Push!"*

Stacey took a deep breath, twisted her face into a terrible scowl, and pushed at the retriever's back end until Sunny went over the edge with a yelp.

The dog hit both boys when she landed, sending them into a deep snowdrift. Sunny got up and shook herself hard, splattering snow all over Jason and Nicky. They looked at each other for a minute, then broke into a fit of muffled giggles.

While they were still climbing out of the snowdrift, Stacey pushed herself over the railing and came sliding down the post. She didn't look too happy about it, Jason thought, but at least she did it. Nicky was pretty smart, all right. He had known Stacey wouldn't stay up there alone.

"Come on," Nicky said breathlessly, hauling himself up and pounding the snow off his coat. "We have to get away from here and go help Teddy and your dad."

He grabbed his sister's hand, and the three of them slogged through the snow with Sunny to hide behind the row of bushes that ringed the cabin.

"What about Mommy?" Jason whispered as they huddled down behind the shrubs.

Nicky looked at him. "You're right." He drew in a deep breath. "We have to get Boone and Arno out of the cabin."

"But how?"

Nicky pressed his lips together, looking away into the distance. When he finally spoke, his voice was so soft Jason could scarcely hear him. "When they realize we're gone, Arno's going to send Boone outside to look for us. If we can keep Boone from going back into the cabin, Arno will get antsy and come out, too. He has your mom tied up, so he won't worry about leaving her alone for a few minutes."

He stopped, looking soberly at Jason. "We'll have to take care of Boone *and* Arno." A funny look crossed his face. "Then we'll go after Wolf."

As Jason watched Nicky, he felt his stomach quiver. Nicky was really smart, and Jason wished he could think even half that fast. But did Nicky really think he was smart enough to outsmart three grown-ups—grown-ups with *guns?*

"All of them?" Jason asked apprehensively. "How?"

"One at a time." Nicky looked pretty sure of himself, and Jason tried not to be afraid. "We can do it. Boone won't be any problem. Arno—" He shrugged. "I'll just have to think of something when the time comes."

Jason was still worried. "Why did you bring that stuff?" He pointed to the big bandanna and the blue pillowcase Nicky had taken from the bedroom.

"You'll see," the other boy answered. "Stay down, now. We have to watch for Boone."

Crouching down out of the wind, they waited. After a minute or two, they heard a furious pounding upstairs.

"That's Boone," Nicky whispered, "trying to get back into the bedroom."

The window was still open, and they could hear Boone shouting and banging on the bedroom door. The uproar went on for another two or three minutes, then stopped.

After another minute, they heard voices coming from the great room. Angry voices. But they couldn't make out what they were saying.

Nicky motioned for the others to stay put, then crept out from the bushes and tiptoed up the steps onto the deck.

Jason held Stacey's hand as he watched Nicky press himself against the wall beside the window. When the muffled voices inside the room grew louder, Nicky sprinted across the deck and back to the bushes. "Boone's coming out! I'm going to hide beside the steps. When he gets about halfway down, I'll trip him. As soon as you see him fall, come and help me."

"But then what will we do?" Jason asked.

Nicky touched Jason's shoulder and grinned. "We'll take care of old Boone! Don't worry. Just trust me."

Jason swallowed hard and nodded. Then Nicky was gone, running back to the cabin steps. He reached under his coat as he ran, pulling out a belt. When he got to the steps, he crawled into the bushes at the side, crouching down low so he couldn't be seen.

Within seconds, the door opened, and Boone stepped out onto the deck, the snow crunching under his feet. Carrying his gun in one hand and gripping the porch railing with the other, he trudged over to the steps, then started down.

Jason held his breath as he watched Boone take one step at a time, looking back and forth around the yard as he descended. He was only two steps away from the bottom when Nicky's hand reached out and yanked his left foot out from under him.

With a startled cry, Boone went flying off the steps. His gun sailed out of his hand and landed several feet away. At the same time, Nicky jumped out of the bushes and hurled himself onto the man's back. Taking their cue, Jason and Stacey ran to help, followed by Sunny, who planted herself in front of Boone and lifted her lip in a silent snarl.

Boone was lying face down in the snow, apparently stunned. Nicky sat on his back, pulling Boone's arms behind him. "Help me tie him up! Hurry!" he whispered hoarsely.

Jason threw himself onto Boone, pressing his arms down as hard as he could. Nicky reached around and stuffed the bandanna into Boone's mouth, then pulled the pillowcase over his head.

"Stacey—hold his head down!" Nicky commanded, raising up just enough to pull out his belt.

Boone struggled, trying to get up. Stacey frowned at her brother for a second, then flung herself across the man's shoulders. She pushed down, forcing his head even deeper into the snow.

While Stacey and Jason held the mobster down, Nicky used his belt to bind Boone's hands behind his back.

"Come on, you guys—help me! We'll put him in the fruit cellar!"

Jason went around to the other side of Boone, and the two boys jerked the stunned man to his feet, pushing him across the yard toward the fruit cellar. Stacey followed, and every now and then Sunny gave a low growl from behind, as if she was warning Boone not to give them too much trouble.

The fruit cellar was pitch black and cold. They pushed Boone up against one wall, and on Nicky's instructions, Jason lifted the pillowcase up over the man's head. Nicky pulled out the bandanna and tied it into a gag before Boone could do anything except let out an angry grunt.

When Nicky seemed satisfied that Boone wasn't going anywhere, he grabbed the pillowcase and headed back outside. He held the door open for Jason and Stacey, then locked it with the wooden crossbar.

"What do we do now?" Jason whispered when they reached their hiding place in the bushes.

Nicky looked at him. "Now we take care of Arno."

EIGHTEEN

G ABE stepped down from the cab of the tow truck, waving his thanks to the driver who had given him a lift from town. The man had offered to turn off the main highway and try his luck on the narrow country road leading to the Farm. Even though the sturdy old wrecker could probably have made it through the snow-clogged lane without any difficulty, Gabe had insisted on walking the rest of the way. The man had already done enough, and besides, he needed some time alone before he faced the others with the news about Lyss.

With considerable effort he limped down the road toward the entrance gate. The road was heavily drifted, but the snow had finally stopped. The worst of the storm was probably over, although that was small comfort now.

As soon as he passed the weathered old barn and empty farmhouse that had once belonged to Yancey's Dairy, Gabe began to watch for light from the main cabin. He was almost halfway down the road before the darkened security lights reminded him of the power outage.

As he plugged along the snow-covered road, Gabe tried to think of anything other than Lyss. But even when he wasn't actively thinking about her, he was still fervently praying for her. He had prayed all the way into town, holding Lyss's blood-soaked form in the cab of the wrecker as he repeatedly thanked the Lord for the tow-truck driver.

The burly young man—"Tom"—apparently owned a small towing business consisting of only two wreckers. During storms like this, he had explained to Gabe, he and his other driver made a practice of being out and available, monitoring the emergency frequencies for news of accidents or stranded vehicles. There had been no word of Gabe and Lyss's accident, of course. He had merely come upon them by chance. "Just a lucky break," he'd said.

Gabe knew better. It hadn't been luck. If the wrecker hadn't shown up when it did, he might have had even worse news for the others waiting in the cabin.

Coolheaded and efficient, the wrecker driver had radioed for the police and an ambulance before even going to check the cab of the semi. Then, to Gabe's amazement and enormous gratitude, he had not only waited with him until the ambulance arrived, but had actually followed them to the hospital in Elkins. And there he had stayed, waiting with Gabe for word of Lys's condition.

His final act of kindness had been to drive Gabe back to the farm.

Gabe had been touched by the kindness of strangers before tonight, but never like this—and never when he had needed it more. When he had waved his thanks to the young tow truck driver, he'd felt as though he were saying good-bye to his guardin angel.

Idly, he wondered how Tom had felt, when he'd told him he was an answer to prayer.

Now, as he trudged through the snow on the way to the cabin, his mind replayed those hours at the hospital. It occurred to him that, if there had been worse times in his life than this night, he couldn't think of any.

He had spent the first hour at the hospital in a near daze, praying desperately for Lyss the entire time the doctors were checking his injuries, later pacing the deserted waiting room as Tom sat nearby, watching him. Occasionally one of them would question the admitting clerk for word on Lyss. By the time one of the emergency-room physicians—Dr. Kline—finally appeared, Gabe was almost incoherent. He was shaking so violently that the doctor made him sit down before he would even discuss Lyss's injuries.

"Mr. Denton, please—over here."

A surge of panic roared up through Gabe. "Lyss—"

"Your wife is still unconscious," Dr. Kline told him, waiting until Gabe sank down into the chair. "It's going to be another two or three hours before we have the test results back so we can give you any kind of a prognosis."

"But she's alive. . . ."

"Yes." Dr. Kline paused. "But I should tell you—"

"Can I see her? I have to see her! Please—"

"Soon," Dr. Kline said firmly. "She's being moved to intensive care right now. Someone will come and take you to her. But please understand, Mr. Denton, your wife won't know you're there. I'm afraid she's in . . . very serious condition."

Fear washed over Gabe, and he gripped the arms of the chair to steady himself. He was surprised to feel a light touch on his shoulder. "Easy, friend. God's in control now."

Gabe stared up at the young truck driver; he had almost forgotten about him. Tom smiled, and for some reason this unexpected kindness nearly undid Gabe. His eyes burned with tears, and his hands began to shake even harder.

"Mr. Denton, are you sure you're all right?" Dr. Kline asked, watching Gabe with concern. "Maybe we'd better take a closer look at *you*."

Gabe raised a hand. "No, I'm fine. I'm OK. Just . . . tell me about my wife. Please. How badly is she injured?" His eyes caught the doctor's and held his gaze. "I want the truth," he added.

The physician nodded briefly, then gave him a thorough description of Lyss's condition, explaining that she had a number of external injuries—cuts, lacerations, and abrasions—but that these were all "treatable."

The longer the doctor spoke, the worse it sounded.

"Her right arm is broken, and she has a compound fracture in her right leg, as well." Dr. Kline stopped when he saw Gabe wince. "Those will cause her some pain and discomfort," he admitted, "but, again, they're treatable." He hesitated, and an unreadable expression passed over his face.

"What else?" Gabe asked, his throat tight.

The doctor sighed. "She has some fractured ribs, and I'm afraid that's creating a more serious problem."

Gabe pulled in a deep breath, waiting.

"One lung has been punctured. We've applied drainage tubes for now. We'll watch it closely and in a few more hours do further x-rays to see if the lung is reexpanding. If it is, she won't need surgery."

"Do you think it *will* . . . reexpand?"

"It's too soon to tell. But I'm hopeful."

Gabe swallowed hard against the knot of anxiety in his throat. He could wait no longer to ask. "Her face . . ."

Dr. Kline nodded, watching him carefully. "Yes," he said quietly, his eyes gentle with understanding. "Glass from the window resulted in some facial lacerations. But we've removed all the glass, and she doesn't seem to have any nerve damage." He paused. "She will need some cosmetic surgery, but the cuts weren't as deep or as severe as we originally thought. Right now, that lung is our main concern."

Gabe looked away. Lovely Lyss . . . she had the face of a model. Perfect features, flawless bone structure, exquisite skin . . .

Oh, Lord . . . just let her live . . . please. I'll help her through all the rest. I'll love her through it, Lord. Nothing matters except her life. . . . Please, Lord, just let her live.

Again he struggled for a deep breath. "She was unconscious . . . ," he began, then lost his voice to a tremor that racked his entire body.

The doctor frowned, measuring him as if he expected him to collapse at any instant. He gave a brief nod. "Yes, and that may last awhile. She was in shock when you brought her in. Until I saw the x-rays, I thought she might have a ruptured spleen, but she doesn't. She has lost a lot of blood, however." He managed a tired smile. "We're working, Mr. Denton. We'll do our best for her, I promise you."

Gabe searched the doctor's eyes. "There's one thing I don't hear you saying."

Dr. Kline met his gaze. "You want to know if she's going to be all right."

Gabe waited, saying nothing, his pulse thundering in his ears.

The doctor hesitated. "I can't give you any guarantees. But you asked me for the truth, and I *am* trying to give you that. Your wife is in serious condition. She has sustained some life-threatening injuries, but prompt treatment can make a real difference. We're going to do everything we can to get her through this, and right now I feel that we have her fairly well stabilized. But I can't promise you anything. Not yet."

Gabe pressed a fist against his mouth. He squeezed his eyes shut for a moment, then opened them, ignoring the tears that threatened to spill over. "Thank you . . . for leveling with me."

He pulled in a long ragged breath, then abruptly asked, "The driver of the truck that hit us—how is he?"

The doctor's face brightened a little. "He's going to be just fine. He has a concussion and a broken collar bone, but he's doing nicely."

Gabe nodded. "That's good," he said softly. "Lyss will be glad for that. It wasn't his fault, you know. The road . . ." His words fell away.

No, it wasn't the truck driver's fault. The blame . . . all of it . . . belonged to someone else. Teddy Giordano, that low-life little hood who had sucked all of them into this nightmare—the blame was his.

A blast of white-hot rage roared up in him, a rage accompanied by a raw, unmitigated wave of hatred. He shook his head, as if to shake off the fury that threatened to send him over the edge. "Please," he said, his voice thick, "may I see her now?"

They allowed him only a few brief minutes with Lyss before insisting that he leave, but Gabe knew he would carry the memory with him for the rest of his life. Nothing could have prepared him for the sight of her, lying there as still as death, tubes running everywhere. Casts and splints and bandages . . . so many bandages, especially on her face.

He couldn't see much of her face—only her closed eyes and a bit of pale skin around her chin—and for just an instant he felt a shameful pang of relief. He *had* seen her face, in the headlights of the tow truck. And he would see it again and again, he thought, for years to come. His mind had photographed it in one stark, agonizing second, and the image was now an indelible part of his memory. He would never forget the wave of abject terror that had seized him until something deep inside his soul had cried out the reminder that the face still belonged to Lyss—his wife, his lovely, beloved Lyss. . . .

Now, as he crossed the yard and headed toward the cabin, Gabe shivered, not so much from the cold as from the impact of all that had happened during this long night. Suddenly he felt exhausted, physically and emotionally depleted. But the night wasn't over. A heavy weight of dread settled over his heart as he considered that, thanks to Teddy Giordano and his cronies, it might *never* be over.

NINETEEN

AT the steps to the deck, Gabe took a deep breath and waited for the throbbing in his head to subside. Something above him, something . . . out of place . . . caught his attention. His eyes scanned the front of the cabin, the deck, the windows, then the second floor—

"Uncle Gabe!"

He heard the loud whisper at the same time his eye caught the open window upstairs. He whirled around to find Jason tugging urgently at his coat, then turned again to note the curtain billowing in and out of the upstairs window.

Jason grabbed his hand, and Gabe realized now that the boy seemed to be terrified.

"Uncle Gabe! You've got to help!"

"Jason? What are you doing out here?"

Jason began tugging violently on Gabe's hand. He seemed close to tears.

Quickly, Gabe enfolded the small hand between both of his and squatted down to put himself at Jason's level. "What's wrong, cub? What is it?"

"The men! The bad men are here!"

Gabe saw the boy's trembling, saw the glint of fear in his eyes, and felt himself turn cold.

"The bad men?"

Jason nodded fiercely. He launched into an explanation, but his whispered words ran together in a white heat of desperation.

Gabe's head began to spin. Then Nicky appeared out of the bushes with his little sister in tow. Without a word, the boy drew Gabe back to their hiding place.

Nicky, too, was breathless and excited but, thankfully, more coherent than Jason. With his words shooting out like bullets, he told Gabe their astonishing story, beginning with the arrival of the three men and ending with their capture and detention of Boone.

"You put him *where?*" Gabe gasped with amazement as the recital ended.

"In the fruit cellar," Nicky replied matter-of-factly. "Then we came back here to hide until we could figure out how to get rid of Arno."

"Arno?"

"The man inside with Mrs. Kaine," Nicky reminded him.

Gabe's mind reeled. Still dazed and disoriented from his own earlier ordeal, he found it nearly impossible to take in the boy's incredible tale.

He rubbed a hand over his eyes. "So you told this . . . Boone . . . that *you* hid the notebook. This is the notebook Teddy's supposed to deliver to the federal marshal?"

"Yes, sir. My papa's notebook."

"Well . . . *did* you? Hide the notebook?" For some reason, Gabe found the boy's apparent calm infuriating.

Nicky met his gaze for an instant, then turned to Jason. "Jason, Sunny's prancing. Maybe you and Stacey had better take her over there beside the tree."

Sure enough, the retriever was circling Jason restlessly, pawing at the snow-covered ground.

"You have to go, Sunny?" Jason queried, as if he expected the dog to answer him.

The retriever stopped and gave a soft whimper, waiting. Quickly, Jason caught Stacey by the hand, and the two of them led Sunny off to the side of the cabin.

As soon as they were out of earshot, Nicky turned back to Gabe. "The notebook is inside Stacey's doll—Mrs. Whispers."

Dumbfounded, Gabe could do nothing but stare at the boy. *"You put the notebook in your sister's doll?"* he finally managed to say.

"I didn't," Nicky said evenly. "Papa did. Before . . . they killed him."

In spite of the cold, Gabe felt a wide band of perspiration break out on his forehead. "Stacey doesn't know?"

Nicky looked at him with mild disdain. "Of course not. She doesn't *need* to know. She's as careful with that doll as if it were a real baby. Papa knew where the notebook would be safest."

Gabe shook his head, trying to clear his mind, trying to get a grip on himself. *These people weren't real. . . . Real people didn't live this way. . . .*

His gaze went to the cabin. A figure moved, silhouetted against the window from the glow of an oil lamp, then disappeared from view.

Before Gabe could muster a rational thought, much less a reply to Nicky's remark, Jason and Stacey returned, along with Sunny.

"Mr. Denton?"

Gabe looked at Nicky.

"I think we'd better see about Arno first. Wolf told him if he wasn't back in an hour, Arno was to—" He faltered, looking at Jason. "He was to shoot Mrs. Kaine."

Gabe's throat closed. "Jennifer?" he mouthed softly. "Would he—would he do that?"

The boy nodded solemnly, looking at Gabe as if he were surprised he'd even ask. "Yes, sir. He would. And once Wolf realizes that Teddy lied to him—" He stopped, but his gaze never wavered. "Wolf is crazy. He'll kill anyone who crosses him," he added softly.

"Uncle Gabe?"

Gabe turned to look at Jason.

"Where's Aunt Lyss?"

"She's . . . in the hospital, Jason. There was an accident."

The boy's eyes widened. "Aunt Lyss got hurt?"

Gabe moistened his lips, cracked almost painfully from the cold and the dryness of his fear. "Yes. A truck hit the Cherokee not long after we left. Your Aunt Lyss . . . was badly injured."

Jason's lower lip trembled. "But she'll get better?"

"Yes, of course she will." Gabe couldn't take much more. He felt as if he had been hurled full-force into the middle of a nightmare.

He suddenly became aware of a gentle but persistent tug on his coat sleeve, then on his hand. Glancing down, he met the dark-eyed gaze of a sober-faced Stacey. "Nora says Jesus helps people. I'll ask Jesus to make Jason's Aunt Lyss all well again."

Unable to answer her, Gabe squeezed her hand before he looked away, struggling to gain control of his emotions.

"What are we going to do, Uncle Gabe?" Jason's whisper was choked. "How can we get Daddy and Mommy—and Teddy—away from the bad men?"

Gabe lifted an unsteady hand and glanced around wildly. What should he do? Storm the cabin with three kids and a guide dog? For a moment, he had an almost hysterical urge to laugh. What *should* he do? That was rich. What *could* he do?

"Mr. Denton?"

Nicky's voice was soft, little more than a guarded whisper.

Gabe shot him an impatient glance. The kid had grated on him from the beginning, at first because of what Lyss had called his *precociousness.* Now, however, Gabe looked at Nicky and saw a reflection of Teddy Giordano.

It was unfair. It was immature. It was probably even unchristian. But at this moment, he could barely stand the sight of Nicky Angelini.

His response was curt, even gruff, but the boy simply looked at him with that steady, older-than-time wisdom. His dark, unreadable gaze appeared to register Gabe's anger, even understand it.

"Sir? I think I may have an idea," he said quietly.

TWENTY

W HEN Chuck Arno first heard the moaning, he thought it was the wind. Even when it grew louder and more insistent, he merely thought the storm had picked up again.

It was the dog's barking that made him go to the window and look out. Dogs made him nervous, even more nervous when they barked. He glanced back at the woman. "Is that the guide dog?"

She hesitated, then nodded. "It sounds like Sunny, yes."

"Then Boone must've found the kids." Seeing nothing, he turned, left the window, and returned to stand in front of the woman.

"Oughta teach those kids a lesson, pulling a stunt like that," he growled, watching her.

He didn't like the way she stared back at him. Who did she think she was, anyway? *She* was the one mixed up with a bunch of defects, not him. She needed to be taken down a notch or two, like most women. Once Boone got the kids back inside, he'd settle her dust—teach her how to show a little respect around a real man.

When the dog began to bark even more savagely, he jumped and whipped around. The low moaning sounded closer now, louder.

Arno muttered a curse under his breath as he went to the door that opened onto the deck. The top half of the door was glass, but the louvered shutters were closed. Cautiously, Arno peered through the slats into the black night. The window was fogged, but even when he cleared it, he still couldn't see anything.

The eerie keening started again, louder than before. The dog went on barking.

Arno swallowed hard, glancing back at the woman. She was staring at him with a hollow-eyed, contemptuous look—an expression that made his blood boil.

He opened the opposite shutter, but he still could see nothing except the thick, snow-veiled darkness, a darkness that could hide anything.

It was the sound of his own name drifting in off the wind that finally snapped his control.

"Chuuckk . . ."

He froze. It had to be Boone! He must be hurt.

Suddenly, the barking stopped. There was nothing but snow-filled silence.

Arno released his breath, at the same time tightening his grip on the gun.

Then it came again. *"Chuuckk . . . help meee. . . ."*

Arno jerked violently, his heart lurching to a stop against his rib cage. He reached for the doorknob, turned it a little, then more. When the lock released, he cracked the door, opening it an inch at a time.

He stood in the doorway, looking and listening. There was nothing. Nothing but darkness and that mind-chilling moaning.

He stepped out, easing over the threshold and onto the deck, the gun extended as he went. He waited, took another step, then stopped.

"Help meee. . . ."

Arno's head whipped to the right, and he choked out a cry of panic as the huge dog came roaring around the side of the cabin

154

at full speed. Its head was low, its mouth open in a furious, snarling rage as it raced toward him. The ground seemed to tilt under him, and Arno felt his bones turn to butter.

The gun in his hand began to shake violently.

Terrified, he screamed as the vicious-looking dog reached the bottom of the steps—and stopped. Stopped on command.

Before Arno could even catch a breath, a heavy, boot-clad foot came swinging up from somewhere beside him. It cracked his wrist in a painful blow and sent the gun flying across the steps and into the snow-laden bushes.

Arno whirled, raising his arm to strike out. But he was too late. A blond-haired man in a blue ski jacket whacked him with a high kick and a straight-line punch, knocking the wind from him.

He reeled and fell backward, slamming against the wall of the cabin. Again Arno struck out, blindly this time, twisting, kicking, clawing in panic as he wheezed for air.

The man came at him again, and Arno felt his blood turn to ice when he glimpsed the expression of raw fury on the guy's face. He saw the punch coming and scrambled to duck it, but suddenly lights went off in his head, and the night erupted in a blinding white flash.

Two fleeting thoughts knifed through the pain as Arno went down. Out of the corner of his eye, he saw the dog turn and go bolting like a crazy thing, away from the cabin and out into the field, and he felt a stroke of insane relief at its leaving.

Then, seeing the rage on the face of the man who had attacked him, he wondered if he might not have been safer with the dog.

Jennifer saw most of the scene between Gabe and the thickset mobster through the open door. She watched with dazed astonishment as her brother-in-law efficiently knocked Arno unconscious, then bound his hands with a length of clothesline from the storage pantry.

By the time Gabe, Jason, and the Angelini children came to untie her, she was on the verge of screaming with relief. Instead, she began to sob, losing the last thin shred of her self-control.

She made two or three attempts to pull herself together while Gabe worked on the rope, but once he had freed her hands and feet, she could no longer restrain the effects of the night's terror. Jason threw his arms around her, and the little girl, Stacey, shyly touched her face. Jennifer only cried harder. After a moment, Nicky walked away, going to the other side of the room to stand quietly and watch Jennifer and his sister.

Still on his knees beside her, Gabe tossed the rope aside and clasped her shoulders. "Jenn—are you all right?"

She nodded weakly, wiping her tear-stained face with the back of one hand. "Yes . . . I'm . . ." She tried to tell him about Daniel, but her lips were trembling so fiercely she couldn't make him understand.

"Jennifer . . . take it easy," he soothed her, still gripping her shoulders firmly. "It's OK now. You're all right."

She shook her head violently and finally forced out the words. *"Daniel!* He's out there with that awful man! Wolf—he took Daniel and Teddy . . . and he has a gun. . . ." Her entire body began to shake as she was once more overcome by the horror of the past few hours.

Jason backed off a little, glancing at his uncle with frightened eyes. Gabe quickly reassured him with a nod, then grasped Jennifer's shoulders even more tightly. "Jenn, I need to go after Dan. You've got to pull yourself together so I can leave the kids with you." He watched her. "Jennifer?"

She nodded, struggling for control. She pulled in deep breaths, hugging her arms tightly to her body. Finally, Gabe dropped his hands away from her shoulders. She squeezed her eyes shut once, hard, then opened them.

Gabe helped her to her feet. "I'm . . . I'm all right," Jennifer assured him, rubbing her wrists where the rope had burned her skin.

Gabe watched her, his expression skeptical. "Sure?"

Again Jennifer nodded. Then, turning to Jason, she exclaimed, "Where *were* you? They said you went out the bedroom window. I was *terrified!*"

"Jennifer." Gabe's voice broke off her questioning, and for the first time Jennifer saw how awful he looked. His face was scratched—or was it cut? There was a small bandage below his ear. His eyes were deeply shadowed and bloodshot. He looked positively stricken.

Suddenly a thought hit her. "Where's Lyss?"

When he didn't answer, Jennifer looked at him more closely. "Gabe? Where's Lyss?"

She caught her breath at the anguish in his eyes. "Lyss is in the hospital. There was an accident . . . not long after we left here."

Too stunned to reply, Jennifer could only stare at him, listening with growing horror as he began to explain.

Would this nightmare never end? The children held hostage . . . Lyss injured . . . Daniel . . .

Daniel!

She turned back to Gabe, but he was already starting toward the door. "Bolt the door behind me," he told her, his voice now steadier, even firm. He actually managed a weak smile. "I'll let the kids fill you in on what *they've* been up to."

"Gabe, be careful. . . ."

"Count on it. You just stay put. Listen, Jenn, I called Giordano's contact people from the hospital. They're snowed in, too, so they couldn't promise me anything. But at least they know where we are, and they'll come when they can." When Jennifer started to question him further, Gabe cut her off. "I also told the hospital to call the police, to send them out here. They'll probably show up anytime now. We're going to be OK."

Jennifer studied him. "Gabe, you know as well as I do that with this storm, there's no telling how long it might be before anyone gets through to us."

"The police will get through," he insisted, not quite meeting her gaze as he again made for the door.

"Mr. Denton?" Nicky Angelini's voice stopped Gabe. He turned, frowning.

"Arno's gun," the boy reminded him. "Shouldn't you take it with you?"

As Jennifer watched, a muscle in Gabe's jaw tightened, and his mouth went hard. "Not everyone settles their problems with a gun," he bit out.

"Gabe, maybe you should take it, just—" Jennifer swallowed her warning at the dark scowl that came over his features.

"I've never had a gun in my hand, and I don't intend to start now. I can take care of that greasy little punk without a gun."

"Would you let me go with you, Mr. Denton?" Nicky pressed. "I know Wolf, how his mind works. . . ."

"Oh, I'll just bet you do, kid," Gabe snapped, his expression ugly. "But I'll take my chances alone, all the same."

The boy looked as if he'd been struck as Gabe whirled around and went out the door, slamming it shut behind him.

After a moment, Jennifer turned to Jason. "Where's Sunny? Is she still outside?"

The boy hesitated. "Sunny went to Daddy," he replied quietly, his face solemn. "I told her to go help Daddy."

Jennifer looked at him, then moved to slide the bolt on the door with a trembling hand, praying with all her heart that Sunny and Gabe wouldn't be too late.

TWENTY-ONE

F ROM his position near the wall of the barn, Daniel heard Wolf's voice thicken with menace.

"You lied to me, didn't you, Teddy?" His tone was soft, but every word was oiled with warning.

Teddy's reply bounded down from overhead. "Hey, man, I was nervous! And it was dark. But I hid it in this hayloft, so it's got to be here."

Listening intently, Daniel could almost feel the electric tension between the two men.

"Oh, you were nervous, were you?" Wolf sneered. "Teddy-boy, I'm disappointed in you. It's not like you don't know better. You worked for Nick long enough to learn *some* smarts, didn't you?"

When Teddy didn't answer, Wolf went on, his words falling quietly off his tongue with a sinister smoothness. "Surely you learned, Teddy. You can't play games with us. Not with the Family. "

"I'm not playing games! This *is* where I hid the notebook. It was dark, and I was in a hurry. You're just going to have to give me a little time, that's all." There was an edge of desperation in Teddy's voice, his words shooting out fast and sharp, like jagged pieces of glass.

"Get down here, punk!"

Daniel stiffened at the change in Wolf's tone. The snide, almost playful note of banter was gone, exchanged for a malevolent hiss of anger, an anger that sounded potentially explosive.

"Hey, Wolf, give me a second, will you?" Uneasily, Daniel heard the change in Teddy's voice, too. The brash assurance seemed to have fled, replaced by a distinct note of fear. "Listen, if you'd just take that gun off me, it would help. You're making me so nervous I can't even think. Give me a break."

"Shut up, punk! Just—*shut up!*" The mobster's voice turned shrill. "I'm not wasting any more time with you! We'll let those smart-mouthed Angelini brats dig up the notebook!"

Daniel flinched when he heard a sudden movement from the hayloft. If Teddy panicked and tried to jump this maniac, he wouldn't have a chance.

"Wolf, I told you, the kids don't know where it is! They don't know anything about it. Leave them alone!"

"We'll see, punk. We'll see."

"Wolf, will you be reasonable—"

Daniel heard the click of the gun. He took a cautious step toward Wolf, judging his distance from the mobster to be only a few inches, no more than a yard. "Give him a chance," he said quietly. "You haven't even given him time to look."

"Dan, don't!" Teddy warned.

Ignoring him, Daniel took another step. "Put the gun on me," he said evenly. "Let him look, however long it takes. No man can think with a gun pointed at him."

The only sound in the barn was the rasp of agitated breathing—his own, as well as that of the other two men.

Suddenly Wolf laughed. The brittle, humorless cackle made Daniel feel as if an icy blast of wind had howled through the building.

"What's this?" Wolf jeered, abruptly sobering. "You looking to be a hero, blind man? Huh? You want to play games, too, is that it?"

Suddenly Wolf's arm slammed hard around Daniel's throat in a vicious grip. At the same time, he prodded the gun roughly into his back.

Daniel choked and stumbled, fighting for breath. He sucked in air to ease the pressure on his windpipe.

"Sure, blind man! Have it your way!" Again Wolf laughed. "Hey, punk—your buddy here wants to die in your place! Which one of you wants to go first, huh? You or your pal?"

Daniel tried to think. He had already judged the mobster to be at least a head shorter than him. Even with Wolf's arm around his throat and a gun in his back, if he were quick enough, he thought he could swing forward, roll Wolf over his back, shake the gun free. . . .

Then he heard Teddy shout, heard him move, and suddenly he knew there was no time. Teddy was going to jump.

Daniel twisted, trying to break free of the headlock.

He heard Teddy cry, *"Nooo!"* as he hurled himself from the loft. With one furious surge of strength, Daniel wrenched himself free of Wolf's arm, turned, and threw himself at the mobster. The gun went off, and he heard Teddy utter a small, odd sound of surprise as he hit the ground. At the same instant, the grayness Daniel lived with every day of his life suddenly exploded into a brilliant blaze of flashing colors. He went down, and the light show fizzled and faded to black.

TWENTY-TWO

T HROUGH a gray haze of pain, Teddy's eyes began to focus. He saw the golden retriever nuzzle Daniel's shoulder, then begin to lick his face. She whimpered softly a couple of times. Once she looked up, toward the far end of the barn.

When the dog saw that Teddy's eyes were open, she transferred her attention to him, padding over to his side and pulling gently at his coat with her teeth. Teddy lifted a weak hand to the retriever, then, remembering, anxiously scanned their surroundings. There was no sign of Wolf.

He raised himself up from the ground, moaning with the effort. He ran a hand over his arm, then his head and neck, surprised when he found no blood. He hadn't been shot, after all.

He turned to Daniel, pushing himself up to his knees, catching his breath with the effort. His upper left arm was on fire, and something pulled in his back when he moved. But he forced himself to crawl to Daniel. Sunny was beside her master. Gently, she touched her nose to the side of Daniel's face, but he lay silent and unmoving.

"Dan?"

Quickly, Teddy examined the big man, his gaze locking on the blood seeping from his upper arm. Daniel stirred then, groaning as he opened his eyes. He turned his head slightly, lifting a hand to his throat, then to his shoulder, yanking it away when he touched the wetness on his sleeve.

"Dan . . . just lie still. You took a hit in your arm."

Daniel scowled and uttered another groan of pain. "My shoulder?"

"Yeah. I need to find something to tie it off until we can get you out of here."

"Wolf . . ."

"He's gone."

Sunny began to whimper and lick Daniel's face. He lifted a hand to stroke her ears, then frowned. "Sunny? Where'd you come from, girl?"

The retriever burrowed her nose into the side of his neck for a moment, then sat down beside him, giving Teddy an expectant look.

"Are you all right?" Daniel asked Teddy dully.

"Fine," Teddy replied, studying Daniel. "Thanks to you. I think I may have a dislocated shoulder and a sprained back, but no bullet holes."

Daniel gave a nod. "I should have a clean handkerchief in my pocket," he mumbled thickly. He pushed himself up enough to get to the pocket of his jeans. "Help me wrap this around my arm, will you?"

Carefully, Teddy helped him free his arm from the sleeve of his jacket, then tied the handkerchief firmly around the wound.

"All right?" he asked, watching Daniel with concern as he helped him back into his coat.

Daniel nodded, propping himself against the wall of the barn.

Teddy searched the other man's face for a long moment. "Why'd you do a crazy thing like that, anyway?" he asked abruptly. "Wolf might have killed you!"

"Instinct," Daniel muttered.

"I don't think so," Teddy said quietly, still watching him. "You meant to save my life."

Daniel tried to smile, but it was more of a grimace. "Had to buy you some time," he said cryptically.

Teddy frowned. "What are you talking about?"

"You don't want to die yet, Teddy," Daniel said. "Not until you're ready for heaven." He broke into a spasm of coughing.

Teddy thought the man might be delirious, but a careful look at the expression on Daniel's face indicated otherwise. He swallowed hard but said nothing.

Daniel let his head loll back weakly against the wall, stroking Sunny's ears with his good hand. "We can talk about that later. Right now, we've got to get out of here, get back to the cabin." Suddenly more alert, he leaned forward. "Wolf—that's where he'll go, isn't it? To the cabin?"

"Probably. He thinks the kids have the notebook—or at least know where it is. He'll stop at nothing to get it."

"We have to stop *him*." Daniel started to drag himself to his feet.

"He's still got the gun, Dan." Teddy moved to help him, slumping under the other's weight as Daniel leaned against him.

"But he's coming unglued," Daniel pointed out. "I think the two of us can take him. It will have to be before he gets back to the cabin, though. We might handle one at a time but not all three of them together."

Again Teddy surveyed their surroundings, his gaze stopping on the big red Massey-Ferguson tractor parked in the middle of the barn. He studied it a moment, then turned back to Daniel. "That tractor—does it drive pretty much like a car?"

Daniel considered the question, then nodded. "They're not hard to drive. Not if it's the MF. Gabe said Mac had left it in the barn."

"You think I could drive it?"

"I used to drive one every summer when I worked up here for my uncle. If I could drive it, I'm sure you can. Why?"

"I don't suppose the keys would be in it?"

"The keys?" Daniel shrugged. "Probably are. I doubt if Mac ever worries much about anyone stealing anything out here."

"Even if there are no keys, I can probably hot-wire it," Teddy said, mostly to himself. "Let's go for a ride, Dan."

"Are you sure you're able?"

Not answering, Teddy braced himself to support Daniel's weight, and the two of them moved slowly toward the tractor. Sunny guided Dan on the opposite side. Even without her harness, the retriever herded her master expertly, blocking him from stumbling over a milk can.

"I don't know how far I'd get on foot," Teddy said, thinking out loud. "My back feels like someone's been jumping rope on my spinal cord. But I can still drive. Maybe we can chase Wolf down before he gets to the cabin."

Daniel staggered, then steadied himself against Teddy.

"You all right?" Teddy darted a worried look at him.

Daniel rubbed his throat and nodded, but Teddy didn't like the way he looked. He was pale as a ghost and drenched with perspiration.

They found the keys in the tractor's ignition. "All right!" said Teddy. "Let's go get him." He hoisted himself up to the tractor seat, then gave Dan a hand up.

Daniel settled himself and gave a brief nod to Sunny, who backed off a little, then came at a run, jumping up onto the tractor and squirming into the tight space beside Teddy's foot.

Teddy watched the dog, then turned his attention to the instrument panel. "OK. What do I do first?"

Daniel thought a minute. "Push in your clutch. There should be a switch around the middle of the panel, maybe a little to the left. That's your fuel shutoff switch. Push it in. Then put it in neutral and turn the key."

"That simple, huh?"

"Let's hope."

Teddy rolled his tongue inside his cheek, took a deep breath, and followed Daniel's directions. When he turned the key, he was afraid the engine wasn't going to catch, but after a couple of seconds, the tractor roared to life.

"Whoa," he said with a soft whistle. "How many horses are in this baby?"

"A bunch," Daniel said. "You ready?"

"What now?"

"Put it in gear and give it some fuel. There's a throttle on the floor. Then let your clutch out and go."

"Right," Teddy said under his breath. Finally the tractor lurched, chugged, and moved forward. "Here goes! Has this thing got any lights on it?"

"Below the steering wheel. A little to the right. You've got work lights and flashers. You can run them separately or together."

"I want it all."

"Then turn the switch to the right as far as it will go."

Teddy turned the switch. "All *right!* We've got *lights!* Hey, this is one tough machine. What's that attachment on the back? Looks like some kind of a motor with a metal pipe."

"Must be the PTO—the power takeoff. That's your power machine to drive other equipment," Daniel explained, shifting a little to steady himself. "Mac was probably using it for the grinder-mixer, to grind feed for the cows. You want to stay well away from one of those if it's running," he cautioned. "It'll eat a man alive within seconds."

They left the barn, lights flashing. Teddy was impressed. Then another thought struck him. "Is the snow going to be a problem for us?"

Daniel shook his head. "City boys," he said with a grin. "No, the snow won't be a problem. This is a four-wheel drive. It'll go through just about anything."

"Good thing. We've got some pretty impressive drifts out here."

Even without a moon or stars, there was plenty of light. The snow-covered field caught the glare of the tractor's headlights, illuminating the night around them.

"See anything?" Daniel asked.

Teddy shook his head, then caught himself. "Nothing yet. Hang on, I'm going to turn and head toward the cabin." He was surprised at how easy it was to turn the big machine around and start it in the other direction. They moved slowly around the side of the barn toward the field that led to the main cabin.

Under other circumstances, Teddy thought, he probably would have enjoyed this. He liked to drive—*loved* to drive, in fact—and he had driven just about every kind of machine on wheels. He had even tried a semi a couple of times, but gave it up when he realized he would need a lot more training in order to get the hang of it. He liked the feel of the big Massey-Ferguson under him, its solid strength, the sound of its power. He even got a childish kick out of the flashing lights. *Yeah,* he decided, *this could be kind of fun if it weren't for . . .*

Wolf! The lights caught him a hundred, maybe a hundred and fifty yards ahead, off to the right. Teddy saw the man in the field turn, stopping to stare at the tractor.

"There he is," he said softly to Daniel. "And you were right. He's headed toward the main cabin."

"Does he see us?"

"Oh, yeah," Teddy murmured as he continued to eye the mobster. "But I don't think he was *expecting* us."

Sunny sat up and began to bark.

To Teddy's surprise, Wolf didn't run. He stood like a statue in the snow, watching their approach as if he were too stunned to move.

They closed the distance by several more yards, the tractor roaring like an angry lion over the retriever's frenzied barking.

Then Teddy saw Wolf raise the gun. "Get down, Dan! He's going to shoot!"

Daniel ducked down as best he could, his hand snaking out to hold Sunny. "Watch yourself!" he yelled at Teddy.

Not answering, Teddy continued to grip the wheel, arrowing in on Wolf with fierce determination.

The mobster fired the gun once, then began to run, awkwardly tripping in the deep snow. Teddy gave a grim little smile of satisfaction. It was impossible for the man to make any real headway. The field was layered with one enormous drift after another, and Wolf obviously wasn't wearing boots. Twice he stumbled and went down.

The tractor was closing the distance fast, and Wolf stopped running, again taking time to aim and fire.

"Stay down, Dan!" Teddy shouted without turning to look. "He's close enough to hit us now."

Wolf fired once, missed, and fired again, more wildly than the first time. He shouted something at Teddy, then turned and ran.

Out of the corner of his eye, Teddy saw that Daniel was having a hard time crouching down, and even more difficulty restraining the retriever. Apparently, the combination of the tractor noise and gunshots had agitated the dog. She twisted under Daniel's hand, barking and snarling angrily.

"Sunny, *no!*" Daniel ordered sharply. The dog quieted her barking but continued to pitch feverishly back and forth.

They were closing in on the running man. Teddy could see him clearly now. Without stopping, Wolf pivoted and fired. Seeing that he had missed again, he fired once more, this time stopping for a better aim.

The bullet sailed past Teddy's head, close enough that he could hear it whistle as it went by. But it missed, and he did a mental check on Wolf's ammunition.

Counting the shot that had wounded Daniel, Wolf's gun should be empty. Teddy decided to make sure.

He stood up from the tractor seat and yelled, "Hey, Wolf—want a ride?"

He was close enough to see the mobster's furious expression as he turned and raised the gun. Teddy ducked when the man aimed and fired, but nothing happened. The gun was empty.

With a sharp breath of relief, Teddy lowered himself to the seat. He gripped the wheel, heading straight for the man in the snow.

Wolf threw his useless gun away and began to hurtle as best he could through the snow, looking wildly over his shoulder every few seconds.

"You can get up now, Dan. He's running on empty," Teddy said tersely, his hands glued to the wheel.

Daniel hauled himself up, removing his hand from Sunny's back as he did. Apparently, that was the chance the retriever had been waiting for. She squirmed out of the cramped area, lunged from the tractor, and pounded across the remaining few feet of snow between her and Wolf, barking fiercely as she ran.

"*Sunny!*" Daniel looked as if he was about to jump after her, and Teddy reached to hold him back, still keeping his eyes on Wolf. "She's all right! Stay put until I stop this thing!" He looked at the panel. "How *do* I stop it, anyway?"

At last Teddy found the brake pedal and brought the tractor to a gradual halt. He took it out of gear but let the motor idle. "Stay here, Dan. I'm going after Wolf!"

Without hesitating, he jumped to the snow-covered ground, ignoring the sudden roar that surged to life behind him. He bolted for Wolf, who was still running as hard as he could.

Sunny beat him there. She charged the mobster, leaped into the air, and hit Wolf's back, a golden fireball of fierce, high-powered fury.

"Way to go, *Sunny!*" Teddy yelled, adding his own weight to the retriever's as he, too, tackled Wolf. The mobster flailed his arms, groping, lashing out at nothing. Then he screamed and went down hard.

TWENTY-THREE

G ABE saw the trio from across the field. Running as fast as he could in his heavy hiking boots, he jumped over a snow-covered tree stump and went on, watching with amazement as Sunny took the mobster down.

He cried out a shout of encouragement to the dog and felt a thrill of grudging relief when he saw Teddy Giordano leap off the tractor to help. He watched Wolf go down, admitting to himself that Teddy was surprisingly good with his punches. One efficient chop, and the mobster's hands stopped grabbing air and fell limply to his sides.

Gabe was only yards away from the scene when he became aware of another noise, a noise that made his stomach constrict with horror—the loud burst of power roaring from the PTO. Someone must have hit the lever.

He stopped dead for an instant, his eyes going to Dan. Somewhere deep inside him a blast of fear exploded. He saw Dan jump from the tractor, then weave unsteadily as his feet hit the ground.

Gabe took off, pushing himself so hard that he was almost flying across the field. The cold stung his face and burned his eyes as he ran. He kept his panic-stricken eyes fixed on Dan, who at first stood unmoving, as if to get his bearings. Suddenly he stepped backward, the movement taking him an inch too close to the rapidly turning, grinding PTO shaft.

Gabe tried to scream, but nothing came out. His chest burned, and his heart banged painfully against his rib cage as he stretched his legs and continued to fly.

Finally he got it out. *"Dan! Don't move! Dan . . . the PTO!"*

Dan froze, but it was too late. Gabe saw the bottom of his jacket touch the uncovered shaft. Over 500 rpms of power grabbed the material and started to wrap the coat.

Gabe's last warning was one long, unbroken scream of sheer terror as he watched Dan throw up a hand to grab something—anything. The movement only made him stumble closer to the PTO. The grinding machine was pulling him into certain death with furious, relentless speed.

With dreadful clarity, Gabe saw that he would never reach his friend in time. Dan cried out, a terrible sound of helplessness.

Gabe pushed himself to the absolute limit. His chest was about to explode, but he was close now, close enough to reach out with both hands to Dan. Then suddenly Teddy Giordano hurled himself at the trapped blind man. The force of his weight ripped Dan free of the PTO with sudden fierceness as Teddy offered himself up to the machine like some kind of pagan sacrifice.

Gabe moved to grab Teddy, but the sleeve of his jacket was too far into the machine to get him free. Throwing himself against the side of the tractor, Gabe hit the lever beside the seat and pushed it back—

It stopped. Stopped just before it would have ground Teddy's arm to the bone.

Even though the tractor was still running, the sudden drop in noise was almost startling as the PTO came to a halt. Sunny, who had deserted the unconscious Wolf to go to Dan, stopped barking.

Gabe killed the motor of the tractor, then ran and dropped down in the snow next to Teddy Giordano, who lay unconscious and bleeding but alive. Gabe pulled off his ski jacket and draped it over Teddy, then started toward Dan.

Shaking, but otherwise all right, Dan had already hauled himself up from where he had fallen after being knocked free of the PTO. He stood, not moving for a moment as he listened. "Gabe?"

Gabe reached for him, grasping his forearm. "Are you all right?" he choked out, his voice roughened by the fear still lodged in his throat. "You're bleeding."

Dan waved off his concern. "It's nothing." After only an instant's hesitation, the two men embraced each other fiercely.

Dan stepped back, but Gabe still held him at arm's length.

"Teddy?" Dan questioned. "Is he—"

"Unconscious. The shaft caught his arm," Gabe explained. "He's losing a lot of blood." He guided Dan over to Teddy. "We need to get him to a hospital fast, but—"

"*Jennifer!*" Dan suddenly grabbed Gabe's arm, a look of dread settling over his features. "Where is she? Is she all right?"

"Jennifer's fine, buddy," Gabe reassured him. "Everything's under control—" He stopped suddenly. He had to tell Dan about Lyss, but now wasn't the time.

"Thank you, Lord," Dan murmured shakily, raking a hand down his face. "We've got to get an ambulance out here for Teddy," he said urgently. "But how—"

He stopped. Both men stiffened as they heard a whirring noise.

For a moment neither spoke as the thrumming sound of an engine grew gradually louder.

Gabe looked up. "It's a chopper!" He watched the approaching lights in the night sky above them with excitement. "It must be Teddy's people from Virginia!"

In his relief, he grabbed Dan's injured shoulder, realizing what he had done when Dan grimaced with pain. "Ah, Dan, I'm sorry."

Dan made a weak dismissing motion with his hand. "I'm OK. Do they see us?"

"I can't tell yet."

"Do you think they can land in this much snow?"

"It's heavy enough to be packed pretty solid. The best place would be down by the gate, where I plowed earlier. Stay here," he said. "I'm going to turn on the tractor lights so they can't miss us!"

Teddy's hoarse whisper stopped him. "Gabe?"

Startled, Gabe froze, staring down at him.

Teddy's face was pale and pinched, his eyes barely open. "Thanks, man."

Gabe looked at him, saying nothing. He wasn't angry anymore. He was simply exhausted. Exhausted and sick at heart. He felt nothing for Teddy Giordano. He hadn't the strength to feel anything.

He tore his eyes away from the man on the blood-soaked snow and ran for the tractor. He climbed up, switched on the headlights and flashers, then began to jump up and down, waving his arms and yelling. "Down here! *Hey! Here!* Here we are!"

The helicopter dropped low, hovering long enough for Gabe to see the pilot wave one hand in acknowledgment.

"They see us, Dan!" he shouted. He made a pointing motion with one hand in the direction of the plowed lane leading to the gate.

The chopper came a little lower, circled, and headed in the direction Gabe had indicated.

Putting the MF into gear, Gabe started forward. "I'll be back!" he yelled to Dan. "I'm going down to the gate with the tractor. The lights will help guide them in!"

He bumped across the snow in the tractor, mumbling a hurried prayer of thanks as he went. When he reached the gate, he jumped from the tractor, leaving the lights on full and the engine idling.

The helicopter hovered, veered a little to the right, then began to descend. Gabe continued to pray. He didn't know how much traction one of those things had on snow or ice.

The chopper was down. It landed rough and hard, but safely. Gabe could have wept with relief.

Both the pilot and his passenger jumped from the cockpit and ran toward him.

"Mr. Denton?" a man in a business suit said. "I'm Keith Frye. We talked on the phone." He reached for Gabe's hand and shook it firmly. "Why don't you fill us in on what's happened?"

Gabe's mind reeled, and he groped for words.

"Mr. Denton?" Frye repeated. "Are you able to talk with us, sir?"

Gabe squared his shoulders and took a deep breath. Then, like the professional newscaster that he was, he began a brief, concise, and surprisingly unemotional report of the past few hours' events.

As he drove the tractor back across the field toward Teddy and Dan, Gabe explained how the kids had taken care of Boone, then recited a sketchy account of his own run-in with Arno. He described the scene he had witnessed between Teddy Giordano and Wolf—including how the former had saved Dan's life at the risk of his own. He ended his monologue by revealing the hiding place of Nick Angelini's notebook in Stacey's doll.

"And good luck on getting that doll away from her," he told the marshal with a rueful smile. "You'd better figure out a way to get the notebook out of the doll without . . . *wounding* Mrs. Whispers, or you're going to have a major battle on your hands."

While Keith Frye and the pilot began to work on Teddy, administering first aid and getting him settled onto a stretcher, Gabe told Dan about the accident . . . and Lyss. He tried to be reassuring, answering Dan's questions as fully and optimistically as he could. The whole time, however, he wished he *felt* as confident as he was trying to sound for Dan's benefit.

Once they had loaded Teddy Giordano and the barely conscious Wolf onto the helicopter, Frye headed for the main cabin to check on Jennifer and the kids—and to round up the other two mobsters. Gabe stayed behind, waiting for the backup helicopter the marshal had requested.

The pilot had set flares for the incoming chopper and was now back inside his own aircraft, keeping an eye on Wolf. Gabe stood off by himself, close enough that he could see inside the chopper, where Dan was balanced on his knees beside Teddy Giordano's stretcher, Sunny nearby. At the moment, Gabe didn't think Dan looked much better than the man on the stretcher. He was pale and perspiring, and obviously in pain whenever he moved his shoulder.

Teddy was conscious, at least enough that he was attempting to carry on a feeble conversation with Dan. His face was pale and pinched, but he clutched Dan's hand as he spoke in a weak, faltering voice.

Gabe didn't especially want to hear anything Teddy Giordano had to say, but he didn't want to let Dan out of his sight, so he stayed put, listening.

"Dan . . . you were right. . . ."

"Right about what, Teddy?" Dan leaned closer to him.

"Both of you . . . you and Gabe. Both of you put your lives . . . on the line for me tonight." He gasped, then choked, "Remember, Dan? I said no one would do that for . . . someone like me." His grip on Dan's hand tightened.

Dan nodded. "But you did the same thing, Teddy—for me. I owe you my life."

Teddy attempted a weak grin. "Yeah, but you're . . . a good man, Daniel. A good man is worth . . . a little pain."

Gabe's eyes burned. Irritably, he wiped the back of his hand across them. The little mobster had that much right, anyway. A man like Dan was worth a *lot* of pain.

Dan's voice was almost as soft as Teddy's when he answered, and Gabe had to strain to hear. "What you have to remember,

Teddy, is that in the eyes of God, we're *all* worth a great deal of pain. That's what the Cross was all about." He paused, then went on. "It was God's way of showing each one of us just how very special we are to him. The Cross was for you, too, Teddy. Not just for a few people who measure up. It was for all of us."

Gabe swallowed hard. He suddenly felt certain that Dan knew he was listening, and that his last remark had been meant as much for him as for Teddy Giordano.

It seemed that even blind, Dan could still read his feelings. He had known all along that Gabe resented Teddy Giordano, that the little mobster had grated on him something fierce.

Gabe squeezed his eyes shut, then opened them. Sick at heart, he realized he had forgotten the truth in what Dan had just told Teddy—that the Lord didn't offer his love and forgiveness only to those who measured up. He also offered it to the Teddy Giordanos of the world. The *outsiders.*

Gabe's thoughts suddenly turned to Nicky Angelini. He remembered with a sick feeling the way the boy had looked at him back at the cabin when Gabe had rejected his offer of help.

He had rejected a *child,* all the while knowing the boy wasn't the problem. His father might have been corrupt, but that didn't mean Nicky was.

The heaviness in his spirit grew as he seemed to hear a voice somewhere deep inside him reminding him that, to God, Teddy Giordano was also a child.

Suffer the children . . . let them come to Me. . . .

Awareness rose slowly at the back of Gabe's mind. Had it not been for Daniel—and Daniel's family—he might have turned out to be a Teddy Giordano or a Nicky Angelini himself.

Or even a Wolf or an Arno . . .

Dan's parents had taken him into their home and their hearts years ago. They had loved him and accepted him and given him a haven from his bitter, alcoholic mother, to whom he had been only an inconvenience. They had taken Gabe to church with their own family week after week for years, teaching him—mostly by example—about the all-inclusive, unconditional love of Jesus Christ. Had the Kaines not . . . *suffered the child,* Gabe might never have become *God's* child.

Overwhelmed by this sudden realization, Gabe watched the two men in the helicopter, straining to hear their conversation.

"Dan, if I come out of this," Teddy Giordano was saying, "I want—I *need*—to talk with you. About . . . some of the stuff I read in Jennifer's Bible." His voice was growing weaker, his eyes fluttering, but he seemed to have Dan's hand in a desperate grip.

Dan bent over him. "We'll talk, Teddy. All you want." He paused. "Besides, there's something I've been wanting to talk with *you* about." A faint smile broke over his haggard features. "I'd like to offer you a job. A job here at the Farm."

Teddy tried to speak but managed nothing more than a choked sound of disbelief.

"You know," Dan went on quietly, "a farm is a great place to raise kids. When you're stronger, we'll talk about that, too. About Stacey and Nicky."

Gabe waited another minute, then climbed up into the helicopter. With tears now spilling from his eyes, clouding his vision, Gabe dropped to his knees beside Dan, studying Teddy Giordano, who was no longer conscious. He touched Dan lightly on the shoulder, then reached for the hand of the man lying on the stretcher.

"Pray for us, Dan," he murmured, as he gripped Teddy's hand. "Pray for him . . . and for me."

"The camp has turned out to be even more of a success than you dreamed it would, hasn't it, Daniel?" Jennifer asked quietly.

He nodded contentedly and squeezed her hand. They sat on the porch swing on the deck of the main cabin, enjoying the uncommon quiet of the evening and trying to catch their second wind before vespers. This was their Sunday at the camp. Every third week, Daniel, Jennifer, and Jason drove up to be a part of the Sunday worship and fellowship activities.

"It still doesn't feel right, not having Lyss and Gabe with us on Sundays," Jennifer murmured sadly.

Daniel draped an arm around her shoulders to pull her closer. "Next year," he said confidently. "Next year things will be a little more normal for all of us again. What with the upcoming trial and everything else . . ." Daniel let the sentence trail off, rubbing his arm absentmindedly.

Jennifer noticed the motion and involuntarily shivered at the memory of what might have happened . . . what had *almost* happened. Even after four months, the bullet wound in Daniel's shoulder still gave him a twinge. "It's hard to believe that one little notebook can destroy a criminal ring," she mused. "It's taking a long time to get this trial underway. But I suppose it will be even longer before it's over." She paused. "They *will* go to jail, won't they? The three of them?"

Daniel nodded. "And their boss, I expect. Sabas." They sat in silence for a few more minutes, lulled by the evening's sultry warmth and the sounds of the day gently winding down. They could hear creek water lapping at the rocks along the bank, and the crickets were already tuning up in anticipation of a long summer evening chorus. Every now and then a child laughed or a dog barked, but most of the camp had settled.

Jennifer looked down at Sunny, dozing at Daniel's feet. The retriever's visits were always a treat for Nicky and Stacey, and Jason and the Angelini children had kept her busy most of the afternoon. Now all of them were off with Teddy, helping to collect wood for tonight's bonfire. Apparently Sunny had decided to take advantage of their absence and catch a quick nap.

Jennifer leaned her head against Daniel's shoulder, sighing when he pressed a gentle kiss onto the top of her head. "I'm getting nervous about seeing Lyss tomorrow." She turned to look up at him. "Oh, Daniel—I don't know how she's endured all this surgery!"

His expression betrayed his own concern for his sister. "Hopefully, the worst is over now. Gabe said that from here on, the rest should be easy." He took a deep breath. "Considering the accident, it could have been a lot worse. She could have needed major reconstruction—which would have taken years, not months."

"I only pray this last surgery is a success. She's had bandages on for months, and she's so hopeful," Jennifer said. "I think she's also frightened. But, then, who wouldn't be? If *I'm* this apprehensive about the outcome, what must *Lyss* be feeling?"

"Lyss will be fine. She's said all along that the Lord gave her this face, and he was capable of putting it back together." He shook his head. "That's faith."

"She's been wonderful. She *is* wonderful."

Smiling faintly, Daniel nodded his agreement. "Poor Gabe.

When all this first started, he was determined to be so strong for Lyss. *He* was going to get *her* through it, remember?"

Jennifer chuckled. "Lyss told me last week that he's given the word *hover* a whole new meaning."

"I can imagine," Daniel laughed. "When we stopped over there Friday morning, she was threatening to lock him in the garage for the weekend."

Jennifer yawned contentedly. A warm drowsiness crept over her, and she snuggled closer to Daniel. "I think Stacey is really enjoying her birthday," she murmured. "She loved her cornshuck doll. Naturally, she gave me to understand that it would have to share her affections with Mrs. Whispers."

"She's a doll baby herself." Daniel paused. "I hope we'll have a little girl someday. I think I could do a really good job of spoiling a little girl."

"You're already doing a fine job of that with your little boy," Jennifer said dryly. "Nicky and Stacey are both thriving on their new life, aren't they?" she went on, her tone more serious. "I've never seen two happier children. Teddy is just great with them."

"He's great with *all* the kids. Mac told me again today that he doesn't know what he'd do without him. He says Teddy has more energy and works harder than any man he's ever known. And the kids are absolutely crazy about him. Coming from Mac," he added, "that's quite a tribute."

Jennifer nodded to herself. "It's sad that Nicky and Stacey's aunt didn't want to be bothered with them. She doesn't know what she's missing."

"That's true," Daniel agreed, "but I've got a hunch the children are better off. This farm is a great place to grow up, and between the MacGregors and Teddy, they'll have all the love and attention they need."

"Teddy says they should adjust well to school. I'm sure a small rural school will be awfully different for them, especially for Nicky, coming from a private school for the gifted."

"He'll probably be filling in as a substitute teacher in no time," Daniel said with a grin. "Wonder what that boy's going to be when he grows up? A nuclear physicist or a space lab designer?"

"As a matter of fact," a voice said behind them, "he's decided to be a farmer."

"Teddy!" Jennifer jumped, startled. "You're as quiet as a cat!"

"Nicky wants to be a *farmer?*" Daniel asked with unmistakable amusement.

"Yep," Teddy said, coming around the swing to perch on the wide banister. "The entire future of agriculture has new hope."

Teddy had changed, Jennifer thought. His arm had healed without any permanent damage, and he had gained some weight— not too much, but enough to make him look a little healthier.

He looked happy, too. He no longer appeared so tense and *hunted*. Now his eyes held a perpetual twinkle—along with the familiar glint of mischief—and he was seldom without a smile.

"Everything going all right?" Daniel asked him.

"Everything's great," Teddy replied, smiling at Jennifer. "I'll never be able to thank you enough for giving me a chance at this job, Daniel. I like it so much, I almost feel guilty taking a salary for it."

"Well, now, that could be a real problem, Teddy," Daniel said gravely. "Mac's dead set on giving you a raise next month."

Teddy grinned. "I'll either learn to deal with the guilt or give the extra to charity."

It occurred to Jennifer that Teddy Giordano was an extremely likeable fellow. It also occurred to her that he ought to have a nice girl, someone who would appreciate him—and the children.

She would certainly have no problem recommending him to any of the young women in their church family. He was nice-looking, intelligent, amusing, brave. Any man willing to take on two children like Nicky and Stacey as a single parent had to be *extremely* brave, not to mention the way he had saved Daniel's life. That. of course, was what would endear Teddy Giordano to her forever.

On the more practical side, he was a hard worker, and he had a good, steady job. Best of all, he was now an enthusiastic Christian, thanks to Daniel's and Gabe's interest and involvement in his life. Yes, she decided, staring at Teddy with a somewhat conniving smile, she'd definitely have to do some girl-shopping on his behalf.

Teddy looked at her curiously, started to say something, then glanced across the field at the road. "Someone's coming."

Jennifer leaned forward. "That's Gabe's T-bird!" She jumped up from the swing and walked to the end of the deck. "Daniel—I think Lyss is with him!"

Gabe pulled in and parked on the turnaround across from the cabin, then helped Lyss from the car. She was wearing a pink floral sundress and had pulled her hair to one side with a pink silk scarf.

"The bandages! The bandages are off, Daniel!"

"How does she look?" he asked, his voice low and tense.

"I can't tell yet."

Lyss and Gabe came toward them, and Jennifer held her breath. Gabe was smiling—no, not smiling—*beaming*. His face was positively *glowing* with happiness and pride.

Lyss was smiling, too, looking from Daniel to Jennifer. Then she stopped walking and started running. She rushed into Jennifer's arms, and Jennifer held on until Daniel cut in for a big-brother hug.

"You look wonderful!" Jennifer choked out between tears. "Better than we could have possibly hoped!"

Jennifer stood back, holding her sister-in-law at arm's length to study her more carefully. Around her right cheek and ear, hairline scars were still visible, as well as a crescent-shaped scar above her right eye. But Jennifer thought she had never seen a more beautiful sight. It was Lyss—whole and healed and herself again.

"Most of the scars around my hairline will fade," Lyss explained without self-consciousness. "And the stitch marks, too. It'll never be perfect, but—"

"But then it never was," Daniel jibed. It was the expected big-brother wisecrack, and he smiled when Lyss punched him playfully in the rib cage.

"Aren't you going to look at me, Daniel?" Her expression sobered as she took her brother's hands and placed them on either side of her face.

"You bet I am," he said with a wobbly grin. "We need an objective opinion on this."

His fingertips went over her face in light, deft movements, lingering on the scars as if he longed to heal them. "Well, Pip," he said lightly, his voice none too steady as he completed his inspection, "it seems to me that you're looking good. Real good." He paused. "There's just one thing, though. . . ."

"What, Daniel?"

His index finger lightly traced her nose. "Since you were getting all that work done anyway, I'm surprised you didn't go ahead and get a nose job while you were at it."

Lyss laughed. "Ah, yes, the Kaine nose. I always said I'd get it fixed, didn't I?" She paused and winked at Jennifer. "But I wasn't sure I'd recognize myself when I came out of all this," she went on. "I figured I should keep my most prominent landmark intact."

Jennifer grinned. "I've always liked the Kaine nose. It gives your face—and Daniel's—a kind of strength."

"In Dan's case, a *great* deal of strength," Gabe said gleefully.

Before Daniel could retaliate, Jason came running up with the Angelini children and Teddy Giordano. Lyss hugged everyone, including a suddenly shy Teddy.

"Gabe, would you get that package out of the trunk for me, please?" Lyss asked, turning to her husband.

"That's the *real* reason I wanted to come today," she explained as Gabe went back to the car. Her gaze went to Stacey, who was staring up at Lyss with solemn, awe-filled eyes.

"We have a very special delivery to make," Lyss went on. "I was told that today is someone's birthday." Stacey bobbed her head up and down excitedly.

Gabe returned with the package, and Lyss placed the long, brightly wrapped box in the little girl's arms. "This is for you, Stacey." She paused, then added softly, "Just for you. With my love."

With dancing eyes, Stacey dropped down on the ground to open the gift. "Oohhh!" she breathed as she carefully lifted from the wrapping a brand-new, curly maple fiddle with its bow.

She studied it lovingly for a long moment before turning her gaze on Lyss and then Gabe. "My very own fiddle?"

"Truly your own, dumpling," Gabe answered. "Lyss made it just for you."

"I've never made a fiddle before, Stacey. Only dulcimers. I hope it turns out to be a good one."

The little girl clutched the fiddle to her heart as if it were a rare and precious treasure. She looked up then and said, with great dignity, "It's the most perfect fiddle in the world. It's even more better than Uncle Gabe's."

At that, Gabe smiled and dug down in his pants pocket to pull out a small package wrapped in plain brown paper. He looked at Nicky, then handed him the package.

"Nicky? I know it's not your birthday," he said quietly, "but I asked Lyss to make something for you, too. Something . . . special." He looked the boy squarely in the eye and added, "After all, you're an adopted member of our family now."

Wide-eyed, Nicky hesitated, then took the package. "May I

open it now, Mr. Denton?" he asked, obviously trying to restrain his enthusiasm.

"Please do," Gabe said dryly.

Jennifer saw her brother-in-law's suppressed smile, and she watched, curious, as Nicky slowly and methodically removed the wrapping and opened the lid of a small, delicately carved wooden box.

The boy caught a sharp breath. He looked up at Gabe in disbelief for a long time before returning his gaze to the box in his hand. With great care, he lifted from the box an exquisitely carved wooden replica of a golden retriever. The figurine looked exactly like Sunny.

Gabe cleared his throat awkwardly. "Did you see the inscription on the box lid?"

Nicky looked at him, glanced down at the box, then read aloud in a faltering voice:

"For Nicky Angelini: Because I owe him." Nicky swallowed hard, then added, "It's signed . . . *Gabe.*"

Nicky stared up at Gabe with a stunned expression. After a long silence, he extended his hand. "I—I don't know what to say, sir."

"How about, 'Thank you, Uncle Gabe'?" A corner of Gabe's mouth quirked. Then he grinned and took Nicky's hand. "I'm getting a little tired of *sir.*"

Jennifer held her breath as she watched. After all that had happened, she knew this was difficult for both of them.

Nicky stared at Gabe for another few seconds. Suddenly, in what Jennifer was certain must have been the first impulsive gesture of this strange little man-child's life, the boy moved in and hugged Gabe tightly around the waist. Gabe's face creased with pleasure as he wrapped Nicky in his arms, releasing him only when Lyss put her arms around both of them.

"Hey! How about a hug for the whittler?"

Laughing, Nicky threw his arms around her and thanked her. Not about to be left out of this display of affection, Stacey jumped up and joined her brother in Lyss's arms.

Gabe stooped and whispered something to the Angelini children. They turned, glanced over at Jennifer and Daniel, and came toward them, carrying their gifts.

Stacey looked up at Daniel, then very carefully took one of his large hands and placed it on her precious new fiddle.

"Here, Uncle Dan—do you want to look at my fiddle?"

"And my retriever, too," Nicky added, smiling at Jennifer.

His expression solemn, Daniel took the fiddle and went over it with careful hands. Shifting it under one arm, he then took the small wooden figurine from Nicky and examined it.

"These are absolutely beautiful," he said as he returned the children's treasures. "But I'm not surprised. Lyss has always had her own unique way of taking something that might not look like much to anyone else and turning it into something really special."

He paused, a fleeting look of wry amusement scurrying across his features as he shot a grin in Gabe's direction. "Of course, at times," he added, "she's had her work cut out for her. But even then I'd have to say she's managed to work wonders."

Collect all the titles in the Daybreak Mysteries series by B. J. Hoff